Lord E.H. of Cherbury, Sidney Lee

The Autobiography of Edward, Lord Herbert of Cherbury

With introd., notes, appendices, and a continuation of the life

Lord E.H. of Cherbury, Sidney Lee

The Autobiography of Edward, Lord Herbert of Cherbury
With introd., notes, appendices, and a continuation of the life

ISBN/EAN: 9783337118341

Printed in Europe, USA, Canada, Australia, Japan

Cover: Foto ©Raphael Reischuk / pixelio.de

More available books at **www.hansebooks.com**

THE AUTOBIOGRAPHY

OF

EDWARD, LORD HERB[ERT]

OF CHERBURY

With Introduction, Notes, Appendices,
a Continuation of the Life

BY

SIDNEY L. LEE, B.A.

BALLIOL COLLEGE, OXFORD

With Four Etched Portraits

LONDON
JOHN C. NIMMO
14, KING WILLIAM STREET, STRAND, W.C.
1886

PREFACE.

It may be of service to the reader to explain the arrangement of this volume. In the Introduction which precedes the Autobiography, I have attempted—firstly, to describe Lord Herbert's varied character, as displayed in his own writings and in historical records; and secondly, to review his eminent achievements in literature and philosophy, of which he himself has given no account. In the essay which succeeds the Autobiography, I have tried to trace his political career in detail from 1624— the year when his own memoirs abruptly terminate—to 1648, the date of his death. In an appendix I have printed several original illustrative documents, many extracts from Herbert's unpublished correspondence, and some historical notes on topics to which frequent allusion is made in the Autobiography on the assumption—no longer justifiable—that they are matters of common knowledge. Former editors have treated the work as a mere curiosity of literature. I have endeavoured in my notes and elsewhere to prove that it deserves the serious attention of the student, not only of English literature, but of English social history in the early seventeenth century.

My text is that of the first printed edition issued from Horace Walpole's private press in 1764. I differ from that text alone in my treatment of proper names. Soon after I had set myself the task of identifying the persons mentioned by Lord Herbert, I came to the conclusion that the names had very often been wrongly transcribed, and my notes will, I trust, justify the changes I have made. Thus, on p. 49, I replace *Ti*lesius by *Te*lesius, on p. 55 *S*cordus by Cordus, on p. 116 William Cro*fts* by William Cro*sse*, and so forth. I greatly regret that I have been unable to consult the original manuscript, but my search for it, as I explain elsewhere, has proved unavailing.

I have to thank the Earl of Powis, the Rev. T. Burd of Chirbury, and the Rev. Dr. Sewell, Warden of New College, Oxford, for the readiness with which they replied to the various inquiries I addressed to them while preparing the book. I also desire to acknowledge my obligations to M. de Rémusat's admirable little volume, *Lord Herbert de Cherbury, sa Vie et ses Œuvres*, and to the Archæological Collections published by the Powysland Club, which are invaluable to the student of Welsh history and biography.

CONTENTS.

LIST OF ETCHED ILLUSTRATIONS.

b

INTRODUCTION.

"It would not be altogether absurd if a man were to thank God for his vanity among the other comforts of life." Benjamin Franklin sets these words in the forefront of his autobiography, and they deserve to be set in the forefront of all successful works of the kind. A man may think to apply a record of his own life to various purposes. He may fashion it as a text-book of conduct for his children, as a history of his relations with the politics, religion, or literature of his time, as a generous panegyric of his friends, or as an ill-natured denunciation of those who have shared his life's successes or defeats. But from whatever point of view the successful autobiographer approaches his subject, unconsciously the same spirit moves him. He is convinced not merely that his life has been worth living, but that he has lived it to eminent advantage. He is self-centred; he is self-satisfied; he loves himself better than his neighbour; he weighs others in the balance, and finds them wanting; he knows himself to be of full weight. All professions to the contrary may safely be ignored. Absolute truthfulness is the last thing we expect of the successful autobiographer. No man can give an impartial estimate of himself; failure is only courted by attempting it, and success in autobiography is not attainable unless this condition receive practical recognition. But although "vain opinions, flattering hopes, false valuations, imaginations as one would, and the like," are the salt of autobiography, sincerity of a kind we do require of it. The writer must be true to his own self-conceit. He must have no self-conscious misgivings about his own real value. The austere may condemn his attitude with what warmth they will. The man of human sympathies will give vanity fair quarter wherever he meet it, and no better reward for his forbearance can be promised him than the power of rightly appreciating that small circle of literature in which Lord Herbert's autobiography holds a central place.

The rigid moralist should devote himself to the "poor shrunken things" of autobiography where the true autobiographical spirit is held in check, or whence it is altogether excluded. Let him not at any rate sit in judgment on the vainglorious performance of Lord Herbert of Cherbury. Mr.

Swinburne has claimed for this autobiography a place among the hundred best books of the world. On no other work of its class has the critic conferred similar rank. Questions of literary precedence can never hope for final answers, and there may be points of view from which this judgment is disputable. But it is doubtful if any other autobiography breathes quite as freely the writer's overweening conceit of his own worth, which is the primary condition of all autobiographical excellence. At every turn Lord Herbert applauds his own valour, his own beauty, his own gentility of birth. At home and abroad he flatters himself that he is the cynosure of neighbouring eyes. He, in fact, conforms from end to end to all the conditions which make autobiography successful. He is guilty of many misrepresentations. No defect is more patent in his memoirs than the total lack of a sense of proportion. Lord Herbert's self-satisfaction is built on sand. It is bred of the trivialities of fashionable life,—of the butterfly triumphs won in court society. He passes by in contemptuous silence his truly valuable contributions to philosophy, history, and poetry. But the contrast between the grounds on which he professed a desire to be remembered and those on which he *deserved* to be remembered by posterity, gives his book almost all its value. Men of solid mental ability and achievements occasionally like to pose in society as gay Lotharios ; it is rare,

however, for them to endeavour, even as autobiographers, to convey the impression to all succeeding generations that they were gay Lotharios
and not much else besides. Yet it is such transparent errors of judgment that give autobiography
its finest flavour.

Lord Herbert professes " to relate to his posterity those passages of his life which he conceives
may best declare him and be most useful to them."
He asserts that he writes " with all truth and sincerity, as scorning to deceive or speak false to any."
When he took the work in hand he was more than
sixty years old, and it was therefore fitting (he
argued) that he should review his life so as to
reform what was amiss and comfort himself with
those actions " done according to the rules of conscience, virtue, and honour." No worthier object
could he have proposed to himself in his declining
years ; yet so easily are autobiographers diverted
from their avowed purposes, that with the exception of the notices of his very early life and a
digression on education, there is no passage in the
book which could serve any useful end in the hands
of the " young person." There is nothing very
interesting in the record of Lord Herbert's youth.[1]

---

[1] Enthusiastic admirer of the book as was Horace Walpole,
he told Mason that he had better skip the first fifty pages,
and Montagu that the first forty pages would make him

Born in 1583—twenty-two years after Bacon, and nineteen after Shakespeare—he was brought up in the luxury that became the eldest son of an old county family. He lost his father when he was thirteen or fourteen years old; was "exceedingly inclined" to his studies and to music; and at the age of fifteen or thereabouts was married, while still at Oxford, to a wealthy cousin far older than himself, in accordance with an unromantic family arrangement, in which his own inclinations were not considered. Herbert was not a very spirited boy; and his mother, who took great pride in him, governed him and his wife rigorously during his minority. When approaching manhood he avoided "the evil example" of other young men, but, in the closing years of Elizabeth's reign, "curiosity rather than ambition" brought him to court. Then temptation spread its net for him for the first time, and he enjoyed the entanglement. He came to recognise that he was singularly handsome. Queen Elizabeth suggested that it was a pity he should have married so young, and twice clapped him gently on the cheek, while he kissed her aged hands. He was one of a crowd of persons

---

sick (Letters, iv. 156, 252). This is rather unfair to Lord Herbert; but the unique interest of the book is certainly not to be found in the early pages.

created Knight of the Bath at James I.'s corona-
tion. " I could tell," he remarks on this occasion,
" how much my person was commended by the
lords and ladies that came to see the solemnity
then used ; but I shall flatter myself too much "
—a tell-tale reservation—" if I believed it " (p.
83). He affected to take seriously the words of
the formal oath, which bound him to defend
all unprotected females, and he soon afterwards
resolved to adopt the profession of knight-errantry.
He had now, he boasts, lived with his wife in
all conjugal loyalty for ten years, and had successfully resisted all allurements to the contrary.
He was twenty-five years old, and deemed it desirable to see something more of the world. He told
his wife that it became him to seek adventures
" beyond sea." Mistress Herbert took another
view of the situation, but her husband had his
way, and in the next decade lived a very restless
life.

He went first to France ; made friends with the
Duc de Montmorency, an elderly French beau, and
while staying at his attractive castle of Merlou
tried to find occasion for his first duel in the
playful endeavour of a French chevalier to take
" a knot of ribbon " from a little girl's head-dress.
He rode the great horse, played the lute, and sang
with great applause. He visited Henri IV. at the
Tuileries, and the King "embraced him in his arms,

and held him some while there." The divorced
Queen Margaret invited him to her balls, and gave
him a place next her own chair, to the wonder and
envy of the assembled company. He flirted with
the Princess of Conti, who had a less than doubtful
reputation. The ladies, however, did not confine
their attention to him ; they admired another man
—one M. Balagni—" who could not be thought at
most but ordinary handsome," and the puzzling
circumstance caused Lord Herbert no little dis-
quietude.

Having tasted of foreign travel, Lord Herbert
returned home, only to set out again on another
expedition in the Low Countries, where there was
a prospect of war. The town of Juliers was to be
besieged by Dutch, French, and English troops.
No command was offered Herbert, and he performed no service of real importance in the campaign, although he hints at quite another conclusion.
But he had the satisfaction of meeting M. Balagni
again. He dared his gay rival to all manner of
boyishly foolish escapades, in which he contrived
that the Frenchman should come off second-best.
But the exploit that made him most notorious in
this campaign was a quarrel with Lord Howard of
Walden. " There was liberal drinking " one night
in Sir Horace Vere's quarters, and Lord Herbert
spoke merrily to his companions, so merrily that
one of them, Lord Howard, an English officer,

took offence, and came towards him "in a violent manner." Some days later Herbert's sensitive honour was wounded by a Frenchman's taunt that he had not demanded satisfaction of Lord Howard. He therefore sent him a challenge, and the duel would have been fought had not the principals been arrested before they met, and the childish dispute been stayed by the Lords of the Council. Such accidents invariably terminated Herbert's duels. Men of sense complained that he was choleric and hasty. He admitted that this, generally speaking, was true, but with appalling boldness he added, amid all manner of protestations, that he never had a quarrel with a man for his own sake ; he often hazarded himself for his friends, but when injury was offered him in his own person, he sheathed his sword, and contented himself with an inward feeling of resentment. On his return to England he describes himself as carrying with him the reputation of a hero: "And now, if I may say it, and without vanity, I was in great esteem both in court and city, many of the greatest desiring my company" (p. 127). The public generally had heard "so many brave things" of him that his portrait, which he had had painted very many times, was in great demand.[1] Ladies, from the Queen

---

[1] Lord Herbert describes below three portraits of himself —1. (p. 85) in the robes of a Knight of the Bath, by an

downwards, placed it in their cabinets or near their
hearts, and gave occasion " of more discourse " than
he (modest man !) could have wished.   One lady
(Lady Ayres), "a considerable person" according
to Lord Herbert—although history has neglected
her altogether—was discovered by the gallant,
under circumstances reflecting little credit on himself (p. 129), looking upon his picture "with more
earnestness and passion than he could have easily
believed."   He was the more surprised at her intense admiration of him, not because Lady Herbert
was occupying any of his attention, but because at
the moment his own affections were engaged by an
anonymous beauty, whose attractions caused him
real anxiety.   But Lady Ayres' passion supplied
him with congenial food for reflection until her
husband treated him to a very uncomplimentary
buffeting in Whitehall.   In one place he protests
before God that he had at court more favours (appa-

---

unknown artist (now at Powis Castle) ; 2. (p. 111) mounted
on a favourite horse ; 3. (pp. 127, 128) a miniature painted
by "one Larkin" (now at Charlecote). Of the first of these
pictures an etching appears in this volume. Isaac Oliver
is credited with the original painting of Lord Herbert lying
on the ground after a duel, an etching of which also appears
below. An engraving of this picture, which is now at Powis
Castle, formed the frontispiece to Horace Walpole's edition
of the autobiography in 1764. There is at Penshurst Castle
a fifth portrait of Lord Herbert, attributed to Oliver.

rently of this kind) than he desired, but such, he consoles himself, are the penal ties attaching to the possession of rare manly beauty.

To a volatile nature like Lord Herbert's, strong passion was altogether foreign. At the best of times his wife received from him conjugal loyalty ; true love did not enter into their relations with one another ; the lover's fleeting raptures were excited in him by other women's charms. So far as his autobiography informs us, he had no near and dear friends. Affability he had in plenty, but affability is not a staple commodity, and is a poor substitute for the enduring virtue of friendship. Aurelian Townsend, his companion on his first journey, and Ned Sackville, whom he travelled with later, proved pleasant company for a while, but he soon wearied of them and sought new associates. Sir Robert Harley, "being *then* my dear friend," was once insulted in his presence, and the insult was promptly resented by Lord Herbert, who in spite of weak health drew his sword upon the offender. But the story in Lord Herbert's mouth merely becomes a new testimony to his own adventurous disposition. He was good-natured in his dealings with his social inferiors, as is usually the case with the vainglorious. Richard Griffiths, his servant, found him a kindly master. He generously used his influence with Count Maurice of Nassau to spare the life of a

soldier who had killed his companion, and he recounts the circumstance for the most part attrac-
tively; but he spoils the effect of the narration by
finally making the Count address all the high
officers of the camp in the words: " Do you see
this cavalier, with all that courage you know, hath
yet that good-nature to pray for the life of *a poor
soldier?*" Lord Herbert clearly infers that his
generosity, like his amours, added something to
his own reputation. He shows himself more disinterested in his affection for his horses, which he
rode to advantage; he lamented their sickness,
entrusted them to careful keeping in his absence
from home, and left provision for them in his
will.

Lord Herbert found the sowing of the wild oats
which he had neglected to sow in early youth a
satisfying pastime in manhood, and did not lightly
relinquish the recreation. In 1614 he reappeared
in the Low Countries. The Spaniards under
Spinola were in the field against the Dutch.
Herbert and the Dutch commander (Count Maurice
of Nassau) were now the best of friends, and when
the fighting was interrupted they played chess with
each other, or discussed horses. The Count also
made Herbert his companion in his love-making,
and "yet so that I saw nothing openly (the modest
autobiographer apologises) more than might argue
a civil familiarity." On one occasion Herbert

wanted to decide the dispute between the Dutch
and the Spaniards by challenging a Spanish
champion in the name of his mistress to single
combat, but this romantic ambition was promptly
suppressed by his friends. Spinola's high reputation led Herbert, although associated with a hostile
camp, to seek an introduction to him ; Boswell
was not more eager to introduce himself to famous
men. Herbert, therefore, walked across to the
Spanish quarters, caught the General at dinner,
sat down beside him, and on taking his leave,
offered to fight under him, if he ever led an
army against the infidel Turk. Immediately
afterwards Herbert's military ardour cooled, and
he visited the notable towns of Germany, Switzerland, and Italy, paying and receiving high-flown
compliments all along the route. He twice visited
the Elector-Palatine and his wife at Heidelberg.
At Rome the master of the English College received
him hospitably, because (Herbert is careful to re-
mind us) he had heard men oftentimes speak of
him "both for learning and courage." On the
return journey he spent much time in Savoy,
where the Duke and his minister Scarnafissi had
also heard that he was a cavalier of great worth,
and treated him accordingly. He promised to
raise a troop of horse in Languedoc in behalf of
the Duke, who was engaged in war with Spain.
On the journey to Languedoc he went out of

his road to see the daughter of an innkeeper, who
(he had been told), was the handsomest woman
in Europe, and the sight was peculiarly refresh-
ing. Like adventures accompanied him until his
arrival in England in 1618, when the Duke of
Buckingham suddenly chose him to go as English
ambassador to France.

The responsibility of office somewhat sobered
him, and he performed his diplomatic duties with
energy and discretion. He lived at Paris in
great state, as befitted, in his opinion, the representative of a great nation ; spent far more than
his salary or his private resources justified, and
was jealous of his privileges. By an eccentric
ruse he asserted his right to have precedence of
the Spanish ambassador in court ceremonies. It
goes without saying that he continued his gallant-
ries at the French court. He was, in fact, in such
robust health, that he was disposed (he tells us)
to some follies which he afterwards repented.
He comforted his conscience, however, with the
knowledge that he was neither intemperate nor
deceitful in his pleasures, and that he could, an'
he would, extenuate his fault by telling circumstances that would have operated adversely on
the most sober-minded of men. His repartees
were of course the delight of French society,
and he was a universal favourite. The only
person who did not make himself agreeable to him

was M. de Luynes, the French king's favourite. Luynes was a man of low breeding, and was little likely to be influenced by Lord Herbert's graces of demeanour. When, therefore, Luynes supported a policy of aggression against the French Protestants, and Herbert, in accordance with his instructions, remonstrated on their behalf, the two soon came to high words. Luynes sent a special messenger to James I. to complain of his representative's misconduct, and Herbert followed to explain matters. Herbert suggested that he should fight Luynes, but James I. did not take kindly to the proposal, although he was satisfied with Herbert's explanations. On Luynes' death in 1621, Herbert returned to the French court, and remained there till the early months of 1624, when he was suddenly and permanently recalled. In the closing years of his embassy Herbert showed himself to real advantage; he used all his influence at Paris in behalf of the Protestant Elector-Palatine, the titular King of Bohemia; he sought to cement an alliance between England and France as opposed to Spain, and to consolidate the union of England and Holland. But with the bitter disappointment of his recall his autobiography comes to an abrupt termination.

Lord Herbert's lack of strict veracity, which I have already laid to his charge, is not a defect with which he has been previously credited. Horace

Walpole judged him to be the incarnation of truthfulness; but Walpole applied no tests, and saved himself trouble by his willingness to be deceived. Herbert, of course, is no common liar. With plausible amiability he suppresses the truth rather than commits deliberate perjury. When he is detected his purpose looks so innocent or so aimless that the lover of autobiography will mercifully attribute some of his inaccuracies to the failure of a sexagenarian's memory. But failure of memory is not always a satisfactory theory. The most significant misstatements in Herbert's autobiography occur in the early pages. There Lord Herbert has not only his own but his forefathers' reputation to maintain, and he sets his shoulder valiantly to the wheel. There is a picturesque description of the founder of his own branch of his family, Sir Richard Herbert of Colebrook. Sir Richard and his brother (the first of the Herberts to be created Earl of Pembroke) bore themselves bravely in Edward IV.'s behalf at Hedgcote Field in 1469. Lord Herbert's glowing story of their noble deeds passes with startling abruptness into an account of their tombs. He discreetly omits to mention that his great-great-grandfather and his great-great-granduncle were taken prisoners on the battlefield, and *beheaded at Northampton.* Their death was not disgraceful, but a well-developed sense of respectability apparently forbids the mention of the ghastly detail.

Lord Herbert makes many genealogical errors, and
such errors are usually excusable whenever and by
whomsoever they may be made. But there is method
visible in Herbert's madness on these points. He
overlooks intervening heirs and heiresses, so that
he may show that the cousin who became his wife
was maliciously deprived of much of her inheritance, and that he had a share of suffering in
her wrongs, all of which is purely imaginary.[1] Of
his widowed mother he tells us less than her
maternal care of him deserved. She was living
throughout the years covered by the autobiography,
and Herbert acquaints us with some circumstances
of her declining days, but he forgets to notice that
she married a second time. It was a strange marriage, and could not easily have been forgotten.
She, a thoughtful woman over forty years old, was
wedded to a youth (Sir John Danvers) less than
half her age; but Donne tells us that the disparity
bred no unhappiness—that the union fostered the
fullest harmony. Yet Herbert, the lady's eldest
son, leaves all this unsaid; he declines to tread on
such delicate ground; and when he has occasion to
refer to his stepfather by name, gives no hint of
the relationship. Other kindly protectors fare no
better at his hands. Donne, his mother's friend
and his own counsellor throughout his youth, is

---

[1] See p. 17.

barely mentioned.[1]   Sir George More of Losely, who, as it happens, became involuntarily Donne's father-in-law, was Herbert's guardian after his father's death.   Extant letters prove Herbert's boyish liking for Sir George;[2] but not only is his name blotted out of the autobiography—a circumstantial story is introduced to show that his uncle, Sir Francis Newport, was the guardian of his minority, and poor Sir George's many acts of kindness are assigned to others.   Ben Jonson and Selden, both lifelong acquaintances, are similarly ignored.[3]

---

[1] Donne had the highest opinion of Herbert, and encouraged him in his studies and in his love of books.   Cf. Donne's Letter—No. lvi.—to Herbert sent with a copy of his *Biothanatos*, and Donne's poem addressed to Herbert "at the siege of Juliers," first printed in the 1633 quarto of Donne's poems, pp. 82–84.   Herbert wrote an elegy on Donne (*d.* 1631) which appears among his poems.

[2] See Appendix vii.

[3] The earliest proof of Selden's intimacy with Herbert is a very friendly note addressed to him under date 3d February 1619–20 (Brit. Mus. MS. Addit. 32,092, f. 314); the latest proof is the appearance of Selden's name as an executor in Herbert's will.   To Ben Jonson Herbert dedicated his *Satyra Secunda*, and he eulogised Jonson in some very complimentary lines prefixed to Jonson's translation of Horace's *Ars Poetica*.   Ben returned the compliment in the following :—

> "If men get name for some one virtue, then
> What man art thou, that art so many men,
> All-virtuous Herbert ! on whose every part
> Truth might spend all her voice, fame all her art ?

For many years Herbert's right to Montgomery
Castle was successfully disputed by his kinsman,
Shakespeare's William Herbert, Earl of Pembroke,
but here again all is silence in Herbert's memoirs.
If the reader place by the side of Lord Herbert's account of his ridiculous quarrel with Lord
Howard of Walden the correspondence and account given by Lord Howard's second,[1] he will
note very strange discrepancies. Lord Herbert
does not tell us (although his letters prove it) that
he was a party to a formal public reconciliation,
and immediately afterwards sent a private challenge; neither would it please him did he know
that posterity had convinced itself, in spite of all
his protestations to the contrary, that he never set
foot in the place appointed for the duel. In France
he would have us infer that from the first he saw
through Luynes' mean character, yet in his private

> Whether thy learning they would take or wit,
> Or valour, or thy judgment seasoning it,
> Thy standing upright to thyself, thy ends
> Like straight, thy piety to God and friends:
> Their latter praise would still the greatest be,
> And yet they, all together, less than thee."

Another of Herbert's poetic aquaintances was Thomas
Carew, who went with him to Paris (see p. 190). On p. 198
Thomas *Caage* is clearly a transcriber's error for Thomas
Carew. Herbert has a reference to "my witty Carew" in
his elegy on Donne.

[1] See Appendix v.

correspondence, penned during the first years of their acquaintance, he praises Luynes without reserve. And in spite of the political foresight on which he plumes himself, with some justice in the last years of his embassy, he overlooks the rise of Richelieu, the most notable fact in contemporary French history.[1]

The reader will recognise that to attain a complete conception of Lord Herbert's character he must not solely confine his attention to the autobiography. It deals with a fragment of Lord Herbert's life, and imperfectly with that fragment. It offers us testimony that for purposes of serious criticism needs corroboration and amplification. To arrive at a final estimate we must probe many topics which are barely alluded to in the memoirs; the details of the last years of Lord Herbert's life, which are untouched by his memoirs, must be consulted; and we must appraise the evidence of mental and imaginative capacity offered us in his philosophical speculations and in his poetry.

Lord Herbert's public life in the years covered by his autobiography was a triumphal progress; it was almost without shadow. His public life in

---

[1] Minor inaccuracies are illustrated by Herbert's contradictory statements as to his own age (p. 29). He represents himself to have been two years younger than was the fact at the date of his marriage.

after years is a dreary series of disasters. It is indeed regrettable that Lord Herbert should have lacked the opportunity, or rather (it may be) the disposition, to pen the record of his misfortunes. The extant letters and papers written by him in his decline, show that defeat and disgrace did not destroy his self-conceit. But the effort to sustain the same self-satisfaction under stress of perplexing difficulties as in the face of smiling fortune, must have exercised all his ingenuity, and would have probably proved the most heroic instance on record of the sustaining power of vanity. The facts of his later life, which, in the absence of any connected presentation of them from his own pen, form no very pleasing picture, are soon told. He was suddenly dismissed from the French embassy; the abruptness of his dismissal ruined his political reputation; and although he petitioned James I., and subsequently Charles I., again and again for compensation, he found all avenues to dignified office closed to him.[1] "I ever loved my book and a private life more than any busy preferments," he writes with curious inconsistency near the close of his autobiography. He certainly did not yield to his exclusion from political place without a struggle,

---

[1] I have given a detailed account of Herbert's later public life on pp. 251-302.

in which other men would have been conscious
of painful humiliation. In season and out of
season, he pressed for a hearing. In plain, un-
varnished terms he pointed out the besotted blind-
ness of neglecting such political merit as his. As
long as Buckingham lived he clung tenaciously to his
former patron ; he sought Charles's favour as Buckingham's friend, and, to flatter the king, defended the
favourite from unfriendly critics after he was laid in
his grave. He was rewarded for his pains, not with
high office, as he desired, but with the cheapest of
all honours of the time—an Irish and an English
peerage. Buckingham's murder practically deprived
Herbert of all hold on the court, and with characteristic versatility he laboured for his end through
new channels. He set himself to write a history
of the reign of Henry VIII., in which Charles I.'s
ancestor was to appear as a man of virtue, and the
Reformation the apotheosis of righteousness. He
really took little interest in either subject, as he confessed to the Papal legate, but, time out of mind,
he tried to impress the King with his disinterested
enthusiasm in taking up the work. Doles of money
and grants of disused apartments in royal palaces
were occasionally flung to him in answer to the
petitions in which he lauded himself and his achievements past and to come. But unmistakable marks
of royal recognition never reached him. He certainly deserved these as well as any diplomatist of

the day, but under the Stuarts, within and without
the court, no man got his deserts. At length the
Civil War grew imminent, and Herbert feigned at
first the enthusiasm of a staunch Royalist. He took
advantage of a general invitation to join the King's
Council at York in 1640, and protested against the
bare thought of conceding any demand to the
enemies of the Crown. But a new generation of
courtiers had arisen since he played a really prominent part in court society, and none heeded
his words. He retired to Montgomery Castle in
dudgeon, pondered his grievances, assumed a cyni-
cal indifference to the current party divisions, and
resolved to suffer as little personal inconvenience
from the war as possible. At the same time as the
Parliament gave him a taste of its growing power,
and threatened him with the confiscation of his
property, Rupert, his sovereign's nephew, and the
son of that Electress Palatine to whom he had
been in earlier years chivalrously attached, came
to Shrewsbury. The Prince asked for his aid,
and for an interview, and offered to put his castle
in a state of defence. Lord Herbert replied by
letter that he could defend himself; that he disliked
soldiers about the house ; and that he had just entered
on a new course of physic which would forbid his
meeting the Royalist leader. Soon afterwards the
Parliamentary general in the district invited him to
surrender ; he hesitated for a day or two ; found

the prospect of resistance uncongenial, and assented
to the demand. He remained joint-master of his
castle with the Parliamentarians, and the Royalists
straightway laid siege to it. His new friends
relieved him, and he put himself wholly in their
hands. He went to London, lived to all outward
appearance on the happiest of terms with the
Parliament men, received a substantial pension
from them, pursued his philosophical studies, grew
irritable in temper, declined in health, and died in
1648 at the age of sixty-five. Before his death he
wrote a long series of epitaphs upon himself, in
which he announced his belief in the soul's im-
mortality, and his anticipations of a happier life
hereafter. His sons and all surviving relatives remained true to their Royalist colours to the last,
and lost everything in the struggle. Lord Herbert
saved his property at the expense of his honour,
and clearly had a poor opinion of those who re-
versed the process. He showed some sense of
parental responsibility in making before his death
pecuniary provision for his children. His theo-
retical devotion to military pursuits also received
illustration in his will, where he promised a pension
in perpetuity to two wounded soldiers, to be chosen
by his younger son—a Royalist captain, and these
pensioners were to stand permanently, fully armed,
at the gates of Montgomery Castle. He asked
the Parliament, with characteristic complacency, to

pay the arrears of his pension to his elder son and heir, to enable the young man to discharge the large fine inflicted on him for his consistent devotion to his sovereign. At the date of his death Lord Herbert had renounced the political ambitions which had distracted him for the first fifty years and more of his life. His political temperament belonged, in fact, to an earlier epoch—to the reign of Elizabeth, in which politicians were true to none but themselves; and such a temperament was ill adapted for a crisis that involved great political principles. The vanity and harmless peculiarities of his earlier life were misinterpreted by a generation that had not known him as a young man, and they consequently degenerated into an absorbing selfishness and confirmed eccentricities of conduct. Herbert's old age lacked "honour, love, obedience, troops of friends," and in their stead came curses both loud and deep. It was overlooked that he was a vainglorious man, disappointed, through little fault of his own, of the worldly successes he loved, or that outside politics he had laid the foundation of a real and lasting reputation. Parliamentarian and Royalist combined to christen him on his death-bed "the black Lord Herbert."

And here let us part with Lord Herbert in the *rôle* of courtier and politician. Let us glance at him now in his study, when he has closed the door on the distractions of court or political life. The change

is a striking one.   Apologetic tones are no more
needed.   The fashionable man of pleasure is one
no longer.   The near-sighted politician, whose political horizon was limited by hopes of his own
advancement, becomes a far-seeing philosopher.   In
the solitude of his library the frivolous worldling
faces boldly the problems of human life ; seeks the
final cause of the processes of the human mind, and
brings all religious systems to the test of reason.
He accepts no man's judgment in place of his own; he
passes by all acknowledged contemporary authorities,
and anticipates opinions and methods that are junior
to him by at least two centuries.   The nature of
truth is the central theme of his earliest speculations, and he is the only Englishman who has
devoted a large treatise to a purely metaphysical
treatment of the topic.   The relations of abstract
truth with religion next absorbed his attention,
and he was the first to seek a conception of the
essentials of religion by applying the comparative
method to all the systems with which he was able
to acquaint himself.   Such are the labours of the
man who pretended that his autobiography recorded
all the achievements to which posterity ought to
attach a serious value.

Lord Herbert gives two or three passing hints
in his autobiography that he had in his leisure
moments dabbled in philosophy, but it is so difficult
and so dangerous to take him seriously in his

memoirs, that the reader who confines himself to that part of his work alone, will altogether misjudge him on these points. As soon as he could speak without fear of imperfection or impertinence in his utterances, he worried himself and his nurses (he tells us) with speculations as to how he had come into the world, and how he should go out of it. In the general digression on education which figures somewhat inaptly in the early pages of the book, Herbert contemns the subtleties of logic as being "only tolerable in a mercenary lawyer," and recommends the pupil to devote himself solely to that part of the science which will enable him to detect fallacies in "vicious argumentations." "Some good sum of philosophy . . . which may teach him both the ground of the Platonic and Aristotelian philosophy," should be acquired subsequently; it will not be amiss to learn the "Paracelsian principles," and the arguments controverting "the ordinary Peripatetic doctrine." But all this, Lord Herbert adds, in a characteristically light-hearted vein, "may be performed in one year; that term being enough for philosophy, as I conceive, and six months for logic, *for I am confident a man may have quickly more than he needs of these arts.*" At the close of the memoirs Herbert shyly confesses to the reader his love of books and of a private life, and adds with conscious pride that he was an author himself. He had begun a book in England, and had continued it in France in the intervals of flirtation and negotiation. He had shown his handiwork to two great scholars, Grotius and Tilenus, who, " after they had perused it, and given it more commendations than is fit for me to repeat, exhorted me earnestly to print and publish it." The title of the book—*De Veritate prout distinguitur a Revelatione verisimili, possibili et à falso*—alone raises the suspicion that Lord Herbert is not speaking in his usual manner, or that the bases of truth had all along divided his attention with the frivolities of society. But it is necessary to turn to the book itself to realise the significance of these suggestions.

It is only desirable to point out here the salient features of Lord Herbert's philosophy,—to treat it as evidence of his reflective and dialectical power, and of the note of seriousness in his mental constitution. Lord Herbert writes in Latin. " Libere philosophemur. . . . Veritatem sine dote quæramus," he says in an opening address to the reader, and the appeal characterises the whole work. Lord Herbert attacks his subject without delay. He lays down as an axiom that truth exists, and thence deduces a series of propositions as to its permanence, its universality, and the general capacity of the mind to perceive truth. His theory of perception is very hazily expressed, and is practically ignored in the latter part of the treatise ; but the fact that he should have introduced such a theory at all is proof of the thoroughness of his method and the sincerity of his aims. The mind, he says, consists of an almost infinite number of what he terms "faculties," and each thing has a form corresponding to one of these "faculties." Whenever a thing is brought into contact with the mind, the corresponding faculty becomes active, immediately conforms to the thing, and the harmonious conforming of the one with the other (*intellectûs cognoscentis cum re cognitâ congruentia*) establishes a perception of truth. Thus the mind is no *tabula rasa*, or blank book, on which objects inscribe themselves; it is rather a closed book, only opened on the presentation of objects. But although the "faculties" of the mind are as numerous as things, and there is thus a virtual analogy between the human mind and the world, the mental "faculties" may be roughly reduced to four great classes, to which Herbert gives the titles—Natural Instinct, Internal Sense, External Sense, and *Discursus*, or Reason.[1] And here (so far as I understand the system) Lord Herbert deviates a little from his old path, and makes no attempt to strictly maintain his original theory of perception. He discusses at length Natural Instinct,

---

[1] Sir William Hamilton calls the last head "the discursive faculty;" Hallam calls it "reason;" M. de Rémusat "raisonnement."

his first class of faculties, which might more justly be designated Intellectual Instinct : it closely corresponds to the Aristotelian νοῦς, the Schoolmen's Intelligentia, the common sense of other philosophy, and the light of nature of popular parlance.   It is the source of the common notions, primary truths, common principles (κοιναὶ ἔννοιαι, *notitiæ communes*), which exist in every human being of sound and entire mind.   These notions are not the product of experience or observation ; they are intuitions. External objects may excite them in us, but do not convey them to us : they are implanted in us at our birth ; they come direct from God ; they are the part of the divine image and the divine wisdom with which every human being is impregnated.   Lord Herbert carefully defines their distinguishing qualities ; they have the priority of all other kinds of notions ; they are established independently of all secondary considerations supplied by the conscious exercise of reason ; they invite such universal consent that to deny them is to abnegate human nature ; they are necessary to the conservation of mankind.   The other three classes of faculties act under the direction of the natural or intellectual instinct.   The "internal sense" distinguishes the agreeable from the disagreeable, and good from evil ; it is identical with the conscience. The "external sense" is nothing more than what is commonly known as sensation.   The "discursive faculty" determines the relations between the various conceptions produced by the other sets of faculties : it deals with quiddity, quality and quantity, time and space. Herbert finally insists that man's capacity for religion distinguishes him from animals rather than reason.[1]

Herbert's religious views show as striking an originality as his purely philosophical speculations. He develops them in the concluding sections of the *De Veritate* as well as in two treatises—*Religio Laici*[2] and *De Religione Gentilium*[3]—which practically form

---

[1] M. de Rémusat has given the fullest account of Lord Herbert's system in his *Lord Herbert, sa Vie et ses Œuvres*, pp. 120–212. Sir William Hamilton has briefly described its characteristic features in his "Notes on Reid's Philosophy of Common Sense" (Reid's Works, ed. Hamilton, ii. pp. 781, 782). Ueberweg touches on it in his "History of Philosophy," ii. 34, 40, and in the Appendix to the English translation (ii. 354, 355) an elaborate notice is to be found. Though translated into French in 1639, the *De Veritate* has never appeared in English.

[2] This treatise was published in London for the first time in 1645, together with an appendix to the *De Veritate*, entitled *De Causis Errorum*, an exposition of the logical fallacies. The *Religio Laici* occupies twenty-seven pages at the close of the work, and is followed by an Appendix *Ad Sacerdotes de Religione Laici* and three Latin poems, two of which are reprinted in the autobiography. Another edition of the volume was issued in 1656.

[3] This work was published posthumously at Amsterdam in 1663 (2d edit. 1700). It was translated into English by

appendices to the work on Truth. His doctrine, briefly expressed, runs thus :—Religion is common to the human race. Stripped of accidental characteristics, and reduced to its essential form, it consists of five *notitiæ communes,* or innate ideas, which spring from the natural instinct. The common notions are—(1.) That there is a God. (To confirm the existence of a God, Herbert relies on the argument of design in the created world, and he anticipates Paley in illustrating his argument by the example of a watch.)[1] (2.) That He ought to be worshipped. (3.) That virtue and piety are essential to worship. (4.) That man ought to repent of his sins. (5.) That there are rewards and punishments in a future life. It is unnecessary and unreasonable to admit any articles of religion other than these. The dogmas of the Churches, reputed to embody divine revelations, are the work of priests, who have endea-

---

W. Lewis in 1709. This is the only English version of any of Lord Herbert's philosophical writings.

[1] " Et quidem si horologium per diem et noctem integram horas signanter indicans, viderit quispiam non mente captus, id consilio arteque summa factum judicaverit. Ecquis non plane demens, qui hanc mundi machinam non per viginti quatuor horas tantum, sed per tot secula circuitus suos obeuntem animadverterit, non id omne sapientissimo utique potentissimoque alicui autori tribuat ?"—*De Religione Gent.,* cap. xiii. The idea has been traced to Cicero, *De Natura Deorum,* ii. 34. It is to be found in many writers intermediate between Paley and Herbert.

d

voured to establish their own influence for their
own advantage by shrouding these five ideas in
obscurely worded creeds.   To prove the universality of these ideas, Herbert submits the religion
of the Gentiles to an historical examination, and
adduces the testimony of Seneca and Plato, of Cicero,
Lucretius, and Ovid to show that the religious
belief of the Greeks and Romans, when stripped of
sacerdotal superstition, is identical with his five
articles.   Certain of the articles in fact maintained
a purer shape in the ancient than in the modern
world.   Death and a future life were more vividly and
profitably realised by the believers in Elysium and
Tartarus than by those who christened the hereafter Heaven and Hell.   Aristotle has defined the
common notions of virtues more effectively than any
other writer.   Thus revealed religion is practically
rejected by Lord Herbert as the artifice of an hierarchy.   Moreover, no one form of revealed religion
receives universal assent ; every form of it is matter
of endless controversy : no one form of it, therefore,
can be true, since universality of assent is one of
the axiomatic conditions of truth.   Any theory of
revelation which represents God to have repeatedly
favoured one part of the human race, to the exclusion
of all the rest of it, is demonstrably inconsistent
with the notion of the divine attributes, inculcated by
the natural instinct.   But to test reputed revelation
we must not rely upon the faculty of natural instinct,

but on the discursive faculty. We must examine
the character and condition of the person to whom
the revelation is presumably made, and this examination is to be conducted on such searching
lines that no received revelation answers the test.
With some inconsistency Lord Herbert adds that
the only revelation that a man can reasonably
accept as true is one made immediately to himself,
and so far is he from denying the possibility of
this kind of personal revelation, that he solemnly
asserts in his autobiography that when he was
hesitating as to whether he ought to publish his
treatise on Truth, God gave him a direct sign of
approval, on which he acted.[1]   In his *Religio Laici*,
and its appendix *Ad Sacerdotes*, priesthoods are
generally denounced, and Lord Herbert explains
his attitude towards Christianity.   He takes up the
neutral position—that it is the best religion because
it is most readily reducible to the five essential
articles.   He sees in its rites an endeavour to give
prominence to the common notions of religion, but

---

[1] Page 248, *infra*, and see also the account of Lord
Herbert's death on p. 298.   Herbert believed in the efficacy
of prayer, and a prayer of his, expressing his gratitude to God
for having given him a knowledge of His greatness, is published in Warner's "Epistolary Curiosities."   Herbert's will
opens with a bequest of "my rational soul, with all its divine
faculties, being, understanding, will, faith, hope, love, and joy
to God, my creator, redeemer, and preserver."

he renounces its claim to a special revelation and all sympathy with those professors of Christianity who believe themselves to be in any wise specially favoured by God—"the impious enemies of the universal Divine Providence." Lord Herbert insists, that whatever form of religion a virtuous man adopt, or whatever government he live under, he will obtain inward peace now and eternal happiness hereafter.

Ethics do not enter very materially into Lord Herbert's philosophy, and in his sparse references to the subject, he inclines, in spite of his eulogies of virtue, to a lax system of morals. He does not set himself up, he reminds us, as an apologist for wicked men, but sin (he argues) is very often attributable to hereditary physical causes, to an inherent and irresistible propensity to vice, which invites a very mild censure from rational beings. Lord Herbert holds the sanguine belief that none are so wicked as to sin purposedly, and with an high hand, against the eternal majesty of God.[1] He urges men to pass over injuries done to themselves, because a great and good God will hereafter assign *double* punishment to those aggressors who do not suffer for their aggressions in this world.[2] But while he treats ethics loosely and unsystematically, Herbert insists on the high importance of educa-

---

[1] P. 61, *infra.*   [2] P. 63, *infra.*

tion. The only obviously serious passages in the
autobiography are those devoted to an exposition of
an educational system which has much of Milton's
loftiness of aim and Locke's sober sense.[1] Hereditary disease must be counteracted in infancy;
manners are as important as learning, " for among
boys all vice is easily learned;" Greek should be
studied before Latin; the logic of the Schools
should not occupy much of the pupil's time, nor
should philosophy nor mathematics; the rudiments
of medical and botanical and ethical science should
be at the command of all men, and athletic exercises
must never be neglected. Botany Herbert especially commends as "a fine study:" "it is worthy
a gentleman to be a good botanic, that so he may
know the nature of all herbs and plants, being our
fellow-creatures and made for the use of man."[2]
Herbert was not quite satisfied that he had treated
education with adequate fulness in his autobiography. "I confess," he writes there,[3] "I have
collected many things to this purpose which I forbear to set down here, because, if God grant me

---

[1] Pp. 43–80, *infra.*

[2] P. 57, *infra.* Herbert's medical knowledge, of which he
gives several examples below (pp. 52–57), is derived from the
works of Paracelsus and his disciples. My friend, Dr.
Norman Moore, points out to me that it is of no scientific
value whatever, and has the worst defects of empiricism.

[3] P. 80, *infra.*

life and health, I intend to make a little treatise concerning these points." This " little treatise" was written later, and after remaining long in an anonymous manuscript, was printed with Lord Herbert's name in 1768, under the title of " A Dialogue between a Tutor and a Pupil." Its authorship is assuredly proved by internal evidence,[1] but its purpose is less practical than might be expected. After the tutor has appraised the value of various studies, in which botany holds, as before, a high place, the pupil asks why, in matters of religion, priests should advise him to rely on faith rather than on reason ? The tutor replies by pointing out the evils of an irrational faith, brings the argument round to Lord Herbert's five points of religion, and corroborates them by an examination of Christian and heathen theology. This " little treatise," therefore, though professedly an appendix to Lord Herbert's educational disquisition in his autobiography, is virtually a final restatement of his religious position. But it is of value as positively proving the author's earnest desire to supplant the received religious teaching by free and unrestricted

---

[1] See the notes on pp. 50, 51, 57, 72, and 80. Abraham Seller presented the MS. in 1704 to Dr. Woodward. It subsequently passed into the hands of Colonel King, Dr. Woodward's executor, and thence apparently to W. Bathoe, the bookseller, who published it in 1768. The MS. is now in the Bodleian Library.

thought in the minds of young as well as of old men.

Lord Herbert's treatment of philosophy and cognate themes is not without defect. In his purely metaphysical works his diction is obscure where precision is least dispensable;[1] wire-drawn distinctions are made between terms and propositions which are for all practical purposes identical, and the author excludes all illustration of his meaning from matters of common knowledge. In the discussion of his five points of religion, he often falls a victim to the theological bias which he so severely denounces in others. His deduction of a future life from the natural instinct which prompts men to imagine its existence, is only worthy of the professed theologian, and much else of his reasoning on religious topics is obviously circular. But the defects are few compared with the undoubted merits of Lord Herbert's achievement. He has the greatest virtue of all speculative writing, the virtue of originality. He had read such books as were accessible to him on the subjects with which he dealt. None of them satisfied him, and rejecting all their conclusions, he worked the questions they professed to

---

[1] Herbert apologises for *sphalmata et errata* at the close of the *De Veritate*, and asks the reader to correct them for himself. Hallam is especially severe on him for his obscurities of terminology.

answer out for himself. No authority, he said, deserved a slavish adherence. A philosopher must think for himself, and have no personal nor professional ends to serve. He must be *ingenuus et sui arbitrii.*[1] This in itself was a sure sign that Herbert was a sincere progressionist. The idol of authority was still worshipped by the mass of his contemporaries, but he resolutely set his face against it. Not the least important part of his work is his dignified and rational plea for universal toleration in matters of religious belief.

It is somewhat characteristic of his temper that Herbert should have made no mention of Bacon in his philosophical works, and have regarded himself as the one man of the age who dared to think for himself. In the whole of his writings there is but a single reference to the greatest of contemporary thinkers. Herbert confesses that he followed Bacon's example in turning his attention to the history of Henry VIII.; but although he admits that his model—Bacon's "Life of Henry VII."—was a performance that did honour to its author, and that its author was "a great personage," he affects to be more depressed by Bacon's disgraceful end than impressed by his literary achievements.[2]

---

[1] *De Veritate* is dedicated *Lectori cuivis integri et illibati judicii.*

[2] See p. 265.

Bacon was the friend of George Herbert the poet,[1] and was in all likelihood personally known to George's brother. But Herbert's silence is very intelligible. The two men were in their characters and in the results of their labours as the poles asunder. Unlike Herbert, Bacon measured accurately the trivialities of court life : he plied them for his own advantage, but he fully recognised their hollowness ; he knew his own superiority to them and to those who found pleasure in them. But as philosophers Herbert and Bacon differ more materially than in the conduct of their lives. The latter sought to extend and systematise knowledge, to put into man's hand and brain the means of conquering nature by enabling him to interpret it, to enlist nature in the service of mankind. " Man is but what he knoweth," and experiment is the only sure road to knowledge. All *à priori* reasoning is to be renounced ; induction is the only method that commands success in the pursuit of knowledge. Elaborating his argument, Bacon surveyed the whole field of human knowledge, and showed how inductive methods advanced its limits and how deductive methods narrowed them. Herbert's scheme was not less ambitious, but did not cover the same ground. He was content to investi-

---

[1] Bacon dedicated his translation of the Psalms (1625) to George Herbert.

gate the mental processes by which man could acquire any knowledge at all, and here he declared experiment to be of no avail. He therefore relied on deductive argument alone. Bacon has hinted that if he had attacked this subject he would have applied inductive methods to it as to all his other speculations. He had no sympathy with metaphysics, which he defined as a temporary substitute for physics ; he asserted that when scientific induction had been sufficiently systematised, metaphysics would succumb at its approach, would (we may take it) form part of psychology, and be as amenable to practical experiment as any other branch of science. For the present he deemed it well to let the topic alone. Religious speculation was in much the same case. He tacitly assumed a vague relationship between religion and morality, but he avoided a discussion which could neither strengthen nor weaken the framework of his scientific system. He was content to describe religion as it was, and to treat it as based " on the word and work of God and upon the light of nature." Reason, he said, must not attempt to prove or examine the mysteries of faith—and these mysteries he identifies with the ordinarily accepted teaching of revelation. In religious debate Herbert was thus logically far in advance of Bacon, and they had few other topics in common. There is nothing, therefore, ungenerous in the failure of the younger writer to make any acknowledgment of the work of the older.[1]

In their immediate effect on contemporary opinion, Herbert's philosophical writings were little better than abortive. Although widely read,[2] their significance was not appreciated. While the purely speculative part proved unintelligible, the religious discussions excited nearly universal hostility, begetting *libros non liberos.* Of the treatise *De Veritate,* Sir William Dugdale writes in 1674 : " It much passeth my understanding, being wholly philosophical." [3] Evelyn notes in his Diary that Herbert's brother, Sir Henry, presented him with a copy,[4] but gives no indication that he put himself to the pains of reading it. The only English writer of the time who attempted a serious discussion of Lord Herbert's philosophy was Nathaniel Culverwel, a fellow of Emanuel College, Cambridge, whose " Discourse of the Light of Nature "

---

[1] They are most closely in agreement in their references to Telesius, who had anticipated some of Bacon's arguments in favour of experiment as the only sure road to knowledge. Herbert advises young men to study Telesius's writings, and clearly attaches high value to them. Bacon similarly applauds them in his treatise *De Principiis,* and owes more to them than he acknowledges. (See note on pp. 49–50, *infra.*)

[2] The first edition of *De Veritate* (1624) was succeeded by a second in 1633, and a third in 1645.

[3] Dugdale's Diary and Correspondence, p. 397.

[4] Evelyn's Diary, ed. Bray and Wheatley, ii. 36.

was first published in 1652. Culverwel is as powerful a writer in support of the doctrine of *à priori* knowledge as Lord Herbert himself, but he opposes the theory of innate ideas, and asserts, in contradiction to Lord Herbert, that the suggesting influence of sense and experience are necessary to the translation of our primary notions into consciousness. But when Culverwel proceeds to erect a theological superstructure upon his speculative theories in close conformity with orthodox Christianity, he will have no further truce with the author of *De Veritate*. Religion, according to Culverwel, "is built upon a surer and higher rock—upon a more adamantine and precious foundation" than Herbert's "common notions," and he finally identifies Herbert with those who have "arrived to that full perfection of error . . . that have a powder-plot against the Gospel; that would very compendiously behead all Christian religion at one blow—a device which old and ordinary heretics were never acquainted withal." [1] In this spirit

---

[1] Culverwel's "Light of Nature," p. 226, in the reprint published at Edinburgh in 1857. See also pp. 128-134, and pp. 211, 212. The preface to this edition, by John Cairns, M.A., is well worthy of study. Sir William Hamilton, in his edition of Reid's works (p. 782), justly calls attention to Culverwel's learning and intelligence. Robert Greville, Lord Brooke, remarkable for his enlightened and tolerant views, was author of a work of a similar kind—"The Nature of Truth," 1641.

Herbert was criticised by Thomas Halyburton, a professor of divinity at St. Andrews, who was especially scandalised by Herbert's identification of the principles of true religion with notions current in pagan writers.[1] Richard Baxter, in " More Reason for the Christian Religion, and No Reason against it " (1672), animadverts in a like temper on Lord Herbert's arguments, and insists that the Scriptures are the sole product of the Spirit's inspiration, and contain no word that is not infallibly true. " Supernatural evidence " alone can produce a satisfactory apprehension of religion ; and there is no supernatural evidence outside the Gospel of Christ. Charles Blount (1654–1693) is the only seventeenth century writer in England who proved himself a disciple of Lord Herbert, but he was no original thinker, but a confirmed plagiarist, and literally borrowed from his master without always acknow-

---

But Lord Brooke confesses that he had not read Herbert's *De Veritate* very recently, and did not remember it (p. 40); he approaches his subject from a purely Christian point of view, while working out the Platonic theory, that all our ideas are remembrances of a former existence. Dr. John Wallis, the mathematician, replied to Brooke in " Truth Tried," 1643, in which he showed the inconsistency of identifying knowledge of matters of fact with implanted ideas.

[1] " Natural Religion Insufficient " (1714) is the title of Halyburton's work.

ledging his obligations. He published a *Religio Laici* in 1682, which is a slavish reproduction of Lord Herbert's volume of the name, and this had been preceded in 1680 by " Great is Diana of the Ephesians ; or, the Original of Idolatry, together with the Politick Institution of the Gentiles' Sacrifices," a feeble adumbration of Herbert's *De Religione Gentilium.*[1] Not until Locke wrote did Herbert, as a philosopher, receive anything like justice from his own countrymen. Locke disagrees with him at every turn, but he honestly explains his position ; and no better introduction to Herbert's system is at present accessible than the first book of Locke's " Essay on the Human Understanding." Locke as an empiricist and sensationalist hunts to the death the theory of innate ideas, but he accepts Herbert's five " common notions " of religion as truths of reason, and in his " Reasonableness of Christianity " he joins hands with Herbert in denouncing the irrational dogmas of priests, although he is content to deduce a definition of faith from an historical examination

---

[1] Blount claimed to have used some unpublished notes by Lord Herbert in his best-known work—" The Two First Books of Apollonius Tyaneus, written originally in Greek, with Philological Notes upon each chapter " (1680), but he apparently only drew upon Herbert's published books. See Mr. Leslie Stephen's article on Blount in the " Dictionary of National Biography."

of Scripture. At a later date, Dr. Leland (1691–1766) christened Herbert the father of English Deism; and while examining his doctrine from an unfriendly point of view, supplies another intelligible exposition of Herbert's religious writings.[1]

Abroad, at an earlier date than at home, Herbert found the recognition that was due to him, but there, too, he failed to make converts or disciples. In 1634 Herbert presented a copy of the *De Veritate* to Charles Diodati, Milton's friend, and Diodati forwarded it to Gassendi, eminent as the champion of Epicurean atomism, and the reviver of systematic materialism. In Gassendi's Works[2] is an adequate discussion of Herbert's system. He agrees in the main with his theory of perception—*intellectûs cognoscentis cum re cognita congruentia;* but complains —very politely, it is true—of Herbert's obscurity, objects that man's reason deals not with the real nature of things, but with such appearances of them as are known to him through the senses, and doubts the universality of Herbert's common notions. Descartes, the most eminent of Herbert's foreign contemporaries, also spoke of Herbert with respect, and made a thorough study of his works.

---

[1] Dr. John Leland's "View of the Principal Deistical Writers," i. 1–34. Charles Blount is placed second on Leland's list of English Deists.

[2] Opera, iii. 411.

But he likewise is not deeply impressed by their
veracity. "J'y trouve," he writes of them, "plu-
sieurs choses fort bonnes, *sed non publici saporis;*
car il y a peu de personnes qui soient capables
d'entendre la metaphysique. Et pour le genéràl du
livre il tient un chemin fort différent de celui que
j'ai suivi. . . . Enfin par conclusion, encore que je
ne puisse m'accorder en tout aux sentiments de cet
auteur, je ne laisse pas de l'estimer beaucoup au-
dessus des esprits ordinaires." Neither as philosopher, mathematician, nor physicist did Descartes
accept Herbert's guidance.[1]

Of the solid seriousness of Lord Herbert's student
life ample proof has already been adduced, but it
is only just to him to supplement the evidence with
a few words on his poetry and his historical work.
Little as we might expect it, he was free from the
puniest of all forms of vanity which prompts the
would-be poet to rush into print as soon as his
verse is committed to paper. So far as Lord
Herbert himself was concerned, the world at large

---

[1] Other hostile attacks on Lord Herbert's position may be
found in J. Musæus' *Examen Cherburianismi sive de Luminis
Naturæ insufficientia ad salutem contra E. Herbertum de
Cherbury* (1675 and 1708) ; C. Kortholt's *De Tribus Impos-
toribus* (*i.e.*, Herbert, Hobbes, and Spinoza),' 1680 and 1700 ;
and J. Ogilvie's "An Enquiry into the Infidelity of the
Times, with Observations on Lord Herbert of Cherbury "
(1783).

might still be without the poems which came from his pen. They were printed for the first time by his brother Henry, seventeen years after their author had been laid in the grave. Yet from youth till he was at least fifty years old did Herbert solace his leisure with the production of English and Latin poetry. And with characteristic versatility he did not restrict his efforts to any one class of composition. Love and philosophy alternately inspire his muse ; sonnets and epitaphs, ditties and satires occupy his attention by turns. As a poet, Herbert proves himself the ablest of all the disciples of Donne. Like his master, he revels in subtleties of thought and diction, and very often exhibits so crude a power of expression as to offend a sensitive reader's ear.[1] No versifier ever lumbered more awkwardly through ten pages of print than does Lord Herbert in his two satires.[2]

---

[1] Ben Jonson told Drummond of Hawthornden in 1619 that " Donne said to him he wrote that Epitaph on Prince Henry, *Look to me, Faith* (1613), to match Sir Ed. Herbert in obscureness" ("Ben Jonson's Conversations with Drummond," p. 8). Herbert also wrote an epitaph on Prince Henry in 1613.

[2] The first is entitled " The State Progress of Ill ; " and the second, " Satyra Secunda of Travellers from Paris," is addressed to Ben Jonson. The former is dated August 1608, the latter September 1608. I give an extract from the second on p. 90, note.

e

..astic echo-poems are too quaint to be
.ng, and far-fetched conceits repel us in the
,.itaphs on his friends.   When at his best, we can
never be certain that the current of his utterances
will not be interrupted by some grotesque discord.
Nevertheless Lord Herbert has every right to the
title of poet.   The author of the " Ditty in Imitation
of the Spanish " possessed true lyrical inspiration.

> " Now that the April of your youth adorns
>   The garden of your face,
> Now that for you each knowing lover mourns,
>   And all seek to your grace,
> Do not repay affection with scorns.
>
> What though you may a matchless beauty vaunt,
>   And all that hearts can move
> By such a power that seemeth to enchant,
>   Yet, without help of love,
> Beauty no pleasure to itself can grant.
>
> Then think each minute that you lose a day.
>   The longest Youth is short,
> The shortest Age is long ; Time flies away,
>   And makes us but his sport,
> And that which is not Youth's is Age's prey."

Verse like this recalls Herrick in his most graceful moods, and evinces far higher powers of reflection.   In his purely contemplative poems, which
chiefly deal with " Platonick Love," Lord Herbert
has reminded a very competent critic of Mr. Robert
Browning's forms of thought and expression ; and a

quaint sonnet addressed to "Black Itself" is not without resemblance to Blanco White's famous sonnet on
" Night."   But Lord Herbert is brought into closest
affinity with modern poetry by the masterly command he displayed over the metre which Lord
Tennyson has carried to perfection in his " In
Memoriam."   He has anticipated the Laureate in
many of the finest effects of which the latter has
proved the metre capable, as the following examples
prove :—

> " You are the first were ever lov'd,
>   And who may think this not so true,
>   So little knows of love or you,
> It need not otherwise be prov'd.
>
>   .   .   .   .   .   .
>
> Yet, as in our Northern clime
>   Rare fruits, though late, appear at last ;
>   As we may see, some years being past,
> Our orange trees grow ripe with time ;—
>
> So think not strange, if Love to break
>   His wonted silence now makes bold :
>   For [when] a love is seven years old,
> Is it not time to learn to speak ? " [1]

---

[1] These verses are from the " Ditty," pp. 41–43, in J.
Churton Collins' edition of the poems.   But " An Ode
upon a question moved whether love should continue for
ever," pp. 92–98, should also be examined, and would deserve
quotation if space permitted it.   Mr. Churton Collins
remarks on the affinity of Lord Tennyson's and Herbert's
metre in the introduction to his edition, the whole of which

In his Latin verse Lord Herbert often expresses himself clumsily and inharmoniously, but taken as a whole his Latin poems form a substantial testimony to his scholarship and general culture.

Herbert's " History of Henry VIII." is his most ambitious essay in English prose. The work was undertaken, as I have shown below, with political objects, and unfortunately exhibits little of that independent criticism which gives value to Lord Herbert's philosophical writings. It is an unmeasured eulogy of Henry VIII.'s statesmanship, and a laboured endeavour to condone the crimes of his private life.[1] Yet, in apparent contradiction of his aims, Herbert acknowledged the obligation which lies upon the historian to deduce his facts from original research. How far he personally engaged in the examination of the documents which are incorporated in the history has been matter of dispute. He employed many clerks to search the Paper Office at Whitehall, and one of these, Thomas Master, a Fellow of New College, Oxford, was popularly reputed to have had a large share

---

is well worthy the perusal of the student of Lord Herbert's writings. Herbert seems to have suggested another poem of the Laureate in the lines beginning—

> " Tears, flow no more, or if you needs must flow,
>   Fall yet more slow."

[1] See pp. 264 *et seq.*

in the construction of the published book.[1] But no solid argument has been produced to rob Herbert of the substantial credit of its authorship, or to prove that his assistants lent him more than mechanical service. He therefore deserves recognition as the

---

[1] Wood, in his "Athenæ Oxon," ed. Bliss, iii., says of Master : " He was a drudge to, and assisted much, Edward, Lord Herbert of Cherbury, when he was obtaining materials for the writing of the 'Life of King Henry VIII.' Four thick volumes in folio of such materials I have lying by me now, in every one of which I find his handwriting, either in inter-lining, adding, or correcting, and one of these four, which is entitled *Collectaneorum lib. Secundum,* is mostly written by him, collected from Parliament Rolls, the Paper Office at Whitehall, Vicar-General's Office, books belonging to the Clerks of the Council, MSS. in Cotton's Library, books of Convocations of the Clergy, &c., printed authors, &c. And there is no doubt that as he had an especial hand in com-posing the said 'Life of King Henry VIII.' (which, as some say, he turned mostly into Latin, but never printed), so had he a hand in latinising that Lord's book, *De Veritate,* or others." An affectionate Latin epitaph on Master, who died in 1643, and some Latin hexameters, entitled "*Mensa Lusoria,* or a Shovelboard-Table to Mr. Master," appear among Her-bert's poems. Aubrey states that Master lived with Herbert till 1642. The MS. volumes containing Herbert's materials for his history are now in Jesus College Library. The work was first published in 1649 by a London stationer named Whitaker. Whitaker had some litigation in the House of Lords with Lord Herbert's grandson Edward as to his right to print the book, each litigant affirming that Lord Herbert had given the MS. to him for his sole use.

producer of a standard historical authority, which is vitiated, but not rendered nugatory, by its frank acknowledgment of partisanship. The style of Lord Herbert's history is as unequal as that of the autobiography, and proves that whether as prose-writer or poet, he did not possess full command of the instrument of language. He depreciates his style very frequently in his private letters,[1] and although self-depreciation from his lips must not be assumed to be sincere, his remarks about his failings in this respect deserve to be taken literally. The construction of his sentences is often suspiciously involved. Where concentrated energy of utterance is necessary to give full effect to his meaning, he sometimes grows tediously loquacious. In his philosophical works he acknowledged conciseness and precision to be of prime importance, and wisely took refuge from himself, not perhaps with complete success, in the artificial restraints imposed by the Latin language. But although his English prose lack the niceties of a great style, his vocabulary is so simple and so copious that he can rarely be misunderstood. He is perspicuous even when he is ungrammatical. He is never pretentious in his choice of words, and has no mannerisms. His diction is without the majesty of Milton or of Sir Thomas Browne; but it has the historical merit of

---

[1] Cf. pp. 263 and 330.

reflecting the best characteristics of the everyday speech of its day.[1]

I have endeavoured to place before the reader a just estimate of Lord Herbert's character in all its contradictory aspects; to make manifest that the light-hearted vainglorious man of the world whose autobiography is printed below was, contrary to all the expectations which that work excites, a poet and a subtle-souled psychologist. Inconsistencies are apparent in all Lord Herbert's actions, and in all his speculations; and a far-reaching theory, which Mr. Browning probably among living men would alone be able to construct, is necessary to weld them in one harmonious whole. It should be remembered, however, that Lord Herbert's complicated character does not stand alone in his own age, and that Bacon and Raleigh present as puzzling enigmas to the biographer. Probably in the

---

[1] Lord Herbert also apparently interested himself in mechanical inventions. He sent to Windebank in 1635 a series of inventions suggested to him by an anonymous Frenchman, which included improvements in warships, gun-carriages, and a proposal for the construction of a floating bathing-palace on the Thames, opposite Somerset House (Cal. State Papers, 1635, pp. 62, 63). In 1638 he showed much interest in Thomas Bushnell's survey of North Wales for the purpose of discovering the presence of silver ore (Cal. State Papers, 3rd Oct. 1638.)

spirit of the time a solution of such riddles may
be discoverable.   That spirit was a strange con-
coction, formed of simples that could not readily
mingle.   Ideas that sprang from modern and from
ancient Italy, from classicism and mediævalism, from
base and pure forms of Christianity, all sought at
once, in the late sixteenth and the early seventeenth
centuries, to gain the mastery over Englishmen's
minds. In the seething strife high ideals were formed
and translated into act, but low ideals were also
generated, and demanded an equal share of recognition.   Torn asunder by conflicting ambitions, men's
conduct lacked internal unity. Greatness allied
itself with littleness, virtue with vice.   Romancers
have figured men living two lives, men combining
two distinct personalities in a single corporeal
frame.   Such freaks of nature are commonly believed to find their homes in dreamland ; but they
are confined to no impalpable realm ; the divided
aims of Herbert's, and of Bacon's, and of Raleigh's
lives prove indubitably that the romancers do not
always romance.

THE history of the publication of the Autobiography deserves attention. In his will Lord Herbert writes:—"And whereas I have begun a manifest of my action in these late troubles, but am prevented in the review thereof, I do hereby leave it to a person, whom I shall by word instruct, to finish the same, and to publish it to the world by my direction, and as having the expresse charge layd upon him by me for doing it." But the friend's name, if ever spoken, has not reached us. Two copies of the MS. remained in Lord Herbert's family, one with his grandson Edward, and the other with his brother Sir Henry, and, according to Oldys, the Lady Dowager Herbert, widow of Henry, the fourth lord of Cherbury, had lent the first copy to the Earl of Clarendon, on June 11, 1696 (Oldys' Diary, p. 25). Clarendon returned it, but it was found many years later in an illegible state at Lady Herbert's house, Lymore, Montgomeryshire, and was apparently destroyed. The second copy was sold with Sir Henry's estate at Ribbisford, but the owner restored it to the Earl of Powis about 1738. Under date, 29th December 1763, Walpole refers to this second copy in his correspondence. He was printing the MS. at his own press at Strawberry Hill, and promises Mason an impression " of the most curious and entertaining book in the world . . . the Life of the famous Lord Herbert of Cherbury " (Walpole's Letters, ed. Cunningham, iv. 156). On 16th July 1764, Herbert writes to George Montagu that the Life is " the most curious book that ever set its foot into the world," and gives the history of the undertaking. " I found it a year ago at Lady Hertford's, to whom Lady Powis had lent it. I took it up and soon threw it down again, as the dullest thing I ever saw. She persuaded me to take it home. My Lady Waldegrave was here in all her grief : Gray and I read it to amuse her. We could not get on for laughing and screaming. I begged to have it in print. Lord Powis, sensible of the extravagance, refused. I insisted—he persisted. I told my Lady Hertford it was no matter, I would print it, I was determined. I sat down and wrote a flattering dedication to Lord Powis, which I knew he would swallow : he did, and gave up his ancestor" (ibid. 252). On 16th December Walpole writes, that " the thing most in fashion is my edition of Lord Herbert's Life ; people are mad after it ; I believe, because only two hundred were printed " (ibid. 302). It is reasonable to suppose that the MS. was returned to Lord Powis, but the present Earl, a descendant, through the female line, of Walpole's friend, has informed me that he is ignorant of its present whereabouts. Walpole's edition was reprinted in 1770, 1809, and in 1826.

f

THE LIFE

EDWARD, LORD HERBERT

OF CHERBURY.

—⊬—

I DO believe that, if all my ancestors had set down
their lives in writing and left them to posterity,
many documents necessary to be known of those
who, both participate of[1] their natural inclinations
and humours, must in all probability run a not
much different course, might have been given for
their instruction ; and certainly it will be found
much better for men to guide themselves by such
observations as their father, grandfather, and great-
grandfather might have delivered to them, than by
those vulgar rules and examples, which cannot in
all points so exactly agree unto them.   Therefore,
whether their life were private and contained only
precepts necessary to treat with their children,

---

[1] *i.e.*, sharing.

A

servants, tenants, kinsmen, and neighbours, or
employed abroad in the university, or study of the
law, or in the court, or in the camp, their heirs
might have benefited themselves more by them
than by any else ; for which reason I have thought
fit to relate to my posterity those passages of my
life, which I conceive may best declare me, and be
most useful to them.   In the delivery of which, I
profess to write with all truth and sincerity, as
scorning ever to deceive or speak false to any ; and
therefore detesting it much more where I am under
obligation of speaking to those so near me : and if
this be one reason for taking my pen in hand at
this time, so as my age is now past threescore,[1]
it will be fit to recollect my former actions, and
examine what had been done well or ill, to the
intent I may both reform that which was amiss,
and so make my peace with God, as also comfort
myself in those things which, through God's great
grace and favour, have been done according to the
rules of conscience, virtue, and honour.   Before
yet I bring myself to this account, it will be necessary I say somewhat concerning my ancestors, as far
as the notice of them is come to me in any credible way ;[2] of whom yet I cannot say much, since

---

[1] Lord Herbert was probably writing in 1643.

[2] Lord Herbert apparently possessed a number of family
papers.   Dugdale, in his account of the family (Baronage,
ii. 256), quotes several particulars about William Herbert,

I was but eight years old when my grandfather died, and that my father lived but about four years after ; and that for the rest I have lived for the most part from home, it is impossible I should have that entire knowledge of their actions which might inform me sufficiently ; I shall only, therefore, relate the more known and undoubted parts of their lives.

My father was Richard Herbert, Esq., son to Edward Herbert, Esq., and grandchild to Sir Richard Herbert, Knight, who was a younger son of Sir Richard Herbert of Colebrook, in Monmouthshire, of all whom I shall say a little. And first of my father, whom I remember to have been black-haired and bearded, as all my ancestors of his side are said to have been, of a manly or somewhat stern look, but withal very handsome and well compact in his limbs, and of a great courage, whereof he gave proof, when he was so barbarously assaulted by many men in the churchyard at

---

the first Earl of Pembroke, from "a certain manuscript book in the custody of Edward, now Lord Herbert of Cherbury," and he notes in the margin (ibid. ii. 258), when speaking of Sir Richard Herbert, Lord Herbert's great grandfather "ex cod. MS. penes Edward D. Herbert de Chirbury." I have collected a few additional facts about Lord Herbert's ancestry in Appendix I. Izaak Walton says generally of the Herberts—"A family that hath been blessed with men of remarkable wisdom and a willingness to serve their country, and indeed to do good to all mankind, for which they are eminent " (Life of G. Herbert).

Llanerfyl,[1] at what time he would have apprehended a man who denied to appear to justice;
for, defending himself against them all, by the
help only of one John ap Howell Corbet, he
chased his adversaries, until a villain, coming behind him, did, over the shoulders of others, wound
him on the head behind with a forest-bill until
he fell down ; though recovering himself again, notwithstanding his skull was cut through to the
pia mater of the brain, he saw his adversaries fly
away, and after walked home to his house at
Llyssyn,[2] where, after he was cured, he offered
a single combat to the chief of the family, by whose
procurement it was thought the mischief was committed ; but he [*i.e.*, the chief] disclaiming wholly
the action as not done by his consent, which he
offered to testify by oath, and the villain himself fly-
ing into Ireland, whence he never returned, my father
desisted from prosecuting the business any farther
in that kind, and attained, notwithstanding the said
hurt, that health and strength, that he returned to
his former exercises in a country life, and became
the father of many children.   As for his integrity
in his places of deputy lieutenant of the county,

---

[1] In the hundred of Caereimion, Montgomeryshire.
[2] There is still a large farm of this name in the parish
of Llanerfyl.   It doubtless occupies the site of Richard
Herbert's house (see p. 28, note 4).

justice of the peace, and *custos rotulorum*,[1] which he, as my grandfather before him, held, it is so memorable to this day, that it was said his enemies appealed to him for justice, which they also found on all occasions. His learning was not vulgar, as understanding well the Latin tongue, and being well versed in history. My grandfather was of a various life; beginning first at court, where, after he had spent most part of his means, he became a soldier, and made his fortune with his sword at the siege of St. Quentin in France,[2] and other wars, both in the north, and in the rebellions happening in the times of King Edward the Sixth, and Queen Mary, with so good success, that he not only came off still with the better, but got so much money and wealth, as enabled him to buy the greatest part of that livelihood which is descended to me; although

---

[1] He was Sheriff of Montgomeryshire in 1576 and 1584, and is probably the Richard Herbert who sat as M.P. for Montgomeryshire in the Parliament of 1585–86. He died in 1596, and was buried in Montgomery Church on 15th October of that year (see p. 10, note 1).

[2] Edward Herbert, as captain-general over 500 men, under his kinsman, William Herbert (created Earl of Pembroke, 11th October 1551), joined the Spaniards in the storming and sacking of St. Quentin two days after it had been taken (10th August 1557) from the French. The latter were commanded by Anne, Duc de Montmorency, Constable of France, whose son and grandson are often mentioned by Lord Herbert below.

yet I hold some lands which his mother, the Lady
Anne Herbert,[1] purchased, as appears by the deeds
made to her by that name, which I can show ; and
might have held more, which my grandfather sold
under foot at an under value in his youth, and
might have been recovered by my father, had my
grandfather suffered him.   My grandfather was
noted to be a great enemy to the outlaws and
thieves of his time, who robbed in great numbers
in the mountains of Montgomeryshire, for the sup-
pressing of whom he went often, both day and
night, to the places where they were ; concerning
which, though many particulars have been told me,
I shall mention one only.[2]   Some outlaws being
lodged in an alehouse upon the hills of Llandinam,
my grandfather and a few servants coming to
apprehend them, the principal outlaw shot an arrow
against my grandfather, which stuck in the pummel
of his saddle ; whereupon my grandfather coming
up to him with his sword in his hand, and taking
him prisoner, he showed him the said arrow,
bidding him look what he had done ; whereof the
outlaw was no farther sensible, than to say, he was
sorry that he left his better bow at home, which he

---

[1] Anne, daughter of Sir David ap Evan (or Euion) ap
Llewellyn Vaughan, Knt., and wife of Sir Richard Herbert
of Montgomery (see p. 10).

[2] A few notes on the general condition of Wales in Lord
Herbert's youth are collected in Appendix II.

conceived would have carried his shot to his body ; but the outlaw, being brought to justice, suffered for it. My grandfather's power was so great in the country, that divers ancestors of the better families now in Montgomeryshire were his servants, and raised by him.[1] He delighted also much in hospitality; as having a very long table twice covered every meal with the best meats that could be gotten, and a very great family. It was an ordinary saying in the country at that time, when they saw any fowl rise, " Fly where thou wilt, thou wilt light at Blackhall ; " which was a low building, but of great capacity, my grandfather erected in his age ;[2] his father and himself, in former times, having lived in Montgomery Castle. Notwithstanding yet these expenses at home, he brought

---

[1] He was appointed deputy-constable of Aberystwith Castle (16th March 1543-4), by his cousin Sir William Herbert (see extract from Lord Powis' MSS. in Powysland Collections, xi. 361); was Sheriff of Montgomeryshire in 1537 and 1568 ; was M.P. for the county in 1553 and 1556-7; was knighted in 1574 (Metcalfe's Knights, p. 128). His local influence is illustrated by a correspondence with Leicester in November 1580, as to the appointment of a sheriff of the county. He successfully insisted on the choice of Griffith Lloyd and the rejection of John Vaughan (Cal. State Papers, 1577-80, p. 686). He was at one time esquire of the body to Queen Elizabeth.

[2] This house, also called Lymore, was standing in the middle of the seventeenth century. Lord Herbert retired to it during the troubles of the civil wars.

up his children well, married his daughters to the
better sort of persons near him,[1] and bringing up
his younger sons at the university; from whence
his son Matthew [2] went to the Low Country wars;
and, after some time spent there, came home, and
lived in the country at Dolguog, upon a house and
fair living, which my grandfather bestowed upon
him.   His son also, Charles Herbert,[3] after he had
passed some time in the Low Countries, likewise
returned home, and was after married to an in-
herétrix,[4] whose eldest son, called Sir Edward
Herbert, Knight, is the king's attorney-general.[5]

---

[1] He had seven daughters.   Mary, the eldest, married
Thomas Purcell of Nantcribbe, who was Sheriff of Mont-
gomeryshire in 1597; Ann, the third daughter, married
Charles Lloyd of Leighton, Sheriff in 1601; and Jane, the
fourth daughter, married Jenkin Lloyd, Sheriff in 1588.
(See Powysland Club Collections, ii. 387.)

[2] Admitted a student of the Inner Temple, November
1582 (Admission Register, 1571–1625, p. 41).   He married
Ann, daughter of Charles Fox of Bromfield, and from him
was descended in the fourth generation Henry Arthur
Herbert, created Earl of Powis in 1748 (second creation).

[3] He is probably the " Charles Herbert e co. Montgom."
who matriculated at Magdalen College, Oxford, 11th May
1582, at the age of fifteen.   He lived at Aston, and was
Sheriff of Montgomeryshire in 1608.

[4] Jane, sole heiress of Hugh ap Owen (Dwnn's Visitations, i. 312).

[5] Of the Inner Temple.   Appointed the Queen's Attorney-
General, 1635; Solicitor-General, 1640; Attorney-General,

His son, George, who was of New College, in
Oxford,[1] was very learned, and of a pious life, died
in a middle age of a dropsy. Notwithstanding all
which occasions of expense, my grandfather purchased much lands,[2] without doing anything yet
unjustly or hardly, as may be collected by an offer
I have publicly made divers times, having given
my bailiff in charge to proclaim to the country,
that if any lands were gotten by evil means, or so
much as hardly, they should be compounded for or
restored again ; but to this day, never any man yet
complained to me in this kind. He died at the
age of fourscore, or thereabouts, and was buried in
Montgomery Church,[3] without having any monu-

29th January 1640–1 ; impeached by the Commons, 8th
March 1641–2 ; Charles II.'s Lord Keeper of the Great
Seal, 1653 ; died at Paris 1657.

[1] The name of George Herbert does not appear on the
books of New College, Oxford, and I believe this statement
to be an error. Together with the Charles Herbert mentioned above, a George Herbert matriculated at Magdalen
College, 11th May 1582, at the age of sixteen.

[2] In 1553, Sir William Herbert, Earl of Pembroke,
granted him the hundred of Cherbury and probably the
castle of Montgomery. On 15th May 1570, he received
a royal grant of the castle of Lyons, or Holt Castle, with
several Shropshire manors.

[3] 20th May 1593, according to the parish register. His
wife, Elizabeth, daughter of Matthew Price of Newtown,
Montgomeryshire, was buried in the same place on 26th
May 1588.

ment made for him, which yet for my father is there set up in a fair manner.[1]

My great-grandfather, Sir Richard Herbert, was steward, in the time of King Henry the Eighth, of the lordships and marches of North Wales, East Wales, and Cardiganshire, and had power, in a martial law, to execute offenders; in the using thereof he was so just, that he acquired to himself a singular reputation; as may appear upon the records of that time, kept in the Paper-Chamber at Whitehall, some touch whereof I have made in my History of Henry the Eighth:[2] of him I can say little more, than that he likewise was a great suppressor of rebels, thieves, and outlaws, and that he was just and conscionable; for if a false or cruel

---

[1] This monument, in the Lymore Chancel of the church, was erected by Lord Herbert's mother in 1600. It is a large alabaster canopied tomb with recumbent figures of Richard Herbert (in complete armour) and of his wife, while small images of their seven sons and three daughters stand beside them. Drawings of the tomb, which is still well preserved, appear in the Powysland Collections, vi. 409; and in Dr. Grosart's edition of George Herbert's Works (vol. ii. frontispiece).

[2] Under date 1520, Lord Herbert says in his History: —" In the greater part [of Wales] and particularly those [parts] in the East, West, and North Wales being about this time administered by my great grandfather, Sir Richard Herbert . . . such justice was used as I find him in our records highly commended to the King's Council by Rowland Lee, now President of Wales."

person had that power committed to his hands, he would have raised a great fortune out of it, whereof he left little, save what his father gave him, unto posterity. He lieth buried likewise in Montgomery : the upper monument of the two placed in the chancel being erected for him.[1]

My great [great] grandfather, Sir Richard Herbert of Colebrook, was that incomparable hero, who (in the History of Hall and Grafton, as it appears[2]) twice passed through a great army of northern men alone, with his pole-axe in his hand, and returned without any mortal hurt, which is more than is famed of Amadis de Gaul, or the Knight of the Sun.[3] I shall, besides this relation of Sir

---

[1] One of two tombs of different dates with recumbent armoured figures on them in Montgomery Church (on the east side of the monument to Lord Herbert's father) is locally believed to be the tomb of Sir Richard Herbert. Sir Richard was alive in 1535, though in ill-health, but the tomb does not appear to be of a date later than Henry VII.'s reign.

[2] 1469. "Sir Richard Herbert so valiauntly acquited himselfe that with his Polleaxe in his hand (as his enemies did afterward reporte) he twise by fine force passed through the battail of his adversaries and without any mortall woonde returned." Hall's "Union of the Two Noble Families" (1548), fol. ccij.b ; cf. Grafton's Chronicle (1569), p. 676. This exploit was part of the action described at length below.

[3] A proverbial reference ; cf. Overbury's Characters (1616) : "It is neither Amadis de Gaule nor the Knight of the Sunne that is able to resist them." Shadwell uses the phrase in his Virtuoso (1676).

Richard Herbert's prowess in the battle at Banbury, or Edgecot Hill,[1] being the place where the late battle was fought,[2] deliver some traditions concerning him, which I have received from good hands; one is, that the said Sir Richard Herbert being employed, together with his brother William, Earl of Pembroke,[3] to reduce certain rebels in North Wales, Sir Richard Herbert besieged a principal person of them at Harlech Castle in Merionethshire;[4] the captain of this place had been a soldier in the wars of France; whereupon he said, he had kept a castle in France so long, that he made the old women in Wales talk of him; and that he

---

[1] See p. 15, note.

[2] The battle of Edgehill (midway between Kineton, Warwickshire, and Banbury), fought on Sunday, 23d October 1642.

[3] Of Raglan, Monmouthshire, "a strict adherer to the House of York in divers bloudy encounters with the Lancastrians;" created a baron by Edward IV. 3d February 1461–2, and Earl of Pembroke 27th May 1468. Dugdale, in his Baronage (ii. 255) gives an extraordinary long list of Welsh castles and offices conferred on him in the early years of Edward IV.'s reign.

[4] Harlech in 1468 was held by David ap Jevan ap Einion in behalf of the Lancastrian, Jasper Earl of Pembroke. The Herberts ravaged all the neighbourhood in the service of Edward IV., seized the castle, and granted a safe-conduct to the defenders, if they would parley with them. See Wynne's Gwydir Family (1878), p. 249. Thomas

would keep the castle so long, that he would make the old women in France talk of him : and indeed, as the place was almost impregnable but by famine, Sir Richard Herbert was constrained to take him in by composition ; he surrendering himself upon condition that Sir Richard Herbert should do what he could to save his life : which being accepted, Sir Richard brought him to King Edward IV., desiring his Highness to give him a pardon, since he yielded up a place of importance, which he might have kept longer upon this hope. But the king replying to Sir Richard Herbert, that he had no power by his commission to pardon any, and therefore might, after the representation hereof to his Majesty, safe deliver him up to justice ; Sir Richard Herbert answered, he had not yet done the best he could for him ; and therefore most humbly desired his Highness to do one of two things—either to put him again in the castle

---

Churchyard describes the exploit in his " Worthines of Wales," 1587. Edward IV. is speaking—

" Our castle then of Hardelach that from our first daies raigne
  A refuge for all Rebels did against us still remaine :
  A fort of wondrous force besiege about did he,
  And tooke it, where in most men's mynds, it could not taken be.
  He won it, and did make them yeeld, who then theire safetie
    sought :
  And all the countrie thereabout to our obedience brought."

where he was, and command some other to take
him out ; or, if his Highness would not do so,
to take his life for the said captain's, that being
the last proof he could give that he used his uttermost endeavour to save the said captain's life.
The king finding himself urged thus far, gave Sir
Richard Herbert the life of the said captain, but
withal he bestowed no other reward for his service.
The other history is, that Sir Richard Herbert,
together with his brother the Earl of Pembroke,
being in Anglesea, apprehending there seven
brothers, which had done many mischiefs and
murders ; in these times the Earl of Pembroke
thinking it fit to root out so wicked a progeny,
commanded them all to be hanged ; whereupon the
mother of them coming to the Earl of Pembroke,
upon her knees desired him to pardon two, or at
leastwise one of her said sons, affirming, that the
rest were sufficient to satisfy justice or example,
which request also Sir Richard Herbert seconded ;
but the earl finding them all equally guilty, said,
he could make no distinction betwixt them, and
therefore commanded them to be executed together ;
at which the mother was so aggrieved, that, with a
pair of woollen beads on her arms (for so the relation goeth), she, on her knees, cursed him, praying
God's mischief might fall to him in the first battle
he should make.   The earl after this, coming with

his brother to Edgecote Field,[1] as is before set down, after he had put his men in order to fight, found his brother, Sir Richard Herbert, in the head of his men, leaning upon his pole-axe in a kind of sad or pensive manner; whereupon the earl said, "What! doth thy great body (for he was higher by the head than any one in the army) apprehend anything that thou art so melancholy, or art thou weary with marching, that thou doest lean thus upon thy pole-axe?" Sir Richard Herbert replied, that he was neither of both, whereof he should see the proof presently; "only I cannot but apprehend

---

[1] In 1469 some northern men led by Robert Hilyard, otherwise Robin of Redesdale, marched south to attack the Yorkist government with the object of restoring Henry VI. They were aided by Sir John Coniers and Lords Latimer and FitzHugh, relatives of the Earl of Warwick (who was on the point of deserting from Edward IV.) The Herberts, and Humphrey, Lord Stafford (created Earl of Devonshire), were ordered to intercept the rebels. The two Yorkist forces met at Banbury, where Stafford quarrelled with the elder Herbert and led his men away. On 26th July the rebels attacked the Herberts with their six or seven thousand Welsh followers, and gained a decisive victory at Edgecote Field near the town. *Both brothers were taken prisoner and beheaded at Northampton,* 28th July. Hall states that the Earl of Warwick, who, doubtless, was mainly responsible for the fate of the Herberts, had had a private quarrel with the elder brother respecting the wardship of Lord Bonvile's daughter. (See Hall's Chronicle and Warkworth's Chronicle (Camden Soc.), pp. 7, 8, 44, 45).

on your part, lest the curse of the woman with the woollen beads fall upon you." This Sir Richard Herbert lieth buried in Abergavenny, in a sumptuous monument for those times, which still remains;[1] whereas his brother, the Earl of Pembroke, being buried in Tintern Abbey, his monument, together with the church, lie now wholly defaced and ruined.[2] This Earl of Pembroke had a younger son, which

---

[1] His wife, Margaret, was buried by his side. A description of the tomb, now in ruins, is given in Coxe's "Tour in Monmouthshire" (1801), p. 187; cf. Churchyard's "Worthines of Wales" (1587), p. 53:—

" In tombe as trim as that before	Here buryed was as 1 haue said
Sir Richard Harbert lyes: *	In sumptuous Tombe full well. †
He was at Banbrie field of yore	His wife Dame Margaret by his side ‡
And through the battaile twise :	Lyes there likewise for troth :
He past with Pollax in his hands,	Their armes as yet may be tryed
A manly act in deede	(In honor of them both)
To preace among so many bands	Stands at their heads, three Lyons white
As you of him may rede.	He giues as well as he might :
This valiant knight at Colbroke dwelt	Three Rauens blacke in shielde she giues
Nere Aborgaynie towne :	As daughter to a knight.
Who when his fatall destnie felt	A sheafe of Arrows vnder head
And fortune flong him downe,	He hath as due to him.
Among his enemies lost his head,	Thus there this worthie couple lye
A ruefull tale to tell :	In tombe full fine and trim."

[2] According to the Earl's will (27th July 1469), printed in Dugdale (ii. 257), he bequeathed much property to Tintern Abbey, but desired to be buried at Abergavenny —a direction which was not observed.

---

* Churchyard's marginal notes are as follows :—" Sir Richard Harbert of Colbroke, Knight."

† "On the left hand of the chappell they lye."

‡ "She was daughter to Thomas ap Griffith, father to Sir Rice ap Thomas, Knight."

had a daughter which married the eldest son of the Earl of Worcester,[1] who carried away the fair castle of Raglan, with many thousand pounds yearly, from the heir-male of that house, which was the second son[2] of the said Earl of Pembroke, and ancestor of the family of St. Julians [Monmouthshire], whose daughter and heir I after married, as shall be told in its place.[3] And here it is very remarkable, that the younger sons of the said Earl of Pembroke, and Sir R. Herbert, left their posterity after them, who, in the person of myself and my wife, united both houses again;[4] which is the more memorable, that when the said Earl of Pembroke and Sir R. Herbert were taken prisoners in defending the just cause of Edward IV. at the battle above-said, the earl never entreated that his own life might be saved, but his brother's,

---

[1] This is a loose statement. The reference is to Elizabeth, daughter of William Herbert (created Earl of Huntingdon 1479), *son and heir, and not younger son, of the Earl of Pembroke.* She married, about 1490, Charles Somerset, illegitimate son of Henry, *Duke of Somerset.* Charles became Earl of Worcester, and Lord Herbert of Gower and Chepstow (1514), and held high office under Henry VIII. He died in 1525. (See Lord Herbert's Henry VIII. and Dugdale's Baronage, ii. 258, 292–294.)

[2] The reference is to Sir George Herbert of St. Julians, the *third* son ; he married Jane, daughter of Sir Richard Crofts.

[3] See p. 40.   [4] See the Genealogical Table.

as it appears by the said history.[1] So that joining
of both houses together in my posterity, ought to
produce a perpetual obligation of friendship and
mutual love in them one to another, since by these
two brothers, so brave an example thereof was
given, as seeming not to live or die but for one
another.

My mother was Magdalen Newport, daughter of
Sir Richard Newport[2] and Margaret his wife,
daughter and heir of Sir Thomas Bromley, one of
the privy council, and executor of King Henry the
Eighth,[3] who, surviving her husband, gave rare
testimonies of an incomparable piety to God, and
love to her children, as being most assiduous and
devout in her daily both private and public prayers,

---

[1] Hall reports the dying speech : " Masters, let me dye,
for 1 am olde, but save my brother which is yonge, lusty,
and hardye, mete and apt to serve the greatest prince of
Christendom " (f. cciij.)

[2] Knighted 1566 ; buried at Wroxeter, 12th September
1570. His epitaph, and that of his wife, who was buried
with him, are printed in Dr. Grosart's edition of George
Herbert's works, i. 27.

[3] Bromley was made a judge of the King's Bench in
1544 ; was a member of Edward VI.'s council of regency ;
was made the Chief-Justice of the Common Pleas by
Mary in 1553 ; died in 1555, and was buried at Wroxeter.
He bought Eyton, Lord Herbert's birthplace, of the crown
in 1547, and received a legacy of £300 under Henry VIII.'s
will.

and so careful to provide for her posterity, that though it were in her power to give her estate (which was very great) to whom she would, yet she continued still unmarried, and so provident for them, that, after she had bestowed all her daughters, with sufficient portions, upon very good neighbouring families, she delivered up her estate and care of housekeeping to her eldest son Francis,[1] when now she had for many years kept hospitality with that plenty and order as exceeded all either of her country or time ; for, besides abundance of provision and good cheer for guests, which her son Sir Francis Newport continued, she used ever after dinner to distribute with her own hands to the poor, who resorted to her in great numbers, alms in money, to every one of them more or less, as she thought they needed it. By these ancestors I am descended of Talbot, Devereux, Grey, Corbet, and many other noble families, as may be seen in their matches, extant in the many fair coats the Newports bear. I could say much more of my ancestors of that side likewise, but that I should exceed my proposed scope : I shall, therefore, only say somewhat more of my mother, my brothers, and

---

[1] Knighted in 1603 ; married Beatrice, daughter of Rowland Lacon of Kinlet. His son Richard became first Lord Newport (1642), and his grandson Francis first Earl of Bradford (1694). Both were prominent royalists.

sisters.   And for my mother, after she lived most
virtuously and lovingly with her husband for many
years, she, after his death, erected a fair monument
for him in Montgomery Church; [1] brought up her
children carefully, and put them in good courses
for making their fortunes, and, briefly, was that
woman Dr. Donne hath described in his funeral
sermon of her printed.[2]   The names of her children
were—Edward, Richard, William, Charles, George,
Henry, Thomas ; her daughters were, Elizabeth,
Margaret, Frances ; of all whom I will say a little
before I begin a narration of my own life, so I
may pursue my intended purpose the more entirely.

My brother Richard, after he had been brought up
in learning, went to the Low Countries, where he
continued many years with much reputation, both in
the wars and for fighting single duels, which were

---

[1] See p. 10, note.

[2] She re-married in 1608, her second husband being Sir
John Danvers, third son of Sir John Danvers of Dauntsey,
Wilts, and twenty years Lady Herbert's junior.   She was
buried in Chelsea Church, 8th June 1627.   Dr. Donne's
funeral sermon bears the title : "A Sermon of Commemo-
ration of the Lady Dāuers, late Wife of Sʳ Iohn Dāuers.
Preach'd at Chilsey, where she was lately buried, by Iohn
Donne, D. of St. Paul's, London, I. July 1627.   Together
with other Commemorations of her, by her sonne, George
Herbert.   London, 1627, 12mo."   Extracts from this
volume, and from Walton's account of her in his Life of
George Herbert, are given in Appendix III.

many; insomuch, that between both, he carried, as I have been told, the scars of four-and-twenty wounds upon him to his grave, and lieth buried in Bergen-op-zoom.[1] My brother William, being brought up likewise in learning, went afterwards to the wars in Denmark, where, fighting a single combat, and having his sword broken, he not only defended himself with that piece which remained, but, closing with his adversary, threw him down, and so held him until company came in ; and then went to the wars in the Low Countries, but lived not long after.[2] My brother Charles[3] was fellow of New College in Oxford, where he died young, after he had given great hopes of himself every

---

[1] He probably served with his brothers, Edward and Thomas, at Juliers, 1610; joined the English contingent in Germany under Sir Horace Vere in 1618, and was with Count Mansfeldt at the relief of Bergen-op-Zoom in 1622, where he doubtless met his death.

[2] In 1617 William Herbert raised a troop of horse in Holland for the Duke of Savoy (see p. 176).

[3] Born in 1592, Charles Herbert was admitted to Winchester School in 1603, became a scholar of New College, Oxford, 4th June 1611, and fellow, 3d June 1613, and died in 1617. For these dates I am indebted to the Warden of New College, the Rev. Dr. Sewell. Verses by Charles Herbert appear in Dr. Zouch's " The Dove," and the lines signed " C. H." in the Travels of Sir Thomas Herbert (1634) have been attributed to him, but the dates make this identification doubtful.

wa:y. My brother George [1] was so excellent a
scholar, that he was made the public orator of the
University in Cambridge; some of whose English
works are extant; which, though they be rare in
their kind, yet are far short of expressing those
perfections he had in the Greek and Latin tongue,
and all divine and human literature : his life was
most holy and exemplary; insomuch, that about
Salisbury, where he lived, beneficed for many years,
he was little less than sainted. He was not exempt
from passion and choler, being infirmities to which
all our race is subject, but that excepted, without
reproach in his actions. Henry,[2] after he had been

---

[1] Born at Montgomery Castle, 3d April 1593 ; educated
at Westminster School ; proceeded to Trinity College,
Cambridge, in 1608 ; B.A., 1611 ; M.A., 1615 ; elected
fellow of his College; public orator of the University, 1619–
27; spent some time at court ; ordained after 1625 ;
chaplain to his kinsman, Philip, Earl of Pembroke ; rector
of Fugglestone and Bemerton, near Salisbury, from 1630 ;
buried at Bemerton, 3d March 1632–3. Two volumes of
poems were issued after his death ; " The Temple," in 1633,
and " The Synagogue," in 1640. Poems to his mother's
memory were published with Donne's sermon in 1627.

[2] Born 1595 at Montgomery ; became Master of the
Revels about 1621 ; was knighted by James I., 7th August
1623 ; was very intimate with Charles I., and was a consistent royalist throughout the civil wars. He was twice
married, his second wife being Elizabeth, daughter of Sir
Robert Offley of Lincolnshire. At the Restoration he
again became Master of the Revels, and died in 1673.

brought up in learning, as the other brothers were, was sent by his friends into France, where he attained the language of that country in much perfection; after which time he came to court, and was made gentleman of the king's privy chamber, and master of the revels; by which means, as also by a good marriage, he attained to great fortunes, for himself and posterity to enjoy. He also hath given several proofs of his courage in duels, and otherwise; being no less dexterous in the ways of the court, as having gotten much by it. My brother Thomas was a posthumous, as being born some weeks after his father's death.[1] He also, being brought up a while at school, was sent as a page to Sir Edward Cecil,[2] lord-general of his Majesty's auxiliary forces to the princes in Germany, and was particularly at the siege of Juliers,[3] A.D. 1610,

---

He was a frequent correspondent of his brothers, Edward and George. His invaluable MS. Diary of plays licensed by him between 1621 and 1641, is in the possession of the Earl of Powis, and has never been fully printed. He edited Lord Herbert's poems in 1665.

[1] The Register of Montgomery Church gives the date 15th May 1597. The father died in the previous October.

[2] Third son of the famous Lord Burghley's elder son Thomas, first Earl of Exeter. After serving in the Low Countries for nearly thirty-five years, he was created Baron Cecil of Putney (1625), and Viscount Wimbledon (1626). He died 16th November 1638.

[3] Lord Herbert gives an account of this campaign, p. 112 *et seq.*

where he showed such forwardness, as no man in
that great army before him was more adventurous
on all occasions. Being returned from thence, he
went to the East Indies, under the command of
Captain Joseph, who, in his way thither, meeting
with a great Spanish ship, was unfortunately killed
in fight with them;[1] whereupon, his men being
disheartened, my brother Thomas encouraged them
to revenge the loss, and renewed the fight in that
manner (as Sir John Smyth, governor of the East
India Company,[2] told me at several times), that
they forced the Spanish ship to run aground,
where the English shot her through and through
so often, that she run herself aground, and was
left wholly unserviceable. After which time, he,
with the rest of the fleet, came to Surat, and from

---

[1] In December 1616, Captain Benjamin Joseph sailed
in the *Globe* as commander of the East India Company's
fleet. Early in the following March the fleet was attacked
by a Portuguese carrack, and Captain Joseph, "a man of
extraordinary note and respect," was killed. (See Sainsbury's Calendar of Colonial Papers.)

[2] Sir *Thomas* Smyth, the first Governor of the Company,
was appointed in 1600, and was re-elected to the post for
every year between 1607 and 1621. He died towards the
end of 1625. Mr. W. N. Sainsbury of the Record Office
informs me that Sir *John*, Sir Thomas Smyth's son,
admitted to the freedom of the Company by patrimony,
30th June 1619, was never Governor. (See Calendar of
Colonial Papers.)

thence, went with the merchants to the Great Mogul; where, after he had stayed about a twelve-month, he returned with the same fleet back again to England.[1] After this, he went in the navy which King James sent to Algiers, under the command of Sir Robert Mansel, where our men being in great want of money and victuals, and many ships scattering themselves to try whether they could obtain a prize, whereby to relieve the whole fleet;[2] it was his hap to meet with a ship, which he took, and in it, to the value of eighteen hundred pounds, which, it was thought, saved the whole fleet from perishing. He conducted, also, Count Mansfeld to

---

[1] Sir Thomas Roe, the first accredited envoy to the Great Mogul, notes, in a despatch dated Mandow, 3d November 1617, that " Mr. Herbert, weary of the progress (*i.e.*, with the English merchants to the Great Mogul's court) is bound for England." He apparently returned to Surat at the end of 1617, and sailed in the *Globe*, the ship in which he came, very early in the following year. (See Cal. of Colonial Papers, 1617–18.) Care must be taken to distinguish this Thomas Herbert from his kinsman of the same name, who was at Surat ten years later, and then paid a visit to the Great Mogul, a full account of which is given in his published Travels (1634).

[2] Sir Robert Mansell arrived with twenty ships in the roads of Algiers, 27th November 1620, to punish the Dey for his piratical attacks on English ships in the Mediterranean. Failure of supplies from home brought the expedition to grief, and after much suffering the fleet was recalled in July 1621. Gardiner's History of England, iv. 223–225.

the Low Countries,[1] in one of the king's ships,
which, being unfortunately cast away not far from
the shore, the count, together with his company,
saved themselves in a long-boat, or shallop, the
benefit whereof my said brother refused to take
for the present, as resolving to assist the master of
the ship, who endeavoured by all means to clear
the ship from the danger ; but finding it impossible,
he was the last man that saved himself in the long-
boat ; the master thereof yet refusing to come away,
so that he perished together with the ship. After
this, he commanded one of the ships that were sent
to bring the prince from Spain ; where, upon his
return, there being a fight between the Low Countrymen and the Dunkirkers, the prince, who thought
it was not for his dignity to suffer them to fight in
his presence, commanded some of his ships to part
them : whereupon my said brother, with some other
ships, got betwixt them on either side, and shot so
long, that both parties were glad to desist. After
he had brought the prince safely home, he was
appointed to go with one of the king's ships to the
Narrow Seas.[2] He also fought divers times with

---

[1] On his return to Flushing with an English army in
January 1624–5. Gardiner's History, v. 285.

[2] 1625, September 25, Buckingham, as Admiral of the
Narrow Seas, appointed Captain Thomas Herbert captain
of the *Dreadnought.* Cal. State Papers, Dom. 1625–6,
p. 111.

great courage and success, with divers men in single fight, sometimes hurting and disarming his adversary, and sometimes driving him away. After all these proofs given of himself, he expected some great command; but finding himself, as he thought, undervalued, he retired to a private and melancholy life, being much discontented to find others preferred to him; in which sullen humour having lived many years, he died and was buried in London, in St. Martin's near Charing Cross;[1] so that of all my brothers none survives but Henry.

Elizabeth, my eldest sister,[2] was married to Sir Henry Jones[3] of Abermarles [Carmarthenshire], who had by her one son and two daughters; the latter end of her time was the most sickly and miserable that hath been known in our times; while, for the space of about fourteen years, she languished and pined away to skin and bones, and at last died in London, and lieth buried in a church

---

[1] Lord Herbert's younger brother apparently died midway between 1626 and 1642. I have had the burial registers of the Church of St. Martin's-in-the-Fields searched in vain for an entry respecting his death. The registers do not seem to have been kept with very scrupulous care at this period.

[2] Baptized in Montgomery Church, 10th November 1583.

[3] Sheriff of Carmarthenshire 1574 and 1584, and for Brecknockshire, 1580. Two letters of Sir Henry appear in the Stradling Correspondence, ed. Traherne, pp. 163, 164.

called ——— near Cheapside. Margaret was married to John Vaughan, son and heir to Owen Vaughan of Llwydiarth;[1] by which match some former differences betwixt our house and that were appeased and reconciled.[2] He had by her three daughters and heirs, Dorothy,[3] Magdalen, and Katherine; of which the two latter only survive. The estate of the Vaughans yet went to the heirs-male, although not so clearly but that the entail which carried the said lands was questioned.[4] Frances, my youngest sister, was married to Sir John Brown, Knight, in Lincolnshire, who had by her divers children; the eldest son of whom, although young, fought divers duels, in one of which it was his fortune to kill one Lee, of a great family

---

[1] Entered in the Montgomery parish register, 3d November 1606.

[2] On 7th January 1588-9, Shrewsbury was much disturbed by a conflict between the retainers of the Herbert and the Newport families, and those of the Vaughans. A tedious lawsuit between Sir Edward Herbert of Powis, third cousin of Lord Herbert's father, and the Vaughans seems to have involved all the Herbert family. Cf. Owen and Blakeway's Shrewsbury, i. 390, 391.

[3] Dorothy's will was proved at Canterbury by her uncle, George Herbert the poet, on 9th October 1632.

[4] John Vaughan died before his wife. She died 14th August 1623, and is buried in Montgomery Church, *inter majores et consanguineos.* She is described in the parish register as *habitans Llussin in parochia Llan-ervell in Diocæsi Asaphensi.*

in Lancashire.[1]   I could say many things more concerning all these, but it is not my purpose to par-
ticularise their lives.   I have related only some
passages concerning them to the best of my memory,
being assured I have not failed much in my relation
of them.   I shall now come to myself.

I was born at Eyton, in Shropshire[2] [being a
house which, together with fair lands, descended
upon the Newports by my said grandmother,]
between the hours of twelve and one of the clock
in the morning;[3] my infancy was very sickly, my

---

[1] Peter Legh, eldest son of Piers Legh of Lyme, Lancashire, by Anne, daughter of Sir John Savile, was killed in
a duel in 1640.   Baines' Lancashire, iii. 644.

[2] Owen and Blakeway's History of Shrewsbury, i. 278 :—
" Eyton [on Severn, near Wroxeter] was a very ancient
possession of the monks of Shrewsbury, granted to them
by their founder, Earl Roger, and it became one of the
country seats of the abbot.   On the dissolution it was
purchased of the crown by Chief-Justice Bromley, whose
only child conveyed it to her husband, Sir Richard Newport.   Sir Richard made this beautiful spot one of his
favourite residences.   After the demolition of Ercall [an-
other seat of the Newports], in the civil wars, Eyton
became their chief seat."   Cf. Dugdale's Monasticon (1821),
iii. 525, 529 ; Eyton's Shropshire, viii. 26–36.   All that
now remains is a garden wall, running along the side of a
terrace, with a tower at the end.

[3] Unfortunately the extant registers at Wroxeter, whence
some information respecting Lord Herbert might have been
expected, begin in 1613.   Anthony à Wood states that
Herbert was fourteen years old in 1595.   He himself

head continually purging itself very much by the
ears ; whereupon also it was so long before I began
to speak, that many thought I should be ever dumb.
The very furthest thing I remember, is, that when
I understood what was said by others, I did yet
forbear to speak, lest I should utter something that
were imperfect or impertinent.   When I came to
talk, one of the furthest inquiries I made was, how
I came into this world ?   I told my nurse, keeper,
and others, I found myself here indeed, but from
what cause or beginning, or by what means, I could
not imagine ; but for this, as I was laughed at by
nurse, and some other women that were then present,
so I was wondered at by others, who said, they
never heard a child but myself ask that question ;
upon which, when I came to riper years, I made

---

states (p. 42) that he was fifteen in 1598–9, and (p. 80)
eighteen or nineteen in 1600.   According to his opening
remarks he was twelve years old (p. 3) when his father
died (1596), and eight when his grandfather died (1593).
These statements are too self-contradictory to prove anything.   On the whole, I am inclined to regard 3d March
1582–3 as the date of his birth.   That his birthday was
3d March appears from his own published verses :—

"*In Diem Natalitium, viz.,* 3 *Mar.*"

" Vere novo lux usque redit quâ nascor, et una
    Dum tempus redit, et fit numerosa dies ;
Ver, olim vires renovans roburque recendens,
    Æ[s]tas fit tandem tristis hyemsque mihi."

this observation, which afterwards a little comforted me, that, as I found myself in possession of this life, without knowing anything of the pangs and throes my mother suffered, yet, doubtless, they did no less press and afflict me than her, so I hope my soul shall pass to a better life than this without being sensible of the anguish and pains my body shall feel in death. For as I believe then I shall be transmitted to a more happy estate by God's great grace, I am confident I shall no more know how I came out of this world, than how I came into it; and because, since that time, I have made verses to this purpose, I have thought fit to insert them here as a place proper for them. The Argument is,

V I T A.[1]

PRIMA fuit quondam genitali semine vita
Procurasse suas dotes, ubi plastica virtus
Gestiit, et vegeto molem perfundere succo,
Externamque suo formam cohibere recessu,
Dum conspirantes possint accedere causæ,
Et totum tuto liceat proludere fœtum.

Altera materno tandem succrevit in arvo
Exiles spumans ubi spiritus induit artus,
Exertusque simul miro sensoria textu

---

[1] This and the following poem appeared in Lord Herbert's lifetime at the close of his *De Causis Errorum* (1645), together with a third Latin poem, "Hæred. et Nepot. suis Præcepta et Auxilia." The first poem is much abbreviated here, and has undergone a few verbal alterations.

Cudit, et hospitium menti non vile paravit,
Quæ cœlo delapsa suas mox inde capessat
Partes, et sortis tanquàm præsaga futuræ
Corrigat ignavum pondus, nec inutile sistat.

Tertia nunc agitur, quâ scena recluditur ingens,
Cernitur et festum cæli, terræque theatrum ;
Congener et species, rerum variataque forma ;
Et circumferri, motu proprioque vagari
Contigit, et leges æternaque fœdera mundi
Visere, et assiduo redeuntia sidera cursu.
Unde etiam vitæ causas, nexumque tueri
Fas erat et summum longè præsciscere Numen ;
Dum varios mirè motus contemperat orbis,
Et Pater, et Dominus, Custos, et conditor idem
Audit ubique Deus ; Quid ni modò Quarta sequatur ?
Sordibus excussis cùm mens jam purior instat,
Auctaque doctrinis variis, virtuteque pollens
Intendit vires, magis et sublimia spirat,
Et tacitus cordi stimulus suffigitur imo,
Ut velit huic quisquam sorti superesse caducæ,
Expetiturque status felicior ambitiosis
Ritibus, et sacris, et cultu religioso,
Et nova succedit melioris conscia fati
Spes superis hærens, toto perfusaque cœlo,
Et sese sancto demittit Numen amori,
Et data celestis non fallax tessera vitæ,
Cumque Deo licuit non uno jure pacisci,
Ut mihi seu servo reddatur debita merces,
Filius aut bona adire paterna petam, mihi sponsor
Sit fidei Numen ; mox hanc sin exuo vitam,
Compos jam factus melioris, tum simul uti
Jure meo cupiam liber, meque asserit inde
Ipse Deus (cujus non terris gratia tantùm,
Sed Cœlis prostat) quid ni modo quinta sequatur,
Et Sexta, et quicquid tandem spes ipsa requirat ?

DE VITA CELESTI CONJECTURA.

TOTO lustratus genio mihi gratulor ipsi,
Fati securus, dum nec terroribus ullis
Dejicior, tacitos condo vel corde dolores,
Sed lætus mediis ærumnis transigo vitam,
Invitisque malis (quæ terras undique cingunt)
Ardenti virtute viam super æthera quærens,
Proxima Cœlestis præcepi præmia vitæ,
Ultima prætento, divino nixus amore,
Quô simul exuperans creperæ ludibria sortis,
Barbara vesani linquo consortia Sæcli,
Auras infernas defflans, spiransque supernas,
Dum sanctis memet totum sic implico flammis,
Hisce ut suffultus penetrem laquearia cœli,
Atq. novi latè speculer magnalia Mundi,
Et notas animas, proprio jam lumine pulchras
Invisam, Superûmque choros, mentesque beatas,
Quêis aveam miscere ignes, ac vincula sacra,
Atq. vice alternâ transire in gaudia, Cœlum
Quæ dederit cunctis, ipsis aut indita nobis,
Vel quæ communi voto sancire licebit,
Ut Deus interea cumulans sua præmia, nostrum
Augeat inde decus, proprioque illustret amore,
Nec Cæli Cælis desint, æternavè Vitæ
Sæcula, vel Sæclis nova gaudia, qualia totum
Ævum nec minuat, nec terminat Infinitum.
His major desit nec gratia Numinis alma,
Quæ miris variata modis hæc gaudia crescant,
Excipiatque statum quemvis fœlicior alter ;
Et quæ nec sperare datur sint præstita nobis,
Nec, nisi sola capit quæ mens divina, supersint ;
Quæ licet ex sese sint perfectissima longe,
Ex nobis saltem magè condecorata videntur :

C

Cum segnes animas, cælum quas indit ab ortu,
Exacuat tantum labor ac industria nostra;
Ac demum poliat doctrina, et moribus illis,
Ut redeant pulchræ, dotem cœloque reportent :
Quum simùl arbitriis usi, mala pellimus illa,
Quæ nec vel pepulit cælum, vel pelleret olim,
Ex nobis ita fit jam gloria Numinis ingens,
Auctior in cælos quoque gloria nostra redundat,
Et quæ virtuti sint debita præmia, tandem
Vel Numen solito reddunt fælicius ipsum.
Amplior unde simul redhibetur Gratia nobis,
Ut vel pro voto nostro jam singula cedant.
Nam si libertas chara est, per amœna locorum
Conspicua innumeris Cœlis discurrere fas est,
Deliciasq. loci cujusvis carpere passim.
Altior est animo si contemplatio fixa,
Cuncta adaperta patent nobis jam scrinia Cœli,
Arcanasque Dei rationes nôsse juvabit :
Hujus sin repetat quisquam consortia sæcli,
Mox agere in terris, ac procurare licebit
Res heic humanas, et justis legibus uti !
Sin magè cælesti jam delectamur amore,
Solvimur in flammas, quæ se lambuntq. foventq
Mutuò, et impliciti sanctis ardoribus, unà
Surgimus amplexi, copulâ junctique tenaci,
Partibus, et toto miscemur ubique vicissim ;
Ardoresque novos accendit Numinis ardor.
Sin laudare Deum lubeat, nos laudat et ipse,
Concinit Angelicusque chorus, modulamine suavi
Personat et cælum, prostant et publica nobis
Gaudia, et eduntur passim spectacula læta ;
Fitque theatralis quasi Cæli machina tota.
Hanc mundi molem sin vis replicaverit ingens
Numinis, atque novas formas exculpserit inde
Dotibus ornatas aliis, magis atque capaces ;
Nostras mox etiam formas renovare licebit,

Et dotes sensusque alios assumere, tandem
Consummata magis quo gaudia nostra resurgant,
Hæc si conjecto mortali corpore fretus
Corpus ut exuerim, Quid ni majora recludam ?

And certainly since in my mother's womb this
plastica, or formatrix, which formed my eyes, ears,
and other senses, did not intend them for that
dark and noisome place, but, as being conscious
of a better life, made them as fitting organs
to apprehend and perceive those things which
should occur in this world : so I believe, since my
coming into this world, my soul hath formed or
produced certain faculties which are almost as
useless for this life, as the above-named senses
were for the mother's womb; and these faculties
are, hope, faith, love, and joy, since they never rest
or fix upon any transitory or perishing object in
this world, as extending themselves to something
further than can be here given, and indeed acquiesce
only in the perfect, eternal, and infinite : I confess
they are of some use here ; yet I appeal to everybody, whether any worldly felicity did so satisfy
their hope here, that they did not wish and hope for
something more excellent, or whether they had
ever that faith in their own wisdom, or in the help
of man, that they were not constrained to have
recourse to some diviner and superior power, than
they could find on earth, to relieve them in their
danger or necessity ; whether ever they could place

their love on any earthly beauty, that it did not
fade and wither, if not frustrate or deceive them,
or whether ever their joy was so consummate in
anything they delighted in, that they did not want
much more than it, or indeed this world can afford,
to make them happy.   The proper objects of these
faculties, therefore, though framed, or at least appearing in this world, is God only, upon whom
faith, hope, and love, were never placed in vain,
or remain long unrequited.[1]   But to leave these
discourses, and come to my childhood again.

I remember this defluxion at my ears above-
mentioned continued in that violence, that my
friends did not think fit to teach me so much as
my alphabet until I was seven years old, at which
time my defluxion ceased, and left me free of the
disease my ancestors were subject unto, being the
epilepsy.   My schoolmaster in the house of my
said lady grandmother began then to teach me the
alphabet, and afterwards grammar, and other books
commonly read in schools; in which I profited so
much, that upon this theme *Audaces fortuna juvat*,
I made an oration of a sheet of paper, and fifty or
sixty verses in the space of one day.   I remember
in that time I was corrected sometimes for going
to cuffs with two schoolfellows being both elder

---

[1] See the Introduction for a discussion of Lord Herbert's
philosophical system.

than myself, but never for telling a lie or any
other fault; my natural disposition and inclination
being so contrary to all falsehood, that being demanded whether I had committed any fault whereof
I might be justly suspected, I did use ever to
confess it freely, and thereupon choosing rather to
suffer correction than to stain my mind with telling
a lie, which I did judge then, no time could ever
deface; and I can affirm to all the world truly,
that, from my first infancy to this hour, I told not
willingly anything that was false, my soul naturally
having an antipathy to lying and deceit. After I
had attained the age of nine, during all which time
I lived in my said lady grandmother's house at
Eyton, my parents thought fit to send me to some
place where I might learn the Welsh tongue, as
believing it necessary to enable me to treat with
those of my friends and tenants who understood no
other language; whereupon I was recommended to
Mr. Edward Thelwall, of Plas-y-ward in Denbighshire.[1] This gentleman I must remember with
honour, as having of himself acquired the exact

---

[1] Son and heir of Symond Thelwall, one of the Councillors
of the Marches of Wales. He named one of his sons
Herbert, doubtless after his pupil. He died 29th July
1610. His brother Eubule was Principal of Jesus College,
Oxford, 1621–30. Dwnn's Visitations, 1566–1613, ed. Mey-
rick, ii. 335, 336.

knowledge of Greek, Latin, French, Italian, and
Spanish, and all other learning, having for that
purpose neither gone beyond seas, nor so much as
had the benefit of any universities. Besides, he
was of that rare temper in governing his choler,
that I never saw him angry during the time of my
stay there, and have heard so much of him for
many years before. When occasion of offence was
given him, I have seen him redden in the face, and
after remain for a while silent, but when he spake,
his words were so calm and gentle, that I found he
had digested his choler, though yet I confess I
could never attain that perfection, as being subject
ever to choler and passion more than I ought, and
generally to speak my mind freely, and indeed
rather to imitate those, who, having fire within
doors, choose rather to give it vent than suffer it to
burn the house. I commend yet much more the
manner of Mr. Thelwall; and, certainly, he that can
forbear speaking for some while, will remit much of
his passion; but as I could not learn much of him
in this kind, so I did as little profit in learning the
Welsh, or any other of those languages that worthy
gentleman understood, as having a tertian ague for
the most part of nine months, which was all the
time I stayed in his house. Having recovered my
strength again, I was sent, being about the age of
ten, to be taught by one Mr. Newton at Didlebury

in Shropshire,[1] where, in the space of less than
two years, I not only recovered all I had lost in
my sickness, but attained to the knowledge of the
Greek tongue and logic, insomuch, that at twelve
years old my parents thought fit to send me to
Oxford to University College,[2] where I remember
to have disputed at my first coming in logic, and to
have made in Greek the exercises required in that
college, oftener than in Latin. I had not been
many months in the University, but news was
brought me of my father's death, his sickness being
a lethargy, *caros*,[3] or *coma vigilans*, which continued
long upon him; he seemed at last to die without
much pain, though in his senses.[4] Upon opinion
given by physicians that his disease was mortal,
my mother thought fit to send for me home, and
presently, after my father's death, to desire her
brother Sir Francis Newport to haste to London to

---

[1] Doubtless Thomas Newton, eldest son of Edward
Newton, of Barley, Cheshire; a graduate of both Cambridge
and Oxford, and a well-known classical scholar. He "taught
school," says Wood, "at Macclesfield, or near it, with
good success." He died in May 1607 (see Wood's "Athenæ
Oxon.," ed. Bliss, ii. 5). Didlebury is near Macclesfield.

[2] Matriculated as a gentleman-commoner in 1595, aged
fourteen years; "being put under the tuition of an eminent
tutor." Wood's "Athenæ Oxon," ed. Bliss, iii. 239.

[3] In old medical books *carus* or *carosis* is applied to
various kinds of coma.

[4] 1596.

obtain my wardship for his and her use jointly, which he obtained.[1]   Shortly after I was sent again to my studies in Oxford, where I had not been long but that an overture for a match with the daughter and heir of Sir William Herbert of St. Julian's [2] was made, the occasion whereof was this : Sir William Herbert being heir-male to the old Earl of Pembroke above-mentioned by a younger son of his (for the eldest son had a daughter, who carried away those great possessions the Earl of Worcester now holds in Monmouthshire, as I said before), having one only daughter surviving, made a will, whereby he estated all his possessions in Monmouthshire and Ireland upon his said daughter, upon condition she married one of the surname of Herbert, otherwise the said lands to descend to the heirs-male of the said Sir William ; and his daughter to have only a small portion out of the lands he had in Anglesey and Carnarvonshire ; his lands being thus settled, Sir William died shortly afterwards.[3] He was a man much conversant with books, and especially given to the study of divinity, insomuch,

---

[1] The wardship was not obtained by Newport, but by his kinsman Sir George More, afterwards Donne's father-in-law. Kempe's Loseley MSS., p. 347.   (See Appendix VI. below.)

[2] Between Caerleon and Newport.   Thomas Churchyard, in his "Worthines of Wales" (1587), says : "Saint Gyllians is a fair house where Sir William Harbert dwelles."

[3] He died at St Julian's, 4th March 1592-3, and was buried at Monmouth a week later.   Powysland Coll., xi. 364.

that he writ an Exposition upon the Revelations,
which is printed ;[1] though some thought he was as
far from finding the sense thereof as he was from
attaining the philosopher's stone, which was another
part of his study :[2] howsoever, he was very understanding in all other things, he was noted yet to
be of a very high mind; but I can say little of
him, as having never seen his person, nor otherwise had much information concerning him. His
daughter and heir, called Mary,[3] after her father

---

[1] "A Letter written by a trve Christian Catholike to a
Romaine pretended Catholike vppon occasion of contro-
uersie touching the Catholike Church : the 12, 13, and
14 chapters of the Reuelations are breifly and trulie ex-
pounded." London, John Windet, 1586. Small 4to. 86 pp.
The book is anonymous, but Sir William's arms are at the
back of the title-page. A copy is in the British Museum.
The interpretation is very quaint and unconvincing. Ames
refers to the book under the author's name, and credits
him with another work, " Sidney or Baripenthes " (1586), a
poem on the death of Sir Philip Sidney. Typograph. Antiquities, ed. Herbert, p. 1226. (See also Strype's Parker, ii.
166 ; and Wood's Athenæ, ed. Bliss, ii. 483.)

[2] Sir William was the intimate friend of Dr. Dee, and
took a house at Mortlake in 1581 in order to pursue his
studies in astrology and alchemy with the doctor. See Dr.
Dee's Diary, published by Camden Society, pp. 3, 10, &c.

[3] The earliest reference to Lord Herbert's wife is in Dr.
Dee's Diary, under date 22d January 1581-2 :—"Arthur
Dee (*b.* 19th July 1579) and Mary Herbert, they being but
3 yere old the eldest, did make, as it wer, a shew of childish
marriage, of calling ech other husband and wife " (p. 14).

died, continued unmarried until she was one-and-twenty; none of the Herberts appearing in all that time, who, either in age or fortune, was fit to match her. About this time I had attained the age of fifteen,[1] and a match at last being proposed, yet, notwithstanding the disparity of years betwixt us, upon the eight-and-twentieth of February 1598[–9], in the house of Eyton, where the same man, vicar of ————, married my father and mother, christened and married me, I espoused her. Not long after my marriage I went again to Oxford, together with my wife and mother, who took a house, and lived for some certain time there;[2] and now, having a due remedy for that lasciviousness to which youth is naturally inclined, I followed my book more close than ever, in which course I continued until I attained about the age of eighteen, when my mother took a house in London, between which place and Montgomery Castle I passed my time till I came to the age of one-and twenty, having in that space divers children, I having now none remaining but Beatrice, Richard, and Edward. During this time of living in the University or at home, I did, without any master or teacher, attain the knowledge of the

---

[1] See p. 29, note 3. The age is probably seventeen.
[2] Walton says Lady Herbert lived for four years at Oxford. (See Appendix III.)

French, Italian, and Spanish languages, by the help of some books in Latin or English translated into those idioms, and the dictionaries of those several languages ; I attained also to sing my part at first sight in music, and to play on the lute with very little or almost no teaching ;—my intention in learning languages being to make myself a citizen of the world as far as it were possible ; and my learning of music was for this end, that I might entertain myself at home, and together refresh my mind after my studies, to which I was exceedingly inclined, and that I might not need the company of young men, in whom I observed in those times much ill example and debauchery.[1]

Being gotten thus far into my age, I shall give some observations concerning ordinary education, even from the first infancy till the departure from the University ; as being desirous, together with the narration of my life, to deliver such rules as I conceive may be useful to my posterity. And first, I find, that in the infancy those diseases are to be remedied which may be hereditary unto them on

---

[1] One is reminded of Sir Philip Sidney's advice to his brother to give good heed to the learning of music. Sidney always regretted that he himself had neglected it in youth. " You will not believe what a want I find of it in my melancholy times." Sidney Papers, i. 283–285. First-rate accomplishment in music was not very common : Puttenham says in his " Arte of Poesie "—" It is hard to find in these dayes of noblemen or gentlemen any excellent musitian " (p. 16).

either side ; so that, if they be subject to the stone
or gravel, I do conceive it will be good for the
nurse sometimes to drink posset drinks, in which
are boiled such things as are good to expel gravel
and stone ; the child also himself when he comes
to some age may use the same posset drinks of
herbs, as milium solis,[1] saxifragia,[2] &c., good for
the stone many are reckoned by the physicians, of
which also myself could bring a large catalogue,
but rather leave it to those who are expert in that
art. The same course is to be taken for the gout ;
for which purpose I do much commend the bathing
of children's legs and feet in the water wherein
smiths quench their iron,[3] as also water wherein
alum hath been infused, or boiled, as also the
decoction of juniper berries, bay berries, chamædrys,[4]
chamæpitys,[5] which baths also are good for those

---

[1] "Gromell [*i.e.*, Gromwell, or grey millet] is called in
shops and among the Italians *milium solis.*"—Gerard's
Herbal (1597), p. 487.

[2] Wall spleenwort, or stone-breaker, so named from the
belief that it was capable of dissolving stones in the bladder.
Gerard, p. 891.

[3] Gervase Markham, in his "English Huswife" (1616),
p. 28, recommends wine in which a red hot "lump of yron or
steele has been quenched." Many other homely prescriptions resembling those suggested by Lord Herbert are met
with in Markham's book.

[4] Wall or tree germander. Gerard, p. 523.

[5] Ground pine, or herb ivy. Gerard, p. 422.

that are hereditarily subject to the palsy, for these
things do much strengthen the sinews; as also
olium castorii, and sucini,[1] which are not to be
used without advice.   They that are also subject
to the spleen from their ancestors, ought to use
those herbs that are splenetics : and those that
are troubled with the falling sickness, with cepha-
niques, of which certainly I should have had need
but for the purging of my ears above mentioned.
Briefly, what disease soever it be that is derived
from ancestors of either side, it will be necessary
first to give such medicines to the nurse as may
make her milk effectual for those purposes; as
also afterwards to give unto the child itself such
specific remedies as his age and constitution will
bear.   I could say much more upon this point, as
having delighted ever in the knowledge of herbs,
plants, and gums, and in few words the history
of nature, insomuch, that coming to apothecaries'
shops, it was my ordinary manner when I looked
upon the bills filed up, containing the physicians'
prescriptions, to tell every man's disease ; howbeit,
I shall not presume in these particulars to prescribe
to my posterity, though I believe I know the best
receipts for almost all diseases, but shall leave
them to the expert physician ; only I will recommend again to my posterity the curing of hereditary

---

[1] Oil of amber.

diseases in the very infancy, since, otherwise, without much difficulty, they will never be cured.

When children go to school, they should have one to attend them, who may take care of their manners, as well as the schoolmaster doth of their learning ; for among boys all vice is easily learned ; and here I could wish it constantly observed, that neither the master should correct him for faults of his manners, nor his governor for manners for the faults in his learning. After the alphabet is taught, I like well the shortest and clearest grammars, and such books into which all the Greek and Latin words are severally contrived, in which kind one Comenius[1] hath given an example : this being done, it would be much better to proceed with Greek authors than with Latin ; for as it is as easy to learn at first the one as the other, it would be much better to give the first impressions into the child's memory of those things which are more rare than usual : therefore I would have them begin at Greek first, and the rather that there is not that art in the world wherein the

---

[1] In the "Janua Linguarum" (1st ed. 1631) of John Amos Comenius the equivalents of common phrases in different languages were arranged side by side in parallel columns. The book was frequently published in an English version, known as the "Gate of Tongues :" of which some editions dealt with the Latin, Greek, and English, and others solely with modern languages.

Greeks have not excelled and gone before others ; so that when you look upon philosophy, astronomy, mathematics, medicine, and briefly all learning, the Greeks have exceeded all nations.[1]   When he shall be ready to go ́to the University, it will be fit also his governor for manners go along with him ; it being the frail nature of youth, as they grow to ripeness in age, to be more capable of doing ill, unless their manners be well guided, and themselves by degrees habituated in virtue, with which if once they acquaint themselves, they will find more pleasure in it than ever they can do in vice ; since everybody loves virtuous persons, whereas the vicious do scarce love one another.   For this purpose, it will be necessary that you keep the company of grave, learned men, who are of good reputation, and hear rather what they say, and follow what they do, than follow the examples of young, wild, and rash persons ; and certainly of those two parts which are to be acquired in youth, whereof one is goodness and virtuous manners, the other learning and knowledge, I shall so much prefer the first before the second, as I shall ever

---

[1] Cf. Ascham's "Scholemaster,"ed. Mayor, p. 52 : "And trewelie, if there be any good in them [*i.e.*, Latin and modern writings], it is either lerned, borowed, or stolne from some one of these worthie wittes in *Athens.*" Ascham's marginal note runs—" Lernyng chiefly conteined in the Greke, and in no other tong."

think virtue, accompanied with ordinary discretion, will make his way better both to happiness in this world and the next, than any puffed knowledge which would cause him to be insolent and vainglorious, or minister, as it were, arms and advantages to him for doing a mischief; so that it is pity that wicked dispositions should have knowledge to acuate their ill intentions, or courage to maintain them; that fortitude which should defend all a man's virtues, being never well employed to defend his humours, passions, or vices. I do not approve for elder brothers that course of study which is ordinary used in the University, which is, if their parents perchance intend they shall stay there four or five years, to employ the said time as if they meant to proceed masters of art and doctors in some science; for which purpose, their tutors commonly spend much time in teaching them the subtleties of logic, which, as it is usually practised,[1] enables them for little more than to be excellent wranglers, which art, though it may be tolerable in a mercenary lawyer, I can by no means commend in a sober and well-governed gentleman. I approve

---

[1] Bacon repeatedly complains that logic and rhetoric, " arts fitter for graduates than children and novices," were begun by scholars at the universities at too early an age, and that, as a consequence, they had degenerated into "ridiculous affectation," and their wisdom become contemptible.—Advancement of Learning, in Spedding's ed., Book ii. p. 601.

much those part of logic which teach men to deduce
their proofs from firm and undoubted principles,
and show men to distinguish betwixt truth and falsehood, and help them to discover fallacies, sophisms,
and that which the schoolmen call vicious argumentations, concerning which I shall not here enter
into a long discourse.   So much of logic as may
serve for this purpose being acquired, some good
sum of philosophy may be learned, which may
teach him both the ground of the Platonic and
Aristotelian philosophy.   After which it will not
be amiss to read the *Idea Medicinæ Philosophicæ*,[1]
written by Severinus (Danus), there being many
things considerable concerning the Paracelsian
principles written in that book, which are not to be
found in former writers ; it will not be amiss also
to read over Franciscus Patricius,[2] and Telesius,[3]

---

[1] ". . . fundamenta continens totius doctrinæ Paracel-
sicæ, Hippocraticæ et Galenicæ," Basle, 1571 ; Erfurt,
1616 ; Hagæ Comitis, 1660. The author, Peter Severin, the
most celebrated champion of Paracelsian medicine in the
sixteenth century, was doctor to the King of Denmark,
and died in 1602. *Cf.* Bacon's De Augmentis, lib. iii. in
Spedding's edition of the Philosophical Works, i. 564.

[2] Francis Patrizi, "qui Platonicorum fumos sublimavit,"
is well known for his inefficient attacks on Aristotle in his
Discussiones Peripateticæ (1571 and 1581). See Bacon's
De Augmentis, ed. Spedding, i. 564.

[3] Telesius of Cosenza (b. 1509) wrote De Rerum Natura,
(1565 and 1586). This work greatly influenced Bacon,

who have examined and controverted the ordinary
Peripatetic doctrine ; all which may be performed
in one year, that term being enough for philosophy, as I conceive, and six months for logic,
for I am confident a man may have quickly more
than he needs of these two arts.   These being
attained, it will be requisite to study geo-
graphy with exactness, so much as may teach a
man the situation of all countries in the whole
world, together with which, it will be fit to learn
something concerning the governments, manners,
religions, either ancient or new, as also the
interests of states, and relations in amity, or
strength in which they stand to their neighbours ;
it will be necessary also, at the same time, to learn
the use of the celestial globe, the studies of both
globes being complicated and joined together.   I
do not conceive yet the knowledge of judicial astrology so necessary, but only for general predictions ;
particular events being neither intended by nor
collected out of the stars.[1]   It will be also fit to

---

who repeatedly refers to it in his philosophical books.   In
the De Augmentis Bacon says of Telesius, " Parmenidis
philosophiam instaurans arma Peripateticorum in illos ipsos
vertit."   See Bacon's De Principiis atque Originibus, and R.
L. Ellis's introduction to the treatise in Spedding's edition,
iii. 74 *et seq.*

[1] *Cf.* Herbert's Religio Gentilium (1663), cap. viii. p. 49.
" Hasce (*i.e.* stellas) consulat sapiens, non quidem juxta

learn arithmetic and geometry in some good measure, but especially arithmetic, it being most useful
for many purposes, and, among the rest, for keeping
accounts, whereof here is much use.   As for the
knowledge of lines, superficies, and bodies,[1] though
it be a science of much certainty and demonstration, it is not much useful for a gentleman, unless
it be to understand fortifications, the knowledge
whereof is worthy of those who intend the wars ;
though yet he must remember, that whatsoever art
doth in way of defence, art likewise, in way of
assailing, can destroy.   This study hath cost me

---

superstitiosas et vulgares astrologorum formulas, sed ex
eventuum observatione, ubi earum motus, conjunctiones,
oppositiones, et aspectus varii inter se comparantur."   See
also Herbert's Dialogue, p. 179 :—" When it [*i.e.* astrology]
is rightly understood and applied, it be not only a lawful, but
a most necessary art for a wise man ; as long as he takes
only general predictions from thence, without presuming to
foretell particular and single events, otherwise then, as they
depended upon the general causes, since they who descend
too far into particulars either err or speak truth by chance."

[1] Of mathematics Lord Herbert writes in A Dialogue
between a Tutor and a Pupil : " I told you also the end
of this mathematical doctrine was but ignoble in respect
of other [sciences] as tending only to the measuring of
heights, depths, and distances, or the making of some
excellent engines and the like ; all which are of so mean
consideration that they can be no ways esteemed as objects
adequated or proportioned to the dignity of our souls,
whose speculations reach much further " (p. 2).   Lord Herbert seems totally ignorant of the higher pure mathematics.

much labour, but as yet I could never find how any place could be so fortified, but that there were means, in certain opposite lines, to prevent or subvert all that could be done in that kind. It will become a gentleman to have some knowledge in medicine, especially the diagnostic part, whereby he may take timely notice of a disease, and by that means timely prevent it, as also the prognostic part, whereby he may judge of the symptoms either increasing or decreasing in the disease, as also concerning the crisis or indication thereof. This art will get a gentleman not only much knowledge, but much credit; since seeing any sick body, he will be able to tell, in all human probability, whether he shall recover, or if he shall die of the disease, to tell what signs shall go before, and what the conclusion will be; it will become him also to know not only the ingredients, but doses, of certain cathartic or purging, emetic or vomitive medicines, specific or choleric, melancholic, or phlegmatic constitutions, phlebotomy being only necessary for those who abound in blood. Besides, I would have a gentleman know how to make these medicines himself, and afterwards prepare them with his own hands; it being the manner of apothecaries so frequently to put in the succedanea, that no man is sure to find with them medicines made with the true drugs which ought to enter into the composition when it is

exotic or rare; or when they are extant in the
shop, no man can be assured that the said drugs
are not rotten, or that they have not lost their
natural force and virtue. I have studied this art
very much also, and have, in case of extremity,
ministered physic with that success which is
strange, whereof I shall give two or three examples: Richard Griffiths of Sutton, my servant,
being sick of a malignant pestilent fever,[1] and tried
in vain all our country physicians could do, and his
water at last stinking so grievously, which physicians note to be a sign of extension of natural
heat, and consequently of present[2] death, I was
entreated to see him, when as yet he had neither
eaten, drank, slept, or known anybody for the
space of six or seven days; whereupon demanding
whether the physicians had given him over, and it
being answered unto me that they had, I said it
would not be amiss to give him the quantity of an
hazle-nut of a certain rare receipt which I had,
assuring that if anything in the world could
recover him, that would: of which I was so confident, that I would come the next day at four of
the clock in the afternoon unto him, and at that
time I doubted not but they should find signs of
amendment, provided they should put the doses I
gave them, being about the bigness of a nut, down

---

[1] A case of typhus fever.   [2] Immediate.

his throat ; which being done with much difficulty, I came the morrow after at the hour appointed, when, to the wonder of his family, he knew me, and asked for some broth, and not long after recovered. My cousin, Athelston Owen, also of Rhiew Saeson,[1] having an hydrocephale also in that extremity that his eyes began to start out of his head, and his tongue to come out of his mouth, and his whole head finally exceeding its natural proportion, insomuch that his physicans likewise left him ; I prescribed to him the decoction of two diuretic roots, which after he had drank four or five days, he urined in that abundance that his head by degrees returned to its ancient figure, and all other signs of health appeared ; whereupon also he wrote a letter to me, that he was so suddenly and perfectly restored to his former health, that it seemed more like a miracle than a cure ; for those are the very words in the letter he sent me. I cured a great lady in London of an issue of blood, when all the physicians had given her over, with so easy a medicine, that the lady herself was astonished to find the effects thereof. I could give more examples in this kind, but these shall suffice ; I will for the rest deliver a rule I conceive for finding

---

[1] In the hundred of Cyveiliog, Montgomeryshire. Athelston was the son of Maurice Owen by Elizabeth, daughter of Matthew Herbert of Dolguog, Lord Herbert's uncle.

out the best receipts not only for curing all inward
but outward hurts, such as are ulcers, tumours,
contusions, wounds, and the like : you must look
upon all pharmacopæias or antidotaries [1] of several
countries, of which sort I have in my library the
Pharmacopœia Londinensis,[2] *Parisiensis,*[3] *Amstelre-
damensis,*[4] that of Quercetanus,[5] Bauderonus,[6]
Renodæus,[7] Valerius Cordus,[8] *Pharmacopœia Colo-*

---

[1] Antidotaries were properly collections of antidote-
recipes, but the term was often used synonymously with
Dispensary or *Dispensatorium, i.e.* a general collection of
simple medical prescriptions.   See Dr. Murray's English
Dictionary.

[2] First edition, called PRIMA, 1618 ; second edition,
called SECUNDA, 1650.

[3] Codex Medicamentarius seu Pharmacopœa Parisiensis,
editore Phil. Harduino, Paris, 1639.

[4] 1636.

[5] Josephus Quercetanus or Du Chesne, a voluminous
writer, published a Pharmacopœia Dogmaticorum Restituta,
1607, 4to, Paris.   He was the chief French champion of
Paracelsian medicine.

[6] Brice Bauderon, Pharmacopœia et Praxis Medica,
1620, Paris.   This work was issued by Philemon Holland,
together with J. Du Boy's Pharmacopœi Parisiensis Obser-
vationes, in London in 1639.

[7] Joannes Renodæus, Dispensatorium Medicum et Antidotarium, 1609, 4to, Paris ; Geneva, 1645.   An English
translation by Richard Tomlinson was published in London
in 1657.

[8] Valerius Cordus, Dispensatorium.   Antw.   1568 ;
Leyden, 1637.

niensis,[1] Augustana,[2] Venetiana,[3] Vononiensis, Flor-
entina, Romana, Messanesis;[4] in some of which are
told not only what the receipts there set down are
good for, but the doses of them.   The rule I here
give is, that what all the said dispensatories, antidotaries, or pharmacopæis prescribe as effectual for
overcoming a disease is certainly good; for as
they are set forth by the authority of the physicians
of these several countries, what they all ordain must
necessarily be effectual : but they who will follow
my advice shall find in that little short antidotary
called Amstelodamensis, not long since put forth,
almost all that is necessary to be known for curing
of diseases, wounds, &c.   There is a book called
Aurora Medicorum, very fit to be read in this kind.[5]
Among writers of physic, I do especially commend,
after Hippocrates and Galen, Fernelius,[6] Lud. Mer-

---

[1] Dispensarium usuale pro Pharmacopœis . . . reipubl.
Coloniæ, Cologne, 1565.   Pharmacopœia sive Dispensatorium Coloniense, Cologne, 1627.

[2] Pharmacopœas were issued at Augsburg in 1573,
1597, 1623, 1643.

[3] Pharmacopœa a Medicorum Venetorum Collegio Com-
probata, Curtio Martinello autore, Venice, 1617.

[4] Antidotarium Speciale sacræ Domus Magni Hospitalis
urbis Messanæ, by Placidus Truglio, Venice, 1642.

[5] Probably Aurora Thesaurusque Philosophorum Theoph.
Paracelsi, by Paracelsus' pupil, Gerard Dorn.   Basle 1577,
and Frankfort 1585.

[6] Johannes Fernelius (physician to Henry II. of France)
published Opera Medicinalia et Universa Medicina, 1564,
4to, and 1577, fol.

catus,[1] and Dan. Sennertus,[2] and Heurnius:[3] I could name many more, but I conceive these may suffice. As for the chemic or spagyric medicines, I cannot commend them to the use of my posterity; there being neither emetic, cathartic, diaphoretic, diuretic medicines extant among them, which are not much more happily and safely performed by vegetables; but hereof enough, since I pretend no further than to give some few directions to my posterity. In the meanwhile, I conceive it is a fine study, and worthy a gentleman to be a good botanic, that so he may know the nature of all herbs and plants, being our fellow-creatures, and made for the use of man;[4] for which purpose it will be fit for him to cull out of some good herbal all the icones[5] together, with the descriptions of

---

[1] Ludovicus Mercatus (physician to Philip II. and III. of Spain) was author of Opera Medica et Chirurgica, fol. Franco. 1620.

[2] Daniel Sennert (1572–1637), an eminent German doctor, published Institutionum Medicinæ, Lib. v., Wittemberg, 1611 and 1628.

[3] Jan van Heurn (1543–1601), a well-known Dutch doctor, was the author of many practical treatises issued between 1587 and 1609.

[4] "I could tell you also of many other strange herbs, but had rather you should read them in herbals, the greatest knowledge of them being a thing I much recommend unto you" (Dialogue, p. 172).

[5] *i.e.* εἰκόνες, figures.

them, and to lay by themselves all such as grow
in England, and afterwards to select again such as
usually grow by the highway-side, in meadows, by
rivers, or in marshes, or in cornfields, or in dry
and mountainous places, or on rocks, walls, or in
shady places, such as grow by the seaside ; for
this being done, and the said icones being ordinarily carried by themselves, or by their servants,
one may presently find out every herb he meets
withal, especially if the said flowers be truly coloured.[1] Afterwards it will not be amiss to distinguish by themselves such herbs as are in gardens,
and are exotics, and are transplanted hither. As
for those plants which will not endure our clime,
though the knowledge of them be worthy of a
gentleman, and the virtues of them be fit to be
learned, especially if they be brought over to a
druggist as medicinal, yet the icones of them are
not so pertinent to be known as the former, unless
it be where there is less danger of adulterating the
said medicaments ; in which case, it is good to

---

[1] In 1639 Thomas Johnson, the learned editor of Gerard's
Herbal, undertook, with companions, the first professedly
botanical tour in Wales. From Machynlleth the travellers
went through Montgomeryshire, and at Montgomery Castle
were hospitably received and entertained by Lord Herbert.
In the neighbourhood, "inter Dudson (Dudeston) et Guarthe-
low," they gathered *Solidaginem etiam Saracenicam*, one of
our rarest British plants (Powysland, Collections, xi. 370).

have recourse to not only the botanics, but also to
Gesner's Dispensatory,[1] and to *Aurora Medicorum*,
above mentioned, being books which make a man
distinguish betwixt good and bad drugs : And this
much of medicine may not only be useful but
delectable to a gentleman, since which way soever
he passeth, he may find something to entertain
him. I must no less commend the study of anatomy, which whosoever considers, I believe will
never be an atheist ; the frame of man's body
and coherence of his parts being so strange and
paradoxal, that I hold it to be the greatest miracle
of nature ; though when all is done, I do not find
she hath made it so much as proof against one
disease, lest it should be thought to have made it
no less than a prison to the soul.

Having thus passed over all human literature,
it will be fit to say something of moral virtues and
theological learning. As for the first, since the
Christians and the heathens are in a manner agreed
concerning the definitions of virtues, it would not
be inconvenient to begin with those definitions
which Aristotle in his Morals hath given, as being
confirmed for the most part by the Platonics,
Stoics, and other philosophers, and in general by
the Christian Church, as well as all nations in the

---

[1] Conrad Gesner's Apparatus et Delectus Simplicium
Medicamentorum, Leyden, 1542.

world whatsoever; they being doctrines imprinted in the soul in its first original, and containing the principal and first notices by which man may attain his happiness here or hereafter; there being no man that is given to vice that doth not find much opposition both in his own conscience, and in the religion and law as taught elsewhere; and this I dare say, that a virtuous man may not only go securely through all the religions,[1] but all the laws in the world, and whatsoever obstructions he meet, obtain both an inward peace and outward welcome among all with whom he shall negotiate or converse; this virtue, therefore, I shall recommend to my posterity as the greatest perfection he can attain unto in this life, and the pledge of eternal happiness hereafter; there being none that can justly hope of an union with the supreme God, that doth not come as near to him in this life in virtue and goodness as he can; so that if human frailty do interrupt this union, by committing faults that make him incapable of his everlasting happiness, it will be fit, by a serious repentance, to expiate and emaculate those faults, and for the rest, trust to the mercy of God his Creator, Redeemer, and Preserver, who being our Father, and knowing well in what a weak condition through

---

[1] This is the view so admirably insisted on in Lord Herbert's De Religione Gentilium. See Introduction.

infirmities we are, will, I doubt not, commiserate
those transgressions we commit when they are
done without desire to offend his Divine Majesty,
and together rectify our understanding through
his grace; since we commonly sin through no
other cause, but that we mistook a true good for
that which was only apparent, and so were deceived,
by making an undue election in the objects proposed to us; wherein, though it will be fit for
every man to confess that he hath offended an
infinite Majesty and Power, yet, as upon better
consideration, he finds he did not mean infinitely
to offend, there will be just reason to believe that
God will not inflict an infinite punishment upon
him if he be truly penitent, so that his justice may
be satisfied, if not with man's repentance, yet at
least with some temporal punishment here or hereafter, such as may be proportionable to the offence;
though I cannot deny but when man would infinitely offend God in a despiteful and contemptuous
way, it will be but just that he suffer an infinite
punishment: but as I hope none are so wicked as
to sin purposedly, and with an high hand against
the eternal Majesty of God; so when they shall
commit any sins out of frailty, I shall believe,
either, that unless they be finally impenitent, and,
(as they say, sold ingeniously over to sin) God's
mercy will accept of their endeavours to return
into a right way, and so make their peace with

him by all those good means that are possible.
Having thus recommended the learning of moral
philosophy and practice of virtue, as the most
necessary knowledge and useful exercise of man's
life, I shall observe, that even in the employing of
our virtues, discretion is required ; for every virtue
is not promiscuously to be used, but such only
as is proper for the present occasion.   Therefore,
though a wary and discreet wisdom be most useful
where no imminent danger appears, yet, where an
enemy draweth his sword against you, you shall
have most use of fortitude, prevention being too
late, when the danger is so pressing.   On the
other side, there is no occasion to use your fortitude against wrongs done by women or children,
or ignorant persons, that I may say nothing of
those that are much your superiors, who are magistrates, &c., since you might by a discreet wisdom
have declined the injury, or when it were too late
to do so, you may with more equal mind support
that which is done, either by authority in the one,
or frailty in the other.   And certainly to such kind
of person's forgiveness will be proper ; in which
kind I am confident no man of my time hath
exceeded me ; for though whensoever my honour
hath been engaged, no man hath ever been more
forward to hazard his life, yet where, with my
honour I could forgive, I never used revenge, as
leaving it always to God, who, the less I punish

mine enemies will inflict so much the more punishment on them ;[1] and to this forgiveness of others
three considerations have especially invited me.

1. That he that cannot forgive others breaks the
bridge over which he must pass himself, for every
man hath need to be forgiven.

2. That when a man wants or comes short of an
entire and accomplished virtue, our defects may be
supplied this way, since the forgiving of evil deeds
in others amounteth to no less than virtue in us ;
that therefore it may be not unaptly called the paying our debts with another man's money.

3. That it is the most necessary and proper work
of every man ; for, though when I do not a just
thing, or a charitable, or a wise, another man may
do it for me, yet no man can forgive my enemy but

---

[1] Horace Walpole (Lord Orford) remarks on this passage : " This is a very unchristian reason for pardoning our
enemies, and can by no means be properly called forgiveness. Is it forgiveness to remit a punishment on the
hope of its being doubled ? " Bacon, from an equally utili-
tarian point of view, puts the case better : " Certainly in
taking revenge a man is but even with his enemy ; but in
passing it over he is superior ; for it is a prince's part to
pardon. And Solomon, I am sure, saith, *It is the glory of
a man to pass by an offence.* That which is past is gone
and irrevocable : and wise men have enough to do with
things present and to come. A man does wrong in order
to profit himself. Therefore why should I be angry with
a man for loving himself better than me ? " (Essay on
Revenge).

myself. And these have been the chief motives
for which I have been ever inclined to forgiveness ;
whereof, though I have rarely found other effect
than that my servants, tenants, and neighbours
have thereupon more frequently offended me, yet at
least I have had within me an inward peace and
comfort thereby; since I can truly say, nothing
ever gave my mind more ease than when I had
forgiven my enemies, which freed me from many
cares and perturbations, which otherwise would
have molested me.

And this likewise brings in another rule concerning the use of virtues, which is, that you are
not to use justice where mercy is most proper ; as,
on the other side, a foolish pity is not to be preferred before that which is just and necessary for
good example. So likewise liberality is not to be
used where parsimony or frugality is more requisite ;
as, on the other side, it will be but a sordid thing in
a gentleman to spare where expending of money
would acquire unto him advantage, credit, or
honour : and this rule in general ought to be
practised, that the virtue requisite to the occasion
is ever to be produced, as the most opportune and
necessary. That, therefore, wisdom is the soul of
all virtues, giving as unto her members life and
motion, and so necessary in every action, that whosoever by the benefit of true wisdom makes use of
the right virtue, on all emergent occasions, I dare

say would never be constrained to have recourse
to vice, whereby it appears that every virtue is not
to be employed indifferently, but that only which
is proper for the business in question; among
which yet temperance seems so universally requisite,
that some part of it at least will be a necessary
ingredient in all human actions, since there may
be an excess even in religious worship, at those
times when other duties are required at our hands.
After all, moral virtues are learned and directed
to the service and glory of God, as the principal
end and use of them.

It would be fit that some time be spent in learning rhetoric or oratory, to the intent that upon all
occasions you may express yourself with eloquence
and grace; for, as it is not enough for a man to
have a diamond unless it is polished and cut out
into its due angles, and a foil be set underneath,
whereby it may the better transmit and vibrate its
native lustre and rays; so it will not be sufficient
for a man to have a great understanding in all
matters, unless the said understanding be not only
polished and clear, but underset and holpen a
little with those figures, tropes, and colours which
rhetoric affords, where there is use of persuasion.
I can by no means yet commend an affected eloquence, there being nothing so pedantical, or
indeed that would give more suspicion that the
truth is not intended, than to use overmuch the

E

common forms prescribed in schools. It is well said by them, that there are two parts of eloquence necessary and recommendable; one is, to speak hard things plainly, so that when a knotty or intricate business, having no method or coherence in its parts, shall be presented, it will be a singular part of oratory to take those parts asunder, set them together aptly, and so exhibit them to the understanding. And this part of rhetoric I much commend to everybody; there being no true use of speech, but to make things clear, perspicuous, and manifest, which otherwise would be perplexed, doubtful, and obscure.

The other part of oratory is to speak common things ingeniously or wittily; there being no little vigour and force added to words, when they are delivered in a neat and fine way, and somewhat out of the ordinary road, common and dull language relishing more of the clown than the gentleman. But herein also affectation must be avoided; it being better for a man by a native and clear eloquence to express himself, than by those words which may smell either of the lamp or inkhorn; so that, in general, one may observe, that men who fortify and uphold their speeches with strong and evident reasons, have ever operated more on the minds of the auditors, than those who have made rhetorical excursions.

It will be better for a man who is doubtful of

his pay to take an ordinary silver piece with its
due stamp upon it, than an extraordinary gilded
piece which may perchance contain a baser metal
under it; and prefer a well-favoured wholesome
woman, though with a tawny complexion, before
a besmeared and painted face.

It is a general note, that a man's wit is best
showed in his answer, and his valour in his defence;
that therefore as men learn in fencing how to ward
all blows and thrusts, which are or can be made
against him [? them], so it will be fitting to debate
and resolve beforehand what you are to say or do
upon any affront given you, lest otherwise you
should be surprised. Aristotle hath written a book
of rhetoric, a work in my opinion not inferior to his
best pieces, whom therefore with Cicero de Oratore,
as also Quintilian, you may read for your instruction
how to speak; neither of which two yet I can think so
exact in their orations, but that a middle style will be
of more efficacy, Cicero in my opinion being too long
and tedious, and Quintilian too short and concise.

Having thus by moral philosophy enabled yourself
to all that wisdom and goodness which is requisite
to direct you in all your particular actions, it will
be fit now to think how you are to behave yourself
as a public person, or member of the commonwealth
and kingdom wherein you live; as also to look into
those principles and grounds upon which government is framed, it being manifest in nature that the

wise doth easily govern the foolish, and the strong
master the weak, so that he that could attain most
wisdom and power, would quickly rule his fellows ;
for proof whereof, one may observe that a king is
sick during that time the physicians govern him,
and in day of battle an expert general appoints
the king a place in which he shall stand ; which
was anciently the office of the constables de France.
In-law also the judge is in a sort superior to his king
as long as he judgeth betwixt him and his people.
In divinity also, he, to whom the king commits the
charge of his conscience, is his superior in that particular. All which instances may sufficiently prove,
that in many cases the wiser governs or commands
one less wise than himself, unless a wilful obstinacy
be interposed ; in which case recourse must be had
to strength, where obedience is necessary.

The exercises I chiefly used, and most recommend to my posterity, were riding the great horse [1]

---

[1] This very well-known phrase was first fully explained
by Richard Berenger in his " History and Art of Horsemanship " (London, 1771), i. 169, 170. Great horses, he says,
[called also *Dextrarii* (Lat.), *Destriere* (Ital.), and *Destrier*
(Fr.), from *dextra*, as being carefully handled, dressed, or
managed], are opposed to Palfreys, Coursers, and Nags, and
are exclusively used in war and for the exercises of the
Tournament. They are usually of prodigious weight, because their riders are clothed in complete armour. Their
size made it necessary for soldiers to learn the art of
managing them after certain fixed rules, and hence came

and fencing, in which arts I had excellent masters, English, French, and Italian.[1]   As for dancing, I could never find leisure enough to learn it, as employing my mind always in acquiring of some art or science more useful; howbeit, I shall wish these three exercises learned in this order.[2]

---

the expression to "ride the great horse."   The passage is quoted fully by Mr. T. W. Jackson in the Oxford Historical Society's Collectanea, i. 273.   Mr. Jackson quotes from the "Gentleman's Dictionary" (1705), that "a horse for war should be 16 or 18 Hands high."   Reference should be made to Markham's "Country Contentments" (1615), pp. 35–86, and "Cavalerice" (1617), to Sir William Hope's "Compleat Horseman" (1717), and to the Duke of New-castle's splendid folios—the *Methode Nouvelle de Dresser des Chevaux* (Antw., 1658), and *A New Method . . . to Dress Horses* (Lond.. 1667)—for fuller information as to seventeenth-century horsemanship.

[1] French masters were most usually employed.   Prince Henry was given by Sully a French riding and a French fencing master.   References to such foreign teachers are common in the dramatists : see an interesting note in W. B. Rye's "England as Seen by Foreigners," p. 253.

[2] Sir R. Southwell thus describes the accomplishments of Lord Ossory, son of the first Duke of Ormonde (about 1650), a perfect specimen of the educated youth of the seventeenth century:—" He rides the great horse very well; is a good tennis-player, fencer, and dancer.   He understands music, and plays on the guitar and lute ; speaks French elegantly: reads Italian fluently, is a good historian, and so well versed in romances that if a gallery be full of pictures or hangings he will tell the stories of all of them that are described."   Cf. Thomas Lorkin's letter to Adam Newton,

That dancing may be learnt first, as that which doth fashion the body, gives one a good presence in and address to all companies, since it disposeth the limbs to a kind of *souplesse* (as the Frenchmen call it) and agility, insomuch as they seem to have the use of their legs, arms, and bodies, more than any others, who, standing stiff and stark in their postures, seem as if they were taken in their joints, or had not the perfect use of their members.[1] I speak not this yet as if I would have a youth never stand still in company, but only, that when he hath occasion to stir, his motions may be comely and graceful, that he may learn to know how to come in and go out of a room where company is, how to make courtesies handsomely, according to the several degrees of persons he shall encounter, how to put off and hold his hat; all which, and many other things which become men, are taught by the more accurate dancing-masters in France.

Prince Henry's tutor, respecting the completion of a young gentleman's education at Paris in 1610.   Horse-riding, fencing, and dancing were to be practised at stated hours daily.   Ellis's Orig. Letters, second series, iii. 220, 221.

[1] Cf. Locke "On Education," 1693, p. 307. "Dancing . . . gives graceful motions all the life, and above all things manliness and a becoming confidence to young children." Locke warns the pupil, however, against "apish, affected postures," and only values the accomplishment "as it tends to perfect graceful carriage."

The next exercise a young man should learn (but not before he is eleven or twelve years of age) is fencing ;[1] for the attaining of which the Frenchman's rule is excellent, *bon pied bon œil*, by which to teach men how far they may stretch out their feet when they would make a thrust against their enemy, lest either should overstride themselves, or, not striding far enough, fail to bring the point of their weapon home. The second part of his direction adviseth the scholar to keep a fixed eye upon the point of his enemy's sword, to the intent he may both put by or ward the blows and thrusts made against him, and together direct the point of his sword upon some part of his enemy that lieth naked and open to him.

The good fencing-masters, in France especially, when they present a foil or fleuret[2] to their scholars, tell him it hath two parts, one of which he calleth the fort or strong, and the other the foyble[3] or weak. With the fort or strong, which extends from the part of the hilt next the sword about a third part of the whole length, thereof he teacheth his scholars to defend themselves, and put by and ward the thrusts and blows of his

---

[1] Of fencing Locke says "it seems to me a good exercise for the health, but dangerous to the life, the confidence of their skill being apt to encourage in quarrels those that think they have learned to use their swords "—which was certainly the case with Lord Herbert.

[2] Mod. Fr. = foil.　　　　[3] *i.e.*, Mod. Fr., faible.

enemy, and with the other two-third parts to strike
or thrust as he shall see occasion ; which rule also
teacheth how to strike or thrust high or low as his
enemy doth, and briefly to take his measure and
time upon his adversary's motions, whereby he
may both defend himself or offend his adversary,
of which I have had much experiment and use both
in the fleuret, or foil, as also when I fought in
good earnest with many persons at one and the
same time, as will appear in the sequel of my life.
And, indeed, I think I shall not speak vaingloriously
of myself, if I say, that no man understood the use
of his weapon better than I did, or hath more dex-
terously prevailed himself thereof on all occasions ;
since I found no man could be hurt but through
some error in fencing.

I spent much time also in learning to ride the
great horse, that creature being made above all
others for the service of man, as giving his rider
all the advantages of which he is capable, while
sometimes he gives him strength, sometimes agility
or motion for the overcoming of his enemy, insomuch, that a good rider on a good horse, is as
much above himself and others, as this world can
make him.[1]   The rule for graceful riding is, that

---

[1] Cf. Lord Herbert's remarks in the Dialogue, p. 225 :
" In which number [*i.e.*, of the animals most useful to man]
the horse must have the precedence, being the animal

a man hold his eyes always betwixt the two ears,
and his rod [1] over the left ear of his horse ; which
he is to use for turning him every way, helping
himself with his left foot and rod upon the left
part of his neck, to make his horse turn on the
right hand, and with the right foot and help of his
rod also (if needs be), to turn him on the left
hand ; but this is to be used rather when one
would make a horse understand these motions,
than when he is a ready horse, the foot and stirrup
alone applied to either shoulder being sufficient,
with the help of the reins, to make him turn any
way.   That a rider thus may have the use of his
sword, or when it is requisite only to make a horse
go sidewards, it will be enough to keep the reins
equal in his hand, and with the flat of his leg and
foot together, and a touch upon the shoulder of the
horse with the stirrup to make him go sideward
either way, without either advancing forward, or
returning backwards.

The most useful *aer*,[2] as the Frenchmen term it,

---

which exalts man so much, that he takes strength, motion,
and even comeliness from a good posture on horseback."

[1] *i.e.*, whip.

[2] *Aer* or air, is a word applied generally to the artificial
movements of a managed horse.   Dr. Murray quotes in
his Dictionary from Brooke, Eng. Episc., I. ii. 5 (1641) :
" Horses which are designed to a lofty Ayre and generous
manege must be of a noble race."

is territerr ;[1] the courbettes, cabrioles, or *un pas et un sault*,[2] being fitter for horses of parade and triumph than for soldiers ; yet I cannot deny but a demivolte[2] with courbettes, so that they be not too high, may be useful in a fight or *mêlée;* for, as Labroue hath it in his book of horsemanship,[3] Monsieur de Montmorency having a horse that was excellent in performing the demivolte, did with his sword strike down two adversaries from their horses in a tourney, where divers of the prime gallants of France did meet ; for taking his time when the horse was in the height of his courbette, and discharging a blow, then his sword fell with such weight and force upon the two cavaliers one after another, that he struck them from their horses to the ground.[4]

---

[1] *i.e.,* terre-à-terre, a forward jump.

[2] Technical terms for various leaps, fully described and illustrated by Pluvinel and Labroue.

[3] The first edition is entitled *Preceptes principaux qve les bons Caualerises doivent exactement obseruer en leurs Escoles. . . . Composez par Sieur de la Broue.* La Rochelle, 1593. The second and more elaborate edition bears the title : " La Cavalarice François : composé par Salomon de la Brove, Escuyer de escuirie du Roy et de Monseigneur Le Duc d'Espernon." Paris, 1602. A copy presented by the author to James I. is in the British Museum. Lord Herbert's remarks on equestrian evolutions are summarised extracts from Labroue's book.

[4] This story, told by Labroue in his eighteenth chapter of both editions—(*Passade a demy air*)—relates to Lord Herbert's friend, Henri Duc de Montmorency, when he was

The manner of fighting a duel on horseback I was taught thus. We had each of us a reasonable stiff riding-rod in our hands, about the length of a sword, and so rid one against the other ; he, as the more expert, sat still to pass me and then to get behind me, and after to turn with his right hand upon my left side with his rod, that so he might hit me with the point thereof in the body ; and he that can do this handsomely, is sure to overcome his adversary, it being impossible to bring his sword about enough to defend himself or offend the assailant ; and to get this advantage, which they call in French, *gagner la crouppe*, nothing is so useful as to make a horse to go only sideward until his adversary be past him, since he will by this means avoid his adversary's blow or thrust, and on a sudden get on the left hand of his adversary in the manner I formerly related ; but of this art let Labroue and Pluvinel[1] be read, who are excellent

---

known as "Monseigneur le Mareschal du Dampuille, maintenant Connestable de France." Montmorency is frequently mentioned by Labroue as the best horseman he had seen, and the second book of the second edition is dedicated to him. He is stated to have twice performed the feat here mentioned, once at Bayonne, and again in presence of the Court in the Louvre Garden at Paris.

[1] Antoine de Pluvinel, Ecuyer to Louis XIII., author of *Instruction du Roi en l'exercice de monter à cheval* (Paris, 1619), with plates by Crispin Pass, exhibiting the whole system of the manege.

masters in that art, of whom I must confess I learned much; though, to speak ingenuously, my breaking two or three colts, and teaching them afterwards those *aers* of which they were most capable, taught me both what I was to do, and made me see mine errors, more than all their precepts.

To make a horse fit for the wars, and embolden him against all terrors, these inventions are useful: to beat a drum out of the stable first, and then give him his provender: then beat a drum in the stable by degrees, and then give him his provender upon the drum.   When he is acquainted herewith sufficiently, you must shoot off a pistol out of the stable, before he hath his provender; then you may shoot off a pistol in the stable, and so by degrees bring it as near to him as you can till he be acquainted with the pistol, likewise remembering still after every shot to give him more provender. You must also cause his groom to put on bright armour, and so to rub his heels and dress him. You must also present a sword before him in the said armour, and when you have done, give him still some more provender.   Lastly, his rider must bring his horse forth into the open field, where a bright armour must be fastened upon a stake, and set forth in the likeness of an armed man as much as possible; which being done, the rider must put his horse on until he make him not only approach the said image, but throw it down; which being done,

you must be sure to give him some provender, that
he may be encouraged to do the like against an
adversary in battle.   It will be good also that
two men do hold up a cloak betwixt them in the
field, and then the rider to put the horse to it until
he leap over, which cloak also they may raise as
they see occasion, when the horse is able to leap
so high.   You shall do well also to use your horse
to swimming; which you may do, either by trail-
ing him after you at the tail of a boat, in a good
river, holding him by the head at the length of the
bridle, or by putting a good swimmer in a linen
waistcoat and breeches upon him.[1]

It will be fit for a gentleman also to learn to
swim, unless he be given to cramps and convul-
sions;[2] howbeit, I must confess, in my own particular, that I cannot swim; for, as I was once in
danger of drowning, by learning to swim, my
mother, upon her blessing, charged me never to
learn swimming, telling me further, that she had
heard of more drowned than saved by it; which
reason, though it did not prevail with me, yet her

----

[1] Locke, in opposition to Lord Herbert, warns his pupil
against making "a business of" learning to ride the great
horse, and urges that "a firm and graceful seat on horseback" is all that is desirable.

[2] Cf. Everard Digby's "De Arte Natandi," 1587, the
first book on the subject produced in England.   The plates
are very curious.

commandment did. It will be good also for a gentleman to learn to leap, wrestle, and vault on horseback ; they being all of them qualities of great use. I do much approve likewise of shooting in the long-bow, as being both an healthful exercise and useful for the wars, notwithstanding all that our firemen speak against it ; for, bring an hundred archers against so many musqueteers, I say if the archer comes within his distance, he will not only make two shoots, but two hits for one.[1]

The exercises I do not approve of are riding of running horses,[2] there being much cheating in that kind ; neither do I see why a brave man should delight in a creature whose chief use is to help him to run away. I do not much like of hunting horses, that exercise taking up more time than can be spared from a man studious to get knowledge ; it is enough, therefore, to know the sport, if there be any in it, without making it an ordinary practice ; and, indeed, of the two, hawking is the

---

[1] Lord Herbert makes similar remarks in his Henry VIII., when speaking of the statutes for the encouragement of archery (1534 and 1541). He condemns the caliver as more costly than the bow, and more difficult to use. Sir John Smythe, in his " Discourses of Weapons," 1590, writes emphatically in the same sense, calling the long-bow " our [*i.e.*, Englishmen's] peculiar and singular weapon " (p. 27).

[2] *i.e.*, racing. Newmarket was acquiring its first fame in the fashionable world while Lord Herbert was a young man.

better, because less time is spent in it.[1]   And upon these terms also I can allow a little bowling; so that the company be choice and good.

The exercises I wholly condemn, are dicing and carding, especially if you play for any great sum of money, or spend any time in them; or use to come to meetings in dicing-houses, where cheaters meet and cozen young gentlemen of all their money. I could say much more concerning all these points of education, and particularly concerning the discreet civility which is to be observed in communication either with friends or strangers, but this work would grow too big; and that many precepts conducing thereunto may be had in *Guazzo de la Civile Conversation,*[2] and *Galeteus de Moribus.*[3]

---

[1] James I., like many other writers on education, takes just the opposite view in his Basilikon Doron, lib. iii. p. 122. He says that hawking is to be praised sparingly, because it is an extreme stirrer-up of passions, and neither resembles war nor makes a man hardy as hunting does.

[2] *La Civil Conversatione del Signor Stefano Guazzo* (Venice, 1575). An English translation was published at London in 1586, in four books, the first three being the work of George Pettie, and the fourth of Bartholomew Young.

[3] This is an Italian book usually known as *Il Galatheo;* translations exist in Latin and almost all modern languages. The author was Giovanni della Casa (1503–1556), Archbishop of Benevento from 1544 till his death. The work was written about 1550, and first published at Milan in 1559. It was long a standard educational work in Italy.

It would also deserve a particular lecture or *recherche*, how one ought to behave himself with children, servants, tenants, and neighbours; and I am confident, that precepts in this point will be found more useful to young gentlemen, than all the subtleties of schools.   I confess I have collected many things to this purpose, which I forbear to set down here; because, if God grant me life and health, I intend to make a little treatise concerning these points.[1]   I shall return now to the narration of mine own history.

When I had attained the age betwixt eighteen or nineteen years, my mother, together with myself and wife, removed up to London, where we took house, and kept a greater family than became either my mother's widow's estate, or such young be-

---

Alfieri the poet complains bitterly in his autobiography of the pain its perusal caused him in his youth.   Extracts from it are given by Mr. W. M. Rossetti in his "Essay on Italian Courtesy Books" appended to the English Tracts on Courtesy, edited by Dr. F. J. Furnivall for the Early English Text Society (1879).   Della Casa wrote another book on a similar subject, entitled *Trattato degli Uffici Comuni tra gli Amici Superiori e Inferiori*, which probably suggested to Herbert the next paragraph.

[1] See the account given in the introduction of "A Dialogue between a Tutor and a Pupil," attributed rightly (as I judge) to Lord Herbert, and first published in 1768.   A manuscript copy is in the Bodleian Library, Oxford (MS. Rawlinson, c. 95).

ginners as we were ; especially, since six brothers
and three sisters were to be provided for, my father
having either made no will, or such an imperfect one,
that it was not proved.   My mother, although she had
all my father's leases and goods, which were of great
value, yet she desired me to undertake that burden
of providing for my brothers and sisters ; which, to
gratify my mother, as well as those so near me, I
was voluntarily content to provide thus far, as to
give my six brothers thirty pounds apiece yearly,
during their lives, and my three sisters one thousand
pound apiece, which portions married them to
those I have above mentioned.   My younger sister,
indeed,[1] might have been married to a far greater
fortune, had not the overthwartness of some neighbours interrupted it.

   About the year of our Lord 1600 I came to
London, shortly after which the attempt of the Earl
of Essex, related in our history, followed ;[2] which
I had rather were seen in the writers of that argument than here.   Not long after this, curiosity,
rather than ambition, brought me to court ; and as
it was the manner of those times for all men to
kneel down before the great Queen Elizabeth, who

---

[1] The wife of Sir John Brown of Lincolnshire (p. 28,
supra).

[2] Essex's fruitless rising in London took place on Sunday,
7th February 1600–1.   The Earl was executed 28th February.

F

then reigned, I was likewise upon my knees in the presence-chamber, when she passed by to the Chapel at Whitehall. As soon as she saw me, she stopped, and, swearing her usual oath,[1] demanded, " Who is this ? " Everybody there present looked upon me, but no man knew me, until Sir James Croft, a pensioner,[2] finding the Queen stayed, returned back and told who I was, and that I had married Sir William Herbert of St. Julian's daughter. The Queen hereupon looked attentively upon me, and swearing again her ordinary oath, said it is pity he was married so young, and thereupon gave her hand to kiss twice, both times gently clapping me on the cheek. I remember little more of myself, but that, from that time until King James's coming to the crown, I had a son which died shortly afterwards, and that I attended my studies seriously ;

---

[1] Naunton gives *God's Death* as the Queen's " wonted oath." Fragmenta Regalia (1641), ed. Arber, p. 17.

[2] Third son of Sir James Croft, of Croft Castle, Herefordshire, the well-known Controller of Queen Elizabeth's household ; was knighted 23d July 1603 ; took a prominent part in Queen Anne's funeral in 1619 ; was alive in 1626 (Retrospective Review, second ser. i. 491). The pensioners were young gentlemen of rank and fortune, selected by Queen Elizabeth for her bodyguard on account of their handsome faces and figures (cf. " Midsummer Night's Dream," ii. 1. 10, and " Merry Wives of Windsor," ii. 2. 79, and Osborne's Elizabeth in " Court of James I.," i. 55).

the more I learnt out of my books, adding still a desire to know more.

King James being now acknowledged King, and coming towards London, I thought fit to meet his Majesty at Burleigh, near Stamford.[1]   Shortly after I was made Knight of the Bath, with the usual cere- monies belonging to that ancient order.[2]   I could tell how much my person was commended by the lords and ladies that came to see the solemnity then used ; but I shall flatter myself too much if I believed it.

I must not forget yet the ancient custom, being that some principal person was to put on the right spur of those the King had appointed to receive that dignity.[3]   The Earl of Shrewsbury, seeing my

---

[1] James I. stayed at Burleigh or Burghley House, the property of Thomas Cecil, the eldest son and successor of the first Lord Burghley, from Saturday the 23d, till Wed- nesday 27th April 1603.

[2] " Sunday the 24th [July 1603], was performed the solemnity of Knights of the Bath, riding honorably from Saint James to the Courte, and made shew with their Squires and Pages about the tilt-yarde, and after went into the Parke of Saint James and ther lighted all from there horses, and went uppe to the King's Majestie's presence in the gallery, where they received the Order of Knighthood of the Bathe."—Howes' Chronicle, p. 827.   Some sixty persons received the honour besides Lord Herbert.

[3] An elaborate account of the ceremonial observed at the creation of Knights of the Bath is printed at the end of " The Order . . . of the creation . . . of Prince Henry,

esquire there with my spur in his hand, voluntarily
came to me, and said, "Cousin, I believe you will be
a good knight, and therefore I will put on your
spur;" whereupon, after my most humble thanks
for so great a favour, I held up my leg against the
wall, and he put on my spur.

There is another custom likewise, that the knights
the first day wear the gown of some religious order,
and the night following to be bathed; after which
they take an oath never to sit in place where in-
justice should be done, but they shall right it to the
uttermost of their power; and particularly ladies and
gentlewomen that shall be wronged in their honour,
if they demand assistance, and many other points,
not unlike the romances of knight errantry.[1]

The second day to wear robes of crimson taffety

Prince of Wales . . . " Lond. 1610; and is reprinted both
in Somers' Tracts and in Nicholls' "Progresses of James I.,"
ii. 336–341.

[1] This oath, which Lord Herbert kept very quixotically,
was (according to Howes' Chronicle) administered in these
words:—"Right deere brother . . . you shall honoure
God above all thinges; you shall be stedfast in the faith
of Christ, and the same maintaine, and defend to your
power; you shall love your Soveraigne above all earthly
creatures, and for your Soveraigne's right and dignity live
and dye; you shall defend widdowes, maydens, and orphans
in their right; you shall suffer no extortion as farre forth as
you maye, nor sit in any place where any wrongful judgement shall be given to your knowledge."

(in which habit I am painted in my study,)[1] and
so to ride from St James's to Whitehall, with our
esquires before us ; and the third day to wear a
gown of purple satin, upon the left sleeve whereof
is fastened certain strings weaved of white silk and
gold tied in a knot, and tassels to it of the same,
which all the knights are obliged to wear until they
have done something famous in arms, or until some
lady of honour take it off, and fasten it on her
sleeve, saying, I will answer he shall prove a good
knight. I had not long worn this string, but a
principal lady of the court, and, certainly, in most
men's opinion, the handsomest,[2] took mine off, and
said she would pledge her honour for mine. I do
not name this lady, because some passages happened
afterwards which oblige me to silence ; though

---

[1] This picture, by an unknown artist, is now at Powis
Castle in the possession of the Earl of Powis. An etching
appears in the present edition.

[2] It is impossible to determine with certainty who this lady
was. Reference is made to her again on p. 129. Selden
reports a *liaison* between Herbert and Lady Kent, probably
Mary the daughter of Sir George Cotton, and wife of Henry,
sixth Earl of Kent, about which Herbert is discreetly silent,
but the lady may be covertly alluded to here. " Lady
Kent," says Selden, " articled with Sir *Edward Herbert*
that he should come to her when she sent for him and
stay with her as long as she would have him, to which he
set his hand ; then he articled with her, that he should go
away when he pleas'd, and stay away as long as he pleas'd,
to which she set her hand."—Table-Talk, ed. Arber, p. 41.

nothing could be justly said to her prejudice or wrong.

Shortly after this I intended to go with Charles, Earl of Nottingham, the Lord Admiral, who went to Spain [1] to take the King's oath for confirmation of the articles of peace betwixt the two crowns. Howbeit, by the industry of some near me, who desired to stay me at home, I was hindered ; and, instead of going that voyage, was made Sheriff of Montgomeryshire,[2] concerning which I will say no more, but that I bestowed the place of under-sheriff, as also other places in my gifts, freely, without either taking gift or reward ; which custom also I have observed throughout the whole course of my life ; insomuch that when I was ambassador in France, and might have had great presents, which former ambassadors accepted, for doing lawful courtesies to merchants and others, yet no gratuity, upon what terms soever, could ever be fastened upon me.

This public duty did not hinder me yet to follow my beloved studies in a country life for the most part ; although sometimes also I resorted to court, without yet that I had any ambition there, and

---

[1] In Feb. 1604–5 (Winwood's Memorials, ii. 50).

[2] In 1605. His deputy or under-sheriff was Edward Whittingham, son of William Whittingham, bailiff of Montgomery 1590–1, and chief steward of Llanowthen to Lord Herbert's father in 1595–6. Lloyd's "Sheriffs of Montgomeryshire" in Powysland Coll., v. 479–481.

much less was tainted with those corrupt delights incident to the times.[1]   For, living with my wife in all conjugal loyalty for the space of about ten years after my marriage, I wholly declined the allurements and temptations whatsoever, which might incline me to violate my marriage bed.

About the year 1608, my two daughters, called Beatrice,[2] and Florence[3] who lived not yet long after, and one son Richard being born, and come to so much maturity, that, although in their mere childhood, they gave no little hopes of themselves for the future time, I called them all before my wife,

---

[1] From 1605 onwards Lord Herbert's name appears on the roll of Montgomeryshire magistrates, but there is no evidence to show that he spent much time in the country. Powysland Collections, v. 479–481.   It is singular that Lord Herbert omits to mention that on 9th February 1606–7 James I. granted the Castle of Montgomery, which had been in the possession of Lord Herbert's family since his grandfather's time, to Philip Herbert, a kinsman through another line, who was created Earl of Montgomery 4th May 1605. From the date of this grant till 11th July 1613 the Castle remained in the hands of the Earl of Montgomery, but at the later date he restored it to Lord Herbert in consideration of the payment of £500.   The Castle passed out of his possession again in 1616, but for only a short time.   Documents establishing these facts are now at Powis Castle, and are described in the Powysland Collections, x. p. 168 *et seq.*

[2] Born 13th August 1604, and baptized at Montgomery, 28th August.   Beatrice survived her father.

[3] Born 27th September 1605, and baptized in Montgomery Church 14th October following.

demanding, how she liked them, to which she answering "well;" I demanded then, whether she was willing to do so much for them as I would? whereupon, she replying, demanded what I meant by that. I told her, that, for my part, I was but young for a man, and she not old for a woman; that our lives were in the hands of God; that, if He pleased to call either of us away, that party which remained might marry again, and have children by some other, to which our estates might be disposed; for preventing whereof, I thought fit to motion to her, that if she would assure [1] upon the son any quantity of lands from three hundred pounds a year to one thousand, I would do the like. But my wife not approving hereof, answered, in these express words, that she would not draw the cradle upon her head; whereupon, I desiring her to advise better upon the business, and to take some few days' respite for that purpose, she seemed to depart from me not very well contented. About a week or ten days afterwards, I demanded again what she thought concerning the motion I made; to which yet she said no more, but that she thought she had already answered me sufficiently to the point. I told her then, that I should make another

---

[1] *i.e.*, convey by deed. Cf. Leviticus xxvii. 19: "He shall add the fifth part of the money . . . and it shall be *assured* to him."

motion to her ; which was, that in regard I was too young to go beyond sea before I married her, she now would give me leave for a while to see foreign countries ; howbeit, if she would assure her lands as I would mine, in the manner above-mentioned, I would never depart from her. She answered, that I knew her mind before concerning that point, yet that she should be sorry I went beyond sea ; nevertheless, if I would needs go, she could not help it. This, whether a license taken or given, served my turn to prepare without delay for a journey beyond sea, that so I might satisfy that curiosity I long since had to see foreign countries. So that I might leave my wife so little discontented as I could, I left her not only posterity to renew the family of the Herberts of St Julian's according to her father's desire to inherit his lands, but the rents of all the lands she brought with her ; reserving mine own, partly to pay my brothers' and sisters' portions, and defraying my charges abroad. Upon which terms, though I was sorry to leave my wife, as having lived most honestly with her all this time, I thought it no such unjust ambition, to attain the knowledge of foreign countries ; especially, since I had in great part already attained the languages, and that I intended not to spend any long time out of my country.

Before I departed yet, I left her with child of a son, christened afterwards by the name of Edward ; and now coming to court, I obtained a license to go beyond sea, taking with me for my companion Mr. Aurelian Townsend,[1] a gentleman that spoke the languages of French, Italian, and Spanish, in great perfection, and a man to wait in my chamber, who spoke French, two lacqueys, and three horses. Coming thus to Dover, and passing the seas thence to Calais, I journeyed without any memorable adventure, until I came to Faubourg St. Germain in Paris, where Sir George Carew, then ambassador for the King,[2] lived ; I was kindly received by him, and often invited to his table.[3]   Next to his house dwelt the Duke of Ventadour, who had married a

---

[1] He was the author of two court masques, both published in 1631.   The one is entitled " Albion's Trivmph," and was " personated at Court . . . the Sunday after Twelfe Night 1631 ; " the other, named "Tempe Restord," was performed on Shrove Tuesday following.   Townsend was a patron of the poets, and is introduced by Suckling into the " Session of the Poets."

[2] From 1605 to 1609 (see Brit. Mus. MS. Addit. 20,765, p. 143).   He afterwards became Master of the Court of Wards, and died in 1612.   He must be distinguished from the Irish administrator of the same name.

[3] In a *satyra* called "Travellers from Paris," addressed to Ben Jonson, dated September 1608, Lord Herbert writes thus of his fellow-countrymen in Paris :—

". . . all they learn is
Toys and the languages, but to attain this,
You must conceive they're cosen'd, mocked, and come
To Fourbourgs St. Germans, there take a Room
Lightly about th' Ambassadors, and where
Having no Church, they come Sundays to hear," &c.

daughter of Monsieur de Montmorency, Grand Constable de France. Many visits being exchanged between that Duchess and the lady of our ambassador, it pleased the Duchess to invite me to her father's house, at the castle of Merlou, being about twenty-four miles from Paris;[1] and here I found much welcome from that brave old General, who being informed of my name, said he knew well of what family I was;[2] telling, the first notice he had

---

[1] Near Clermont (Oise). The village whence the castle takes its name is now known as Mello. The old forms Mellou and Meslou are known, but not that of Merlou. M. de Rémusat states that a magnificent castle and park are still in existence there (*Lord Herbert, Sa Vie et ses Œuvres*, p. 30). Several of Lord Herbert's poems are dated from Merlou, and a sonnet "made upon the groves near Merlou Castle" gives vigorous expression to the rare delight with which the beauty of the place inspired him.

[2] Henri de Montmorency was second son of the Constable Anne (who, after taking part in the battle of St. Quentin, was killed at St. Denis in 1567), and brother of François, Duc de Montmorency, who died in 1579. Henri, born in 1534, was known in early life as the Comte de Damville, was present at St. Quentin in 1557, and, like his father, was taken prisoner by the Spaniards and the English. He fought at the battles of Dreux and St. Denis, but gained his chief fame as Governor of Languedoc from 1563 onwards. He ultimately became a supporter of Henri IV., was made by him Constable of France, and died 2d April 1614. (See *Biographie Universelle*, s. v. Montmorency.) His second daughter, Marguerite, married Anne de Levis, Duc de Ventadour, to whom reference is made above.

of the Herberts was at the siege of St Quentin, where my grandfather, with a command of foot under William Earl of Pembroke, was.[1] Passing two or three days here, it happened one evening, that a daughter of the Duchess, of about ten or eleven years of age, going one evening from the castle to walk in the meadows, myself, with divers French gentlemen, attended her and some gentlewomen that were with her. This young lady wearing a knot of ribbon on her head, a French chevalier took it suddenly, and fastened it to his hatband. The young lady, offended herewith, demands her ribbon, but he refusing to restore it, the young lady, addressing herself to me, said, "Monsieur, I pray get my ribbon from that gentleman." Hereupon, going towards him, I courteously, with my hat in my hand, desired him to do me the honour, that I may deliver the lady her ribbon or bouquet again ; but he roughly answering me, " Do you think I will give it you, when I have refused it to her ? " I replied, " Nay then, sir, I will make you restore it by force ; " whereupon also, putting on my hat and reaching at his, he to save himself ran away, and, after a long course in the meadow, finding that I had almost overtook him, he turned short, and running to the young lady, was about to put the ribbon on her hand, when I, seizing

---

[1] See p. 5, note 2, *supra.*

upon his arm, said to the young lady, "It was I that gave it." "Pardon me," quoth she, "it is he that gives it me." I said then, "Madam, I will not contradict you; but if he dare say that I did not constrain him to give it, I will fight with him." The French gentleman answered nothing thereunto for the present, and so conducted the young lady again to the castle. The next day I desired Mr. Aurelian Townsend to tell the French cavalier, that either he must confess that I constrained him to restore the ribbon, or fight with me; but the gentleman seeing him unwilling to accept of this challenge, went out from the place, whereupon, I following him, some of the gentlemen that belonged to the Constable taking notice hereof, acquainted him therewith, who sending for the French cavalier, checked him well for his sauciness, in taking the ribbon away from his grandchild, and afterwards bid him depart his house; and this was all that I ever heard of the gentleman, with whom I proceeded in that manner, because I thought myself obliged thereunto by the oath taken when I was made Knight of the Bath, as I formerly related upon this occasion.[1]

I must remember also, that three other times I engaged myself to challenge men to fight with me, who I conceived had injured ladies and gentle-

---

[1] See p. 84.

women ;[1] one was in defence of my cousin, Sir
Francis Newport's daughter, who was married to
John Barker of Hamon, whose younger brother
and heir [2]   .   .   .   .

.   .   .   .

sent him a challenge, which to this day he never
answered ; and would have beaten him afterwards,
but that I was hindered by my uncle Sir Francis
Newport.

I had another occasion to challenge one Captain
Vaughan, who I conceived offered some injury to
my sister the Lady Jones of Abermarles. I sent
him a challenge, which he accepted, the place between us being appointed beyond Greenwich, with
seconds on both sides. Hereupon, I coming to
the King's Head in Greenwich, with intention the
next morning to be in the place, I found the house
beset with at least an hundred persons, partly sent
by the Lords of the Privy Council, who gave orders
to apprehend me. I hearing thereof, desired my
servant to bring my horses as far as he could from
my lodging, but yet within sight of me ; which
being done, and all this company coming to lay
hold on me, I and my second, who was my cousin,

---

[1] See Appendix IV., where I have collected some notes
on the duelling of the period.

[2] This space is left blank in all the editions : there is
certainly something wanting.

James Price of Hanachly, sallied out of the doors, with our swords drawn, and, in spite of that multitude, made our way to our horses, where my servant very honestly opposing himself against those who would have laid hands upon us, while we got up on horseback, was himself laid hold on by them, and evil treated; which I perceiving, rid back again, and with my sword in my hand rescued him, and afterwards seeing him get on horseback, charged them to go anywhere rather than to follow me. Riding afterwards with my second to the place appointed, I found nobody there; which, as I heard afterwards, happened, because the Lords of the Council, taking notice of this difference, apprehended him, and charged him in his Majesty's name not to fight with me; since otherwise I believed he would not have failed.

The third that I questioned in this kind was a Scotch gentleman, who, taking a ribbon in the like manner from Mrs. Middlemore, a maid of honour, as was done from the young lady above-mentioned, in a back room behind Queen Anne's lodgings in Greenwich, she likewise desired me to get her the said ribbon. I repaired, as formerly, to him in a courteous manner to demand it, but he refusing as the French cavalier did, I caught him by the neck, and had almost thrown him down, when company came in and parted us. I offered likewise to fight with this gentleman, and came to the place appointed

by Hyde Park; but this also was interrupted by
order of the Lords of the Council, and I never
heard more of him.[1]

These passages, though different in time, I have
related here together; both for the similitude of
argument, and that it may appear how strictly I
held myself to my oath of knighthood; since, for
the rest I can truly say, that, though I have lived
in the armies and courts of the greatest princes in
Christendom, yet I never had a quarrel with man
for my own sake; so that, although in mine own
nature I was ever choleric and hasty, yet I never
without occasion quarrelled with anybody, and as
little did anybody attempt to give me offence, as
having as clear a reputation for my courage as
whosoever of my time. For my friends often I
have hazarded myself; but never yet drew my
sword for my own sake singly, as hating ever the
doing of injury, contenting myself only to resent
them when they were offered me. After this
digression I shall return to my history.

---

[1] Chamberlain describes this affair thus in a letter to
Carleton, 23d January 1609–10 :—" There was a quarrel
hatching at Greenwich 'twixt Sir Edward Herbert and one
Boquhan [? Buchan], a Scot gentleman, usher to the Queen,
about a ribbon or favour taken, as it were, by force from
Mrs. Middlemore. But the matter was timely taken up,
and compounded by the Council."—*Court and Times of
James I.*, i. 103 ; Cal. State Papers, 1603–10, p. 583.

That brave Constable in France testifying now more than formerly his regard of me, at his departure from Merlou to his fair house at Chantilly, five or six miles distant, said, he left that castle to be commanded by me, as also his forests and chases, which were well stored with wild boar and stag; and that I might hunt them when I pleased.[1] He told me also, that if I would learn to ride the great horse, he had a stable there of some fifty, the best and choicest as was thought in France; and that his escuyer, called Monsieur de Disancourt, not inferior to Pluvinel or Labroue, should teach me.[2] I did with great thankfulness accept his offer,

---

[1] In the account of the Constable written by a contemporary, Tallemant des Réaux, great stress is laid on his equestrian skill and on his passion for hunting :—" Il aimoit extremement les chevaux, et dès qu'un cheval étoit à lui, il ne changeoit plus de maitre, et, n'eût-il que trois jambes, on le nourrissoit dans une infirmerie qui étoit à Chantilly. . . . C'étoit un grand tyran pour la chasse. Cependant il disoit qu'il falloit permettre à un gentilhomme de poursuivre le gibier qu'il auroit fait lever sur sa propre terre et qu'en ce cas il laisseroit prendre un lièvre jusque dans sa salle."—*Historiettes*, tom. i. p. 173, ed. 1861. As Grand Constable, Montmorency had the general direction of the equestrian education of the French army.

[2] Pluvinel had studied horsemanship under Pignatelli at Naples ; was first Master of the Horse to Henri III., directed Henri IV.'s famous stables, became sub-governor to the Dauphin, and even French Ambassador to Holland. Salomon de la Broue was also Master of the Horse under Henri IV.,

G

as being very much addicted to the exercise of riding
great horses; and, as for hunting in his forests,
I told him I should use it sparingly, as being
desirous to preserve his game. He commanded
also his escuyer to keep a table for me, and his
pages to attend me, the chief of whom was Monsieur
de Mennon,[1] who proving to be one of the best
horsemen in France, keeps now an academy in
Paris; and here I shall recount a little passage
betwixt him and his master, that the inclination of
the French at that time may appear; there being
scarce any man thought worth the looking on, that
had not killed some other in duel.

Mennon (? Menou) desiring to marry a niece of
Monsieur Disancourt, who it was thought should
be his heir, was thus answered by him : " Friend,
it is not time yet to marry; I will tell you what
you must do. If you will be a brave man, you
must first kill in single combat two or three men,
then afterwards marry and engender two or three
children, so the world will neither have got nor lost
by you ; " of which strange counsel Disancourt was

---

but ultimately died in poverty. Both were authors of
works on horsemanship, which Lord Herbert has already
described.

[1] Probably a misprint for M. René de Menou, the friend
of Pluvinel and editor of his book *Le Manège Royale.*
Pluvinel is generally believed to be the founder of riding
schools or academies.

no otherwise the author than as he had been an example at least of the former part ; it being his fortune to have fought three or four brave duels in his time.

And now, as every morning I mounted the great horse, so in the afternoon I many times went a-hunting, the manner of which was this. The Duke of Montmorency having given orders to the tenants of the town of Merlou, and some villages adjoining, to attend me when I went a-hunting, they, upon my summons, usually repaired to those woods where I intended to find my game, with drums and muskets, to the number of sixty or eighty, and sometimes one hundred or more persons ; they entering the wood on that side with that noise, discharging their pieces and beating their said drums, we on the other side of the said wood having placed mastiffs and greyhounds to the number of twenty or thirty, which Monsieur de Montmorency kept near his castle, expected those beasts they should force out of the wood. If stags or wild boars came forth, we commonly spared them, pursuing only the wolves, which were there in great number, of which are found two sorts ; the mastiff wolf, thick and short, though he could not indeed run fast, yet would fight with our dogs ; the greyhound wolf, long and swift, who many times escaped our best dogs, although when he was overtaken, easily killed by us, without making much resistance. Of both these sorts I killed divers with my sword, while I stayed there.

One time also it was my fortune to kill a wild boar in this manner. The boar being roused from his den, fled before our dogs for a good space; but finding them press him hard, turned his head against our dogs, and hurt three or four of them very dangerously: I came on horseback up to him, and with my sword thrust him twice or thrice without entering his skin, the blade being not so stiff as it should be. The boar hereupon turned upon me, and much endangered my horse; which I perceiving, rid a little out of the way, and leaving my horse with my lacquey, returned with my sword against the boar, who by this time had hurt more dogs. And here happened a pretty kind of fight; for, when I thrust at the boar sometimes with my sword, which in some places I made enter, the boar would run at me, whose tusks yet by stepping a little out of the way I avoided, but he then turning upon me, the dogs came in, and drew him off, so that he fell upon them, which I perceiving, ran at the boar with my sword again, which made him turn upon me, but then the dogs pulled him from me again, while so relieving one another by turns, we killed the boar. At this chase Monsieur Disancourt and Mennon (? Menou) were present, as also Mr. Townsend; yet so as they did endeavour rather to withdraw me from, than assist

me in the danger.   Of which boar, some part being
well seasoned and larded, I presented to my uncle
Sir Francis Newport in Shropshire, and found
most excellent meat.

Thus having passed a whole summer, partly in
these exercises, and partly in visits of the Duke of
Montmorency at his fair house at Chantilly ; which,
for its extraordinary fairness and situation, I shall
here describe.

A little river descending from some higher grounds
in a country which was almost all his own, and falling at last upon a rock in the middle of a valley,
which to keep its way forwards, it must on one or
other side thereof have declined.   Some of the
ancestors of the Montmorencies, to ease the river
of this labour, made divers channels through this
rock to give it a free passage, dividing the rock by
that means into little islands, upon which he built
a great strong castle, joined together with bridges,
and sumptuously furnished with hangings of silk and
gold, rare pictures, and statues ; all which buildings,
united as I formerly told, were encompassed about
with water, which was paved with stone (those
which were used in the building of the house were
drawn from thence).   One might see the huge
carps, pike, and trouts, which were kept in several
divisions, gliding along the waters very easily ; yet
nothing in my opinion added so much to the glory
of this castle as a forest adjoining close to it, and

upon a level with the house. For being of a very
large extent, and set thick both with tall trees and
underwood, the whole forest, which was replenished
with wild boar, stag, and roe-deer, was cut out
into long walks every way; so that, although the
dogs might follow their chase through the thickets,
the huntsmen might ride along the said walks, and
meet or overtake their game in some one of them,
they being cut with that art, that they led to all
the parts in the said forest; and here also I have
hunted the wild boar divers times, both then and
afterwards, when his son, the Duke of Montmorency,
succeeded him in the possession of that incomparable place.[1]

And there I cannot but remember the direction
the old Constable gave me to return to his castle
out of this admirable labyrinth; telling me I should
look upon what side the trees were roughest and
hardest, which being found, I might be confident
that part stood northward, which being observed,
I might easily find the east, as being on the right
hand; and so guide my way home.

How much this house, together with the forest,
hath been valued by great princes, may appear by
two little narratives I shall here insert. Charles V.,
the great Emperor, passing in the time of François I.
from Spain into the Low Countries, by the way

---

[1] In 1614 (see p. 199).

of France, was entertained for some time in this house by a Duke of Montmorency, who was likewise Constable de France; after he had taken this palace into his consideration, with the forests adjoining, said he would willingly give one of his provinces in the Low Countries for such a place; there being, as he thought, nowhere such a situation.

Henry IV. also was desirous of this house, and offered to exchange any of his houses, with much more lands than his estate thereabouts was worth; to which the Duke of Montmorency made this wary answer: *Sieur, la maison est à vous, mais que je sois le concierge;* which in English sounds thus: " Sir, the house is yours, but give me leave to keep it for you."

When I had been at Merlou about some eight months, and attained, as was thought, the knowledge of horsemanship, I came to the Duke of Montmorency at St. Ilee,[1] and, after due thanks for his favours, took my leave of him to go to Paris; whereupon, the good old prince embracing me, and calling me son, bid me farewell, assuring me nevertheless he should be glad of any occasion hereafter to testify his love and esteem for me; telling me further, he should come to Paris himself shortly, where he hoped to see me. From hence

---

[1] Probably a blunder of the transcriber for Chantilly.

I returned to Merlou, where I gave Monsieur Disancourt such a present as abundantly requited the
charges of my diet, and the pains of his teaching.
Being now ready to set forth, a gentleman from
the Duke of Montmorency came to me, and told
me his master would not let me go without giving
me a present, which I might keep as an earnest of
his affection ; whereupon also a jennet, for which
the Duke had sent expressly into Spain, and which
cost him there five hundred crowns, as I was told,
was brought to me. The greatness of this gift,
together with other courtesies received, did not a
little trouble me, as not knowing then how to requite them. I would have given my horses I had
there, which were of great value to him, but that I
thought them too mean a present : but the Duke
also suspecting that I meant to do so, prevented
me ; saying, that as I loved him, I should think
upon no requital, while I stayed in France, but
when I came into England, if I sent him a mare
that ambled naturally, I should much gratify him.
I told the messenger I should strive both that way,
and every way else, to declare my thankfulness,
and so dismissed the messenger with a good
reward.

Coming now to Paris, through the recommendation of the Lord Ambassador, I was received to the
house of that incomparable scholar Isaac Casaubon,
by whose learned conversation I much benefited

myself;[1] besides, I did apply myself much to know the use of my arms, and to ride the great horse, playing on the lute, and singing according to the rules of the French masters.

Sometimes also I went to the court of the French king, Henry IV., who, upon information of me in the garden at the Tuilleries, received me with all courtesy, embracing me in his arms, and holding me some while there. I went sometimes also to the court of Queen Margaret at the Hostel, called by her name;[2] and here I saw many balls or masks, in all which it pleased that Queen publicly to place me next to her chair, not without the wonder of some, and the envy of another, who was wont to have that favour. I shall recount one accident which happened while I was there.

All things being ready for the ball, and every one being in their place, and I myself next to the Queen, expecting when the dancers would come in,

---

[1] The great scholar lived at Paris from 1600 to 1610; after which he came to London. (See Mark Pattison's Casaubon.)

[2] *i.e.*, Marguerite of Valois. M. Tallemant des Réaux (i. 165) tells some amusing stories about the ballets given by Queen Marguerite at her hotel. The Queen had been divorced from Henri IV. in 1600, and her reputation was not good. Lord Herbert writes of her with greater justice in his *Satyra* addressed to Ben Jonson (September 1608), as

> " that swol'n vicious Queen Margaret,
> Who were a monster ev'n without her sin !'

one knocked at the door somewhat louder than
became, as I thought, a very civil person. When
he came in, I remember there was a sudden
whisper among the ladies, saying, *C'est Monsieur
Balagny*, or, It is Monsieur Balagny;[1] whereupon
also I saw the ladies and gentlewomen one after
another invite him to sit near them, and, which is
more, when one lady had his company a while,
another would say, You have enjoyed him long
enough, I must have him now; at which bold
civility of theirs, though I were astonished, yet it
added unto my wonder, that his person could not
be thought at most but ordinary handsome; his
hair, which was cut very short, half grey, his
doublet but of sackcloth cut to his shirt, and his
breeches only of plain grey cloth. Informing myself by some standers-by who he was, I was told
that he was one of the gallantest men in the world,

---

[1] Damien de Montluc, Seigneur de Balagni, was the son
of a well-known Marshal of France, who entered the service
of Henri IV. in 1593. Through his mother, Renée de
Clermont, he was the nephew of Bussy d'Amboise, the hero
of Chapman's plays, whom he appears to have resembled
in character. Sir Thomas Edmondes, the English Ambassador in Paris, reports a duel between M. D'Andelot and
Balagny on 11th January 1611–12, and another in the streets
of Paris between M. Pinocin and Balagny, 26th March
1612. In the latter quarrel Pinocin was killed on the
spot, and Balagny died of his wounds two days afterwards.
Winwood's Memorials, iii. 324, 350, 353.

as having killed eight or nine men in single fight, and that for this reason the ladies made so much of him, it being the manner of all Frenchwomen to cherish gallant men, as thinking they could not make so much of any else with the safety of their honour. This cavalier, though his head was half grey, he had not yet attained the age of thirty years, whom I have thought fit to remember more particularly here, because of some passages that happened afterwards betwixt him and me, at the siege of Juliers, as 1 shall tell in its place.

Having passed thus all the winter, until about the latter end of January [1609], without any such memorable accident as I shall think fit to set down particularly, I took my leave of the French king, Queen Margaret, and the nobles and ladies in both courts ; at which time the Princess of Conti[1] desired me to carry a scarf into England, and present it to Queen Anne on her part, which being accepted, myself and Sir Thomas Lucy[2] (whose second I had been

---

[1] 1574–1631. Daughter of the Duc de Guise, and wife of François de Bourbon, Prince de Conti, son of the first Prince de Condé. She enjoyed a very unenviable reputation at the French court. (See *Les Amours du grand Alcandre*, of which she is the heroine ; her own romance, *Les Adventures de la cour de Perse*, 1629 ; Tallemant des Réaux, *Historiettes*, i. 54 ; and the notice in the *Biographie Universelle*, 1856).

[2] Of Charlecote, Warwickshire. Eldest son (born 1584) of the Sir Thomas Lucy with whom Shakespeare is alleged

twice in France, against two cavaliers of our nation, who yet were hindered to fight with us in the field, where we attended them), we came on our way as far as Dieppe in Normandy, and there took ship about the beginning of February, when so furious a storm arose, that with very great danger we were at sea all night. The master of our ship lost both the use of his compass and his reason ; for not knowing whither he was carried by the tempest, all the help he had was by the lightnings, which, together with thunder very frequently that night, terrified him, yet gave the advantage sometimes to discover whether we were upon our coast, to which he thought by the course of his glasses we were near approached. And now towards day we found ourselves, by great providence of God, within view of Dover, to which the master of our ship did make. The men of Dover rising betimes in the morning to see whether any ship were coming towards them, were in great numbers upon the shore, as believing

---

to have come into unpleasant contact ; was Knight of the shire for Warwickshire in six Parliaments between 1621 and 8th December 1640, the date of his death ; married Alice, daughter of Thomas Spencer of Claverdon, and granddaughter of Sir John Spencer of Althorpe. A very elaborate monument was erected to his memory in Charlecote Church by his wife ; it bears a long Latin inscription, in which his charitableness, hospitality, love of learning, and patriotism are specially commended. (See Dugdale's Warwickshire, ed. Thomas, i. 506, 511, 512.)

the tempest, which had thrown down barns and
trees near the town, might give them the benefit of
some wreck, if perchance any ship were driven
thitherwards.   We coming thus in extreme danger
straight upon the pier of Dover, which stands out
in the sea, our ship was unfortunately split against
it ; the master said, *Mes amies, nous sommes perdus ;*
or, My friends, we are cast away.   When myself
who heard the ship crack against the pier, and then
found by the master's words it was time for every
one to save themselves, if they could, got out of
my cabin (though very sea-sick), and climbing up
the mast a little way, drew my sword and flourished
it ; they at Dover having this sign given them,
adventured in a shallop of six oars to relieve us,
which being come with great danger to the side
of our ship, I got into it first with my sword in my
hand, and called for Sir Thomas Lucy, saying, that
if any man offered to get in before him, I should
resist him with my sword ; whereupon a faithful
servant of his taking Sir Thomas Lucy out of the
cabin, who was half dead of sea-sickness, put him
into my arms, whom after I had received, I bid the
shallop make away for shore, and the rather that I
saw another shallop coming to relieve us ; when a
post from France, who carried letters, finding the
ship still rent more and more, adventured to leap
from the top of our ship into the shallop, where
falling fortunately on some of the stronger timber

of the boat, and not on the planks, which he must needs have broken, and so sunk us, had he fallen upon them, escaped together with us two, unto the land.   I must confess myself, as also the seamen that were in the shallop, thought once to have killed him for this desperate attempt ; but finding no harm followed, we escaped together unto the land, from whence we sent more shallops, and so made means to save both men and horses that were in the ship, which yet itself was wholly split and cast away, insomuch that in pity to the master, Sir Thomas Lucy and myself gave thirty pounds towards his loss, which yet was not so great as we thought, since the tide now ebbing, he recovered the broken parts of his ship.

Coming thus to London, and afterwards to court, I kissed his Majesty's hand, and acquainted him with some particulars concerning France.   As for the present I had to deliver to her Majesty from the Princess of Conti, I thought fit rather to send it by one of the ladies that attended her, than to presume to demand audience of her in person : but her Majesty not satisfied herewith, commanded me to attend her, and demanded divers questions of me concerning that princess and the courts in France, saying she would speak more at large with me at some other time ; for which purpose she commanded me to wait on her often, wishing me to advise her what present she might return back again.

Howbeit, not many weeks after, I returned to my wife and family again, where I passed some time, partly in my studies, and partly riding the great horse, of which I had a stable well furnished. No horse yet was so dear to me as the jennet I brought from France, whose love I had so gotten, that he would suffer none else to ride him, nor indeed any man to come near him, when I was upon him, as being in his nature a most furious horse; his true picture may be seen in the chapel chamber in my house, where I am painted riding him, and this motto by me,

Me totum bonitas bonum suprema
Reddas ; me intrepidum dabo vel ipse.[1]

This horse as soon as ever I came to the stable would neigh, and when I drew nearer him would lick my hand, and (when I suffered him) my cheek, but yet would permit nobody to come near his heels at the same time. Sir Thomas Lucy would have given me £200 for this horse, which, though I would not accept, yet I left the horse with him when I went to the Low Countries, who not long after died. The occasion of my going thither was

---

[1] A print of this picture, engraved by J. Bowen, was published in 1768. The picture is there stated to be at Powis Castle in the possession of the Earl of Powis. The present Earl informs me that the picture is not now in his hands, and I have been unable to discover its whereabouts.

thus : hearing that a war about the title of Cleves, Juliers, and some other provinces betwixt the Low Countries and Germany, should be made, by the several pretenders to it, and that the French king himself would come with a great army into those parts ; [1] it was now the year of our Lord 1610, when my Lord Chandos [2] and myself resolved to take shipping for the Low Countries, and from

---

[1] On 25th March 1610, William John, Duke of Cleves, died. There were many pretenders to his Duchy; and two of them—the Elector of Brandenburg and the Palatine of Neuburg—combined to seize it, at the instance of the Protestant princes of the Empire. The Emperor thereupon ordered the Archduke Leopold to occupy the country in his name, and the Archduke entered Juliers, one of the chief towns of the Duchy. Henri IV. announced that he would support the two Protestant claimants by force of arms. Holland and England promised him their assistance. In May, Henri, who intended to head his troops, was killed by Ravaillac, but the Queen-Regent and her advisers subsequently ordered Marshal de la Châtre to proceed against Juliers, where he arrived on 8th August. Already on 17th July, the English (under Sir Edward Cecil) and the Dutch had begun the siege, and Juliers surrendered on 22d August.

[2] Grey Brydges, fifth Lord Chandos, a well-known courtier, was born about 1579, and was made a Knight of the Bath in 1604. Unlike Herbert, who was only a volunteer, he was one of the officers in command of the present expedition (see " Newes out of Cleaveland," 1611). Subsequently he suffered much in health, and died at Spa, 10th August 1621. The hospitality which he dispensed at Sudeley Castle, Gloucestershire, gained for him the title of " King of the Cotswolds."

thence to pass to the city of Juliers, which the
Prince [Philip William] of Orange resolved to besiege.[1] Making all haste thither, we found the siege
newly begun ; the Low Country army assisted by
4000 English under the command of Sir Edward
Cecil.[2] We had not been long there, when the
Marshal de la Châtre,[3] instead of Henry IV., who
was killed by that villain Ravaillac,[4] came with
a brave French army thither, in which Monsieur
Balagny, I formerly mentioned, was a colonel.

My Lord Chandos lodged himself in the quarters where Sir Horace Vere[5] was ; I went and
quartered with Sir Edward Cecil, where I was
lodged next to him in a hut I made there, going
yet both by day and night to the trenches ; we
making our approaches to the town on one side,
and the French on the other. Our lines were

---

[1] Subsequently (p. 176) Herbert speaks of Count
Maurice of Nassau, the Dutch commander, as Prince of
Orange—a title to which he only succeeded on his elder
brother's death in 1618. Their father was William the
Silent.

[2] See p. 23 *supra.*

[3] Marshal of France from 1594 till his death in 1614.

[4] 14th May 1610.

[5] Like his elder brother Francis, Sir Horatio Vere
acquired a very great military reputation by his prolonged
service in the Low Countries. Conway and Monk, subsequently Duke of Albemarle, were among his pupils. He
was created Baron Vere of Tilbury in 1625, and dying in
1635 was buried in Westminster Abbey.

H

drawn towards the point of a bulwark of the citadel
or castle, thought to be one of the best fortifications in Christendom, and encompassed about with
a deep wet ditch.   We lost many men in making
these approaches, the town and castle being very
well provided both with great and small shot, and
a garrison in it of about 4000 men, besides the
burghers.   Sir Edward Cecil (who was a very
active general) used often, during the siege, to go
in person in the night time, to try whether he
could catch any sentinels *perdus;* and for this purpose still desired me to accompany him; in performing whereof, both of us did much hazard our
lives, for the first sentinel retiring to the second,
and the second to the third, three shots were commonly made at us, before we could do anything,
though afterwards chasing them with our swords
almost home unto their guards, we had some sport
in the pursuit of them.

One day Sir Edward Cecil and myself coming
to the approaches that Monsieur de Balagny had
made towards a bulwark or bastion of that city,
Monsieur de Balagny, in the presence of Sir
Edward Cecil and divers English and French captains then present, said, *Monsieur, on dit que vous
êtes un des plus braves de vôtre nation, et je suis
Balagny, allons voir qui faira le mieux—*"They say
you are one of the bravest of your nation, and I
am Balagny, let us see who will do best;" where-

upon leaping suddenly out of the trenches with his sword drawn, I did in the like manner as suddenly follow him, both of us in the meanwhile striving who should be foremost, which being perceived by those of the bulwark and cortine [1] opposite to us, three or four hundred shot at least, great and small, were made against us. Our running on forwards in emulation of each other, was the cause that all the shots fell betwixt us and the trench from which we sallied. When Monsieur Balagny, finding such a storm of bullets, said, *Par Dieu il fait bien chaud*—" It is very hot here ; " I answered briefly thus : *Vous en ires premier, autrement je n'iray jamais*—" You shall go first, or else I will never go ; " hereupon he ran with all speed, and somewhat crouching, towards the trenches. I followed after leisurely and upright, and yet came within the trenches before they on the bulwark or cortine could charge again ; which passage afterwards being related to the Prince of Orange, he said it was a strange bravado of Balagny, and that we went to an unavoidable death.

I could relate divers things of note concerning myself, during the siege ; but do forbear, lest I

---

[1] *i.e.*, curtain—the name applied in fortification to the portion of a rampart situated between two bastions and uniting their flanks.

should relish too much of vanity : it shall suffice, that my passing over the ditch unto the wall, first of all the nations there, is set down by William Crosse, master of arts, and soldier, who hath written and printed the history of the Low Countries.[1]

There happened during this siege a particular quarrel betwixt me and the Lord of Walden,[2]

---

[1] In all previous editions this name is wrongly printed Crofts ; but no person of that name (so far as I have been able to discover), wrote on the siege of Juliers. *William Crosse*, "M! of Arts," however, published in 1627 a second impression of Grimestone's " Generall Historie of the Netherlands," with a continuation of the narrative from 1608—the date of the first edition—to 1627. Crosse writes thus (p. 1294), of the fall of Juliers : " The English sapped or mined first into the wall before *Chatillon* or *Bethun* had advanced so farre ; the truth whereof Sir *Edward Harbert*, now Lord *Harbert* of Castle Island, can approoue ; who carried himselfe most valiantly in all that Service, and brought away a mark of Honour, as beeing the first of all the Nations then passed ouer into the wall. This I speake not out of any nationall partialitie, Truth being neerer to me than my Countrie, but onely that I might quit myselfe from that imputation, which concealment deserues in an historicall consistorie : and there specially, whereas our owne, not other men's actions, are interpreted and questionable." In the margin Crosse quaintly writes : " Gentle reader, if you chance to see any copie with any other name than that of Sir *Edw. Harbert* here specified, know it was mistaken in the printing." There are no other references to Herbert in Crosse's account of the campaign.

[2] Theophilus, created Lord Howard of Walden in 1603,

eldest son to the Earl of Suffolk, Lord Treasurer
of England at that time, which I do but unwillingly
relate, in regard of the great esteem I have of that
noble family ; howbeit, to avoid misreports, I have
thought fit to set it down truly.[1] That Lord having been invited to a feast in Sir Horace Vere's
quarters, where (after the Low Country manner)
there was liberal drinking, returned not long after
to Sir Edward Cecil's quarters, at which time I
speaking merrily to him, upon some slight occasion,
he took that offence at me, which he would not
have done at another time, insomuch that he came
towards me in a violent manner, which I perceiving,

---

was the eldest son of Thomas, first Earl of Suffolk. He
was an officer in the present expedition, was subsequently
Governor of Jersey (1621), succeeded his father as Earl
(1626), was made K.G. (1628), held the offices of Privy
Councillor, Constable of Dover Castle, and Captain of the
Band of Pensioners, and died 3d June 1640. Collins'
Peerage, ed. Brydges, iii. 155.

[1] Peyton, Lord Howard of Walden's second, drew up
an account of this quarrel, which I have printed from
the Lansdowne MS. (XC.) in Appendix V. Winwood
writes to Salisbury, 22d August 1610 : " Sir Edward
Herbert (will they, nill they) hath forced a quarrel since
my coming from the army, first upon my Lord Walden,
after upon Sir Thomas Somersett [see p. 123] . . . Wherein
he hath offered an irreparable injurie to my Lord Generall
[Sir Edward Cecil] who hath treated him, as he hath done
them all, with an exceeding love and kindness."—Winwood's
Memorials, iii. 210.

did more than half-way meet him; but the company were so vigilant upon us, that before any
blow passed we were separated; howbeit, because
he made towards me, I thought fit the next day to
send him a challenge, telling him, that if he had
anything to say to me, I would meet him in such
a place as no man should interrupt us.[1]   Shortly
after this Sir Thomas Peyton[2] came to me on his
part, and told me my Lord would fight with me on
horseback with single sword; "and," said he, "I will
be his second; where is yours?"   I replied, that
neither his Lordship nor myself brought over any
great horses with us; that I knew he might much
better borrow one than myself: howbeit, as soon
as he showed me the place, he should find me there
on horseback or on foot; whereupon both of us

---

[1] According to Peyton's account (printed in Appendix
V.), Sir Edward Cecil intervened early in the quarrel, and
with the consent of both parties arranged a reconciliation.
On 11th September, however, when the troops were returning home, Herbert made some vague rumours an excuse
for renewing the former challenge.   His conduct was
censured on all sides.

[2] In the Lansdowne MS. (printed below) Peyton's
Christian name seems to be "Jo," *i.e.*, John.   Sir Thomas,
who was M.P. for Dunwich in 1587 and Custodian of
Plymouth, had a grandson, John, who settled in Virginia in
1644.   Another Thomas Peyton was the author of a very
rare poem, *The Glasse of Time* (Lond. 1620).   Sir Thomas'
fourth son, Sir Henry, was the most prominent member
of the family at James I.'s court.

riding together upon two geldings to the side of a wood, Peyton said he chose that place, and the time, break of day the next morning. I told him I would fail neither place nor time, though I knew not where to get a better horse than the nag I rid on ; "and as for a second, I shall trust to your nobleness, who, I know, will see fair play betwixt us, though you come on his side." But he urging me again to provide a second, I told him I could promise for none but myself, and that if I spoke to any of my friends in the army to this purpose, I doubted lest the business might be discovered and prevented.

He was no sooner gone from me, but night drew on, myself resolving in the meantime to rest under a fair oak all night ; after this, tying my horse by the bridle unto another tree, I had not now rested two hours, when I found some fires nearer to me than I thought was possible in so solitary a place ; whereupon also having the curiosity to see the reason hereof, I got on horseback again, and had not rode very far, when by the talk of the soldiers there, I found I was in the Scotch quarter, where, finding in a stable a very fair horse of service, I desired to know whether he might be bought for any reasonable sum of money ; but a soldier replying it was their captain's, Sir James Areskin's chief horse,[1] I demanded for Sir James, but the soldier

---

[1] Areskin is probably a misreading for Erskine. James

answering he was not within the quarter, I demanded then for his lieutenant, whereupon the soldier courteously desired him to come to me. This lieutenant was called Montgomery, and had the reputation of a gallant man ; I told him that I would very fain buy a horse, and, if it were possible, the horse I saw but a little before; but he telling me none was to be sold there, I offered to leave in his hands 100 pieces, if he would lend me a good horse for a day or two, he to restore me the money again when I delivered him the horse in good plight, and did besides bring him some present as a gratuity.

The lieutenant, though he did not know me, suspected I had some private quarrel, and that I desired this horse to fight on, and thereupon told me, " Sir, whosoever you are, you seem to be a person of worth, and you shall have the best horse in the stable ; and if you have a quarrel and want a second, I offer myself to serve you upon another horse, and if you will let me go along with you upon these terms, I will ask no pawn of you for the horse." I told him I would use no second, and I desired him to accept 100 pieces, which I had there about me, in pawn for the horse, and he

---

I. gave places at court to several of the name, who had accompanied him from Scotland. I have not been able to specially identify Sir James.

should hear from me shortly again; and that
though I did not take his noble offer of coming
along with me, I should evermore rest much
obliged to him; whereupon giving him my purse
with the money in it, I got upon his horse, and
left my nag besides with him.

Riding thus away about twelve o'clock at night
to the wood from whence I came, I alighted from
my horse and rested there till morning; the day
now breaking I got on horseback, and attended the
Lord of Walden with his second. The first person that appeared was a footman, who I heard
afterwards was sent by the Lady of Walden,[1] who
as soon as he saw me, ran back again with all
speed; I meant once to pursue him, but that I
thought it better at last to keep my place. About
two hours after Sir William St. Leger, now Lord
President of Munster,[2] came to me, and told me he
knew the cause of my being there, and that the
business was discovered by the Lord Walden's
rising so early that morning, and the suspicion
that he meant to fight with me, and had Sir
Thomas Peyton with him, and that he would ride
to him, and that there were thirty or forty sent
after us, to hinder us from meeting. Shortly after
many more came to the place where I was, and

---

[1] Lady Howard of Walden was Elizabeth, daughter of
George Hume, Earl of Dunbar.

[2] He held this post throughout the rebellion of 1641.

told me I must not fight, and that they were sent for the same purpose, and that it was to no purpose to stay there, and thence rode to seek the Lord of Walden. I stayed yet two hours longer, but finding still more company came in, rode back again to the Scotch quarters, and delivered the horse back again, and received my money and nag from Lieutenant Montgomery, and so withdrew myself to the French quarters, till I did find some convenient time to send again to the Lord Walden.

Being among the French, I remembered myself of the bravado of Monsieur Balagny, and coming to him, told him, I knew how brave a man he was, and that as he had put me to one trial of daring, when I was last with him in his trenches, I would put him to another; saying I heard he had a fair mistress, and that the scarf he wore was her gift, and that I would maintain I had a worthier mistress than he, and that I would do as much for her sake as he, or any else durst do for his. Balagny hereupon looking merrily upon me, said, "If we shall try who is the abler man to serve his mistress, let both of us get two wenches, and he that doth his business best, let him be the braver man;" and that, for his part, he had no mind to fight on that quarrel. I, looking hereupon somewhat disdainfully on him, said he spoke more like a paillard [1]

---

[1] *i.e.,* a dissolute fellow (Mod. Fr.)

than a cavalier ; to which he answering nothing,
I rid my ways, and afterwards went to Monsieur
Terant, a French gentleman that belonged to the
Duke of Montmorency, formerly mentioned ; who
telling me he had a quarrel with another gentleman,
I offered to be his second, but he saying he was
provided already, I rode thence to the English
quarters, attending some fit occasion to send again
to the Lord Walden.   I came no sooner thither,
but I found Sir Thomas Somerset [1] with eleven or
twelve more in the head of the English, who were
then drawing forth in a body or squadron, who
seeing me on horseback, with a footman only that
attended me, gave me some affronting words, for
my quarrelling with the Lord of Walden ; whereupon I alighted, and giving my horse to my lacquey,
drew my sword, which he no sooner saw, but he
drew his, and also all the company with him.   I
running hereupon amongst them, put by some of
their thrusts, and making towards him in particular,
put by a thrust of his, and had certainly run him
through, but that one Lieutenant Prichard, at that
instant taking me by the shoulder, turned me
aside ; but I, recovering myself again, ran at him

---

[1] Third son of Edward, Earl of Worcester, Lord Privy
Seal to Queen Elizabeth and King James.   Sir Thomas
was Master of the Horse to Queen Anne, was made a
Knight of the Bath in 1604, and created Viscount Somerset
of Cashel in Ireland on 8th December 1626.

a second time, which he perceiving, retired himself
with the company to the tents which were near,
though not so fast but I hurt one Proger, and some
others also that were with him. But they being all
at last got within the tents, I finding now nothing
else to be done, got to my horse again, having
received only a slight hurt on the outside of my
ribs, and two thrusts, the one through the skirts
of my doublet, and the other through my breeches,
and about eighteen nicks upon my sword and hilt,
and so rode to the trenches before Juliers, where
our soldiers were.

Not long after this, the town being now surrendered,[1] and everybody preparing to go their
ways, I sent again a gentleman to the Lord of
Walden to offer him the meeting with my sword ;
but this was avoided not very handsomely by him
(contrary to what Sir Henry Rich, now Earl of
Holland, persuaded him).

After having taken leave of his Excellency Sir
Edward Cecil, I thought fit to return on my way
homewards as far as Dusseldorf. I had been
scarce two hours in my lodgings when one Lieutenant Hamilton brought a letter from Sir James
Areskin (who was then in town likewise) unto me,
the effect whereof was, that in regard his Lieutenant Montgomery had told him that I had the

---

[1] 22d August 1610.

said James Areskin's consent for borrowing his
horse, he did desire me to do one of two things,
which was, either to disavow the said words, which
he thought in his conscience I never spake, or if I
would justify them, then to appoint time and place
to fight with him.   Having considered a while
what I was to do in this case, I told Lieutenant
Hamilton that I thought myself bound in honour
to accept the more noble part of his proposition,
which was to fight with him, when yet perchance
it might be easy enough for me to say that I had
his horse upon other terms than was affirmed ;
whereupon also giving Lieutenant Hamilton the
length of my sword, I told him that as soon as
ever he had matched it, I would fight with him,
wishing him further to make haste, since I desired
to end the business as speedily as could be.   Lieutenant Hamilton hereupon returning back, met in
a cross street (I know not by what miraculous adventure) Lieutenant Montgomery, conveying divers of
the hurt and maimed soldiers at the siege of Juliers
unto that town, to be lodged and dressed by the
chirurgeons there ; Hamilton hereupon calling to
Montgomery, told him the effects of his captain's
letter, together with my answer, which Montgomery
no sooner heard, but he replied (as Hamilton told
me afterwards), "I see that noble gentleman chooseth
rather to fight than to contradict me ; but my telling
a lie must not be an occasion why either my captain

or he should hazard their lives : I will alight from my horse, and tell my captain presently how all that matter passed ; " whereupon also he relating the business about borrowing the horse, in that manner I formerly set down, which as soon as Sir James Areskin heard, he sent Lieutenant Hamilton to me presently again, to tell me he was satisfied how the business passed, and that he had nothing to say to me, but that he was my most humble servant, and was sorry he ever questioned me in that manner.

Some occasions detaining me in Dusseldorf, the next day Lieutenant Montgomery came to me, and told me he was in danger of losing his place, and desired me to make means to his Excellency the Prince of Orange that he might not be cashiered, or else that he was undone. I told him that either I would keep him in his place, or take him as my companion and friend, and allow him sufficient means till I could provide him another as good as it ; which he taking very kindly, but desiring chiefly he might go with my letter to the Prince of Orange, I obtained at last he should be restored to his place again.

And now taking boat, I passed along the river of Rhine to the Low Countries, where after some stay, I went to Antwerp and Brussels ; and having passed some time in the court there, went from thence to Calais, where taking ship I arrived at

Dover, and so went to London. I had scarce been two days there, when the Lords of the Council sending for me, ended the difference betwixt the Lord of Walden and myself. And now, if I may say it without vanity, I was in great esteem both in court and city; many of the greatest desiring my company, though yet before that time I had no acquaintance with them. Richard, Earl of Dorset,[1] to whom otherwise I was a stranger, one day invited me to Dorset House, where bringing me into his gallery, and showing me many pictures, he at last brought me to a frame covered with green taffeta, and asked me who I thought was there; and therewithal presently drawing the curtain, showed me my own picture; whereupon demanding how his Lordship came to have it, he answered, that he had heard so many brave things of me, that he got a copy of a picture which one Larkin a painter drew for me, the original whereof I intended before my departure to the Low Countries for Sir Thomas Lucy.[2] But not only the Earl of

---

[1] Richard Sackville, third Earl of Dorset, grandson of the Treasurer. He married Anne Clifford, daughter of the Earl of Cumberland. His brother Edward succeeded to the earldom on his death in 1624.

[2] Mr. Spencer Lucy of Charlecote Park, Warwickshire, still has in his possession this portrait (painted on copper), originally presented to Sir Thomas Lucy. No painter named *Larkin* is known. The name may be a misreading

Dorset, but a greater person [1] than I will here nominate, got another copy from Larkin, and placing it afterwards in her cabinet (without that ever I knew any such thing was done) gave occasion to those that saw it after her death, of more discourse than I could have wished; and indeed I may truly say, that taking of my picture was fatal to me, for more reasons than I shall think fit to deliver.

There was a lady also, wife to Sir John Ayres, Knight, who, finding some means to get a copy of my picture from Larkin, gave it to Mr. Isaac [Oliver] the painter in Blackfriars,[2] and desired him to draw it in little after his manner; which being done, she caused it to be set in gold and enamelled, and so wore it about her neck so low that she hid it under her breasts, which I conceive coming afterwards to the knowledge of Sir John

---

for Nicholas *Lockie*, who was in some repute as a portrait-painter in James I.'s reign, and is mentioned in Meres' "Palladis Tamia" (1598). See Walpole's Anecdotes, ed. Wornum, pp. 185 and 865.

[1] Probably Queen Anne. According to Lord Herbert's own account, the Queen repeatedly showed him special marks of favour (*cf.* p. 129).

[2] This famous miniature-painter (1555–1617) drew portraits of all the distinguished men and women of James I.'s time, many of which are now in the national collections. He was buried in St. Anne's Church, Blackfriars (see Walpole's "Anecdotes of Painting," ed. Wornum, i. 176–183).

Ayres, gave him more cause of jealousy than needed, had he known how innocent I was from pretending to anything which might wrong him or his lady; since I could not so much as imagine that either she had my picture, or that she bare more than ordinary affection to me. It is true, that as she had a place in court, and attended Queen Anne, and was beside of an excellent wit and discourse, she had made herself a considerable person; howbeit little more than common civility ever passed betwixt us, though I confess I think no man was welcomer to her when I came, for which I shall allege this passage :—

Coming one day into her chamber, I saw her through the curtains lying upon her bed with a wax candle in one hand, and the picture I formerly mentioned in the other. I coming thereupon somewhat boldly to her, she blew out the candle, and hid the picture from me ; myself thereupon being curious to know what that was she held in her hand, got the candle to be lighted again, by means whereof I found it was my picture she looked upon with more earnestness and passion than I could have easily believed, especially since myself was not engaged in any affection towards her : I could willingly have omitted this passage, but that it was the beginning of a bloody history which followed : [1]

---

[1] I have not discovered any reference to this story elsewhere.

1

Howsoever, yet I must before the Eternal God clear her honour.   And now in court a great person [1] sent for me divers times to attend her, which summons though I obeyed, yet God knoweth I declined coming to her as much as conveniently I could, without incurring her displeasure; and this I did not only for very honest reasons, but, to speak ingenuously, because that affection passed betwixt me and another lady (who I believe was the fairest of her time) [2] as nothing could divert it. I had not been long in London, when a violent burning fever seized upon me, which brought me almost to my death, though at last I did by slow degrees recover my health; being thus upon my amendment, the Lord Lisle, [3] afterwards Earl of Leicester, sent me word, that Sir John Ayres intended to kill me in my bed, and wished me to keep a guard upon my chamber and person; the same advertisement was confirmed by Lucy Countess of Bedford, [4] and the Lady Hoby [5] shortly after.   Here-

---

[1] Queen Anne (see p. 129).

[2] This is in all probability the lady mentioned above on p. 85.   No attempt at identification seems possible.

[3] Robert Sidney, second son of Sir Henry Sidney, and younger brother of Sir Philip, was created Lord Sidney in 1603, Viscount Lisle in 1604, and Earl of Leicester in 1618.   He died in 1626.

[4] The wife of Edward Earl of Bedford, the well-known patroness of Ben Jonson, Drayton, and other poets.

[5] Probably Anne, second wife of Sir Edward Hoby, a patron of Camden.

ANNE, QUEEN OF JAMES I

upon I thought fit to entreat Sir William Herbert,
now Lord Powis,[1] to go to Sir John Ayres, and
tell him, that I marvelled much at the information
given me by these great persons, and that I could
not imagine any sufficient ground hereof; howbeit,
if he had anything to say to me in a fair and noble
way, I would give him the meeting as soon as I
had got strength enough to stand upon my legs; Sir
William hereupon brought me so ambiguous and
doubtful an answer from him, that whatsoever he
meant, he would not declare yet his intention, which
was really, as I found afterwards, to kill me any
way that he could, since, as he said, though falsely,
I had whored his wife. Finding no means thus to
surprise me, he sent me a letter to this effect; that
he desired to meet me somewhere, and that it might
so fall out as I might return quietly again. To
this I replied, that if he desired to fight with me
upon equal terms, I should, upon assurance of the
field and fair play, give him meeting when he did
any way specify the cause, and that I did not think
fit to come to him upon any other terms, having been
sufficiently informed of his plots to assassinate me.

After this, finding he could take no advantage
against me, then in a treacherous way he resolved

---

[1] The eldest son of Sir Edward Herbert, second son
of William, Earl of Pembroke (created 1651). He was
created Lord Powis in 1629. He died in 1655.

to assassinate me in this manner ; hearing I was to come to Whitehall on horseback with two lacqueys only, he attended my coming back in a place called Scotland Yard, at the hither end of Whitehall, as you come to it from the Strand, hiding himself here with four men armed on purpose to kill me. I took horse at Whitehall Gate, and passing by that place, he being armed with a sword and dagger, without giving me so much as the least warning, ran at me furiously, but instead of me wounded my horse in the brisket, as far as his sword could enter for the bone ; my horse hereupon starting aside, he ran him again in the shoulder, which though it made the horse more timorous, yet gave me time to draw my sword. His men thereupon encompassed me, and wounded my horse in three places more ; this made my horse kick and fling in that manner as his men durst not come near me ; which advantage I took to strike at Sir John Ayres with all my force, but he warded the blow both with his sword and dagger ; instead of doing him harm, I broke my sword within a foot of the hilt. Hereupon some passenger that knew me, and observing my horse bleeding in so many places, and so many men assaulting me, and my sword broken, cried to me several times, " Ride away, ride away ; " but I, scorning a base flight upon what terms soever, instead thereof alighted as well as I could from my

horse. I had no sooner put one foot upon the
ground, but Sir John Ayres pursuing me, made at
my horse again, which the horse perceiving, pressed
on me on the side I alighted, in that manner that
he threw me down, so that I remained flat upon
the ground, only one foot hanging in the stirrup,
with that piece of a sword in my right hand.   Sir
John Ayres hereupon ran about the horse, and
was thrusting his sword into me, when I, finding
myself in this danger, did with both my arms
reaching at his legs pull them towards me, till he
fell down backwards on his head ; one of my foot-
men hereupon, who was a little Shropshire boy,
freed my foot out of the stirrup, the other, which
was a great fellow, having run away as soon as he
saw the first assault.   This gave me time to get
upon my legs, and to put myself in the best posture
I could with that poor remnant of a weapon.   Sir
John Ayres by this time likewise was got up,
standing betwixt me and some part of Whitehall,
with two men on each side of him, and his brother
behind him, with at least twenty or thirty persons
of his friends, or attendants of the Earl of Suffolk.[1]
Observing thus a body of men standing in opposition against me, though to speak truly I saw no
swords drawn but by Sir John Ayres and his men,

---

[1] Thomas Howard, father of Theophilus, Lord Howard
of Walden ; with whom Herbert had lately quarrelled.

I ran violently against Sir John Ayres; but he, knowing my sword had no point, held his sword and dagger over his head, as believing I could strike rather than thrust, which I no sooner perceived but I put a home thrust to the middle of his breast, that I threw him down with so much force, that his head fell first to the ground, and his heels upwards. His men hereupon assaulted me, when one Mr. Mansel, a Glamorganshire gentleman, finding so many set against me alone, closed with one of them; a Scotch gentleman also closing with another, took him off also. All I could well do to those two which remained was to ward their thrusts, which I did with that resolution that I got ground upon them. Sir John Ayres was now got up a third time, when I making towards him with intention to close, thinking that there was otherwise no safety for me, put by a thrust of his with my left hand, and so coming within him, received a stab with his dagger on my right side, which ran down my ribs as far as my hip, which I feeling, did with my right elbow force his hand, together with the hilt of the dagger, so near the upper part of my right side, that I made him leave hold. The dagger now sticking in me, Sir Henry Cary, afterwards Lord of Falkland and Lord Deputy of Ireland,[1] finding the dagger thus

---

[1] From 1622 to 1629. Strafford was his successor in

in my body, snatched it out. This while I, being closed with Sir John Ayres, hurt him on the head, and threw him down a third time, when kneeling on the ground and bestriding him, I struck at him as hard as I could with my piece of a sword, and wounded him in four several places, and did almost cut off his left hand ; his two men this while struck at me, but it pleased God even miraculously to defend me ; for when I lifted up my sword to strike at Sir John Ayres, I bore off their blows half a dozen times. His friends now finding him in this danger, took him by the head and shoulders, and drew him from betwixt my legs, and carried him along with them through Whitehall, at the stairs whereof he took boat. Sir Herbert Croft [1] (as he told me afterwards) met him upon the water vomiting all the way, which I believe was caused by the violence of the first thrust I gave him. His servants, brother, and friends, being now retired also, I remained master of the place and his

---

Ireland. He was raised to the Peerage (1622), while Controller of James I.'s household. His son and heir was Lucius Cary, second Viscount Falkland.

[1] Born about 1571 ; eldest son of Edward, the eldest son of Sir James Croft, well-known in Elizabeth's reign (see p. 82, *supra*) ; Knight of the Shire for Hereford, 1592, 1601, 1603, 1614 ; knighted 7th May 1603 ; became a Roman Catholic about 1617, and a monk of Douay, where he died, 1cth April 1622. Retrospective Review, second ser. i. 491–4.

weapons ; having first wrested his dagger from him, and afterwards struck his sword out of his hand.

This being done, I retired to a friend's house in the Strand, where I sent for a surgeon, who searching my wound on the right side, and finding it not to be mortal, cured me in the space of some ten days, during which time I received many noble visits and messages from some of the best in the kingdom. Being now fully recovered of my hurts, I desired Sir Robert Harley[1] to go to Sir John Ayres, and tell him, that though I thought he had not so much honour left in him, that I could be any way ambitious to get it, yet that I desired to see him in the field with his sword in his hand : the answer that he sent was, that I had whored his wife, and that he would kill me with a musket out of a window.

The Lords of the Privy Council, who had first sent for my sword, that they might see the little fragment of a weapon with which I had so behaved myself, as perchance the like had not been heard in any credible way, did afterwards command both him and me to appear before them ; but I absenting myself on purpose, sent one Humphrey Hill with a

---

[1] Master of the Mint from 1626 to 1649 ; grandfather of Harley, Earl of Oxford under Queen Anne. His third wife was Lady Brilliana, daughter of Lord Conway, whose letters (printed by Camden Soc.) are well known.

challenge to him in an ordinary, which he refusing
to receive, Humphrey Hill put it upon the point of
his sword, and so let it fall before him and the
company then present.

The Lords of the Privy Council had now taken
order to apprehend Sir John Ayres; when I, finding nothing else to be done, submitted myself likewise to them.   Sir John Ayres had now published
everywhere, that the ground of his jealousy, and
consequently of his assaulting me, was drawn from
the confession of his wife the Lady Ayres.   She,
to vindicate her honour, as well as free me from
this accusation, sent a letter to her aunt the Lady
Crook, to this purpose : That her husband Sir John
Ayres did lie falsely, in saying that I ever whored
her ; but most falsely of all did lie when he said
he had it from her confession, for she had never
said any such thing.

This letter the Lady Crook presented to me most
opportunely as I was going to the Council table
before the Lords, who having examined Sir John
Ayres concerning the cause of his quarrel against
me, found him still persist in his wife's confession
of the fact ; and now he being withdrawn, I was
sent for, when the Duke of Lennox,[1] afterwards of
Richmond, telling me that was the ground of his

---

[1] Ludovick Stuart, Duke of Lennox, created Earl of
(1613) and Duke of Richmond (1623), was Lord Steward
of the Royal Household.

quarrel, and the only excuse he had for assaulting
me in that manner; I desired his Lordship to peruse
the letter, which I told him was given me as I came
into the room.   This letter being publicly read by
a clerk of the Council, the Duke of Lennox then
said, that he thought Sir John Ayres the most
miserable man living; for his wife had not only
given him the lie, as he found by her letter, but
his father had disinherited him for attempting to
kill me in that barbarous fashion, which was most
true, as I found afterwards.   For the rest, that I
might content myself with what I had done, it being
more almost than could be believed, but that I had
so many witnesses thereof; for all which reasons,
he commanded me, in the name of his Majesty and
all their Lordships, not to send any more to Sir John
Ayres, nor to receive any message from him, in the
way of fighting, which commandment I observed.
Howbeit I must not omit to tell, that some years
afterwards, Sir John Ayres, returning from Ireland
by Beaumaris, where I then was, some of my servants and followers broke open the doors of the
house where he was, and would, I believe, have cut
him into pieces, but that I hearing thereof, came
suddenly to the house and recalled them, sending
him word also, that I scorned to give him the usage
he gave me, and that I would set him free out of
the town; which courtesy of mine, as I was told
afterwards, he did thankfully acknowledge.

About a month after that Sir John Ayres attempted to assassinate me, the news thereof was carried, I know not how, to the Duke of Montmorency, who presently dispatched a gentleman with a letter to me, which I keep, and a kind offer, that if I would come unto him, I should be used as his own son; neither had this gentleman, as I know of, any other business in England. I was told besides by this gentleman, that the Duke heard I had greater and more enemies than did publicly declare themselves, which indeed was true, and that he doubted I might have a mischief before I was aware.

My answer hereunto by letter was, That I rendered most humble thanks for his great favour in sending to me; that no enemies, how great or many soever, could force me out of the kingdom; but if ever there were occasion to serve him in particular, I should not fail to come; for performance whereof, it happening there were some overtures of a civil war in France the next year, I sent over a French gentleman who attended me unto the Duke of Montmorency, expressly to tell him, that if he had occasion to use my service in the designed war, I would bring over 100 horse at my own cost and charges to him, which that good old Duke and Constable took so kindly, that, as the Duchess of Ventadour his daughter, told me afterwards, when I was ambassador, there were few days till the last

of his life that he did not speak of me with much
affection.

I can say little more memorable concerning myself from the year 1611, when I was hurt, until
the year of our Lord 1614, than that I past my
time sometimes in the court, where (I protest
before God) I had more favours than I desired,
and sometimes in the country, without any memorable accident ; but only that it happened one time
going from St. Julian's to Abergavenny, in the
way to Montgomery Castle, Richard Griffiths,[1] a
servant of mine, being come near a bridge over
Usk, not far from the town, thought fit to water
his horse, but the river being deep and strong in
that place where he entered it, he was carried
down the stream.   My servants that were before
me seeing this, cried aloud Dick Griffiths was
drowning, which I no sooner heard, but I put
spurs to my horse, and coming up to the place,
where I saw him as high as his middle in water,
leapt into the river a little below him, and swimming up to him, bore him up with one of my
hands, and brought him unto the middle of the
river, where (through God's great providence) was
a bank of sand.   Coming hither, not without some
difficulty, we rested ourselves, and advised whether
it were better to return back unto the side from

---

[1] See p. 53 *supra.*

whence we came, or to go on forwards ; but Dick
Griffiths saying we were sure to swim if we returned back, and that perchance the river might
be shallow the other way, I followed his counsel,
and putting my horse below him, bore him up in
the manner I did formerly, and swimming through
the river, brought him safe to the other side.
The horse I rode upon I remember cost me £40.
and was the same horse which Sir John Ayres
hurt under me, and did swim excellently well,
carrying me and his back above water ; whereas
that little nag upon which Richard Griffiths rid,
swam so low, that he must needs have drowned,
if I had not supported him.

I will tell one history more of this horse, which
I bought of my cousin Fowler of the Grange,
because it is memorable. I was passing over a
bridge not far from Colebrook, which had no
barrier on the one side, and a hole in the bridge
not far from the middle ; my horse, although lusty,
yet being very timorous, and seeing besides but
very little on the right eye, started so much at the
hole, that upon a sudden he had put half his body
lengthways over the side of the bridge, and was
ready to fall into the river, with his fore-foot and
hinder-foot on the right side, when I, foreseeing
the danger I was in if I fell down, clapt my left
foot, together with the stirrup and spur, flat-long
to the left side, and so made him leap upon all

four into the river, whence, after some three or four plunges, he brought me to land.

The year 1614 was now entering, when I understood that the Low Country and Spanish army would be in the field that year ;[1] this made me resolve to offer my service to the Prince of Orange, who upon my coming did much welcome me, not suffering me almost to eat anywhere but at his table, and carrying me abroad the afternoon in his coach, to partake of those entertainments he delighted in when there was no pressing occasion. The Low-Country army being now ready, his Excellency prepared to go into the field ; in the way to which he took me in his coach, and sometimes in a waggon after the Low-Country fashion,

---

[1] The old dispute (see p. 112 *supra*) concerning Cleves and Juliers broke out again in 1614. The joint-holders of the territory, Wolfgang William, the Palatine of Neuburg, and the Elector of Brandenburg had now quarrelled, and the former joined the Emperor, declaring himself a Catholic. The Spanish general Spinola, with the consent of the Spanish King, levied a large force, and, nominally in support of the Palatine of Neuburg, but really in behalf of the Catholic Emperor, invaded the country. The Dutch, alarmed at the presence of Spinola, also entered the disputed duchies and seized Emmerich and Rees in the duchy of Cleves. Count Maurice of Nassau, as before, led the Dutch troops, and with him served Sir Horace Vere, Lord Herbert, and many other English volunteers. In September 1614, a vain effort was made in England to induce James I. to send an army to the aid of the Elector of Brandenburg and Holland.

to the great envy of the English and French chief commanders, who expected that honour. Being now arrived near Emmerich, one with a most humble petition came from a monastery of nuns, most humbly desiring that the soldiers might not violate their honour nor their monastery, whereupon I was a most humble suitor to his Excellency to spare them, which he granted ; but, said he, we will go and see them ourselves ; and thus his Excellency, and I and Sir Charles Morgan [1] only, not long after going to the monastery, found it deserted in great part. Having put a guard upon this monastery, his Excellency marched with his army on till we came near the city of Emmerich, which upon summoning yielded. And now leaving a garrison here, we resolved to march towards Rees ; [2] this place having the Spanish army, under the command of Monsieur Spinola, on the one side, and the Low-Country army on the other, being able to resist neither, sent word to both armies, that which soever came first should have the place. Spinola hereupon sent word to his

---

[1] Of Herefordshire : knighted at Whitehall, 23d July 1603 (Nichols's Progresses, i. 215). He was the intimate associate of William Herbert, Earl of Pembroke, and saw much service as a volunteer in the Thirty Years' War.

[2] See William Crosse's account of these movements in Grimestone's Historie of the Netherlands (1627), pp. 134 *et seq.*

Excellency, that if we intended to take Rees, he
would give him battle in a plain near before the
town. His Excellency, nothing astonished hereat,
marched on, his pioneers making his way for the
army still, through hedges and ditches, till he
came to that hedge and ditch which was next the
plain ; and here drawing his men into battle, resolved to attend the coming of Spinola into the
field. While his men were putting in order, I
was so desirous to see whether Spinola with his
army appeared, I leapt over a great hedge and
ditch, attended only with one footman, purposing
to change a pistol-shot or two with the first I
met. I found thus some single horse in the field,
who, perceiving me to come on, rid away as fast
as they could, believing perchance that more would
follow me ; having thus past to the further end of
the field, and finding no show of the enemy, I
returned back that I might inform his Excellency
there was no hope of fighting as I could perceive.
In the mean time, his Excellency having prepared
all things for battle, sent out five or six scouts to
discover whether the enemy were come according
to promise ; these men finding me now coming
towards them, thought I was one of the enemies,
which being perceived by me, and I as little
knowing at that time who they were, rode up
with my sword in my hand, and pistol, to encounter them ; and now being come within

reasonable distance, one of the persons there that knew me told his fellows who I was, whereupon I passed quietly to his Excellency and told him what I had done, and that I found no appearance of an army : his Excellency then caused the hedge and ditch before him to be levelled, and marched in front with his army into the middle of the field, from whence sending some of his forces to summon the town, it yielded without resistance.

Our army made that haste to come to the place appointed for the battle, that all our baggage and provision were left behind, in so much that I was without any meat, but what my footman spared me out of his pocket; and my lodging that night was no better, for extreme rain falling at that time in the open field, I had no shelter, but was glad to get on the top of a waggon which had straw in it, and to cover myself with my cloak as well as I could, and so endure that stormy night. Morning being come, and no enemy appearing, I went to the town of Rees, into which his Excellency having now put a garrison, marched on with the rest of his army towards Wezel, before which Spinola with his army lay, and in the way entrenched himself strongly, and attended Spinola's motions. For the rest, nothing memorable happened after this, betwixt those two great generals, for the space of many weeks.

I must yet not omit with thankfulness to re-

K

member a favour his Excellency [1] did me at this
time; for a soldier having killed his fellow soldier,
in the quarter where they were lodged, which is
an unpardonable fault, insomuch that no man would
speak for him; the poor fellow comes to me, and
desires me to beg his life of his Excellency; whereupon I demanding whether he had ever heard of
a man pardoned in this kind, and he saying no,
I told him it was in vain then for me to speak;
when the poor fellow writhing his neck a little,
said, " Sir, but were it not better you shall cast
away a few words, than I lose my life?" This
piece of eloquence moved me so much, that I went
straight to his Excellency, and told him what the
poor fellow had said, desiring him to excuse me,
if upon these terms I took the boldness to speak
for him. There was present at that time the Earl
of Southampton,[2] as also Sir Edward Cecil, and
Sir Horace Vere, as also Monsieur de Châtillon,
and divers other French commanders; to whom
his Excellency turning himself said in French, " Do

---

[1] Count Maurice of Nassau, the Dutch Commander.
See p. 113.

[2] Henry Wriothesley, third Earl of Southampton, the
friend of Shakespeare, had been attainted with the Earl
of Essex in 1600–1, was restored by King James on his
accession, and made Knight of the Garter. He died in
1624. He was captain of the Isle of Wight.

you see this cavalier, with all that courage you
know, hath yet that good nature to pray for the
life of a poor soldier ? Though I had never pardoned
any before in this kind, yet I will pardon this at
his request." So commanding him to be brought
me, and disposed of as I thought fit, whom therefore I released and set free.

It was now so far advanced in autumn, both
armies thought of retiring themselves into their
garrisons, when a trumpeter comes from the
Spanish army to ours, with a challenge from a
Spanish cavalier to this effect, That if any cavalier
in our army would fight a single combat for the
sake of his mistress, the said Spaniard would meet
him, upon assurance of the camp in our army.
This challenge being brought early in the morning,
was accepted by nobody till about ten or eleven of
the clock, when the report thereof coming to me,
I went straight to his Excellency, and told him I
desired to accept the challenge. His Excellency
thereupon looking earnestly upon me, told me he
was an old soldier, and that he had observed two
sorts of men who used to send challenges in this
kind ; one was of those who, having lost perchance
some part of their honour in the field against the
enemy, would recover it again by a single fight.
The other was of those who sent it only to discover
whether our army had in it men affected to give
trial of themselves in this kind ; howbeit, if this

man was a person, without exception to be taken against him, he said there was none he knew, upon whom he would sooner venture the honour of his army than myself; and this also he spoke before divers of the English and French commanders I formerly nominated. Hereupon, by his Excellency's permission, I sent a trumpet to the Spanish army with this answer, That if the person who would be sent were a cavalier without reproach, I would answer him with such weapons as we should agree upon, in the place he offered; but my trumpeter was scarcely arrived, as I believe, at the Spanish army, when another trumpeter came to ours from Spinola, saying the challenge was made without his consent, and that therefore he would not permit it. This message being brought to his Excellency, with whom I then was, he said to me presently :—
"This is strange; they send a challenge hither, and when they have done, recall it. I should be glad if I knew the true causes of it." "Sir," said I, "if you will give me leave, I will go to their army, and make the like challenge, as they sent hither; it may be some scruple is made concerning the place appointed, being in your Excellency's camp, and therefore I shall offer them the combat in their own." His Excellency said, "I should never have persuaded you to this course, but since you voluntarily offer it, I must not deny that which you think to be for your honour." Hereupon

taking my leave of him, and desiring Sir[1] Humphrey Tufton, a brave gentleman, to bear me company, thus we two, attended only with two lackeys,
rode straight towards the Spanish camp before
Wezel; coming thither without any disturbance,
by the way I was demanded by the guard at the
entering into their camp, with whom I would
speak; I told them with the Duke of Neuburg;[2]
whereupon a soldier was presently sent with us to
conduct us to the Duke of Neuburg's tent, who
remembering me well, since he saw me at the siege
of Juliers, very kindly embraced me, and therewithal demanding the cause of my coming thither;
I told him the effect thereof in the manner I
formerly set down: to which he replied only, he
would acquaint the Marquis Spinola therewith;
who coming shortly after to the Duke of Neuburg's
tent, with a great train of commanders and captains
following him, he no sooner entered, but he turned
to me and said, that he knew well the cause of my
coming, and that the same reasons which made
him forbid the Spanish cavalier to fight a combat in
the Prince of Orange's camp, did make him forbid
it in his, and that [none] should be better welcome
to him than I would be, and thereupon entreated

---

[1] Third son of Sir John Tufton, and brother of Nicholas
Earl of Thanet.

[2] *i.e.*, the Elector Palatine of Neuburg, to whose conduct
I have drawn attention on p. 141, note.

me to come and dine with him ; I finding nothing
else to be done, did kindly accept the offer, and so
attended him to his tent, where a brave dinner
being put upon his table, he placed the Duke of
Neuburg uppermost at one end of the table, and
myself at the other, himself sitting below us, presenting with his own hand still the best of that
meat his carver offered him ; he demanded of me then
in Italian, "*Di che moriva Sigr. Francisco Vere?*"
(Of what died Sir Francis Vere ?)   I told him, "*Per
aver niente à fare*" (Because he had nothing to do).
Spinola replied, "*E basta per un generale*" (And it is
enough to kill a general) ; and indeed that brave
commander, Sir Francis Vere, died not in time of
war but of peace.[1]

Taking my leave now of the Marquis Spinola, I
told him that if ever he did lead an army against
the infidels, I should adventure to be the first
man that would die in that quarrel, and together
demanded leave of him to see his army, which he

---

[1] On 28th August 1608. Sir Francis, second son of
Geoffrey, 15th Earl of Oxford, served with the states of
Holland against Spain, throughout Elizabeth's reign.
With the peace between Spain and Holland, concluded by
James I. in 1604, Sir Francis's military service came to
an end.   He was buried in Westminster Abbey.   Among
Herbert's poems is a Latin epitaph on him.   See William
Dillingham's Commentaries of Sir Francis Vere, 1657, and
Fuller's Worthies.

granting, I took leave of him, and did at leisure view it; observing the difference in the proceedings betwixt the Low-Country army and fortifications, as well as I could; and so returning shortly after to his Excellency, related to him the success of my journey. It happened about this time that Sir Henry Wotton mediated a peace by the king's command,[1] who coming for that purpose to Wezel, I took occasion to go along with him into Spinola's army, whence after a night's stay, I went on an extreme rainy day through the woods to Kysarswert, to the great wonder of mine host, who said all men were robbed or killed that went that way. From hence I went to Cologne, where, among other things, I saw the monastery of St. Herbert; from hence I went to Heidelberg, where I saw the Prince and Princess Palatine, from whom having received much good usage,[2] I went to Ulm, and so to Augsbourg, where extraordinary honour was done me; for coming into an inn where an ambassador from Brussels lay, the town sent twenty

---

[1] Sir Henry Wotton, English ambassador at Venice, on the part of James I., and an ambassador from France arranged at Xanten a pacification, 2d Nov. 1614, between the two claimants to the disputed duchies (see Dumont—Corps Diplomatique, v. pt. ii. 259). But neither Spinola nor Maurice would accept it, and the former straightway seized Wezel. The war was continued in the following year.

[2] See p. 175, *infra.*

great flaggons of wine thither, whereof they gave eleven to the ambassador, and nine to me; and withal some such compliments that I found my fame had prevented my coming thither. From hence I went through Switzerland to Trent, and from thence to Venice, where I was received by the English ambassador,[1] Sir Dudley Carleton, with much honour; among other favours showed me, I was brought to see a nun in Murano, who being an admirable beauty, and together singing extremely well, was thought one of the rarities not only of that place but of the time; we came to a room opposite unto the cloister, whence she coming on the other side of the grate betwixt us, sung so extremely well, that when she departed, neither my lord ambassador nor his lady, who were then present, could find as much as a word of fitting language to return her, for the extraordinary music she gave us; when I, being ashamed that she should go back without some testimony of the sense we had both of the harmony of her beauty and her voice, said in Italian, "*Moria pur quando vuol, non bisogna mutar ni voce ni facia per esser un angelo*" (Die whensoever you will, you will neither need to change voice, nor face, to be an angel):

---

[1] Ambassador to Venice, Savoy, and Holland. In 1628 he was appointed Secretary of State, and created Viscount Dorchester. He died on 15th Feb. 1631–2.

these words it seemed were fatal, for going thence to Rome, and returning shortly afterwards, I heard she was dead in the meantime.

From Venice, after some stay, I went to Florence, where I met the Earl of Oxford[1] and Sir Benjamin Rudyerd.[2] Having seen the rarities of this place likewise, and particularly that rare chapel made for the house of Medici, beautified on all the inside with a coarser kind of precious stone, as also that nail which was at one end iron, and the other gold, made so by virtue of a tincture into which it was put, I went to Siena, and from thence, a little before the Christmas holidays, to Rome. I was no sooner alighted at my inn, but I went straight to the English College, where demanding for the regent or master thereof,[3] a grave person not long

---

[1] Henry Vere, 18th Earl of Oxford. He died at the Hague in 1625, of a sickness contracted at the siege of Breda. His wife Diana, daughter of William Cecil, Earl of Exeter, was one of the most celebrated beauties of her time. Her "rare beauty" is the subject of one of Herbert's poems.

[2] Sir Benjamin Rudyerd, a wit and poet, and the intimate friend of William Earl of Pembroke (with whose poems Sir Benjamin's were printed by the younger Donne in 1669), was one of the foremost champions of the policy of English interference in the continental quarrels during James I.'s reign. In Charles I.'s reign, as an active member of Parliament, he sought to hold the balance between the King and Commons. His memoirs were published (1828).

[3] No mention of Herbert is made in the list of visitors to the English College printed in Foley's Records. S. J.

after appeared at the door, to whom I spake in this
manner : " Sir, I need not tell you my country
when you hear my language ; I come not here to
study controversies, but to see the antiquities of the
place ; if without scandal to the religion in which
I was born and bred up, I may take this liberty,
I should be glad to spend some convenient time
here ; if not, my horse is yet unsaddled, and
myself willing to go out of town." The answer
returned by him to me was, that he never heard
any body before me profess himself of any other
religion than what was used in Rome ; for his
part, he approved much my freedom, as collecting
thereby I was a person of honour ; for the rest,
that he could give me no warrant for my stay
there, howbeit that experience did teach that those
men who gave no affronts to the Roman Catholic
religion, received none ; whereupon also he demanded my name.   I telling him I was called Sir
Edward Herbert, he replied, that he had heard
men oftentimes speak of me both for learning and
courage, and presently invited me to dinner ; I told
him that I took his courteous offer as an argument
of his affection ; that I desired him to excuse me, if
I did not accept it ; the uttermost liberty I had
(as the times then were in England) being already
taken in coming to that city only, lest they should
think me a factious person ; I thought fit to tell
him that I conceived the points agreed upon on

both sides are greater bonds of amity betwixt us,
than that the points disagreed on could break them ;
that for my part I loved everybody that was of
a pious and virtuous life, and thought the errors
on what side soever, were more worthy pity than
hate ; and having declared myself thus far, I took
my leave of him courteously, and spent about a
month's time in seeing the antiquities of that place,
which first found means to establish so great an
empire over the persons of men, and afterwards
over their consciences, the articles of confession
and absolving sinners being a greater *arcanum
imperii* for governing the world, than all the arts
invented by statists formerly were.

After I had seen Rome sufficiently, I went to
Tivoli, anciently called Tibur, and saw the fair
palace and garden there, as also Frascati, anciently
called Tusculanum. After that I returned to
Rome, and saw the Pope in consistory, which
being done, when the Pope being now ready to
give his blessing, I departed thence suddenly ;
which gave such a suspicion of me, that some
were sent to apprehend me, but I going a bye
way escaped them, and went to my inn to take
horse, where I had not been now half an hour,
when the master or regent of the English College
telling me that I was accused in the Inquisition,
and that I could stay no longer with any safety,
I took this warning very kindly ; howbeit I did

only for the present change my lodging, and a
day or two afterwards took horse, and went out
of Rome towards Siena, and from thence to
Florence. I saw Sir Robert Dudley,[1] who had
the title of Earl or Duke of Northumberland given
him by the Emperor, and handsome Mrs. Sudel
[Southwell], whom he carried with him out of
England, and was there taken for his wife. I

---

[1] Sir Robert was the son of Queen Elizabeth's Earl of
Leicester, by a daughter of William, Lord Effingham.
Leicester thought it politic in his later years to repudiate
this lady, and to deny that he had married her, although there
is every reason to believe that she was his legitimate second
wife (Amy Robsart being his first). Sir Robert was therefore never able to establish his legitimacy, though he inherited
much of Leicester's property. He left England in anger,
and retired to Italy : on his refusal to return to England his
estates were seized by the crown. He finally resided in
Tuscany and became the intimate friend of the Grand
Duke. He was an exceptionally accomplished man, and
his reputation as an artist reached the Emperor Ferdinand
II., who created him (9th March 1620) Duke of Northumberland. Like his father, he brought serious matrimonial
troubles on himself. He seems to have first married a sister
of Sir Thomas Cavendish the navigator, who died young.
He abandoned his second wife Alice, daughter of Sir Thomas
Leigh, and took with him to the Continent (in the disguise of
a page) a daughter of Sir Robert Southwell of Wood Rising,
Norfolk. Miss Southwell he married abroad. Charles I.
created Sir Robert's discarded wife the Duchess of Dudley
(30th May 1644). See Walpole's Catalogue of Royal and
Noble Authors, vol. ii. ; and Burke's Extinct Peerage.

was invited by them to a great feast the night
before I went out of town ; taking my leave of
them both, I prepared for my journey the next
morning ; when I was ready to depart, a messenger
came to me, and told me if I would accept the
same pension Sir Robert Dudley had, being two
thousand ducats per annum, the Duke would
entertain me for his service in the war against the
Turks.   This offer, whether procured by the
means of Sir Robert Dudley, Mrs. Sudel [South-
well], or Sigr. Loty, my ancient friend, I know
not, being thankfully acknowledged as a great
honour, was yet refused by me, my intention
being to serve his Excellency [1] in the Low-Country
war.

After I had stayed a while, from hence I
went by Ferrara and Bologna towards Padua, in
which university having spent some time to hear
the learned readers, and particularly Cremonini,[2]
I left my English horses and Scotch saddles there,
for on them I rid all the way from the Low
Countries, I went by boat to Venice.   The Lord
Ambassador, Sir Dudley Carleton, by this time

---

[1] Count Maurice of Nassau.

[2] Cesare Cremonini (1550–1631) became Professor of
Philosophy at Ferrara in 1571 and at Padua in 1590.   His
fame as a lecturer was wide spread.   He was a zealous and
sympathetic interpreter of Aristotle, and published a large
number of philosophical tracts.

had a command to reside a while in the court of the Duke of Savoy,[1] wherewith also his Lordship acquainted me, demanding whether I would go thither; this offer was gladly accepted by me, both as I was desirous to see that court, and that it was in the way to the Low Country, where I meant to see the war the summer ensuing.

Coming thus in the coach with my Lord Ambassador to Milan, the governor thereof invited my Lord Ambassador to his house, and sometimes feasted him during his stay there. Here I heard that famous nun singing to the organ in this manner; another nun beginning first to sing, performed her part so well, that we gave her much applause for her excellent art and voice; only we thought she did sing somewhat lower than other women usually did; hereupon also being ready to depart, we heard suddenly, for we saw nobody, that nun which was so famous, sing an eight higher than the other had done: her voice was the sweetest, strongest, and clearest, that ever I heard, in the using whereof also she showed that art as ravished us into admiration.

---

[1] Charles Emanuel I. Negotiations were opened early in James I.'s reign to marry Prince Henry and the Princess Elizabeth to a daughter and son of the Duke. From 1612–15 the Duke was engaged in a harassing war with his brother-in-law, Philip III. of Spain, and in April 1615 James I. sent him a present of £15,000 to aid him in its prosecution.

From Milan we went to Novara, as I remember, where we were entertained by the governor, being a Spaniard, with one of the most sumptuous feasts that ever I saw, being but of nine dishes, in three several services ; the first whereof was, three ollas podridas, consisting of all choice boiled meats, placed in three large silver chargers, which took up the length of a great table ; the meat in it being heightened up artificially, pyramid wise, to a sparrow which was on the top. The second service was like the former, of roast meat, in which all manner of fowl from the pheasant and partridge, to other fowl less than them, were heightened up to a lark. The third was in sweet-meats dry of all sorts, heightened in like manner to a round comfit.

From hence we went to Vercelli, a town of the Duke of Savoy's, frontier to the Spaniard, with whom the Duke was then in war ; from whence, passing by places of least note, we came to Turin, where the Duke of Savoy's court was. After I had refreshed myself here some two or three days, I took leave of my Lord Ambassador with intention to go to the Low Countries, and was now upon the way thither, as far as the foot of Mount Cenis, when the Count Scarnafissi came to me from the Duke,[1] and brought a letter to this effect : That

---

[1] Scarnafissi is best known to English readers by his

the Duke had heard I was a cavalier of great worth, and desirous to see the wars, and that if I would serve him I should make my own conditions. Finding so courteous an invitation, I returned back, and was lodged by the Duke of Savoy in a chamber furnished with silk and gold hangings, and a very rich bed, and defrayed at the Duke's charges in the English ambassador's house. The Duke also confirmed unto me what the Count Scarnafissi had said, and together bestowed divers compliments on me. I told his Highness, that when I knew in what service he pleased to employ me, he should find me ready to testify the sense I had of his princely invitation.

It was now in the time of Carnival, when the Duke, who loved the company of ladies and dancing as much as any prince whosoever, made divers masks and balls, in which his own daughters, among divers other ladies, danced ; and here it was his manner to place me always with his own hand near some fair lady, wishing us both to entertain each other with some discourse, which was a great

---

visit to England in 1616–17, when he sought James I.'s aid in behalf of his master, who had just been forced into a new war with Spain. Raleigh, who was preparing for his expedition to Guiana, seemed anxious to divert his efforts and attack Genoa in support of Savoy, but the negotiations with Scarnafissi were suddenly broken off. See Gardiner's History, iii. 49–52, and p. 176, *infra.*

favour among the Italians. He did many other ways also declare the great esteem he had of me without coming to any particular, the time of the year for going into the field being not yet come; only he exercised his men often, and made them ready for his occasions in the spring.

The Duke at last resolving how to use my service, thought fit to send me to Languedoc in France, to conduct 4000 men of the reformed religion, who had promised their assistance in his war,[1] unto Piedmont. I willingly accepted this offer; so taking my leave of the Duke, and bestowing about £70 or £80 among his officers, for the kind entertainment I had received, I took my leave also of my Lord Ambassador, and Sir Albertus Morton,[2] who was likewise employed there, and prepared for my journey, for more expedition of which I was desired to go post. An old Scotch knight of the Sandilands[3] hearing this, desired to

---

[1] *i.e.* with Spain.

[2] Sent to Savoy in May 1614 as assistant to Sir Dudley Carleton, the English ambassador there. Early in 1616 Morton became secretary to the Electress Palatine (Elizabeth) at Heidelberg. (Cal. State Papers (Dom.) 1611-18.) He was a nephew of Sir Henry Wotton, and served him as secretary at Venice. He died in 1625.

[3] Sir James Sandilands, a Scotch knight, was in 1604 Gentleman Usher of the Privy Chamber. In 1605 the Queen and Prince Henry stood sponsors at the christening of one of his children. He was made *maistre d'hostel* to the

L

borrow my horses as far as Heidelberg, which I granted, on condition that he would use them well by the way, and give them good keeping in that place afterwards.

The Count Scarnafissi was commanded to bear me company in this journey, and to carry with him some jewels, which he was to pawn in Lyons in France, and with the money gotten for them to pay the soldiers above nominated; for though the Duke had put extreme taxations on his people, insomuch that they paid not only a certain sum for every horse, ox, cow, or sheep that they kept, but afterwards for every chimney; and, finally, every single person by the poll, which amounted to a pistole, or 14s. a-head or person, yet he wanted money; at which I did not so much wonder as at the patience of his subjects, of whom I demanded how they could bear their taxations? I have heard some of them answer, " We are not so much offended with the Duke for what he takes from us, as thankful for what he leaves us."

The Count Scarnafissi and I, now setting forth, rid post all day without eating or drinking by the way, the Count telling me still we should come to a good inn at night. It was now twilight when

---

Princess Elizabeth on her marriage in 1613. He was buried at Greenwich 7th June 1618. See Rye's England as seen by Foreigners, pp. 255-6.

the Count and I came near a solitary inn, on the
top of a mountain ; the hostess hearing the noise
of horses, came out with a child new born on her
left arm, and a rush candle in her hand : she
presently knowing the Count de Scarnafissi, told
him, "Ah, Signor, you are come in a very ill
time, the Duke's soldiers have been here to-day,
and have left me nothing." I looked sadly upon
the Count, when he coming near to me whispered
me in the ear, and said, " It may be she thinks we
will use her as the soldiers have done : go you
into the house, and see whether you can find anything ; I will go round about the house, and perhaps I shall meet with some duck, hen, or chicken ; "
entering thus into the house, I found for all other
furniture of it, the end of an old form, upon which
sitting down, the hostess came towards me with a
rush candle, and said, " I protest before God that
is true which I told the Count, here is nothing to
eat ; but you are a gentleman, methinks it is pity
you should want ; if you please I will give you
some milk out of my breasts, into a wooden dish
I have here." This unexpected kindness made
that impression on me, that I remember I was
never so tenderly sensible of anything. My
answer was, " God forbid I should take away
the milk from the child I see in thy arms ; howbeit, I shall take it all my life for the greatest
piece of charity that ever I heard of ; " and there-

withal, giving her a pistole, or a piece of gold of 14s., Scarnafissi and I got on horseback again and rid another post, and came to an inn, where we found very coarse cheer, yet hunger made us relish it.

In this journey I remember I went over Mount Gabelet by night, being carried down that precipice in a chair, a guide that went before bringing a bottle of straw with him, and kindling pieces of it from time to time, that we might see our way. Being at the bottom of a hill, I got on horseback and rid to Burgoine, resolving to rest there a while; and the rather, to speak truly, that I had heard divers say, and particularly Sir John Finet[1] and Sir Richard Newport,[2] that the host's daughter there was the handsomest woman that ever they saw in their lives. Coming to the inn, the Count Scarnafissi wished me to rest two or three hours, and he would go before to Lyons to prepare business for my journey to Languedoc. The host's daughter being not within, 1 told her father and mother that I desired only to see their daughter,

---

[1] Master of the Ceremonies to James I.; and author of a curious book on ceremonies and points of precedence, known as "*Fineti Philoxenis.*" Weldon states that Finet was eminent (ed. James Howell 1656) as a composer of loose songs, which James I. delighted to hear sung after supper. See Court of James I. (1812) i. 399.

[2] A first cousin of Lord Herbert's. See p. 19, n.

as having heard her spoken of in England with so
much advantage, that divers told me they thought
her the handsomest creature that ever they saw.
They answered she was gone to a marriage, and
should be presently sent for, wishing me in the
meanwhile to take some rest upon a bed, for they
saw I needed it. Waking now about two hours
afterwards, I found her sitting by me, attending
when I would open mine eyes. I shall touch a
little of her description : her hair being of a shining
black, was naturally curled in that order that a
curious woman would have dressed it, for one curl
rising by degrees above another, and every bout
tied with a small ribbon of a naccarine,[1] or the
colour that the Knights of the Bath wear, gave a
very graceful mixture, while it was bound up in
this manner from the point of her shoulder to the
crown of her head ; her eyes, which were round and
black, seemed to be models of her whole beauty, and
in some sort of her air, while a kind of light or flame
came from them not unlike that which the ribbon
which tied up her hair exhibited ; I do not remember ever to have seen a prettier mouth, or whiter
teeth ; briefly, all her outward parts seemed to
become each other, neither was there anything
that could be misliked, unless one should say her

---

[1] From the French *nácre*, mother-of-pearl.

complexion was too brown, which yet from the shadow was heightened with a good blood in her cheeks. Her gown was a green Turkey grogram, cut all into panes or slashes, from the shoulder and sleeves unto the foot, and tied up at the distance of about a hand's-breadth everywhere with the same ribbon with which her hair was bound ; so that her attire seemed as bizare as her person. I am too long in describing an host's daughter ; howbeit I thought I might better speak of her than of divers other beauties, held to be the best and fairest of the time, whom I have often seen. In conclusion, after about an hour's stay, I departed thence, without offering so much as the least incivility ; and indeed, after so much weariness, it was enough that her sight alone did somewhat refresh me.

From hence I went straight to Lyons. Entering the gate, the guards there, after their usual manner, demanded of me who I was, whence I came, and whither I went ? to which, while I answered, I observed one of them look very attentively upon me, and then again upon a paper he had in his hand ; this having been done divers times, bred in me a suspicion that there was no good meaning in it, and I was not deceived in my conjecture ; for the Queen-mother of France [1] hav-

---

[1] Marie de Médicis.

ing newly made an edict, that no soldiers should
be raised in France, the Marquis de Rambouillet,[1]
French ambassador at Turin, sent word of my
employment to the Marquis de St. Chaumont, then
governor of Lyons, as also a description of my
person. This edict was so severe, as they who
raised any men were to lose their heads. In this
unfortunate conjuncture of affairs, nothing fell out
so well on my part, as that I had not raised as yet
any men ; howbeit, the guards requiring me to
come before the governor, I went with them to a
church where he was at vespers ; this while I
walked in the lower part of the church, little
imagining what danger I was in had I levied any
men. I had not walked there long, when a single
person came to me, apparelled in a black stuff suit,
without any attendants upon him, when I, supposing this person to be any man rather than the
governor, saluted him without much ceremony.

---

[1] Charles d'Angennes, who succeeded his father as Marquis of Rambouillet in 1611. His wife was the famous
Madame de Rambouillet, who presided over the well-known
assemblies of wits and poets at the Hôtel de Rambouillet,
in the Rue Saint Thomas du Louvre—a house which she in
great part designed. Her daughter Julie (born 1607), afterwards (1645) Duchesse de Montausier, was almost as prominent a figure as herself in Parisian society. Tallemant
des Réaux gives a very amusing account of father, mother,
and daughter in his *Historiettes*, iii. 204-258.

His first question was, whence I came? I
answered, from Turin. He demanded then, whither
I would go? I answered, I was not yet resolved.
His third question was, what news at Turin? to
which I answered, that I had no news to tell, as
supposing him to be only some busy or inquisitive
person. The Marquis hereupon called one of the
guards that conducted me thither, and after he had
whispered something in his ear, wished me to go
along with him, which I did willingly, as believing
this man would bring me to the governor. This
man silently leading me out of the church, brought
me to a fair house, into which I was no sooner
entered, but he told me I was commanded to prison
there by him I saw in the church, who was the
governor; I replied, I did not know him to be
governor, nor that that was a prison, and that if
I were out of it again, neither the governor nor
all the town could bring me to it alive. The
master of the house hereupon spoke me very fair,
and told me he would conduct me to a better
chamber than any I could find in an inn, and
thereupon conducted me to a very handsome
lodging not far from the river. I had not been
here half an hour when Sir Edward Sackville [1]

---

[1] Second son of Robert, second Earl of Dorset, and grandson of Thomas, first Earl, author of *Gorboduc* and Lord
Treasurer of England for many years. He is best known by
his duel with Lord Bruce of Kinloss in 1613. He succeeded

(now Earl of Dorset) hearing only that an English-man was committed, sent to know who I was, and why I was imprisoned. The governor not know-ing whether to lay the fault upon my short answers to him, or my commission to levy men contrary to the Queen's edict, made him so doubtful an answer, (after he had a little touched upon both) as he dismissed him unsatisfied.

Sir Edward Sackville hereupon coming to the house where I was, as soon as ever he saw me embraced me, saying, "Ned Herbert, what doest thou here?" I answered, "Ned Sackville, I am glad to see you, but I protest I know not why I am here." He again said, "Hast thou raised any men yet for the Duke of Savoy?" I replied, "Not so much as one." "Then," said he, "I will warrant thee, though I must tell thee the governor is much offended at thy behaviour and language in the church; (I replied it was impossible for me to imagine him to be governor that came without a guard, and in such mean clothes as he then wore.) I will go to him again, and tell him what you say, and doubt not but you shall be suddenly freed." Hereupon returning to the governor, he

---

to the earldom of Dorset on his elder brother's death in 1624. He married Mary, daughter of Sir George Curzon. Lord Herbert wrote a very quaint epitaph on Sir Edward Sackville's "first child, who died in his birth."

told of what family I was, and of what condition,
and that I had raised no men, and that I knew
him not to be governor; whereupon the Marquis
wished him to go back, that he would come in
person to free me out of the house.

This message being brought me by Sir Edward
Sackville, I returned this answer only: That it
was enough if he sent order to free me.   While
these messages past, a company of handsome young
men and women, out of I know not what civility,
brought music under the window and danced before
me, looking often up to see me; but Sir Edward
Sackville being now returned with order to free
me, I only gave them thanks out of the window,
and so went along with them to the governor.
Being come into a great hall where his lady was,
and a large train of gentlewomen and other persons,
the governor, with his hat in his hand, demanded
of me whether I knew him? when his noble lady,
answering for me, said, how could he know you,
when you were in the church alone, and in this
habit, being for the rest wholly a stranger to you?
which civility of hers, though I did not presently
take notice of it, I did afterwards most thankfully
acknowledge when I was ambassador in France.
The governor's next questions were the very same
he made when he met me in the church; to which
I made the very same answers before them all,
concluding that as I did not know him, he could

think it no incongruity if I answered in those terms : the governor yet was not satisfied herewith, and his noble lady taking my part again, gave him those reasons for my answering him in that manner, that they silenced him from speaking any further. The governor turning back, I likewise, after an humble obeisance made to his lady, returned with Sir Edward Sackville to my lodgings.

This night I passed as quietly as I could, but the next morning advised with him what I was to do ; I told him I had received a great affront, and that I intended to send him a challenge, in such courteous language, that he could not refuse it : Sir Edward Sackville by all means dissuaded me from it; by which I perceived I was not to expect his assistance therein, and indeed the next day he went out of town.

Being alone now, I thought on nothing more than how to send him a challenge, which at last I penned to this effect : That whereas he had given me great offence, without a cause, I thought myself bound as a gentleman to resent it, and therefore desired to see him with his sword in his hand in any place he should appoint ; and hoped he would not interpose his authority as an excuse for not complying with his honour on this occasion, and that so I rested his humble servant.

Finding nobody in town for two or three days by whom I might send this challenge, I resolved for my last means to deliver it in person, and observe how he took it, intending to right myself as I could, when I found he stood upon his authority.

This night it happened that Monsieur Terant, formerly mentioned, came to the town; this gentleman knowing me well, and remembering our acquaintance both at France and Juliers, wished there were some occasion for him to serve me; I presently hereupon, taking the challenge out of my pocket, told him he would oblige me extremely if he were pleased to deliver it, and that I hoped he might do it without danger, since I knew the French to be so brave a nation, that they would never refuse or dislike anything that was done in an honourable and worthy way.

Terant took the challenge from me, and after he had read it, told me that the language was civil and discreet; nevertheless he thought the governor would not return me that answer I expected; howsoever, said he, I will deliver it. Returning thus to my inn, and intending to sleep quieter that night than I had done three nights before; about one of the clock after midnight, I heard a great noise at my door, which awakened me, certain persons knocking so hard as if they would break it; besides, through the chinks thereof I saw light. This made me presently rise in my shirt, when, drawing my sword, I went to the door, and demanded who they

were; and together told them that if they came to
make me prisoner, I would rather die with my
sword in my hand; and therewithal opening the
door, I found upon the stairs half a dozen men
armed with halberts, whom I no sooner prepared
to resist, but the chief of them told me, that they
came not to me from the governor, but from my
good friend the Duke of Montmorency,[1] son to the
Duke I formerly mentioned, and that he came to
town late that night, in his way from Languedoc
(of which he was governor) to Paris; and that he
desired me, if I loved him, to rise presently and
come to him, assuring me further that this was
most true; hereupon wishing them to retire themselves, I drest myself, and went with them. They
conducted me to the great hall of the governor,
where the Duke of Montmorency, and divers other
cavaliers, had been dancing with the ladies; I went
presently to the Duke of Montmorency, who, taking
me a little aside, told me that he had heard of the
passages betwixt the governor and me, and that

---

[1] Henri II., Duc de Montmorency, born 1595, the idol
of the French court in his youth, succeeded his father as
governor of Languedoc in 1613 and to his father's title at
his death in 1614. He resisted the rising power of Richelieu for many years, but ultimately found it too strong for
him. He therefore entered into what was construed to be a
treasonable conspiracy against the king and Richelieu, was
arrested, and was beheaded at Toulouse, 30th Oct. 1632.

I had sent him a challenge; howbeit, that he conceived men in his place were not bound to answer as private persons for those things they did by virtue of their office; nevertheless, that I should have satisfaction in as ample manner as I could reasonably desire. Hereupon, bringing me with him to the governor, he freely told me that now he knew who I was, he could do no less than assure me that he was sorry for what was done, and desired me to take this for satisfaction; the Duke of Montmorency hereupon said presently, *C'est assez;* it is enough. I then turning to him, demanded whether he would have taken this satisfaction in the like case? He said, yes. After this, turning to the governor, I demanded the same question, to which he answered, that he would have taken the same satisfaction, and less too. I kissing my hand, gave it him, who embraced me, and so this business ended.

After some compliments past between the Duke of Montmorency, who remembered the great love his father bore me, which he desired to continue in his person, and putting me in mind also of our being educated together for a while, demanded whether I would go with him to Paris? I told him that I was engaged to the Low Countries, but that wheresoever I was I should be his most humble servant.

My employment with the Duke of Savoy in

Languedoc being thus ended, I went from Lyons to Geneva, where I found also my fame had prevented[1] my coming; for the next morning after my arrival, the state taking notice of me, sent a messenger in their name to congratulate my being there, and presented me with some flaggons of wine, desiring me (if I staid there any while) to see their fortifications, and give my opinion of them; which I did, and told them I thought they were weakest where they thought themselves the strongest; which was on the hilly part, where indeed they had made great fortifications; yet as it is a rule in war, that whatsoever may be made by art may be destroyed by art again, I conceived they had need to fear the approach of an enemy on that part rather than any other. They replied, that divers great soldiers had told them the same; and that they would give the best order they could to serve themselves on that side.

Having rested here some while to take physic (my health being a little broken with long travel) I departed, after a fortnight's stay, to Basle, where taking a boat upon the river, I came at length to Strasbourg, and from thence went to Heidelberg, where I was received again by the Prince Elector and Princess with much kindness, and viewed at leisure the fair library there, the gardens, and other

---

[1] *i.e.* anticipated.

rarities of that place;[1] and here I found my horses
I lent to Sandilands in good plight,[2] which I then
bestowed upon some servants of the Prince, in way
of retribution for my welcome thither.   From hence
Sir George Calvert,[3] and myself went by water, for
the most part, to the Low Countries, where taking
leave of each other, I went straight to his Excellency,[4] who did extraordinarily welcome me, insomuch that it was observed that he did never
outwardly make so much of any one as myself.

It happened this summer that the Low-Country
army was not drawn into the field, so that the
Prince of Orange[5] past his time at playing at chess
with me after dinner; or in going to Ryswick with

---

[1] See p. 151, *supra*.   Lord Herbert's statement of his
intimacy with the Elector Palatine and his wife, the Princess
Elizabeth, is corroborated by the letter from the Princess to
him, which I print below.   An interesting relic of the
Elector's library here referred to, is now in the British
Museum.   It is the Princess's copy of Raleigh's "History
of the World," 1614.   A curious history of the book is given
by Mr. Rye in his "England as seen by Foreigners," p.
222–3.

[2] See note on p. 161.

[3] Appointed Secretary of State in 1619.   He resigned
the post on declaring himself a Catholic in 1625, and was
soon afterwards created Lord Baltimore in the Irish peerage.
See Horace Walpole's Royal and Noble Authors, vol. ii.

[4] Count Maurice of Nassau.

[5] This is apparently another reference to Count Maurice
of Nassau.   See p. 113, note.

him to see his great horses ; or in making love ; in
which also he used me as his companion, yet so
that I saw nothing openly, more than might argue
a civil familiarity.   When I was at any time from
him, I did by his good leave endeavour to raise a
troop of horse for the Duke of Savoy's service, as
having obtained a commission to that purpose for
my brother William,[1] then an officer in the Low
Country.   Having these men in readiness, I sent
word to the Count Scarnafissi thereof, who was now
ambassador in England,[2] telling him, that if he
would send money, my brother was ready to go.

Scarnafissi answered me, that he expected money
in England, and that as soon as he received it, he
would send over so much as would pay an hundred
horse.   But a peace betwixt him and the Spaniard
being concluded not long after at Asti,[3] the whole

---

[1] See p. 21, *supra*.
[2] At the close of 1616.   See p. 159.
[3] Lord Herbert clearly acted precipitately.   The terms
of this treaty between Spain and Savoy were first broached
in 1615.   Scarnafissi received his final answer—England's refusal to aid his master—in January 1616-17,
apparently before Herbert raised his troops, and the treaty
of Asti was permanently determined a few months later.
When Scarnafissi applied for assistance to continue the war, it
is probable that both James I. and his minister Somerset
anticipated that the peace would be ultimately confirmed by
the two powers.   Raleigh's anxiety to divert his expedition
to the service of the Duke of Savoy caused Scarnafissi's

M

charge of keeping this horse fell upon me, without ever to this day receiving any recompense.

Winter now approaching, and nothing more to be done for that year, I went to the Brill to take shipping for England. Sir Edward Conway,[1] who was then governor at that place, and afterwards Secretary of State, taking notice of my being there, came to me, and invited me every day to come to him, while I attended only for a wind ; which serving at last for my journey, Sir Edward Conway conducted me to the ship, into which as soon as I was entered he caused six pieces of ordnance to be discharged for my farewell. I was scarce gone a league into the sea, when the wind turned contrary, and forced me back again. Returning thus to the Brill, Sir Edward Conway welcomed me as before ; and now, after some three or four days, the wind serving, he conducted me again to the ship, and bestowed six volleys of ordnance upon me. I was now about half way to England, when

---

demand to be entertained for a few weeks, but no farsighted politician could have believed that much would come of the negotiation.

[1] Knighted by the ill-fated Earl of Essex at Cadiz in 1596, he afterwards served in the Low Countries, as governor of the Brill. He was made a principal Secretary of State by James I. in 1623 and created Lord Conway in 1624. He was afterwards Lord-President of the Council. He died in 1630.

a most cruel storm arose, which tore our sails and
spent our masts, insomuch that the master of our
ship gave us all for lost, as the wind was extreme
high, and together contrary; we were carried at
last, though with much difficulty, back again to
the Brill, where Sir Edward Conway did congratulate my escape; saying, he believed certainly, that
(considering the weather) I must needs be cast
away.

After some stay here with my former welcome,
the wind being now fair, I was conducted again to
my ship by Sir Edward Conway, and the same
volleys of shot given me, and was now scarce out
of the haven, when the wind again turned contrary,
and drove me back. This made me resolve to try
my fortune here no longer; hiring a small bark,
therefore, I went to the sluice, and from thence to
Ostend, where finding company, I went to Brussels.
In the inn where I lay, here an ordinary was kept,
to which divers noblemen and principal officers of
the Spanish army resorted : sitting among these at
dinner, the next day after my arrival, no man
knowing me, or informing himself who I was, they
fell into discourse of divers matters, in Italian,
Spanish, and French; and at last three of them,
one after another, began to speak of King James,
my master, in a very scornful manner; I thought
with myself then, that if I was a base fellow, I
need not take any notice thereof, since no man

knew me to be an Englishman, or that I did so much as understand their language; but my heart burning within me, I, putting off my hat, arose from the table, and turning myself to those that sat at the upper end, who had said nothing to the King my master's prejudice, I told them in Italian, *Son Inglese;* "I am an Englishman; and should be unworthy to live if I suffered these words to be spoken of the King my master;" and therewithal turning myself to those who had injured the King, I said, "You have spoken falsely, and I will fight with you all." Those at the upper end of the table, finding I had so much reason on my part, did sharply check those I questioned, and, to be brief, made them ask the King's forgiveness, where-with also the King's health being drank round about the table, I departed thence to Dunkirk, and thence to Gravelines, where I saw, though un-known, an English gentlewoman enter into a nunnery there. I went thence to Calais; it was now extreme foul weather, and I could find no master of a ship willing to adventure to sea; how-beit, my impatience was such, that I demanded of a poor fisherman there whether he would go? he answered, his ship was worse than any in the haven, as being open above, and without any deck, besides, that it was old; but, saith he, "I care for my life as little as you do, and if you will go, my boat is at your service."

I was now scarce out of the haven, when a high
grown sea had almost overwhelmed us, the waves
coming in very fast into our ship, which we laded
out again the best we could; notwithstanding
which, we expected every minute to be cast away :
it pleased God yet before we were gone six leagues
into the sea, to cease the tempest, and give us a
fair passage over to the Downs, where, after giving
God thanks for my delivery from this most needless
danger that ever I did run, I went to London. I
had not been here ten days when a quartan ague
seized on me, which held me for a year and a half
without intermission, and a year and a half longer
at spring and fall : the good days I had during all
this sickness, I employed in study, the ill being
spent in as sharp and long fits as I think ever any
man endured, which brought me at last to be so
lean and yellow, that scarce any man did know me.
It happened during this sickness, that I walked
abroad one day towards Whitehall, where, meeting
with one Emerson, who spoke very disgraceful
words of Sir Robert Harley,[1] being then my dear
friend, my weakness could not hinder me to be
sensible of my friend's dishonour ; shaking him
therefore by a long beard he wore, I stept a little
aside, and drew my sword in the street ; Captain
Thomas Scriven, a friend of mine, being not far off

---

[1] See p. 136, *supra*.

on one side, and divers friends of his on the other
side.   All that saw me wondered how I could go,
being so weak and consumed as I was, but much
more that I would offer to fight ; howsoever, Emerson, instead of drawing his sword, ran away into
Suffolk House, and afterwards informed the Lords of
the Council of what I had done ; who not long after
sending for me, did not so much reprehend my
taking part with my friend, as that I would adventure to fight, being in such a bad condition of
health.   Before I came wholly out of my sickness,
Sir George Villiers, afterwards Duke of Buckingham,
came into the King's favour ; [1] this cavalier meeting
me accidentally at the Lady Stanhope's[2] house, came

---

[1] Late in 1614 Villiers, for whom the King had manifested
a liking on first seeing him, was made the King s Cupbearer.
On 23d April 1615 he became a Gentleman of the Royal
Bedchamber, and was knighted.   Somerset's enemies at
court hoped to use him as a check to the power of the older
favourite, but he was shrewd enough to turn the situation to
his own advantage.   Created Viscount Villiers in 1616 and
Earl of Buckingham in 1618, he was at the time of which
Lord Herbert is now writing all powerful in the King's
Council.   Lord Herbert remained faithful to him to the last.

[2] Catherine, daughter of Francis Lord Hastings, heir of
the 4th Earl of Huntingdon, married, in 1605, Philip, created
Lord Stanhope in 1616, and Earl of Chesterfield (4th
August 1628).   She died 28th August 1636, and from her
son, Henry Stanhope, descended the celebrated Lord Chesterfield.

to me, and told me he had heard so much of my worth, as he would think himself happy if, by his credit with the King, he could do me any service; I humbly thanked him, but told him, that for the present I had need of nothing so much as of health, but that if ever I had ambition, I should take the boldness to make my address by him.

I was no sooner perfectly recovered of this long sickness, but the Earl of Oxford and myself resolved to raise two regiments for the service of the Venetians.[1] While we were making ready for this journey, the King having an occasion to send an ambassador into France, required Sir George Villiers to present him with the names of the fittest men for that employment that he knew; whereupon eighteen names, among which mine was, being written in a paper, were presented to him; the King presently chose me, yet so as he desired first to have the approbation of his Privy Council, who, confirming his Majesty's choice, sent a messenger to my house among gardens, near the Old Ex-

---

[1] According to the State Papers, the Earl of Oxford was at Venice throughout 1617. In 1618 the Venetian ambassador in London was raising troops for the service of his republic, and by 30th March had hired eight ships, in which Sir Henry Peyton and Sir Henry Mainwaring were to have leading commands. Neither the Earl of Oxford nor Lord Herbert appears to have taken an active part in this business.

change,[1] requiring me to come presently to them.
Myself little knowing then the honour intended
me, asked the messenger whether I had done any
fault, that the Lords sent for me so suddenly ?
wishing him to tell the Lords that I was going to
dinner, and would afterwards attend them. I had
scarce dined when another messenger was sent ;
this made me hasten to Whitehall, where I was no
sooner come, but the Lords saluted me by the name
of Lord Ambassador of France ; I told their Lordships thereupon, that I was glad it was no worse,
and that I doubted, that by their speedy sending for
me, some complaint, though false, might be made
against me.

My first commission was to renew the oath of
alliance betwixt the two crowns,[2] for which purpose I was Extraordinary Ambassador, which being
done, I was to reside there as ordinary. I had
received now about six or seven hundred pounds,

---

[1] "Old Exchange was," says Stow, "a street so called
of the King's Exchange there kept, which was for the
receipt of bullion to be coined. . . . . This street beginneth
by West Cheape in the north and runneth down south to
Knighriders Street." Survey of London, ed. Thoms, p. 121.

[2] Concluded 19th August 1610, while Louis XIII. was
in his minority. Lord Herbert's instructions were of a
general character, and chiefly dealt with the necessity of
maintaining the existing peaceful relations between the two
countries. They bear the date 7th May 1619. I have
printed them at length in Appendix VI.

towards the charges of my journey, and locked it
in certain coffers in my house ; when the night
following, about one of the clock, I could hear
divers men speak and knock at the door, in that
part of the house where none did lie but myself,
my wife, and her attendants, my servants being
lodged in another house not far off : as soon as I
heard the noise, I suspected presently they came
to rob me of my money ; howsoever, I thought
fit to rise, and go to the window to know who
they were ; the first word I heard was, " Darest
thou come down, Welshman ? " which I no sooner
heard, but, taking a sword in one hand, and a
little target in the other, I did in my shirt run
down the stairs, open the doors suddenly, and
charged ten or twelve of them with that fury that
they ran away, some throwing away their halberts,
others hurting their fellows to make them go faster
in a narrow way they were to pass ; in which dis-
ordered manner I drove them to the middle of the
street by the Exchange, where finding my bare
feet hurt by the stones I trod on, I thought fit to
return home, and leave them to their flight. My
servants, hearing the noise, by this time were got
up, and demanded whether I would have them
pursue those rogues that fled away ; but I answering that I thought they were out of their reach, we
returned home together.

While I was preparing myself for my journey,

it happened that I, passing through the Inner Temple one day, and encountering Sir Robert Vaughan in this country,[1] some harsh words past betwixt us, which occasioned him, at the persuasion of others whom I will not nominate, to send me a challenge ; this was brought me at my house in Blackfriars, by Captain Charles Price, upon a Sunday, about one of the clock in the afternoon. When I had read it, I told Charles Price that I did ordinarily bestow this day in devotion, nevertheless that I would meet Sir Robert Vaughan presently, and gave him thereupon the length of my sword, demanding whether he brought any second with him ; to which Charles Price replying that he would be in the field with him, I told my brother, Sir Henry Herbert then present, thereof, who readily offering himself to be my second, nothing was wanting now but the place to be agreed upon betwixt us, which was not far from the waterside near Chelsea.

My brother and I taking boat presently, came to the place, where, after we had staid about two hours in vain, I desired my brother to go to Sir Robert Vaughan's lodging, and tell him that I now

---

[1] A member of Prince Charles' household (Cal. State Papers, 1611-18, p. 443). Apparently a member of the family with whom Lord Herbert's house had had previous quarrels. (See p. 28, *supra.*)

attended his coming a great while, and that I desired him to come away speedily ; hereupon my brother went, and after a while, returning back again, he told me they were not ready yet ; I attended then about an hour and a half longer, but as he did not come yet, I sent my brother a second time to call him away, and to tell him I catched cold, nevertheless that I would stay there till sunset : my brother yet could not bring him along, but returned himself to the place, where we staid together till half an hour after sunset, and then returned home.

The next day the Earl of Worcester,[1] by the King's command, forbid me to receive any message or letter from Sir Robert Vaughan, and advertised me withal, that the King had given him charge to end the business betwixt us, for which purpose he desired me to come before him the next day about two of the clock ; at which time, after the Earl had told me, that being now made ambassador, and a public person, I ought not to entertain

---

[1] Probably Edward Somerset, 4th Earl of Worcester, Lord Privy Seal and Knight of the Garter, who died in 1627. His son Henry, a devoted royalist, created Marquis of Worcester (2d November 1642), was the father of the second Marquis, the well-known author of the "Century of Inventions." Charles Somerset, the founder of the family, who married Elizabeth Herbert, a very distant relative of Lord Herbert, is referred to p. 17, n. 1.

private quarrels ; after which, without much ado, he ended the business betwixt Sir Robert Vaughan and myself : It was thought by some, that this would make me lose my place, I being under so great an obligation to the King for my employment in France ; but Sir George Villiers, afterwards Duke of Buckingham, told me he would warrant me for this one time, but I must do so no more.

I was now almost ready for my journey, and had received already as choice a company of gentlemen for my attendants, as I think ever followed an ambassador ; when some of my private friends told me, that I was not to trust so much to my pay from the Exchequer, but that it was necessary for me to take letters of credit with me, for as much money as I could well procure. Informing myself hereupon who had furnished the last ambassador, I was told Monsieur Savage, a Frenchman : [1] coming to his house, I demanded whether he would help me with moneys in France, as he had done the last ambassador ; he said he did not know me, but would inform himself better who I was ;

---

[1] Like all the English ambassadors abroad, Herbert found great difficulty in obtaining remittances from home. Among Earl de la Warr's MSS. are a series of letters from Herbert to the Earl of Middlesex praying for payment of his salary in 1623, and frequent mention is made there of sums advanced to Herbert by " his merchant Sauvage." (Historical MSS. Commission, Rep. iv. pp. 299, 311).

departing thus from him, I went to Sigr. Burlamacchi, a man of great credit in those times,[1] and
demanded of him the same ; his answer was, that
he knew me to be a man of honour, and I had
kept my word with everybody ; whereupon also
going to his study, gave me a letter of credit to
one Monsieur de Langherac in Paris, for £2000
sterling : I then demanded what security he expected for this money ? he said, he would have
nothing but my promise; I told him he had put
a great obligation upon me, and that I would strive
to acquit myself of it the best I could.

Having now a good sum of money in my coffers,
and this letter of credit, I made ready for my
journey ; the day I went out of London I remember was the same in which Queen Anne was
carried to burial, which was a sad spectacle to all
that had occasion to honour her.[2]   My first night's
journey was to Gravesend, where being at supper
in my inn, Monsieur Savage formerly mentioned

---

[1] Philip Burlamacchi appears to have been the chief
foreign banker in London.   Through him all payments to
ambassadors abroad were made.   Frequent mention is
made of him in the State Papers.

[2] The Queen died 18th March 1618–19 and was buried
after many delays on 13th May.   Sir Gerard Herbert wrote
to Carleton (19th March) : "Sir Edward Herbert is going
to France and his brother Harry is gone to prepare for
him." (Cal. State Papers, 1619–23, p. 25.)

came to me, and told me, that whereas I had spoken to him for a letter of credit, he had made one which he thought would be to my contentment. I demanded to whom it was directed; he said to Monsieur Tallemant and Rambouillet, in Paris;[1] I asked then what they were worth? he said, above one hundred thousand pounds sterling; I demanded for how much this letter of credit was? he said, for as much as I should have need of: I asked what security he required? he said, nothing by my word, which he had heard was inviolable.

From Gravesend, by easy journeys I went to Dover, where I took shipping, with a train of an hundred and odd persons,[2] and arrived shortly after at Calais, where I remember my cheer was twice as good as at Dover, and my reckoning half as cheap. From whence I went to Boulogne, Monstreville, Abbeville, Amiens, and in two days thence, to St. Denis near Paris, where I was met with a great train of coaches that were sent to receive me, as also by the master of the ceremonies, and Monsieur Mennon,[3] my fellow scholar, with

---

[1] Frequently mentioned in the letters on money-matters addressed by Herbert to the Earl of Middlesex (in the Earl of Warr's MSS.) See also Tallemant des Reáux' Historiettes.

[2] Thomas Carew accompanied Lord Herbert as his Secretary.

[3] Probably René de Menou (see p. 98, *supra*).

Monsieur Disancourt,[1] who then kept an academy, and brought with him a brave company of gentlemen on great horses, to attend me into town.

It was now somewhat late when I entered Paris, upon a Saturday night; I was but newly settled in my lodging, when a secretary of the Spanish ambassador there told me that his Lord desired to have the first audience from me, and therefore requested he might see me the next morning; I replied, it was a day I gave wholly to devotion, and therefore entreated him to stay till some more convenient time : the secretary replied, that his master did hold it no less holy; howbeit, that his respect to me was such, that he would prefer the desire he had to serve me before all other considerations ; howsoever I put him off till Monday following.

Not long after, I took a house in Fauburg St. Germain Rue Tournon, which cost me £200 sterling yearly ; having furnished the house richly, and lodged all my train, I prepared for a journey to Tours and Touraine, where the French court then was : being come hither in extreme hot weather, I demanded audience of the King and Queen, which being granted, I did assure the King of the great affection the King my master bore him, not only out of the ancient alliance betwixt the two crowns,

---

[1] See p. 98, *supra.*

but because Henry the Fourth and the King my
master had stipulated with each other, that whensoever anyone of them died, the survivor should
take care of the other's child: I assured him
further, that no charge was so much imposed upon
me by my instructions, as that I should do good
offices betwixt both kingdoms; and therefore that
it were a great fault in me, if I behaved myself
otherwise than with all respect to his Majesty:
this being done I presented to the King a letter of
credence from the King my master: the King assured
me of a reciprocal affection to the King my master,
and of my particular welcome to his court: his
words were never many, as being so extreme a
stutterer, that he would sometimes hold his tongue
out of his mouth a good while before he could
speak so much as one word; he had besides a
double row of teeth, and was observed seldom or
never to spit or blow his nose, or to sweat much,
though he were very laborious, and almost in-
defatigable in his exercises of hunting and hawking,
to which he was much addicted; neither did it
hinder him, though he was burst in his body, as
we call it, or herniosus; for he was noted in those
sports, though oftentimes on foot, to tire not only
his courtiers, but even his lacqueys, being equally
insensible, as was thought, either of heat or cold:
his understanding and natural parts were as good
as could be expected in one that was brought up

in so much ignorance, which was on purpose so
done that he might be the longer governed; howbeit, he acquired in time a great knowledge in
affairs, as conversing for the most part with wise
and active persons.   He was noted to have two
qualities incident to all who were ignorantly brought
up—suspicion and dissimulation; for as ignorant
persons walk so much in the dark, they cannot be
exempt from fear of stumbling; and as they are
likewise deprived of, or deficient in those true principles by which they should govern both public
and private actions in a wise, solid, and demon-
strative way, they strive commonly to supply
these imperfections with covert arts, which, though
it may be sometimes excusable in necessitous persons, and be indeed frequent among those who
negotiate in small matters, yet condemnable in
princes, who, proceeding upon foundations of reason
and strength, ought not to submit themselves to
such poor helps: howbeit, I must observe, that
neither his fears did take away his courage, when
there was occasion to use it, nor his dissimulation
extend itself to the doing of private mischiefs to
his subjects, either of one or the other religion;
his favourite was one Monsieur de Luynes, who
in his nonage gained much upon the King, by
making hawks fly at all little birds in his gardens,
and by making some of those little birds again
catch butterflies; and had the King used him for

N

no other purpose, he might have been tolerated; but as, when the King came to a riper age, the government of public affairs was drawn chiefly from his counsels, not a few errors were committed.[1]

The Queen-mother, princes, and nobles of that kingdom, repined that his advices to the King should be so prevalent, which also at last caused a civil war in that kingdom.[2] How unfit this man was for the credit he had with the King may be argued by this; that when there was question

---

[1] Charles, Marquis D'Albert and Duc de Luynes (1578–1621), attached in his youth as a page to the household of Henri IV., acquired so much influence with the young prince who afterwards reigned as Louis XIII., that when Herbert arrived in Paris Luynes was virtual ruler of France. He had contrived in 1617 the murder of his chief rival, Concini, the favourite of Marie de Medicis, and Marie herself was dismissed from court to prison at Blois. His success as a bird trainer had obtained for him the appointment of Grand Falconer of France in 1616, and all offices at court were afterwards at his disposal. He became Grand Constable 2d April 1621, although it was said he had never handled a sword. He recommended the suppression of the Protestants by force of arms in 1621 with fatal result to himself. Herbert was treated politely by Luynes in the first year of his embassy (see Appendix VII.)

[2] In 1619 the supporters of the Queen-mother released her from Blois and secured some concessions for her by the peace of Angoulême. An attempt on the part of the Queen-mother's adherents to override the treaty was stoutly resisted by an army under Louis XIII. in the following year.

made about some business in Bohemia, he demanded
whether it was an inland country, or lay upon the
sea ?[1]   And thus much for the present of the King
and his favourite.

   After my audience with the King, I had another
from the Queen, being sister to the King of Spain ;[2]
I had little to say unto her, but some compliments
on the King my master's part, but such compliments as her sex and quality were capable of.
This Queen was exceedingly fair, like those of the
house of Austria, and together of so mild and good
a condition, she was never noted to have done ill
offices to any, but to have mediated as much as
was possible for her, in satisfaction of those who
had any suit to the King, as far as their cause
would bear.   She had now been married divers
years, without having any children, though so
ripe for them, that nothing seemed to be wanting
on her part.   I remember her the more particularly, that she showed publicly at my audiences
that favour to me, as not only my servants, but
divers others took notice of it.   After this my first

---

   [1] Similarly Shakespeare (it is well known) in " Winter's
Tale" treated Bohemia as a maritime country (*cf.* Jonson's
" Conversations with Drummond," p. 16).
   [2] Anne of Austria, daughter of Philip III. of Spain (*d.*
1621), by Margaret, sister of the Emperor Ferdinand II.
Her brother, Philip IV., married (1) a daughter of Henri IV.
of France, and (2) his niece Maria, daughter of his sister
Maria by the Emperor Ferdinand III. (*cf.* p. 241).

audience, I went to see Monsieur de Luynes, and
the principal ministers of state, as also the princes
and princesses, and ladies then in the court, and
particularly the Princess of Conti, from whom I
carried the scarf formerly mentioned ;[1] and this is
as much as I shall declare in this place concerning
my negotiation with the King and state, my purpose being, if God sends me life, to set them forth
apart, as having the copies of all my despatches in
a great trunk, in my house in London ; and considering that in the time of my stay there, there
were divers civil wars in that country, and that
the prince, now King, passed with my Lord of
Buckingham, and others, through France into
Spain ; and the business of the Elector Palatine
in Bohemia, and the battle of Prague,[2] and divers
other memorable accidents, both of state and war,
happened during the time of my employment ; I
conceive a narration of them may be worth the
seeing, to them who have it not from a better
hand ; I shall only therefore relate here, as they
come into my memory, certain little passages,
which may serve in some part to declare the
history of my life.

Coming back from Tours to Paris, I gave the

---

[1] See p. 107, *supra.*

[2] 29th October 1620, one of the early decisive battles of
the Thirty Years' War. Frederick, the Elector Palatine, was
disastrously defeated, and his loss of Bohemia final.

best order I could concerning the expenses of my
house, family, and stable, that I might settle all
things as near as was possible in a certain course,
allowing, according to the manner of France, so
many pounds of beef, mutton, veal, and pork, and
so much also in turkeys, capons, pheasants, part-
ridges, and all other fowls, as also pies and tarts,
after the French manner, and after also this, a
dozen dishes of sweetmeats every meal constantly.
The ordering of these things was the heavier to
me, that my wife flatly refused to come over into
France, as being now entered into a dropsy, which
also had kept her without children for many years:
I was constrained therefore to make use of a
steward, who was understanding and diligent, but
no very honest man; my chief secretary was
William Boswell, now the King's agent in the Low
Countries;[1] my secretary for the French tongue
was one Monsieur Ozier, who afterwards was the
King's agent in France. The gentleman of my
horse was Monsieur de Meny,[2] who afterwards
commanded a thousand horse, in the wars of
Germany, and proved a very gallant gentleman.
Mr. Crofts was one of my principal gentlemen,

---

[1] He was afterwards secretary to Sir Dudley Carleton at
the Hague, and succeeded Carleton as ambassador there in
1633. He died in 1649.

[2] Perhaps René de Menou, to whom I have already referred on p. 97, note.

and afterwards made the King's Cup-bearer;[1] and Thomas Caage, that excellent wit, the King's Carver; Edmund Taverner, whom I made my under secretary, was afterwards chief secretary to the Lord Chamberlain; and one Mr. Smith, secretary to the Earl of Northumberland;[2] I nominate these, and could many more, that came to very good fortunes afterwards, because I may verify that which I said before concerning the gentlemen that attended me.

When I came to Paris, the English and French were in very ill intelligence with each other, insomuch that one Buckly coming then to me, said he was assaulted and hurt upon Pontneuf, only because he was an Englishman: nevertheless, after I had been in Paris about a month, all the English were so welcome thither, that no other nation was so acceptable amongst them, insomuch, that my gentlemen having a quarrel with some debauched French, who in their drunkenness quarrelled with them, divers principal gentlemen of that nation

---

[1] I have been unable to identify these persons elsewhere. Mr. Crofts was doubtless a relative of the Sir James and Sir Herbert Croft who have already been mentioned (see pp. 82 and 135). Master Taverner was a well-known musician of the time (see Meres' "Palladis Tamia," 1598).

[2] I have printed below a series of letters written by Lord Herbert during his embassy, which illustrate most of these incidents.

offered themselves to assist my people with their swords.

It happened one day that my cousin, Oliver Herbert,[1] and George Radney, being gentlemen who attended me, and Henry Whittingham, my butler, had a quarrel with some French, upon I know not what frivolous occasion. It happened my cousin, Oliver Herbert, had for his opposite a fencer, belonging to the Prince of Conde, who was dangerously hurt by him in divers places ; but as the house, or hostel, of the Prince of Conde was not far off, and himself well beloved in those quarters, the French in great multitudes arising, drove away the three above mentioned into my house, pursuing them within the gates ; I perceiving this at a window, ran out with my sword, which the people no sooner saw, but they fled again as fast as ever they entered. Howsoever, the Prince of Conde, his fencer, was in that danger of his life, that Oliver Herbert was forced to fly France, which, that he might do the better, I paid the said fencer 200 crowns, or £60 sterling, for his hurt and cures.

The plague now being hot in Paris, I desired the Duke of Montmorency to lend me the castle

---

[1] Apparently grandson of Herbert's grand-uncle, Oliver Herbert of Machynlleth (see Genealogical Table). He was with Herbert during the siege of Montgomery Castle in October 1644.

of Merlou, where I lived in the time of his most noble father, which he willingly granted.[1] Removing thither, I enjoyed that sweet place and country, wherein I found not a few that welcomed me out of their ancient acquaintance.

On the one side of me was the Baron de Montaterre of the reformed religion, and Monsieur de Bouteville on the other, who, though young at that time, proved afterwards to be that brave cavalier which all France did so much celebrate.[2] In both their castles, likewise, were ladies of much beauty and discretion, and particularly a sister of Bouteville, thought to be one of the chief perfections of the time, whose company yielded some divertisement, when my public occasions did suffer it.

Winter being now come, I returned to my house in Paris, and prepared for renewing the oath of alliance betwixt the two crowns, for which, as I said formerly, I had an extraordinary commission; nevertheless the King put off the business to as long a time as he well could. In the meanwhile Prince Henry of Nassau, brother to Prince Maurice,[3] coming to Paris, was met and much welcomed by

---

[1] See pp. 97 *et seq.* The old Duke died in 1614.

[2] Like Balagni, Bouteville had the reputation of always killing his man in his duels.

[3] Prince Frederick Henry succeeded his brother Maurice as Prince of Orange in 1625 (see p. 113).

me, as being obliged to him no less than to his brother in the Low Countries.[1]   This Prince, and all his train, were feasted by me at Paris with one hundred dishes, costing, as I remember, in all £100.

The French King at last resolving upon a day for performing the ceremony, betwixt the two crowns above mentioned, myself and all my train put ourselves into that sumptuous equipage, that I remember it cost me one way or another above £1000.   And truly the magnificence of it was such, as a little French book was presently printed thereof.   This being done, I resided here in the quality of an ordinary ambassador.[2]

And now I shall mention some particular passages concerning myself, without entering yet any way into the whole frame and context of my negotiation, reserving them, as I said before, to a particular treatise.[3]   I spent my time much in the

---

[1] Herbert announced his appointment in Paris to the Prince of Orange from Tours 17th June (*cf.* British Museum Addit. MS. 7082).

[2] See Appendix VII.   I have not found any proof of the existence of a book on the subject of the ceremonial mentioned above.

[3] There is no proof that this was ever written, but his correspondence supplies the information, which he apologises for passing over here.   The internal history of the French court is best studied in the Memoires of Bassompierre and of Brantôme, in the Historiettes of Tallemant des Réaux and the early memoirs of Richelieu.

visits of the princes, council of state, and great
persons of the French kingdom, who did ever
punctually requite my visits. The like I did also
to the chief ambassadors there, among whom the
Venetian, Low Country, Savoy, and the united
princes in Germany, ambassadors, did bear me that
respect, that they usually met in my house, to
advise together concerning the great affairs of that
time : For as the Spaniard then was so potent that
he seemed to affect an universal monarchy, all the
above-mentioned ambassadors did, in one common
interest, strive to oppose him. All our endeavours
yet could not hinder, but that he both publicly prevailed in his attempts abroad, and privately did
corrupt divers of the principal ministers of state in
this kingdom. I came to discover this by many
ways, but by none more effectually than by the
means of an Italian, who returned over, by letters
of exchange, the moneys the Spanish ambassador
received for his occasions in France ; for I perceived
that when the said Italian was to receive any extraordinary great sum for the Spanish ambassador's
use, the whole face of affairs was presently changed,
insomuch that neither my reasons, nor the ambassadors above mentioned, how valid soever, could
prevail : though yet afterwards we found means
together, to reduce affairs to their former train ;
until some other new great sum coming to the
Spanish ambassador's hand, and from thence to the

aforesaid ministers of state, altered all. Howbeit
divers visits passed betwixt the Spanish ambassador
and myself; in one of which he told me, that
though our interests were diverse, yet we might
continue friendship in our particular persons ; for,
said he, it can be no occasion of offence betwixt us,
that each of us strive the best he can to serve the
King his master.   I disliked not his reasons, though
yet I could not omit to tell him, that I would
maintain the dignity of the King my master the
best I could : And this I said, because the Spanish
ambassador had taken place of the English, in the
time of Henry IV., in this fashion :   They both
meeting in an antechamber to the secretary of state,
the Spanish ambassador, leaning to the wall in that
posture that he took the hand of the English ambassador, said publicly, I hold this place in the right of
the King my master; which small punctilio being not
resented by our ambassador at that time, gave the
Spaniard occasion to brag, that he had taken the
hand from our ambassador.   This made me more
watchful to regain the honour which the Spaniard
pretended to have gotten herein; so that though
the ambassador, in his visits, often repeated the
words above mentioned, being in Spanish, *Que cada
uno haga lo que pudiere por su amo,* " Let every man
do the best he can for his master," I attended the
occasion to right my master.   It happened one
day, that both of us going to the French King for

our several affairs, the Spanish ambassador, between
Paris and Estampes, being upon his way before
me in his coach, with a train of about sixteen or
eighteen persons on horseback, I following him in
my coach, with about ten or twelve horse, found
that either I must go the Spanish pace, which is
slow, or if I hasted to pass him, that I must hazard
the suffering of some affront like unto that our
former ambassador received ; proposing hereupon
to my gentlemen the whole business, I told them
that I meant to redeem the honour of the King my
master some way or other, demanding further,
whether they would assist me ? which they promising, I bid the coachman drive on.   The Spanish
ambassador seeing me approach, and imagining
what my intention was, sent a gentleman to me, to
tell me he desired to salute me ; which I accepting,
the gentleman returned to the ambassador, who,
alighting from his coach, attended me in the middle
of the highway ; which being perceived by me I
alighted also, when, some extravagant compliments
having passed betwixt us, the Spanish ambassador
took his leave of me, went to a dry ditch not far
off, upon pretence of making water, but indeed
to hold the upper hand of me while I passed by
in my coach ; which being observed by me, I
left my coach, and getting upon a spare horse I had
there, rode into the said dry ditch, and telling him
aloud, that I knew well why he stood there, bid

him afterwards get to his coach, for I must ride that
way : the Spanish ambassador, who understood me
well, went to his coach grumbling and discontented,
though yet neither he nor his train did any more
than look one upon another, in a confused manner ;
my coach this while passing by the ambassador on
the same side I was, I shortly after left my horse
and got into it.   It happened this while, that one of
my coach-horses having lost a shoe, I thought fit to
stay at a smith's forge, about a quarter of a mile
before ; this shoe could not be put on so soon, but
that the Spanish ambassador overtook us, and
might indeed have passed us, but that he thought
I would give him another affront.   Attending, therefore, the smith's leisure, he staid in the highway, to
our no little admiration, until my horse was shoed.
We continued our journey to Estampes, the Spanish
ambassador following us still at a good distance.

I should scarce have mentioned this passage, but
that the Spaniards do so much stand upon their
pundonores ; for confirming whereof I have thought
fit to remember the answer a Spanish ambassador
made to Philip II. king of Spain, who, finding
fault with him for neglecting a business of great
importance in Italy, because he could not agree
with the French ambassador about some such
pundonore as this, said to him, *Como a dexado
una cosa di importancia per una ceremonia !*—" How
have you left a business of importance for a cere-

mony!" The ambassador boldly replied to his master, *Como por una ceremonia? Vuessa Majesta misma no es sino una ceremonia.*—" How, for a ceremony ? your Majesty's self is but a ceremony."[1]

Howsoever, the Spanish ambassador taking no notice publicly of the advantage I had of him herein, dissembled it, as I heard, till he could find some fit occasion to resent this passage, which yet he never did to this day.

Among the visits I rendered to the grandees of France, one of the principal I made was to that brave general the Duke of Lesdigueres,[2] who was

---

[1] *Cf.* Shakespeare's Henry V., iv. 1—

" And what have kings, that privates have not too,
Save ceremony, save general ceremony ? "

[2] Francois de Bonne, Duc de Lesdiguères (1543-1626), one of the leading French Protestant commanders throughout the religious wars of the sixteenth century, bore the highest military reputation. As a patriotic Frenchman, he never allowed his religious scruples to prevent his aiding his country against a foreign enemy. Under the influence of a young wife, whom he married in 1617, he practically renounced Protestantism late in life, and fought with Louis XIII. and De Luynes in 1621 against the Protestants. His love of warfare led him to engage in it to the last. The Electress Palatine (Princess Elizabeth) is reported to have said, " Si il y avait en France deux Lesdiguères, j'en demanderais un au roi." Sir Thomas Overbury refers to Lesdiguères' great age in his " Crumms Fal'n from King James' Table," ed. 1856, p. 271. See Tallemant des Réaux, Historiettes, i. 87.

now grown very old and deaf. His first words to
me were, "Monsieur, you must do me the honour
to speak high, for I am deaf;" my answer to him
was, "You was born to command and not to obey;
it is enough if others have ears to hear you." This
compliment took him much, and indeed I have a
manuscript of his military precepts and observations,
which I value at a great price.[1]

I shall relate now some things concerning myself,
which, though they may seem scarce credible, yet,
before God, are true: I had been now in France
about a year and an half, when my tailor, Andrew
Henly of Basel,[2] who now lives in Blackfriars,
demanded of me half a yard of satin, to make me a
suit, more than I was accustomed to give; of which
I required a reason, saying I was not fatter now
than when I came to France. He answered, it
was true, but you are taller; whereunto, when I
would give no credit, he brought his old measures,

---

[1] Lesdiguères' *Discours de l'art militaire*, dedicated to
Henri IV., was first printed from a MS. in the Paris Library
in 1878 in *Actes et Correspondences du Connétable de Lesdi-
guières* (Grenoble), ii. 541–578.

[2] Foreigners were invariably the fashionable London
tailors in James I.'s reign. In 1616 a petition was presented to the King by native workmen protesting against
the presence of so many foreign handicraftsmen in the
metropolis. Special attention is drawn to the fact that 148
tailors were in active practice then. (Foreigners Residents in
England, *Camd. Soc.* p. vi.)

and made it appear that they did not reach to their just places. I told him I knew not how this happened; but howsoever he should have half a yard more, and that when I came into England I would clear the doubt; for a little before my departure thence, I remember William Earl of Pembroke[1] and myself did measure heights together at the request of the Countess of Bedford,[2] and he was then higher than I by about the breadth of my little finger. At my return, therefore, into England, I measured again with the same Earl, and, to both our great wonders, found myself taller than he by the breadth of a little finger: which growth of mine I could attribute to no other cause but to my quartan ague formerly mentioned, which, when it quitted me, left me in a more perfect health than I formerly enjoyed, and indeed disposed me

---

[1] Lord Herbert's kinsman and the friend of Shakespeare (probably the W. H. of the dedication to the Sonnets). His mother was the far-famed Countess of Pembroke of Jonson's epitaph—"Sidney's sister, Herbert's mother." His poems, published in 1666, attest his literary tastes. He was Chamberlain to the Royal Household under James I., and Chancellor of Oxford University. He died 10th April 1630, and was succeeded in his title by his younger brother Philip, created Earl of Montgomery in 1605. To these brothers, it will be remembered, the great folio Shakespeare of 1623 is dedicated. Clarendon's account of them is the most vivid and interesting. (Cf. his History of Rebellion 1705, i. 56–61.)

[2] See p. 130, *supra.*

to some follies which I afterwards repented, and
do still repent of; but as my wife refused to come
over, and my temptations were great, I hope the
faults I committed are the more pardonable.   Howsoever I can say truly, that, whether in France or
England, I was never in a bawdy-house, nor used
my pleasures intemperately, and much less did
accompany them with that dissimulation and falsehood which is commonly found in men addicted to
love women.   To conclude this passage, which I
unwillingly mention, I must protest again, before
God, that I never delighted in that or any other
sin; and that if I trangressed sometimes in this
kind, it was to avoid a greater ill; for certainly if I
had been provided with a lawful remedy, I should
have fallen into no extravagancy.   I could extenuate
my fault by telling circumstances which would have
operated, I doubt, upon the chastest of mankind;
but I forbear, those things being not fit to be
spoken of; for though the philosophers have
accounted this act to be *inter honesta factu*, where
neither injury nor violence was offered, yet they
ever reckoned it among the *turpia dictu*.   I shall,
therefore, only tell some other things alike strange
of myself.

I weighed myself in balances often with men
lower than myself by the head, and in their bodies
slenderer, and yet was found lighter than they, as

o

Sir John Davers, knight,[1] and Richard Griffiths, now living,[2] can witness, with both whom I have been weighed. I had also, and have still, a pulse on the crown of my head. It is well known to those that wait in my chamber, that the shirts, waistcoats, and other garments I wear next my body, are sweet, beyond what either easily can be believed, or hath been observed in any else, which sweetness also was found to be in my breath above others, before I used to take tobacco, which, towards my latter time, I was forced to take against certain rheums and catarrhs that trouble me, which yet did not taint my breath for any long time;[3] I scarce ever felt cold in my

---

[1] Sir John Davers or Danvers was Lord Herbert's step-father, having married Lady Herbert in 1608. See *supra*, p. 20, note 2, and Appendix III.

[2] Lord Herbert's servant, to whom he has already referred more than once.

[3] Nothing is more singular than the rapidity with which the habit of tobacco-smoking spread in England. The herb was first brought to this country, according to Camden, in 1585. Camden, writing in the early years of James I.'s reign, says that "Tobacco or Nicotiana is grown so frequent in use, and of such price that many, nay the most part, with an insatiable desire do take of it, . . . some for wantonness or rather fashion's sake, and *others for health's sake*, insomuch that tobacco shops are set up in greater number than either ale-houses or taverns !" Barnaby Rich, writing in 1614, states that in that year there were 7000 shops in London where tobacco was sold. (*Honestie of the Age.*)

life, though yet so subject to catarrhs, that I think
no man ever was more obnoxious to it; all which
I do in a familiar way mention to my posterity,
though otherwise they might be thought scarce
worth the writing.

The effect of my being sent into France by the
King my master, being to hold all good intelligence
betwixt both crowns, my employment was both
noble and pleasing, and my pains not great, France
having no design at that time upon England, and
King James being that pacific prince all the world
knew.[1] And thus, besides the times I spent in
treaties and negotiations I had either with the
ministers of state in France, or foreign ambassadors
residing in Paris, I had spare time not only for
my book, but for visits to divers grandees, for
little more ends than obtaining some intelligence
of the affairs of that kingdom and civil conversation, for which their free, generous, and cheerful
company was no little motive; persons of all
quality being so addicted to have mutual entertainment with each other, that in calm weather
one might find all the noble and good company
in Paris, of both sexes, either in the garden of

---

[1] Sir Anthony Weldon, no friendly critic, admits of
James I. that "he lived in peace, died in peace, and left all
his kingdoms in a peaceable condition, with his own motto:
Beati Pacifici." Court of James I., ii. 12.

the Tuileries, or in the park of Bois de Vincennes ; they thinking it almost an incivility to refuse their presence and free discourse to any who were capable of coming to those places, either under the recommendation of good parts, or but so much as handsome clothes, and a good equipage. When foul weather was, they spent their time in visits at each other's houses, where they interchanged civil discourses, or heard music, or fell to dancing, using, according to the manner of that country, all the reasonable liberties they could with their honour, while their manner was, either in the garden of the Tuileries, or elsewhere, if any one discoursing with a lady did see some other of good fashion approach to her, he would leave her and go to some other lady, he who conversed with her at that time quitting her also, and going to some other, that so addresses might be made equal and free to all without scruple on any part, neither was exception made, or quarrel begun, upon these terms.

It happened one day, that I being ready to return from the Tuileries, about eight of the clock in the summer, with intention to write a despatch to the King about some intelligence I had received there, the Queen,[1] attended with her principal ladies, without so much as one cavalier, did enter

---

[1] *i.e.* Anne of Austria.

the garden : I staid on one side of an alley, there
to do my reverence to her and the rest, and so
return to my house, when the Queen perceiving
me, staid a while, as if she expected I should
attend her : but as I stirred not more than to
give her that great respect I owed her, the Princess
of Conti, who was next, called me to her, and said
I must go along with her,[1] but I excusing myself
upon occasion of a present despatch which I was
to make unto his Majesty, the Duchess of Antador,[2]
who followed her, came to me, and said I must
not refuse her : whereupon, leading her by her
arms, according to the manner of that country,
the Princess of Conti, offended that I had denied
her that civility which I had yielded to another,
took me off, after she had demanded the consent
of the Duchess : but the Queen then also staying,
I left the Princess, and, with all due humility, went
to the Queen, and led her by the arms, walking
thus to a place in the garden where some orange
trees grew, and here discoursing with her Majesty
bareheaded, some small shot fell on both our
heads. The occasion whereof was this : the King
being in the garden, and shooting at a bird in the
air, which he did with much perfection, the descent

---

[1] See p. 107, *supra.*

[2] *i.e.*, the Duchess de Ventadour, sister of the young Duc
de Montmorency. See p. 90, *supra.*

of his shot fell just upon us : the Queen was much
startled herewith, when I, coming nearer to her,
demanded whether she had received any harm :
to which she answering no, and therewith taking
two or three small pellets from her hair, it was
thought fit to send a gardener to the King, to tell
him that her Majesty was there, and that he should
shoot no more that way, which was no sooner
heard among the nobles that attended him, but
many of them leaving him, came to the Queen and
ladies, among whom was Monsieur le Grand,[1] who,
finding the Queen still discoursing with me, stole
behind her, and letting fall gently some comfits
he had in his pocket upon the Queen's hair, gave
her occasion to apprehend that some shot had
fallen on her again : turning hereupon to Monsieur
le Grand, I said that I marvelled that so old a
courtier as he was could find no means to entertain
ladies but by making them afraid ; but the Queen
shortly after returning to her lodging, I took my
leave of her, and came home.   All which passage

---

[1] This was the popular name of Roger de Saint Lary et de
Termes Duc de Bellegarde (1563–1646), grand écuyer under
Henry III., Governor of Bourgogne under Henri IV., and
created a duke and peer of France by Louis XIII. in 1620.
He is best known by his ambitious amours.   Henri IV.
exiled him as the lover of Gabrielle d'Estrées, and later
Richelieu banished him from court as the lover of Anne of
Austria.

I have thought fit to set down, the accident above-mentioned being so strange, that it can hardly be paralleled.

It fell out one day that the Prince of Condè coming to my house, some speech happened concerning the King my master, in whom, though he acknowledged much learning, knowledge, clemency, and divers other virtues, yet he said he had heard that the King was much given to cursing; I answered that it was out of his gentleness; but the Prince demanding how cursing could be a gentleness, I replied, "Yes, for though he could punish men himself, yet he left them to God to punish:" which defence of the King my master was afterwards much celebrated in the French court.

Monsieur de Luynes [1] continuing still the King's favourite, advised him to war against his subjects of the reformed religion in France, saying, he would neither be a great prince as long as he suffered so puissant a party to remain within his dominions, nor could justly style himself the most Christian king, as long as he permitted such heretics to be in that great number they were, or to hold those strong places which by public edict were assigned to them : and therefore that he

---

[1] See *supra*, p. 193, and extracts from Lord Herbert's correspondence, 1619–21, in Appendix VII.

should extirpate them as the Spaniards had done
the Moors, who are all banished into other countries, as we may find in their histories.   This
counsel, though approved by the young King, was
yet disliked by other grave and wise persons
about him,   and particularly by the Chancellor
Sillery, and the President Jannin,[1] who thought,
better to have a peace which had two religions,
than a war that had none.   Howbeit, the design
of Luynes was applauded, not only by the Jesuit
party in France, but by some princes, and other
martial persons,[2] insomuch that the Duke of

---

[1] Peter Jeannin, usually called President Jeannin, was one
of the most high-minded counsellors that Louis XIII. had
about him.   He brought the finances into something like
order, but a lack of firmness prevented him giving full
effect to his reforms.   His valuable political treatise, " Negotiations " (Paris, 1656), was highly valued by Richelieu.
Herbert announces the death of the good President Jannin
to Viscount Doncaster, 23d March 1622–3.   Lord Herbert's
statement that Luynes pressed the King into a war with the
Protestants is not confirmed by his own despatch to Secretary Naunton (dated 20th February 1620–1), in which he
states that the arbitrament of the sword was first suggested
by Louis XIII. himself.

[2] The Protestants of Béarn had resisted the decree re-estab-
lishing the Catholic religion in their province, issued in 1617.
In 1621 Lewis XIII. entered the province with an army to
enforce the edict.   An assembly of Protestants at Rochelle
declared themselves independent of the crown, raised troops,
and intrusted the command to the Duc de Rohan.   The

Guise [1] coming to see me one day, said, that they should never be happy in France, until those of the religion were rooted out : I answered, that I wondered to hear him say so : and the Duke demanding why, I replied, that whensoever those of the religion were put down, the turn of the great persons, and governors of provinces of that kingdom, would be next : ˙ and that, though the present King were a good prince, yet that their successors may be otherwise, and that men did not know how soon princes might prove tyrants, when they had nothing to fear : which speech of mine was fatal, since those of the religion were no sooner reduced into that weak condition in which now they are, but the governors of provinces were

---

royal troops under Louis and Constable De Luynes made an unsuccessful attack on Montauban, and the Constable marched on Monheurt, where he died of a fever. The war continued till October 1622, when a peace was made between the combatants, practically renewing the Edict of Nantes in favour of the Protestants.

[1] Charles, fourth Duc de Guise (1571–1640), son of the Duc de Guise assassinated at Blois, held office under Henri IV., although at one time the League had put him forward as a rival claimant to the crown of France. He fought against the Rochelle Protestants in 1622, but as a supporter of Marie de Médicis, Richelieu expelled him from France, and about 1631 he settled in Florence. Tallemant des Réaux describes him as a very amiable man, but an inveterate liar.

brought lower, and curbed much in their power
and authority, and the Duke of Guise first of them
all : so that I doubt not but my words were well
remembered. Howsoever, the war now went on
with much fervour : neither could I dissuade it,
although using, according to the instructions I had
from the King my master, many arguments for
that purpose. I was told often, that if the reformation in France had been like that in England,
where, they observed, we retained the hierarchy,
together with decent rites and ceremonies in the
church, as also holidays in the memory of saints,
music in churches, and divers other testimonies,
both of glorifying God, and giving honour and
reward to learning, they could much better have
tolerated it ; but such a rash and violent reformation as theirs was, ought by no means to be
approved ; whereunto I answered, that, though the
causes of departing from the Church of Rome were
taught and delivered by many sober and modest
persons, yet that the reformation in great part was
acted by the common people, whereas ours began
at the prince of state, and therefore was more
moderate : which reason I found did not displease
them. I added further then, that the reformed
religion in France would easily enough admit an
hierarchy, if they had sufficient means among them
to maintain it, and that if their churches were as
fair as those which the Roman Catholics had, they

would use the more decent sorts of rites and ceremonies, and together like well of organs and choirs
of singers, rather than make a breach or schism on
that occasion. As for holidays, I doubted not but
the principal persons and ministers of their religion
would approve it much better than the common
people, who, being labourers, and artisans for the
most part, had the advantages for many more days
than the Roman Catholics for getting their living :
howsoever, that those of the religion had been
good cautions to make the Roman Catholic priests,
if not better, yet at least more wary in their lives
and actions : it being evident that since the
reformation began among those of the religion, the
Roman Catholics had divers ways reformed themselves, and abated not only much of their power
they usurped over laics, but were more pious and
continent than formerly. Lastly, that those of the
religion acknowledged solely the King's authority
in government of all affairs : whereas the other side
held the regal power, not only inferior in divers
points, but subordinate to the papal. Nothing
of which yet served to divert Monsieur de Luynes,
or the King, from their resolutions.

The King having now assembled an army, and
made some progress against those of the religion,
I had instruction sent me from the King my master
to mediate a peace, and if I could not prevail
therein, to use some such words as may both argue

his Majesty's care of them of the religion, and
together, to let the French King know that he
would not permit their total ruin and extirpation.
The King was now going to lay siege to St. Jean
d'Angely, when myself was newly recovered of
a fever at Paris, in which, besides the help of many
able physicians, I had the comfort of divers visits
from many principal grandees of France, and particularly the Princess of Conti, who would sit by
my bedside two or three hours, and with cheerful
discourse entertain me, though yet I was brought
so low, that I could scarce return anything by way
of answer but thanks. The command yet which
I received from the King my master quickened me,
insomuch that, by slow degrees I went into my
coach, together with my train, towards St. Jean
d'Angely. Being arrived within a small distance
of that place, I found by divers circumstances,
that the effect of my negotiation had been discovered from England, and that I was not welcome
thither; howbeit, having obtained an audience from
the King, I exposed what I had in charge to say
to him, to which yet I received no other answer
but that I should go to Monsieur de Luynes, by
whom I should know his Majesty's intention.
Repairing thus to him, I did find outwardly good
reception, though yet I did not know how cunningly
he proceeded to betray and frustrate my endeavours
for those of the religion ; for, hiding a gentleman,

called Monsieur Arnaud,[1] behind the hangings in
his chamber, who was then of the religion, but had
promised a revolt to the King's side, this gentleman, as he himself confessed afterwards to the Earl
of Carlisle, had in charge to relate unto those of
the religion, how little help they might expect from
me, when he should tell them the answers which
Monsieur de Luynes made me.   Sitting thus in
a chair before Monsieur de Luynes, he demanded
the effect of my business ; I answered, that the
King my master commanded me to mediate a peace
betwixt his Majesty and his subjects of the religion,
and that I desired to do it in all those fair and
equal terms, which might stand with the honour
of France, and the good intelligence betwixt the
two kingdoms : to which he returned this rude
answer only, " What hath the King your master to
do with our actions ? why doth he meddle with our
affairs ? "   My reply was, that the King my master
ought not to give an account of the reason which
induced him hereunto, and for me it was enough
to obey him; howbeit, if he did ask me in more
gentle terms, I should do the best I could to give
him satisfaction ; to which, though he answered
no more than the word *bien*, or well, I, pursuing

---

[1] He was son of Anthoine de la Mothe-Arnauld, and
although his father was a Protestant, there is no evidence to
support Lord Herbert's statement that he himself was one.

my instruction, said that the King my master, according to the mutual stipulation betwixt Henry the Fourth and himself, that the survivor of either of them should procure the tranquillity and peace of the other's estate, had sent this message; and that he had not only testified this his pious inclination heretofore, in the late civil wars of France, but was desirous on this occasion also to show how much he stood affected to the good of the kingdom; besides, he hoped that when peace was established here, that the French King might be the more easily disposed to assist the Palatine, who was an ancient friend and ally of the French crown. His reply to this was, "We will have none of your advices:" whereupon I said, that I took those words for an answer, and was sorry only that they did not understand sufficiently the affection and good will of the King my master; and since they rejected it upon those terms, I had in charge to tell him, that we knew very well what we had to do. Luynes seeming offended herewith, said, "*Nous ne vous craignons pas*," or, "We are not afraid of you." I replied hereupon, that if you had said you had not loved us, I should have believed you, but should have returned you another answer; in the meanwhile, that I had no more to say than what I told him formerly, which was, that we knew what we had to do. This, though somewhat less than was in my instructions, so angered him, that in much passion he said, *Par Dieu, si vous n'êties Monsieur l'Ambassadeur, je vous traitterois d'un' autre sorte*—" By God, if you were not Monsieur Ambassador, I would use you after another fashion." My answer was, that as I was an ambassador, so I was also a gentleman; and therewithal, laying my hand upon the hilt of my sword, told him, there was that which should make him an answer, and so arose from my chair; to which Monsieur de Luynes made no reply, but, arising likewise from his chair, offered civilly to accompany me to the door; but I telling him there was no occasion for him to use ceremony, after so rude an entertainment, I departed from him. From thence returning to my lodging, I spent three or four days afterwards in seeing the manner of the French discipline, in making approaches to towns; at what time I remember, that going in my coach within reach of cannon, those in the town imagining me to be an enemy, made many shots against me, which so affrighted my coachman, that he durst drive no farther; whereupon alighting, I bid him put the horses out of danger; and notwithstanding many more shots made against me, went on foot to the trenches, where one Seaton, a Scotchman, conducting me, showed me their works, in which I found little differing from the Low Country manner. Having satisfied myself in this manner, I thought fit to take my leave of the King, being

at Cognac, the city of St. Jean d'Angely being now
surrendered unto him. Coming thus to a village
not far from Cognac, about ten of the clock at
night, I found all the lodgings possessed by
soldiers; so that alighting in the market-place, I
sent my servants to the inns to get some provision,
who bringing me only six rye loaves, which I was
doubtful whether I should bestow on myself and
company, or on my horses, Monsieur de Ponts,
a French nobleman of the religion, attended with
a brave train, hearing of my being there, offered
me lodging in his castle near adjoining: I told him
it was a great courtesy at that time, yet I could
not with my honour accept it, since I knew it
would endanger him, my business to those parts
being in favour of those of the religion, and the
chief ministers of state in France being jealous of
my holding intelligence with him; howbeit, if he
would procure me lodging in the town, I should
take it kindly; whereupon, sending his servants
round about the town, he found at last, in the
house of one of his tenants, a chamber, to which,
when he had conducted me, and together gotten
some little accommodation for myself and horses,
I desired him to depart to his lodgings, he being
then in a place which his enemies, the King's
soldiers, had possessed. All which was not so
silently carried, but that the said nobleman was
accused afterwards at the French court, upon sus-

picion of holding correspondence with me, whereof
it was my fortune to clear him.

Coming next day to Cognac, the Mareschal de
St. Geran,[1] my noble friend, privately met me,
and said I was not in a place of surety there, as
having offended Monsieur de Luynes, who was
the King's favourite, desiring me withal to advise
what I had to do : I told him I was in a place of
surety wheresoever I had my sword by my side,
and that I intended to demand audience of the
King ; which also being obtained, I found not so
cold a reception as I thought to meet with, insomuch that I parted with his Majesty, to all outward
appearance, in very good terms.

From hence returning to Paris shortly after, I
found myself welcome to all those ministers of
state there, and noblemen, who either envied the
greatness, or loved not thé insolencies of Monsieur
de Luynes ; by whom also I was told, that the
said Luynes had intended to send a brother of his
into England with an embassy, the effect whereof
should be chiefly to complain against me, and to
obtain that I should be repealed ;[2] and that he

---

[1] Jean François de la Guiche, Comte de la Palisse and
Mareschal de Saint Geran.   He died in 1632.

[2] Lord Herbert is not quite accurate here.   Luynes' brother
was the Marquis de Cadenet.   He had already visited England in January 1621, some months before Lord Herbert's
quarrel with Luynes had assumed its final form ; he had

P

intended to relate the passages betwixt us at St. Jean d'Angely in a much different manner from that I reported, and that he would charge me with giving the first offence. After thanks for this advertisement, I told them my relation of the business betwixt us, in the manner I delivered, was true, and that I would justify it with my sword; at which they being nothing scandalised, wished me good fortune.[1]

The ambassador into England following shortly after, with a huge train,[2] in a sumptuous manner, and an accusation framed against me, I was sent

---

soon afterwards returned to France, and did not repeat his visit to the English court. He endeavoured in vain to secure an English alliance with France, mainly in anticipation of the rising of the French Protestants. His insolent temper led him into some very curious quarrels, not only with the English courtiers, but with the permanent French ambassador in London, Comte de Tilliers. See Gardiner's Hist., iii. 389.

[1] Howell thus mentions the author's recall : " Sir Edward Herbert is returned, having had some clashings and counter-buffs with the favourite Luynes, wherein he comported himself gallantly." Familiar Letters, Book i. sect. 3, letter v. Chamberlain writes to Carleton under date 14th July 1621 : "Sir Edward Herbert is recalled thence for challenging Luynes the favourite, and Sir Edward Sackville is to succeed him." As a matter of fact, James Hay, Viscount Doncaster and Earl of Carlisle, temporarily took Herbert's place in Paris.

[2] Sieur Dumoulin came to England to make complaint against Lord Herbert in the summer of 1621. See Rémusat's La Vie de Lord Herbert, p. 83.

for home, of which I was glad, my payment being
so ill, that I was run far into debt with my
merchants, who had assisted me now with £3000 or
£4000 more than I was able at the present to
discharge. Coming thus to court, the Duke of
Buckingham, who was then my noble friend,
informed me at large of the objections represented
by the French ambassador; to which when I had
made my defence in the manner above related, I
added, that I was ready to make good all that I
had said with my sword; [1] and shortly after, I
did, in the presence of his Majesty and the Duke

---

[1] The French ambassador in London, Comte de Tilliers,
sent to M. de Puisieux, the French King's secretary of state,
a despatch respecting this interview between Lord Herbert
and James I. This despatch, which M. de Rémusat has
printed in his " Lord Herbert de Cherbury," p. 85, is dated
28th September 1621. It runs as follows :—

De ce propos je suis entré en celui de M. Herbert, disant que
j'avois entendu comme S. M. l'avait reçu avec toutes sortes de faveurs
et de courtoisies, et que même il se promettait de retourner en France,
que cela était bien contraire aux discours qu'il m'avait tenus en ma
dernière audience et aux demonstrations, de colère qu'il avait
temoignées contre le sieur Herbert, et même au désaveu qu'il avait
fait des inconsidérées paroles qu'il avait dites à S. M. et à M. le
connétable [*i.e.* Luynes], ce que j'avois fait savoir par delà. Sur
quoi il m'a repliqué qu' étant roi il devoit retenir une oreille pour la
justification comme pour ouïr les plaintes : ce que j'avois ecrit en
France était vrai, mais que ce qu'il avait dit, ç'avait été sur le fonde-
ment que tout ce que j'avois proposé contre M. Herbert était vrai :
mais que depuis, s'en étant voulu éclaircir, il avait trouvé que les
choses n'allaient pas comme l'on m'en avait instruit.

of Buckingham, humbly desire leave to send a
trumpet to Monsieur de Luynes, to offer him the
combat, upon terms that past betwixt us ; which
was not permitted, otherwise than that they would
take my offer into consideration. Howsoever,
notice being publicly taken of this my desire, much
occasion of speech was given, every man that heard
thereof much favouring me ; but the Duke of
Luynes death following shortly after,[1] the business
betwixt us was ended, and I commanded to return
to my former charge in France. I did not yet
presently go, as finding much difficulty to obtain
the moneys due to me from the Exchequer, and
therewith, as also by my own revenues, to satisfy
my creditors in France. The Earl of Carlisle[2]
this while being employed Extraordinary Ambassador to France, brought home a confirmation of
the passages betwixt Monsieur de Luynes and myself; Monsieur de Arnaud, who stood behind the
hangings, as above related, having verified all I

---

[1] 21st December 1621, at Monheurt, of a fever contracted
while he was leading an attack on the Protestants of Bearn.

[2] James Hay, James I.'s first favourite at the English court,
Viscount Doncaster and Earl of Carlisle (13th September
1622), Knight of the Garter and Master of the Great Ward-
robe. He had lived in France in his youth, and had been
ambassador there in 1616. He died 25th April 1636. Tillieres
specially requested James I. to send him to replace Herbert.
Rémusat, p. 86.

said, insomuch that the King my master was well satisfied of my truth.

Having by this time cleared all my debts, when demanding new instructions from the King my master, the Earl of Carlisle brought me this message, that his Majesty had that experience of my abilities and fidelity, that he would give me no instructions, but leave all things to my discretion, as knowing I would proceed with that circumspection, as I should be better able to discern, upon emergent occasions, what was fit to be done, than that I should need to attend directions from hence, which besides that they would be slow, might perchance be not so proper, or correspondent to the conjuncture of the great affairs then in agitation, both in France and Germany, and other parts of Christendom, and that these things, therefore, must be left to my vigilance, prudence, and fidelity. Whereupon I told his Lordship, that I took this as a singular expression of the trust his Majesty reposed in me; howbeit, that I desired his Lordship to pardon me, if I said I had herein only received a greater power and latitude to err, and that I durst not trust my judgment so far as that I would presume to answer for all events, in such factious and turbulent times, and therefore again did humbly desire new instructions, which I promised punctually to follow. The Earl of Carlisle returning hereupon to the King, brought me yet no other answer back than that I formerly mentioned, and that his Majesty did so much confide in me, that he would limit me with no other instructions, but refer all to my discretion, promising together, that if matters proceeded not as well as might be wished, he would attribute the default to anything rather than to my not performing my duty.

Finding his Majesty thus resolved, I humbly took leave of him and my friends at court, and went to Monsieur Savage;[1] when demanding of him new letters of credit, his answer was, he could not furnish me as he had before, there being no limited sum expressed there, but that I should have as much as I needed; to which, though I answered that I had paid all, yet, as Monsieur Savage replied, that I had not paid it at the time agreed on, he said he could furnish me with a letter only for three thousand pounds, and nevertheless, that he was confident I should have more if I required it, which I found true, for I took up afterwards upon my credit there as much more, as made in the whole five or six thousand pounds.

Coming thus to Paris, I found myself welcomed by all the principal persons, nobody that I found there being either offended with the passages

---

[1] Locke writes to Carleton that Herbert was returning to Paris on 22d February 1621–22 (Cal. State Papers).

betwixt me and Monsieur de Luynes, or that were sorry for his death, in which number the Queen's Majesty seemed the most eminent person, as one who long since had hated him : whereupon also, I cannot but remember this passage, that in an audience I had one day from the Queen, I demanded of her how far she would have assisted me with her good offices against Luynes ? She replied, that what cause soever she might have to hate him, either by reason or by force, they would have made her to be of his side ; to which I answered in Spanish, *No ay feurce por las a reynas*—" There is no force for queens," at which she smiled.

And now I began to proceed in all public affairs according to the liberty with which my master was pleased to honour me, confining myself to no rules but those of my own discretion.   My negotiations in the meanwhile proving so successful, that during the remainder of my stay there, his Majesty received much satisfaction concerning my carriage, as finding I had preserved his honour and interest in all great affairs then emergent in France, Germany, and other parts of Christendom ; which work being of great concernment, I found the easier, that his Majesty's ambassadors and agents everywhere gave me perfect intelligence of all that happened within their precincts ; insomuch, that from Sir Henry Wotton, his Majesty's ambassador at Venice, who was a learned and witty gentleman, I received all

the news of Italy ; as also from Sir Isaac Wake,[1]
who did more particularly acquaint me with the
business of Savoy, Valentina,[2] and Switzerland ;
from Sir Francis Nethersole,[3] his Majesty's agent
in Germany, and more particularly with the united
princes there, on the behalf of his son-in-law, the
Palatine, or King of Bohemia, I received all the news
of Germany; from Sir Dudley Carleton, his Majesty's
ambassador in the Low Countries, I received intelligence concerning all the affairs of that state ;
and from Mr. William Trumbull, his Majesty's
agent at Brussels, all the affairs on that side ;[4] and
lastly, from Sir Walter Aston, his Majesty's

---

[1] A Fellow of Merton College, Oxford (1598), and Orator of
the University (1604). He was at one time Sir Dudley Carleton's secretary ; in April 1619 made ambassador-extraordinary
in Savoy and Piedmont, and ordinary ambassador in Switzerland and Italy. He was an accomplished scholar. A manuscript history by him of the Duchies of Montreux and
Montferrat is in the Bodleian. He died in July 1632.

[2] The Valteline.

[3] He was succeeded by George Herbert in the public
oratorship of Cambridge, 18th January 1619–20, and was
one of the most chivalrous supporters of the Princess Elizabeth of the Palatinate. He repeatedly urged on James I.
the necessity of interfering in the German war on her behalf.

[4] In 1620 he was directed to protest and prevent, as far
as he was able, the invasion of the Palatinate ; but he met
with little success in these negotiations, and was recalled in
1625.

ambassador in Spain,[1] and after him, from the Earl of Bristol[2] and Lord Cottington,[3] I had intelligence from the Spanish court: out of all whose relations being compared together, I found matter enough to direct my judgment in all public proceedings; besides, in Paris, I had the chief intelligence which came to either Monsieur de Langherac, the Low Country ambassador, or Monsieur Postek, agent for the united princes in Germany, and Signior Contarini, ambassador for Venice, and Signior Guiscardi my particular friend, agent for Mantua, and Monsieur Gueretin, agent for the Palatine, or King of Bohemia,[4] and Monsieur Villers, for the Swiss, and Monsieur Ainorant, agent for Geneva, by whose means, upon the resultance of the several advertisements given me, I found what I had to do.

---

[1] From 1620–1625; but the marriage negotiations were entrusted to John Digby, Earl of Bristol, in 1622–3. He was created Lord Aston in the Scottish peerage in 1627; served in Spain again in 1638-9, and died 13th August 1639.

[2] John Digby, afterwards Earl of Bristol, was thrice appointed ambassador in Spain for brief periods between 1611 and 1624. He finally left the Spanish court in January 1623-4, after the marriage negotiation had come to grief. Cottington was often agent at Madrid in Digby's absence. See below.

[3] See p. 238, note 1.

[4] *i.e.*, Frederick the Elector-Palatine.

The wars in Germany were now hot, when several French gentlemen came to me for recom-, mendations to the Queen of Bohemia, whose service they desired to advance, which also I performed as effectually as I could :[1] howbeit, as after the battle of Prague, the Imperial side seemed wholly to prevail, these gentlemen had not the satisfaction expected.[2] About this time, the Duke de Crouy, employed from Brussels to the French court, coming to see me, said, by way of rhodomontade, as though he would not speak of our isles, yet he saw all the rest of the world must bow under the Spaniard ; to which I answered, God be thanked they are not yet come to that pass, or when they were, they have this yet to comfort them, that at worst they should be but the same which you are now ; which speech of mine, being afterwards, I know not how, divulged, was much applauded by the French, as believing I intended that other countries should be put under the same severe government to which the Duke of Crouy, and those within the Spanish dominions, were subject.

---

[1] Several letters concerning offers of aid made to Herbert in behalf of the Elector Palatine are in the letter-book described below.   Brit. Mus. MS. Addit. 7082.

[2] By the battle of Prague (7th November 1619), the Elector-Palatine and his wife were absolutely ruined.   A vivid account of their situation is given in their letters to James I., printed in Ellis's Letters, first scr. iii. 110-4.

It happened one day that the agent from Brussels, and ambassador from the Low Countries, came to see me, immediately one after the other, to whom I said familiarly, that I thought that the inhabitants of the parts of the seventeen provinces, which were under the Spaniards, might be compared to horses in a stable, which, as they were finely curried, dressed, and fed, so they were well ridden also, spurred, and galled; and that I thought the Low Country men were like to horses at grass, which, though they wanted so good keeping as the other had, yet might leap, kick, and fling, as much as they would; which freedom of mine displeased neither : or, if the Low Country ambassador did think I had spoken a little too sharply, I pleased him afterwards, when, continuing my discourse, I told him that the states of the United Provinces had within a narrow room shut up so much warlike provision both by sea and land, and together demonstrated such courage upon all occasions, that it seemed they had more need of enemies than of friends, which compliment I found did please him.

About this time, the French being jealous that the King my master would match the Prince, his son, with the king of Spain's sister, and together relinquish his alliance with France, myself, who did endeavour nothing more than to hold all good intelligence betwixt the two crowns, had enough to

do.[1]   The Count de Gondomar [2] passing now from
Spain into England, came to see me at Paris,
about ten of the clock in the morning, when, after
some compliments, he told me that he was to go
towards England the next morning, and that he
desired my coach to accompany him out of town ;
I told him, after a free and merry manner, he
should not have my coach, and that if he demanded
it, it was not because he needed coaches, the
Pope's nuntio, the Emperor's ambassador, the Duke
of Bavaria's agent, and others, having coaches

---

[1] Lord Herbert had from the first encouraged the French
court in its hopes of a marriage between Henrietta Maria
and Prince Charles, and viewed with little favour, it would
appear, the Spanish proposal of marriage. On 14th August
1620 he had written to James I. that the French marriage
would be highly acceptable to the French nation and that
the religious difficulties could be readily surmounted.

[2] Diego Sarmiento de Acuna, Count de Gondomar, was
Spanish ambassador in England from 1613 to 1618. He
arrived in England again about 1619–20, and Herbert must
have met him at Paris while on the journey. He was the
chief negotiator of the Spanish marriage treaty, and left
England in 1622 to complete it at the Spanish court. He
never returned to this country, and died in 1625 at Bommel
in Flanders. Although loathed by the London populace,
his gaiety made him popular at court. He told a merry
tale, read Shakespeare's plays, bought a first folio, and
liked English wines. (See Howell's Letters, 1630, p. 111.)
Middleton's "Game at Chesse," 1624, is a scathing satire
upon him. (See Middleton's Works, ed. A. H. Bullen,
vol. vii.) His portrait by Mytens is at Hampton Court.

enough to furnish him, but because he would put a jealousy betwixt me and the French, as if I inclined more to the Spanish side than to their's. Gondomar then looking merrily upon me, said, I will dine with you yet; I told him, by his good favour, he should not dine with me at that time, and that when I would entertain the ambassador of so great a King as his, it should not be upon my ordinary, but that I would make him a feast worthy of so great a person; howbeit, that he might see after what manner I lived, I desired some of my gentlemen to bring his gentlemen into the kitchen, where, after my usual manner, were three spits full of meat, divers pots of boiled meat, and an oven, with store of pies in it, and a dresser board, covered with all manner of good fowl, and some tarts, pans with tarts in them after the French manner; after which, being conducted to another room, they were showed a dozen or sixteen dishes of sweetmeats, all which was but the ordinary allowance for my table. The Spaniards returning now to Gondomar told him what good cheer they found, notwithstanding which, I told Gondomar again that I desired to be excused if I thought this dinner unworthy of him, and that when occasion were, I should entertain him after a much better manner. Gondomar hereupon coming near me, said, he esteemed me much, and that he meant only to put a trick upon me, which he found I had

discovered, and that he thought that an Englishman had not known how to avoid handsomely a
trick put upon him under show of civility; and
that I ever should find him my friend, and would
do me all the good offices he could in England,
which also he really performed, as the Duke of
Lennox and the Earl of Pembroke confirmed to
me; Gondomar saying to them, that I was a man fit
for employment, and that he thought Englishmen,
though otherwise able persons, knew not how to
make a denial handsomely, which yet I had done.

This Gondomar being an able person, and dexterous in his negotiations, had so prevailed with
King James, that his Majesty resolved to pursue
his treaty with Spain, and for that purpose, to
send his son Prince Charles in person to conclude
the match, when, after some debate whether he
should go in a public or private manner, it was at
last resolved, that he, attended with the Marquis
of Buckingham, and Sir Francis Cottington, his
secretary,[1] and Endymion Porter,[2] and Mr. Grimes,

---

[1] He came from Madrid, where he had acted as English
agent, to be Charles's secretary, in 1622. He was created a
baronet on 16th February 1623; became Lord Cottington soon
after, being accredited ambassador to Spain in 1631. After
fighting for Charles I., he went into exile with Charles II., and
died at Valladolid in 1653, when the peerage became extinct.

[2] An intimate friend of Charles I. and Buckingham, he
was frequently engaged in diplomatic negotiations with

gentleman of the horse to the Marquis, should pass in a disguised and private manner through France to Madrid ; these five passing, though not without some difficulty, from Dover to Boulogne, where taking post horses, they came to Paris, and lodged at an inn in Rue St. Jacques, where it was advised amongst them whether they should send for me to attend them ; after some dispute, it was concluded in the negative, since, as one there objected, if I came alone in the quality of a private person, I must go on foot through the streets ; and because I was a person generally known, might be followed by some one or other, who would discover whither my private visit tended, besides, that those in the inn must needs take notice of my coming in that manner ; on the other side, if I came publicly with my usual train, the gentlemen with me must needs take notice of the Prince and Marquis of Bucking-ham, and consequently might divulge it, which was thought not to stand with the Prince's safety, who endeavoured to keep his journey as secret as pos-sible ; howbeit, the Prince spent the day following his arrival in seeing the French court, and city of Paris, without that anybody did know his person, but a maid that had sold linen heretofore in Lon-

Spain ; but he is best known as a prominent leader of court society under Charles I., and a patron of literature, in which he occasionally dabbled himself.

don, who seeing him pass by, said, certainly this is the Prince of Wales, but withal suffered him to hold his way, and presumed not to follow him : the next day after, they took post horses, and held their way towards Bayonne, a city frontier to Spain.[1]

The first notice that came to me was by one Andrews, a Scotchman, who, coming late the night preceding their departure, demanded whether I had seen the Prince ? when I demanding what Prince ? "for," said I, "the Prince of Conde is yet in Italy ; " he told me the Prince of Wales, which yet I could not believe easily, until with many oaths he affirmed the Prince was in France, and that he had charge to follow his Highness, desiring me in the meanwhile, on the part of the King my master, to serve his passage the best I could. This made me rise very early the next morning, and go to Monsieur Puisieux, Principal Secretary of State, to demand present audience ; Puisieux hereupon entreated me to stay an hour, since he was in bed, and had some earnest business to despatch for the King his master, as soon as he was ready ; I returned answer, that I could not stay a minute, and

---

[1] The best account of this adventurous journey, which took place in February 1622-3, is given by Sir Henry Wotton, in his "Short View of the Life and Death of the Duke of Buckingham," 1642.

that I desired I might come to his bedside; this
made Puisieux rise and put on his gown only, and
so came to the chamber, where I attended him.
His first words to me were, "I know your business
as well as you; your Prince is departed this morning post to Spain;" adding further, that I could
demand nothing for the security of his passage, but
it should be presently granted, concluding with
these very words; *Vous serez servi au point nommè*,
or, "You shall be served in any particular you can
name." I told him that his free offer had prevented
the request I intended to make, and that because
he was so principal a minister of state, I doubted
not but what he had so nobly promised, he would
see punctually performed; as for the security of
his passage, that I did not see what I could demand
more, than that he would suffer him quietly to hold
his way, without sending after, or interrupting him.
He replied, that the Prince should not be interrupted, though yet he could do no less than send
to know what success the Prince had in his journey.
I was no sooner returned out of his chamber, but
I despatched a letter by post to the Prince, to desire
him to make all the haste he could out of France,
and not to treat with any of the religion in the
way, since his being at Paris was known, and that
though the French secretary had promised he
should not be interrupted, yet that they would send
after his Highness, and when he gave any occasion

Q

of suspicion, might perchance detain him. The
Prince, after some examination at Bayonne (which
the governor thereof did afterwards particularly
relate to me, confessing that he did not know who
the Prince was), held his way on to Madrid, where
he and all his company safely arrived. Many of
the nobility, and others of the English court, being
now desirous to see the Prince, did pass through
France to Spain, taking my house still in their
way,[1] by whom I acquainted his Highness in Spain
how much it grieved me that I had not seen his
Highness when he was in Paris, which occasioned
his Highness afterwards to write a letter to me,
wholly with his own hand, and subscribe his name,
your friend Charles, in which he did abundantly
satisfy all the unkindness I might conceive on this
occasion.

I shall not enter into a narration of the passages
occurring in the Spanish court, upon his Highness's
arrival thither, though they were well known to
me for the most part, by the information the
French Queen was pleased to give me, who, among

---

[1] Mr. Mead writes to Sir Martin Stucville (14th March
1622-3) that besides the Lords Carlisle and Mountjoy who
went to Paris to excuse to Louis XIII. the unceremonious
journey of the Prince of Wales through France, the Prince
and his company were followed to Madrid by the Lords
Andover, Vaughan, Kensington, and about two hundred persons more of nobles, knights, gentlemen, and others. Ellis's
Orig. Letters, 1st ser., iii. 131.

other things, told me that her sister [1] did wish well
unto the Prince.   I had from her also, intelligence
of certain messages sent from Spain to the Pope,
and the Pope's messages to them ; whereof, by
her permission, I did afterwards inform his Highness.   Many judgments were now made concerning the event which this treaty of marriage was
likely to have ; the Duke of Savoy said that the
prince's journey thither was, *Un tiro di quelli caval-
lieri antichi che andavano cosi per il mondo a diffare
li incanti* (that it was a trick of those ancient
knights errant, who went up and down the world
after that manner to undo enchantments) : for as
that Duke did believe that the Spaniard did intend
finally to bestow her on the Imperial house, he
conceived that he did only entertain the treaty
with England, because he might avert the King my
master from treating in any other place, and
particularly in France, howbeit, by the intelligence I received in Paris, which I am confident
was very good, I am assured the Spaniard meant
really at that time, though how the match was
broken, I list not here to relate, it being a more
perplexed and secret business than I am willing to
insert into the narration of my life. [2]

---

[1] Maria, wife of Philip IV. of Spain (see p. 194).

[2] Lord Herbert's report on French public opinion as to
the Prince's journey to and from Spain (dated 31st October
1623) is printed below.

New propositions being now made, and other counsels thereupon given, the Prince taking his leave of the Spanish court, came to St. Andrews in Spain, where, shipping himself, with his train, arrived safely at Portsmouth, about the beginning of October 1623; the news whereof being shortly brought into France, the Duke of Guise came to me, and said he found the Spaniards were not so able men as he thought, since they had neither married the Prince in their country, nor done any thing to break his match elsewhere; I answered, that the Prince was more dexterous than that any secret practice of theirs could be put upon him; and as for violence, I thought the Spaniards durst not offer it.

The war against those of the religion continuing in France,[1] Père Séguerend, confessor to the King, made a sermon before his Majesty upon the text, "That we should forgive our enemies," upon which argument, having said many good things, he at last distinguished forgiveness, and said, We were indeed to forgive our enemies, but not the enemies of God; such as were heretics, and particularly those of the religion; and that his

---

[1] It is curious that Lord Herbert avoids all mention of Richelieu, who succeeded to power early in 1624, and at once embarked on his policy of a forcible suppression of Protestantism.

Majesty, as the most Christian King, ought to extirpate them wheresoever they could be found. This particular being related to me, I thought fit to go to the Queen-mother without further ceremony, for she gave me leave to come to her chamber whensoever I would, without demanding audience, and to tell her, that though I did not usually intermeddle with matters handled within their pulpits, yet because Père Séguerend, who had the charge of the King's conscience, had spoken so violently against those of the religion, that his doctrine was not limited only to France, but might extend itself in its consequences beyond the seas, even to the dominions of the King my master; I could not but think it very unreasonable, and the rather, that as her Majesty well knew that a treaty of marriage betwixt our Prince and the Princess her daughter, was now begun, for which reason I could do no less than humbly desire that such doctrines as these henceforth might be silenced, by some discreet admonition, she might please to give to Père Séguerend, or others that might speak to this purpose. The Queen, though she seemed very willing to hear me, yet handled the business so, that Père Séguerend was together informed who had made this complaint against him, whereupon also he was so distempered, that by one Monsieur Gaellac, a Provençal, his own countryman, he sent me this message; that he knew well who had accused him to her Majesty, and that he was sensible thereof; that he wished me to be assured, that wheresoever I was in the world, he would hinder my fortune.   The answer I returned by Monsieur Gaellac was, That nothing in all France but a friar or a woman durst have sent me such a message.

Shortly after this, coming again to the Queen-mother, I told her, that what I said concerning Père Séguerend, was spoken with a good intention, and that my words were now discovered to him in that manner, that he sent me a very affronting message, adding, after a merry fashion, these words, that I thought Séguerend so malicious, that his malice was beyond the malice of women : the Queen, being a little startled hereat, said, *A moy femme, et parler ainsi ?*—" To me a woman, and say so ? "   I replied gently, *Je parle a vôtre majesté comme reyne, et non pas comme femme*—" I speak to your Majesty as a queen, and not as a woman," and so took my leave of her.   What Père Séguerend did afterwards, in way of performing his threat, I know not; but sure I am, that had I been ambitious of worldly greatness, I might have often remembered his words, though, as I ever loved my book, and a private life, more than any busy preferments, I did frustrate and render vain his greatest power to hurt me.

My book, *De veritate prout distinguitur à revelatione verisimili, possibili, et à falso,* having been

begun by me in England, and formed there in all
its principal parts, was about this time finished;
all the spare hours which I could get from my
visits and negotiations, being employed to perfect
this work, which was no sooner done, but that I
communicated it to Hugo Grotius, that great
scholar, who, having escaped his prison in the
Low Countries, came into France,[1] and was much
welcomed by me and Monsieur Tielenus[2] also, one
of the greatest scholars of his time, who, after
they had perused it, and given it more commendations than is fit for me to repeat, exhorted me
earnestly to print and publish it; howbeit, as the
frame of my whole book was so different from

---

[1] The great Dutch international lawyer and philosopher.
As a leader of the Arminian faction and friend of Grotius,
he was imprisoned in Holland in 1619. Lord Herbert welcomed him to Paris on his release from prison with the
lines :—

> Carcere dum carcer victus, Tenebrisque Tenebræ
> Vinclis cum demum vincla soluta tibi
> Prosiliens mediâ tandem de mole, videris
> Quidquid mortale est, deposuisse simul.

In the fine English play of Barnaveldt (1619), which Mr.
A. H. Bullen recently discovered and printed for the first
time in his "Old Plays," vol. ii., Grotius is one of the
characters. He had visited England in 1613.

[2] Born at Goldberg in Silesia, in 1563, he was for many years
Professor of Theology at Sedan. At the request of James I.
he visited England, but was there suspected of heresy. He

any thing which had been written heretofore, I found I must either renounce the authority of all that had written formerly concerning the method of finding out truth, and consequently insist upon my own way, or hazard myself to a general censure, concerning the whole argument of my book ; I must confess it did not a little animate me, that the two great persons above mentioned did so highly value it, yet as I knew it would meet with much opposition, I did consider whether it was not better for me a while to suppress it. Being thus doubtful in my chamber, one fair day in the summer, my casement being opened towards the south, the sun shining clear, and no wind stirring, I took my book, *De Veritate*, in my hand, and, kneeling on my knees, devoutly said these words :—

" O thou eternal God, Author of the light which now shines upon me, and Giver of all inward illuminations, I do beseech Thee, of Thy infinite

---

abandoned Calvinism for the doctrines of the Remonstrants. He was a voluminous theological writer, and the intimate friend of Grotius. He died at Paris in 1633. Among Lord Herbert's poems is one "in answer to Tilenus, when I had that fatal defluxion in my hand "—

> Quî possim Phoebum successum credere ? Laudes
> Quum facit ut scribas, Docte Tilene, meas.
> Providus atque morum consulto surripit istam
> Ut melius possem nunc superesse tuâ.

goodness, to pardon a greater request than a sinner ought to make ; I am not satisfied enough whether I shall publish this book, *De Veritate ;* if it be for Thy glory, I beseech Thee give me some sign from heaven ; if not, I shall suppress it."

I had no sooner spoken these words, but a loud though yet gentle noise came from the heavens, for it was like nothing on earth, which did so comfort and cheer me, that I took my petition as granted, and that I had the sign I demanded, whereupon also I resolved to print my book. This, how strange soever it may seem, I protest before the eternal God is true, neither am I any way superstitiously deceived herein, since I did not only clearly hear the noise, but in the serenest sky that ever I saw, being without all cloud, did to my thinking see the place from whence it came.[1]

And now I sent my book to be printed in Paris, at my own cost and charges,[2] without suffering it to be divulged to others than to such as I

---

[1] This testimony to a special divine revelation strangely contrasts with the advanced views that Lord Herbert elsewhere advocates respecting the subject of Revelation.   See Introduction.

[2] The first edition in Latin was published in 1624.   A second edition was issued in Paris in 1636.   A French translation appeared in Paris in 1639.   The first London edition is dated 1645 ; the second, 1659.

thought might be worthy readers of it; though afterwards reprinting it in England, I not only dispersed it among the prime scholars of Europe, but was sent to not only from the nearest but furthest parts of Christendom, to desire the sight of my book, for which they promised anything I should desire by way of return; but hereof more amply in its place.

The treaty of a match with France continuing still, it was thought fit for the concluding thereof, that the Earl of Carlisle and the Earl of Holland should be sent Extraordinary Ambassadors to France.[1]

---

[1] In May 1624, James Hay, Earl of Carlisle, and Henry Rich (created Lord Kensington in 1622, but not created Earl of Holland until 24th September 1624), arrived in Paris to negotiate the French marriage between Henrietta Maria and Prince Charles. Herbert returned to England on 24th July 1624, and "hopes," says Chamberlain, writing to Carleton, "to be Vice-chamberlain." Sir Albertus Morton succeeded him at Paris as ordinary ambassador. Herbert's letter of recall, dated 14th April 1624, is printed below.

A

CONTINUATION OF THE LIFE

OF

EDWARD, LORD HERBERT

OF CHERBURY,

FROM 1624 TO 1648.

——+——

In spite of his avowed indulgence in all the frivolous
pleasures of the French capital, Herbert served his
sovereign and his country faithfully during the five
years that he was English Ambassador at Louis
XIII.'s Court.[1] His correspondence bears ample
testimony to his self-denying industry. He set
himself to estimate the political and social forces
that dominated France during the period, and the
record of his observations proves for the most part
his energy and his discrimination.[2] And Herbert

---

[1] I give here a detailed statement of the facts of Herbert's later
life. More general comment is made in the Introduction.
[2] See Appendix vii.

had every reason to believe that his services were
highly valued at home. James I. was a punctilious
master, but in spite of an occasional misunderstanding, which was removed as soon as it was expressed,
James had treated his minister with real consideration. The curt letter of recall which reached Herbert
in April 1624 was the first sign that he had fallen into
disfavour. James I. had found it good (so the note
ran) to dismiss his Minister, and had directed the Earl
of Carlisle and Lord Kensington to take his place.[1]
The rest was silence, and Herbert subsequently
professed himself unable to discover the cause that
prompted the King to cast so marked a slur on his
reputation. But the clue is really not far to seek.

It was not to obtain a suitable partner in marriage
for his son Charles that James I. had made his
fruitless advances to Spain in 1623, and was about
to make similar advances to France in 1624. The
matrimonial alliance was a mere accident in the

---

[1] The letter, dated 14th April, ran thus :—"JAMES R.—Trustie
and well-beloved, we grete you well. We having upon further
deliberation found good to call you from that service you are now
in, we have signified so much by our letters to that King, which
we send you herewith to bee delivered unto him, for as we having
employed thither with our commission our right trustie and well-
beloved cousin and councellor the Earle of Carlisle, and our right
trustie and well-beloved the Lord Kensington, we doe require you to
present them to that King at their first audience, and so to take your
leave and return unto us with what convenient speed you may."—
Powysland Club Collection, vi. 420.

policy that he was in both cases pursuing. His
foremost anxiety was, without engaging England in
a Continental war, to protect his daughter Elizabeth
and her husband, the Elector-Palatine, from the
overwhelming onslaught of the Catholic princes of
Germany. James was a passionate lover of peace;
but if peace became impossible, he wished his battles
fought by anybody rather than himself. And
another sentiment now combined with his love of
peace-at-any-price to force him into a crooked
course of action. James I. knew well enough that a
straightforward war needed money, and that money
implied an appeal to Parliament and a discussion of
popular grievances. Such a prospect always alarmed
him, and it was mainly to avert its realisation
that he flung himself upon the barren hope of
transferring to the shoulders of another nation
his own responsibility in the German strife. He
believed it practicable to introduce into a marriage
treaty with a great Continental power (be it Spain
or France) a clause pledging his new ally to inter-
vene in behalf of his son-in-law, and of his son-
in-law's allies the Protestant princes of Germany.
When, therefore, Spain rejected the proposal, he
coolly handed it on to France.

Herbert, his representative in Paris, saw at once
the fatuity of the scheme, and he spoke out. Four
years before, it is true, he had hinted that a marriage of the Princess Henrietta with the Prince

of Wales might be acceptable to the French nation,
and that the religious obstacles were not insuper-
able.   The suggestion had then taken James I. by
surprise, and no one had paid much attention to it.
But the situation in 1624 differed materially from
that in 1620.   Then Herbert was instructed to do
all in his power to cement an alliance between the
two countries, which offered equal advantages to
each contracting party.   Now England looked for
a union in which her neighbour was to be saddled
with whatever sacrifice the connection involved.
French politicians, with all of whom Herbert was
living on terms of intimacy, had not watched the
tedious negotiation of Spain with England in the
previous year without realising this, and although
the proposals were unattractive, French *amour propre*
was not conciliated by the bestowal on France's
rival, Spain, of the first opportunity of rejecting
them.   When, therefore, directed to open the discussion of terms with the French King, Herbert
plainly told James that it would be necessary to
bring Louis to some real and infallible proofs of
his intention to aid in the recovery of the Elector-
Palatine's territory before placing the matrimonial
offer beyond recall, Herbert was not talking at
random ; he was merely interpreting one of many
important pieces of information which had just
reached him.   Louis XIII. was actually making
proffers of friendship to the Elector's worst enemy,

the Duke of Bavaria. But the English Ministers
failed to recognise the significance of this fact,
and Herbert resolved on his own account to give
the opening discussion the advantage of frankness.
He told the French statesmen that the negotiation
with Bavaria must provoke a breach with England.
The Frenchmen were annoyed by Herbert's freedom
of speech; they addressed a remonstrance to the
English sovereign; and James accepted the remonstrance in the spirit in which it was offered him.
He had no taste for plain dealing; he had always
placed his confidence in the most tortuous forms
of diplomacy. The conduct of his Minister was
as repugnant to him as to his enemies, and he dismissed him without delay.[1] Thus Herbert suffered
for doing no more than his duty—for showing a
little more resolution and fixity of principle than
was habitual either to him or to his contemporaries.
Did he cherish any ill-will against James, the final
result of the negotiation gave him ample satisfaction. Prince Charles and Princess Henrietta Maria
were duly married, but France stirred neither hand
nor foot to retrieve the cause of the Elector and the
Princess Elizabeth.

Herbert was nearing middle age when he had first
entered on a political career, but he had no wish to
retire from it at the early age of forty-two. He

---

[1] Gardiner's "History of England," v. 218.

would probably have lived a happier life had
it been otherwise. He had native capacity that
was fitted for higher purposes than contemporary
diplomacy, and his memory would deserve greater
honour had he yielded readily to the pressure of
circumstance, and forsworn politics when the in-
ducement to exert his abilities in their service was
first removed. But he never looked very far ahead.
He knew that at the moment the student's habits
were not wholly to his liking; he preferred to find
his recreation in literature and philosophy, and to
make the handling of affairs the real business of
life. Compromising imputations had been cast
upon his name by his sudden recall, and these
he was anxious to remove. His pecuniary resources
had been, moreover, severely taxed; he was deep
in debt to French merchants, who were importunate
for payment; much of his salary remained unpaid,
and he knew that, in spite of his numerous acquaintances at court, he needed the influence attaching to
official position to press his claims on the attention
of the Government. And there was certainly every
reason for him to believe that his ambition in this
direction would be gratified. Buckingham, the
Prince of Wales, and other men of influence were
his friends; from an early age he had been accustomed to receive marks of favour from the Crown
itself. On his return home in July 1624, he therefore confidently awaited the offer of further political

employment. But for six months he received only the vaguest promises. At length, on 30th December 1624, came a barren mark of royal approval, which gave its recipient very slender satisfaction. Herbert's wife had inherited the Irish estate of Castle-Island, Kerry, and in this fact James found a shadowy justification for creating Herbert, in reward of his five years' foreign service, my Lord of Castle-Island in the peerage of Ireland. Buckingham hinted that he might be able later to transform the peerage into an English honour, and on this assurance Herbert accepted it. With the cheap distinction went a grant of supporters to the ancient shield of his family, viz., "a lion arg. powdered with roses of England, and a lion az. powdered with fleurs-de-lis of France." * James I. gave Herbert no other reward.

The accession of Charles I. inspired Lord Castle-Island with new hope, and as soon as the King was firmly seated on the throne he addressed himself to him in fairly outspoken language. His letter ran as follows :—

"MAY IT PLEASE YOUR MOST EXCELLENT MAJESTIE,— Havinge given my most faithfull attendance to your Majesties father of blessed memorie from the beginninge of his reigne to the latter ende, and in all that time havinge neyther demanded suite nor had any, your Majestie will easily knowe how small advantage I made of his service ;

---

* Powysland Collection, v. 165.

R

yet, I must confesse, I was chosen Ambassador when I
least thought of it. But as I lived in a more chargeable
fashion than any before mee, and notwithstanding saved
his Majestie a 1000^{li} yearly wch others spent him, and
havinge withall done all marchant's busines freely, wch never
any other did in my place, I spent not only all the means
I had from his Majestie, together wth my owne annuall
rents, but somethinge above, so that still your Majestie
may be pleas'd to consider mee as a looser. But yf the
losse had beene only to my purse I could better have
endured it, but it was (though wthout my fault) in my name
and estimation too, for when after the reconciliage of the
distracted affections of this and that other people where I
served, I hoped in this later treaty of marriage to bee
admitted to the same honor wch was granted to Sr Thomas
Edmonds in the former, I was not only excluded, but
repeald, wch was the most publique disgrace that ever minister in my place did suffer ; neyther have I anything to
comfort mee, but your Majesties many gracious promises,
both in your blessed father's time and sithence, the effect
of wch I cannot doubt of, not only in regard of my many
services and suffrings, but that no man in the memory of
man ever return'd from the charge I had in that cuntrey
that had not some place of honor and preferment given
him. In the meane while I shall crave leave to present
these my most humble suites : 1. That whereas his late
Majestie made mee a Baron in Ireland, as in the way
of beinge made a Baron of Englande (wch my L. Duke
of Buckingham I assure myself well remembers), your
Majestie would be gratiously pleas'd to make good that
promise. 2. Whereas all his late Majesties Ambassadors
in France have at their returne beene sworne of the Privy
Counseile, your good Majestie may be gratiously pleas'd
not to thinke mee lesse worthy that honor. 3. Whereas
I am so farre from beinge payd that wch was promised by
my privy seale, that I am not a saver yet by 3000^{li}, your

good Majestie some way or other would recompense mee ; and for the present to continue mee in your Counseile of Warre, both that I am the sole elder brother of my estate, who have beene on all occasions of that kind, since my minority untill my imployment in France (where I saw the seige of St Jean d'Angely and other memorable services) ; and also that I have done nothing in the warres for wch I have received publiq praise and thankes at the Counseile table here.   I could adde other services, and doubt not but your Majestie may bee pleas'd to thinke on some, but howsoever shall submitt all to your Majestie, as my good kinge and master, who at length may be pleas'd to give a gracious conclusion to all my troubles, which I shall strive to approve myselfe, ever, and to all tryalles, your most excellent Majesties most obedient, most faithfull, and most affectionate subject and servant,

E. HERBERT.[1]

" May 8, 1626."

Although Charles showed little more anxiety than his father to acknowledge Herbert's claim, and Buckingham was not in a position to enforce it, Herbert was not altogether overlooked. His anxiety to serve on the Council of War was a modest ambition, and with some modification it was satisfied.   On 12th December 1626 he joined his kinsman the Earl of Pembroke, his friend Viscount Wimbledon, who, as Sir Edward Cecil, had been his commander in the Low Countries, and many other

---

[1] This letter, discovered by Mr. E. P. Shirley among the papers of the Baroness North at Croxton, Oxfordshire, was first printed in *Notes and Queries*, 4th series, vol. x. p. 222.

courtiers, on a commission to inquire into abuses
in the state of the navy. But he still lacked more
substantial satisfaction. Unfortunately, in March
1627 the French merchants to whom Herbert was
in debt grew more importunate than before, and
appealed to the English Treasury to force Herbert
to pay them £2000. Three months later (21st July
1627) he received very slight compensation for yield-
ing to this demand in the joint grant of the manor
of Ribbesford and other land in Worcestershire, to
himself, his brother George, and another ; but he did
not long retain his share in the property, which ultimately passed to his brother Henry. The succeeding twenty months saw Herbert waiting helplessly
for a more decided change of fortune. He was not
invited to take part in the expedition to the Isle of
Rhé in 1627, although many of his friends accompanied Buckingham in that unlucky enterprise ;
and the murder of the favourite in the following
year (23d August 1628) further depressed his pro-
spects. Meanwhile preferments were lavished on
Herbert's relatives and friends with no sparing
hand, and he began to realise that he was playing
a losing game. A cousin William was elevated to
the English peerage as Baron Powis of Powis Castle,
Montgomeryshire, on 2d April 1629. The news was
not very welcome to him. "Lord Castle-Island,"
wrote one Philip Mainwaring of the effect the an-
nouncement produced upon him, "has run into a

nutshell, and will never appear again." None the less in 1629 Charles gave effect to Buckingham's former assurance that Herbert's admission to the Irish peerage was only the prelude to his admission to the English peerage; and on 7th May in that year Baron Castle-Island became Baron Herbert of Cherbury. Three years later (27th June 1632) he took his long-sought-for place on the Council of War, and helped to draw up "fit instructions for persons in command of garrisons and forts." He was reinstated in this position on 29th May 1637; but this petty employment practically brought Herbert's official life to a close.[1]

Humiliating to his self-esteem as was his inability to obtain a responsible political office by ordinary agencies and by appeals to his former official work, Herbert had too versatile a capacity to submit quietly to the failure of ordinary efforts. If success were attainable by less dignified methods than those he had already tried and tried in vain, he claimed no superior political virtue over his contemporaries, and was ready to give the less dignified methods a trial. He argued, with Bacon, that the architect of his own fortunes must make his "mind pliant and obedient to occasion."

---

[1] The authority for the statements made in this paragraph is the Calendar of State Papers for the years 1626–37. The exact dates, given in each case, will indicate the volumes whence they are derived.

Buckingham, on his return from the Isle of Rhé
in 1627, had drawn up "certain commentaries (hastily
written)" concerning his conduct of the expedition.
His enemies had charged him with gross mismanage-
ment throughout his command, and with personal
cowardice. A vindication was necessary, and he
handed his notes over to Lord Herbert, who was
importunate for the honour of retrieving his patron's
reputation, and saw in the endeavour a means of increasing his own influence at Court. But the task
proved a difficult one, and the Duke died " his nefa-
rious death by the hand of an assassin " before it
was little more than begun. Buckingham's death,
however, was the signal for some attacks of exceptional ferocity upon his life and character in both
France and England. A Frenchman named Isnard
and a Jesuit named Monat both published detailed
accounts of his conduct[1] at Rochelle, and their
libels led Herbert to abandon a momentary intention of sacrificing Buckingham's notes to "privacy
and silence." At Montgomery Castle, on 10th
August 1630, he completed the defence of his friend,
and he dedicated the manuscript to Charles I.

---

[1] The works which (Herbert asserts) called for refutation are : (1.)
*Arcis Sammartianæ Obsidis et Fuga Anglorum a Rea Insula
Scripta Jacobo Isnard*, Paris, 1629 ; (2.) *Treziesme Tome dv Mercvre
Francois*, Paris, 1627-28 ; and (3.) *Capta Rupecula Gracinia Ser-
vata auspiciis ac ductu. . . . Ludovici XIII.: descripta utraque ab
P. Philiberto Monato de Societate Jesu*, Leyden, 1630.

Herbert approached his sovereign deferentially: he applauded his "innate and implanted gentleness," and he apologised for his own incapacity as a writer. "It is not, indeed, as I could wish polished and set foorth: the rough and unmusicall kind of stile admits not the ornaments of words." It must, in all fairness, be confessed that the vindication is a lame affair. On the last page Herbert arrives at a very halting conclusion: "If it be granted that the French did triumph over the vanquished, it must not be denied but the English triumphed even over the victory itself, which, consequently, if they did not make use of and pursue according to the time and occasion, that the night coming on, and defect of horse were the only obstacles." Sir Henry Wotton professed to admire the book,[1] but Charles showed a shrewder judgment in declining to flatter either it or its author. Herbert apparently expected a fee for the performance, but the fee never came, and the writer was vainly reminding Secretary Windebank of the charges to which he had been put by the composition of the pamphlet eight years

---

[1] Cf. *Reliquiæ Wottonianæ*, 1685, p. 226. "This action, as I hear, hath been delivered by a noble gentleman of much learning and active spirits, himself the fitter to do it right; which in truth it greatly wanted, having found more honourable censure, even from some of the French writers than it had generally amongst ourselves at home. Now, because the said book is not yet flowing into the light, I will but sweep the way with a few notes."

later.   Herbert had it translated into Latin by
a lawyer named Timothy Baldwin, but wisely took
no steps to put either the English or the Latin
version into print.[2]

This failure, however, did not daunt Lord Herbert.
If he could not gain royal recognition as the historian
of the present, he would command it as the historian
of the past. As early as 1632 he was engaged on
his elaborate history of the reign of Henry VIII.;
in February 1639 he stated that he had already
spent seven years in the undertaking. On 11th
November 1633 he reminded Charles through Secretary Windebank that he had now served in Court
"without that ever he asked or got anything of
benefit or value for above thirty years,"—a statement
which seems somewhat open to exception. He
therefore prayed, in the first place, that further
official powers over the manor of Cherbury, which
"he conceived to be his right," might be acknowledged by the Crown, and he made a second un-
specified request, admitted to be "wholly in His
Majesty's good pleasure." This request is proved

---

[1] See p. 269.

[2] The Latin version was published by Baldwin in 1658 after
Herbert's death. The English version remained in MS. till 1860,
when it was first printed by the Earl of Powis for the Philobiblon
Society. The date of the completion of the work given above
appears only in the Latin version, which differs in several small
particulars from its original.

by other evidence to have been an appeal for
pecuniary assistance in preparing his great historical treatise.[1]   In a later petition (10th January
1634–35) he sought payment of £600, a fraction
of his arrears of salary as French Ambassador,
in the interests of the same work.   His earlier
request, he stated, had been answered by the grant
of apartments in the royal palace at Richmond,
but he found the situation inconvenient, and he
now begged permission to remove to Whitehall,
or rather to St. James's, "whereby he might have
access to the paper chamber of the one, and the
library of the other house."

But Herbert still stood in need of something
more.   His craving for an unequivocal public testimony of the King's favour had not been satisfied,
and the mental distraction which his new labours
brought him had not abated its intensity.   In
applying himself to historical investigations he
allowed that he was following the example of two
distinguished statesmen, and the result could bring
no loss of honour.   Sir Thomas More was the
author of a life of Richard III. and Bacon the
author of a life of Henry VII.; but although both
were "great personages," he desired to be distinguished "from those who before had taken pains in
this kind."   More and Bacon wrote their histories,

---

[1] Calendar of State Papers, 11th November 1633.

he reminded Charles, "in the time of their disgrace,
and when otherwise they were disabled to appear."
Herbert was differently situated ; and it was, he
urged, the King's business to avert any popular mis-
conception on the subject.[1]

Charles was deaf to these new entreaties. But
Herbert energetically continued the campaign. On
14th May of the same year (1635) he drew up a
paper of observations on the royal supremacy in the
Church. He discussed Old Testament history, and
showed the inconveniences and unscriptural character of a supremacy "invested in a far remote and
obnoxious prelate, who may sometimes want the
power, and sometimes the means of giving that order
which is requisite."[2] He therefore argued that a
powerful king should alone be head of the Church.
Herbert did not merit any advantage from this very
imperfect and servile version of his own theological
opinions, and the King did him a deservedly ill
service by forwarding it some months later to
Archbishop Laud, with whom the writer had
previously maintained a formal intimacy.[3] A

---

[1] Calendar of State Papers, 17th January 1634-35.

[2] Two copies of this tract remain in manuscript—one in the
State Paper Office (Cal. State Papers, 14th May 1635), and the
other in the Library of Queen's College, Oxford (clvii. 158-79).

[3] In Laud's correspondence with Strafford is the following passage :—"Another suit I am to make unto you at the request of
Mr. Herbert, my counsel at law (*i.e.*, Sir Edward Herbert, the

month or two later, Herbert, who still hung about
Court, discussed the same subject with another
authority, Panzani, the Papal Envoy, and took
up a very different line of argument. His fellow-
courtiers were showing Panzani much attention at
the time, and Herbert deemed it prudent to conciliate the men of influence with a courteous bearing towards their protégé. He was, of course, full
of his history of Henry VIII., and he told the
Catholic priest that the hero of his book really
deserved to have little that was good written of
him, and that, so far from upholding the rights
of a secular ruler over a church, he intended to
show as much favour as was possible to the theories
of the Papacy. Anxious to obtain recognition as
an author in any quarter, he went so far as to offer
to submit his philosophical treatise "De Veritate"
to the Pope's criticism.[1] Vain yearning for applause
doubtless moved him to make the offer; he did not
intend his behaviour to cloak any very subtle design.
But Panzani thought Herbert's remarks of sufficient
significance to transmit them to the Holy See.

---

lawyer). And your lordship I know will grant it me. Richard
Herbert, eldest son of the Lord Cherbury, is heir by his mother
to certain lands in Ireland, formerly the possessions of the Earl
of Desmond. My suit is that if the young gentleman come over
to you at spring, you will take notice of him, and let him know
I have desired so much " (Laud's *Works*, vii. 214).

[1] Gardiner's History, ix. 137–138.

Unbaffled still, Herbert returned to the direct
attack on the Crown on 9th February 1638-39.
The scandalous delay of the Treasury in paying
'him his arrears of salary was growing more and
more embarrassing.   His son Edward had lived
riotously and was heavily in debt, and he had
impoverished himself in compounding with the
young man's creditors.   Moreover, Herbert was
sparing himself no expense in collecting materials for his history—a work which he honestly
deemed, in spite of ulterior personal aims, to be
of royal, if not national interest.   And the time
seemed to him more opportune than ever for
pressing his demand for recompense and recognition.   Charles was in the presence of a difficult
crisis.   No one probably saw distinctly the road
that events were taking, but the existing troubles
with Scotland, which proved the prelude to the
civil war in England, impressed Charles and his
advisers with the necessity of closing up their own
ranks, of conciliating their own supporters, and of
presenting a compact front to their enemies, on
whatever side they might threaten attack.   He had
taken the first step in this policy by levying troops
for a military demonstration in Scotland, and by
accusing the Scotch in a royal proclamation of
attempting the overthrow of the monarchy under
colour of a religious agitation.   To lend support to
the cause of monarchy, Charles summoned Herbert

with his fellow-peers to York. It was therefore only just, Herbert argued, that the Crown, before throwing upon him new expenses, should cease to be his debtor, and he wrote to Windebank in a very sanguine strain on the subject:—

" Having (he says) attended, since my return in 1624, some recompense through his Majesty's goodness for extraordinary expenses of about £5300 upon occasion of my embassage there, £2500 whereof rest due to me upon my privy seal (as I made it appear to the late Lord Treasurer and am ready to show to this), you may easily collect how much I have suffered these many years without presuming to trouble his Majesty with any large complaint, as hoping indeed his Majesty would before this time have bestowed on me such honourable place as my predecessors in that employment have enjoyed, as I desire to be represented to his Majesty, not forgetting to inform him how much this reflects upon my reputation. Besides which, my charges for writing the expedition to the Isle of Rhé in Latin and English, as also my keeping scholars and clerks for copying records and making transcripts of the history of Henry VIII., having caused for these last seven years divers new expenses, and having paid the debts of an unthrifty son, you see how many ways I am disabled from bringing the equipage I desire to the rendezvous at York."

Herbert proceeds to express the hope that he may advance his Majesty's cause by taking a command " convenable to my experience, former charge, and present quality," in the Scotch war, but he reminds Charles that he is prosecuting lawsuits in both Ireland and England, and that his absence may cost him dear. He therefore urges in conclusion that, should he not put in an immediate appearance at York, his delay must not be misconstrued.[1]

The terms of this appeal were not likely to give it signal success, and probably did not secure its writer a very warm welcome when he joined his sovereign in the North. It proved that Herbert had lived too long on the outskirts of the political world to command much political foresight. He failed to see that Charles's difficulties were increasing with such velocity that merely personal grievances were incapable of redress in a crisis like the present. We do not know the duties assigned Herbert in the fruitless expedition of 1639, which never reached actual hostilities. The only trace of the episode left on his writings is a characteristically abstract poem entitled "The Idea made of Alnwick in his [*i.e.* the author's] Expedition to Scotland with the Army, 1639."[2] The strains are too thoughtful to suggest that Herbert was in a mood to lend much effective military aid to the royal forces.

In 1640 the relations between King and Commons entered a far more critical stage. The Short Parliament was hastily dissolved (5th May), and Charles summoned a council of peers at York to discuss the situation. For the moment Herbert

---

[1] Calendar of State Papers, 9th February 1638–39.
[2] Poems, edited by J. Churton Collins, pp. 109–113.

forgot his grievances, for a second time joined the
King in the North, and took his place in the
Council (24th September). The immediate question under debate was whether or no an armistice
should be arranged with the Scotch, who had now
invaded the northern counties. Herbert argued
(6th October 1640) in the negative. In spite of
his years and his long lack of active service, in
theory his martial ardour had not cooled, and he
advised Charles to continue the war at all hazards.[1]
The Scots demanded the payment of £40,000 as
the first step towards a treaty of peace. "Treaties,"
said Lord Herbert, "are thin airy things," and
could never be worth so large a sum of money.
No prince "had ever bought a treaty of his subjects at so dear a rate," and it "would reflect upon
the honour of his Majesty abroad when foreign
nations should hear of such an affront given to
his Majesty and this kingdom." But Herbert's
advice was rejected and the temporary treaty of
Ripon signed. Thereupon Herbert took what
proved to be his last farewell of his sovereign, and
at once withdrew to Montgomery. He was not
over-pleased with the result of this new excursion
into politics. He recognised that younger men
were the prime movers in contemporary affairs,

---

[1] Gardiner's History, ix. 212. Rushworth reports the speech in
his Historical Collections, ii. 1293. .

and that his name was practically unknown among
them. The friends of his youth were no longer in
the King's council. His kinsman, William Herbert,
the well-known Earl of Pembroke, had died in
1630, Lord Wimbledon in 1638, and Sir Thomas
Lucy in 1640. His health, moreover, was beginning
to break, and his physicians recommended unexciting
pursuits. Through 1641 and a great part of 1642
Herbert therefore passed his time with his books,
began continuations of his philosophical treatise
" De Veritate " and planned his autobiography and
a work on education. He was clearly hesitating
even then as to the *rôle* he should play in the
coming struggle. His hopes that the King would
redress his personal grievances were growing fainter
and fainter.

The desperate aspect of affairs in May 1642
recalled him to London to study the situation from
the nearest points of view. He attended the sittings
of the House of Lords. When, on 20th May, the
Commons resolved that the King transgressed his
oath if he made war, Herbert spoke with cautious
hesitation, and thought to sail with the wind. He
promised to vote for the resolution if he could
assure himself that the King made war " without
cause." This qualification was ill interpreted by
the Commons: he was committed by them for a
few days to the Tower, and was only released on
making a very handsome apology. The experience

was not a satisfactory one,[1] and Herbert appears to have contemplated retiring to the Continent. He, however, withdrew once more to Montgomery, which he doubtless deemed a safe distance from which to watch events.

It goes without saying that Herbert had mental resources outside politics which ought to have enabled him to take his political disappointments platonically, but until very late in life he would never allow himself to recognise the fact distinctly. Readers of other portions of this work will find illustration of his devotion at this and all other times to science, mechanical inventions and the culture of horses, to history, philosophy, and poetry. But whenever he allowed his mind to dwell upon the habitual neglect to which the politicians subjected him, he was tormented by consciousness of failure. And besides failing health and loss of friends, he had domestic troubles to harass him. His wife died on 29th October 1634, and was laid to rest in Montgomery Church on the following day.[2] One

---

[1] See Lords' Journal, v. 77, and Historical MSS. Commission Report, v. 24. According to the Commons' Journal, ii. 554, Herbert was ready to advance money to the Parliament (cf. Hist. MSS. Com. Rep., v. 21). It is very necessary, and very difficult, to distinguish in the various records of the civil war the various Herberts who took part in it. Lord Herbert of Cherbury has often been mistaken for Lord Herbert, the eldest son of the Earl of Worcester, who led the Royalists in South Wales.

[2] The entries are in the Montgomery parish register.

S

of his sons was a spendthrift. All his brothers were
dead before 1640 except Sir Henry, to whom he
pathetically wrote in 1643, "And here I must
remember that of all of us there remains but I and
you to brother it." Everything contributed to
benumb his political enthusiasm. Montgomery
Castle seems alone to have preserved its attractions
for him; there he was forced back on the happier
memories of his early life, and his neighbours treated
him with respect.[1] Since political honour was
denied him, he set a higher value than of old on
his personal comfort, and he soon resolved to make
that the chief plank in his political platform.

The outbreak of the civil war in 1642 evidently
perplexed him. He prayed for "a good and speedy
end to all these troubles." He tried for a while to
close his eyes to their serious import. Although he
was not inclined to countenance a revolution, his
loyalty (it was clear) would ill bear the severe strain
of repeated menaces of his personal security. His
sufferings at the hands of the Crown had weakened
his regard for its present possessor. The warfare of

---

[1] We obtain a glimpse of Lord Herbert, or Lord Castle-Island
(as he was often called after his accession to an English peerage),
in the Chamberlain's accounts of the corporation of Shrewsbury
in 1636. He visited the town and was feasted by the civic magistrates :—" 1636, November 22, spent on my Lord Castell Islande,
four pottles claret, 5*s*. 4*d*. Two ditto sack, 4*s*. Two dozen fine
cakes.

political parties had never been any concern of his.
All that he immediately aimed at now, therefore,
was a pacific independence. He resolved, as long
as it was practicable, to observe a strict neutrality
in the coming struggle, and to wait on the result.
He cared no longer for his country but for himself.

The presence of Charles and his nephew Prince
Rupert in Chester and Shrewsbury in 1642 feverishly
moved the people of North Wales, and did much to
strengthen their Royalist predilections. Lord Herbert's eldest son, Richard, at once raised a troop of
horse and a regiment of foot at his own expense, and
joined the Royal forces at Shrewsbury. Throughout the war he fought valiantly against the Parliament, together with his brother Edward, and
Edward his eldest son. But Lord Herbert held
aloof from the popular excitement, although it
combined with his other anxieties to cause him
exceptional depression of spirits. "I am thinking," he wrote to his brother Henry on 14th June
1643, "of a journey to the Spa, but I doubt how I
shall be able to go, my body being more infirm
than to endure any labour. And let me assure you
I find myself grown older in this one year than in
fifty-nine years before ; which, as it is true, I should
be glad were known among the best of those to
whom you go."

Ten days later Herbert wrote again in a like
strain to his brother. A slight dispute had arisen

between them. Sir Henry apparently desired Lord
Herbert to take charge of his horses and put them
out to grass in Montgomery, while the midland
counties, where his estates lay, continued in their
disturbed state. Lord Herbert declined to accede
to the request. The letter is of value as an indication of his growing depression, of his fretfulness,
and of his resolute endeavours to blind himself to
the strife that was now approaching Montgomery
Castle very closely. It begins :—

"SIR HENRY,—For the good offices you ever done me,
I thank you. But why thereupon you should fall upon
your old whetting, I marvel. I had rather for my part
forget all unkind passages than remember them, so as to
send you a forgiveness for them.[1]

"Good brother, use no more close repetitions ; and now I
grow old and infirm, do not add affliction and discomforts
to your faithful loving brother,

E. HERBERT."

Two months later (25th August 1643), Lord Herbert began to feel personally the inconveniences of
a civil war; but he confessed to no sentiment
except one of resentment at the interference with

---

[1] "The intervening passages run :—" If Richard Whittingham
sent you word (as he told mee) of the condition of the two parkes,
you would take nothing unkindly, especially when I wished him
to tell you that if you sent a gelding thither, he should be welcome.
But here you may remember the old answer. If you will not take
it unkindly that I denied you a courtesy, I will not take it unkindly
that you asked it."

his comfort. Sir William Brereton was pushing his
Parliamentary successes in Cheshire to the Welsh
border, and on 11th June 1643 Sir Thomas Middleton, of Chirk Castle, Denbighshire, was appointed
by the Parliament Sergeant-Major-General of the
six counties of North Wales. At first Middleton
joined Brereton in consolidating his conquests in
Shropshire and Cheshire, and they interrupted all
communication between Montgomery Castle and
Shrewsbury.

"SIR HENRY" (Lord Herbert writes), "though the
messenger brought no letter from you to my self, yet
because hee tould me you were well, the welcome news
thereof in these troublesome times invites me to congratulate
it with you.[1]

"We are here almost in as great straits as if the warre
were amongst us. Shrewsbury, which is our ordinary
magazine, being exhausted of wine, vinegar, hops, paper,
and pepper at four shillings the pound ; and shortly a
want of all commodities, that are not natives with us, will
follow, the intercourse between us and London being
interdicted.

"My dear and only brother, I wish you all health and
happiness, and so rest, though much broken in my health.
                                        "E. HERBERT."

---

[1] The next sentence concerns the quarrel about the horses. It
runs as follows :—"If it had pleased R. Wittingham to have tould
you that I had stone horses in my lower parke, and no grass in my
upper parke (as he tould me he would), there had been no occasion
for you to demand that I could not conveniently do ; but if you
send a gelding or two untill Michaelmas, they shall be received."

Lord Herbert sends in a postscript his "kind remembrance to your lady and children."[1]

Early in 1644 Charles had recourse to the feeble
expedient of summoning what he termed a Parliament to Oxford. The meeting was scantily attended,
and mainly resulted in the dispatch of a letter to the
Earl of Essex, the Parliamentary general, asking him
to persuade "those whose confidence he possessed" to
treat of peace. All present signed the letter, but
although the name of Richard Herbert, Lord Herbert's son and heir, appears there, his own is absent.
Lord Herbert had declined to make the journey to
Oxford on the ground of ill-health, and his excuse
had been accepted by the King. Up to this time
the public had not suspected Herbert's loyalty.
His name had Royalist associations, and the Parliament, which resented the contemptuous references
made to it by the Royalist assembly at Oxford,
identified him with his relatives. On 9th February
1643–44 a Parliamentary order was issued for the
confiscation and sale of Herbert's property in London
and elsewhere. Directions were not given, however,
for the immediate execution of this order, and Lord
Herbert made good use of the delay. The order
opened his eyes to his personal insecurity, and the
growing necessity of caution.

---

[1] These letters to Sir Henry are printed in all the previous
editions of the Autobiography.

In February 1643-44 Prince Rupert, whose mother's misfortunes had in earlier years excited in Lord Herbert a chivalric devotion, visited Shrewsbury with a view to protecting North Wales from the attacks of Middleton, who had made a very formidable demonstration there a few months before. Lord Herbert was invited to lay suggestions before the Prince, but he was clear-sighted enough to see the danger of openly associating himself with the Royalist leader; he declined the offer, and demanded to be left at peace in his castle. He was well able, he said, to defend himself and his property with the help of his son, and he resented the proposal to introduce a Royalist garrison.

" May it please your Highnes," he wrote (27th February 1643-44), "having now continued for the space of above two yeares in soe bad a condition of health, that I have not beene able to attend his Majesty in person, or otherwise to endure much labour, I shall most humbly desire to bee excused to y^r Highnes if I attend not y^r Highnes in person at this tyme : I have taken the boldnes further to acquaint your Highnes that Mr. Sheriffe of this county hath sent mee word that y^r Highnes intends to send a garrison for defence of this castle ; but because diverse of my sonnes souldiers are inquartered in ye towne, and that for the rest, betweene my servants and neighbours I am always able to put a sufficient garrison in this place, I shall humbly desire y^r Highnes either to leave mee to the defence of my owne house, or if y^r Highnes will have a garrison here, that they may bee inquartered in the towne of Montgomery wherein my castle stands (some few only excepted) which may be lodged in my outworks made to ye castle. Of all which I humbly desire I may have the command, together with the nomination of such officers as are usuall for fifty or threescore men, who (with the helpe of my neighbours) will bee able to make good this place, and that good order may be taken not only for providing the souldiers with all necessaries, but for their constant pay ; though yet by your Highnes good leave I conceive there will bee noe neede of a garrison as long as my sonnes souldiers remayne in this towne, soe that at least I hope y^r Highnes neede not hasten the sending a garrison hither." [1]

Prince Rupert quitted Shrewsbury for a fortnight in March 1644, and returned after relieving Newark. That victory gave the neighbouring Royalists new hopes, and the absence of Middleton in London relieved them of their worst fears. But Rupert was not very successful in his collection of men or money from North Wales, and on 9th April 1644 he forwarded a threatening letter to the gentlemen of Montgomeryshire.[2] In the following

---

[1] This letter is printed (I believe) for the first time from the British Museum MS., Addit., 18, 981, f. 67.

[2] The following papers are printed in the Powysland Collections, vol. x. p. 138, with the prefatory remark :—

"The following letter and document are in the collection of the Rev. Dr. Raffles, now possessed by his son, Mr. T. Stamford Raffles of Liverpool. They show that the loyalty of Montgomeryshire, as well as other parts of Wales, was waning, and that it required the military rigour of the Prince to enforce the contributions."

'GENTLEMEN,—I have thought fitt hereby to give you notice, since I finde the country so deficient in the performance of those

month the Parliamentary Colonel Mitton successfully attacked Oswestry, and in June Prince Rupert
removed to York. These diversions destroyed the
Royalists' rising hopes, and their situation obviously
grew more and more hazardous. Rupert's disastrous
defeat at Marston Moor (2d July) drove him back
once again to the Welsh border to recruit his
depleted force. He was closely watched by Brereton
and Middleton, but he managed to reach either
Chester or Shrewsbury in safety. Thence he re-
issued urgent appeals to all the gentry of North
Wales, including Lord Herbert, but Lord Herbert

---

condicions concerning the contribuciouns of and by Montgomery,
which you soe willinglie offered and agreed upon in their behalfe
with my Commissioners at their being there with you at Welsh
Poole, concerning that affaire, I am now resoluied to raise and
collect the contributions of that countrye after the same manner
that I doe the contribution of Salop, which is by an imposicion of
sixpence in the pound by the moneth out of all men's estates, in
which there can be no particularitie or excuse. And for your
arrears of the contributions formerly granted, I shall verie speedilie
send some troopes of horse to quarter upon that countrie till they
are fullie payd and satisfyed, which will be a thing that I intended
not, had not the country forced me theretoe by a voluntary fayling
on their parts. Thus, I rest, your friend,   RUPERT.

" Showsburye this nineth day of April 1644."

" 6 *May* 1644.—Warrant of Sheriff and Magistrates to the
High Constables of the hundreds of the said county, touching the
assessment of £1500 to be levied therein for the King's service.
The assessors are to appear at 10 am., on Friday the tenth inst., at
the house of Richard Price of Glan Waren."

still refused to bestir himself. On 23rd August
1644 he forwarded from his castle the following
quaint epistle :—

" May it please your most Excellent Highnes, I shall
humbly crave leave to tell your Highnes that though I
have the ambition to kisse your most valorous and
princely hands, yet because I am newly entered into a
course of physiq I do humbly desire to be excused for the
presente, beseechinge your Highnes nevertheless to hold
mee in your former good opinion and favor." [1]

But an attitude of neutrality in a civil war must
always prove impracticable at one period or another,
and the time was fast approaching when Lord
Herbert had to definitely choose a side. About the
first day of September 1644, Sir Thomas Middleton,
who was with Colonel Mitton at Oswestry, received
orders from the Parliament to advance on Montgomeryshire. Although there is little to confirm the
conjecture, the county was regarded in London as a
stronghold of the Royalists, and it was deemed wise
to intercept within it a Royalist convoy of powder
which was passing from Bristol on its way to Chester
and Liverpool. On 3rd September Middleton and his
troops left Oswestry by night. They marched until
morning continuously, and then having seized New-

---

[1] This letter, which has frequently been printed, has been transcribed from the British Museum MS., Addit., 18, 981, f. 229.

town, advanced to Montgomery, "though with much difficulty on account of the foulness of the roads and the breaking of the bridges by the enemy."[1] The town made no resistance, but the castle was strongly fortified, and was expected to show fight; Lord Herbert and his daughter Beatrice were, however, the only members of the family in residence there, and they were in no fighting humour. Middleton summoned Lord Herbert to surrender, and he showed at first a respectable hesitation in replying to the demand. A few days were given him in which to make his final decision. There were many inducements for him to adopt a conciliatory tone. He knew that all his property would be confiscated, both in Montgomery and London, if he resolved on refusal. News had reached him that his books, which were his most valued possessions, were to be sold forthwith under an order of the Commons dated 30th August, and the proceeds handed to Lord Fairfax's army.[2] But he had doubtless also learnt that a few days later the Parliamentary authorities had "forborne the disposing of my lord's goods for one week longer till they heard of his behaviour touching the

---

[1] Full particulars of these military movements are given in J. R. Phillipp's "Civil War in Wales," i. pp. 247-248. Sir Thomas Middleton's letter to John Glyn detailing his action is printed in Hist. MSS. Report, vi., and in "Archæologia Cambrensis" (4th series), xii. 325.

[2] Commons' Journal, iii. 612.

surrender of his castle." This forbearance weighed
with Lord Herbert, and after some parleying he
determined to save his property at the expense of
his honour.[1] Before 7th September he signed an
agreement with Middleton's lieutenant, James Till,
according to which he, his daughter, and his attendants, were to remain in safety in the castle as long
as they pleased; his property was to remain untouched, and was to be re-delivered to him absolutely
in time of peace. It was not very agreeable to Lord
Herbert to consent to the provision that Sir Thomas
Middleton with twenty soldiers should take up his
residence there. But by a special stipulation none
of the new residents were to enter Lord Herbert's
library or the two rooms adjoining it, and the
owner of the castle was to be permitted to quit it
at his pleasure.[2] A few days later Lord Herbert

---

[1] Under date 5th September Middleton wrote to the House of
Commons:—"I have sent to my Lord of Cherbury about the
surrendering of the castle of Mountgomery unto use for the Parliament's service: it is a place of great strength and importance:
and have received a very good and satisfactory answer from him,
the particulars whereof I shall make bold to certifie you of."—
A Perfect Diurnall, No. 59, p. 469.

[2] The text is given in the Hist. MSS. Report, vi. 28. The date
must have been earlier than that stated. The document runs as
follows :—

"1644, Sept. 24.—The Coppie of the Articles of Agreem't
betweene the Lord Cherbury and Seriant Maior Generall S'r Tho
Myddleton touchinge the surrend'r uppe of Montgomery Castle.

"I, James Till, Gent, as Lieutenant Collonell of horse, do hereby,

sent a servant, James Heath, to London to draw the
attention of the Parliament to his alleged patriotic

---

in the name of Sir Thomas Middleton, Knight, promise and
undertake that noe violence shal bee offred to the p'son or goods
of Edward Lord Herbert, or any p'son or p'sons within his
castle of Montgomery ; and that they shall haue free liberty to
goe out of the said castle, and carry away their goods and money
whensoever they will ; and that a good convoy shall bee graunted
for the safe doeing thereof as farr as Coventry ; and recommenda-
tions given to the officers there for the further conveying of the said
persons and goods to London, if it bee required; and that in the
meane while a true inventory shal bee taken of all the household
stuffe vsed in the said castle, and of all the bookes, trunkes, and
wrytings in the said castle, and that all the horses and cattel in
and about the said castle, and all p'visions of victualls, bread,
wine, and beare, shall be imployed for the use of the said Edward
Lord Herbert and his family, and that noe money, silver, gould,
or plate shal bee taken from the said Edward Lord Herbert or any
of his family ; and that the said castle, with all the goods, bookes,
and armes of the said Edward Lord Herbert, shal bee restored
and redelyvered to the said Edward Lord Herbert, if it please God
to send peace, or the Parliament order it so to bee done. And that
in the meane while the said Edward Lord Herbert, with his
daughter and family, shall continue in or returne to the said castle
as formerly they did, if they soe please ; and that they shall carry
into the said castle all provisions necessary for cloathing and diett.
And it is further agreed that Sir Thomas Middleton shall signe
and seale this accord or agreement, if the said Edward Lord
Herbert shall require it ; and shall also further and assist the
bailiffs of the said Edward Lord Herbert in the leavying of his
rents, and also p'serve his woods and deere. Dated halfe an
houre past twelue of the clocke at midnight on Thursday the fifth
day of September, Anno D'ni 1644.

" And it is further agreed that as longe as the said Lord Herbert
or his daughter continue in the said castle, there shall not exceede

action, and to secure his London property indubitably. " His master," the servant said, " went, with

---

the number of twenty p'sons or souldiers, vnlesse some iminent danger appeares ; and that noe trunkes or doores under locks and keyes shal bee broken open. And that if it happen that the said Lord Herbert at any time doe remove from the said castle, that the said Lord Herbert shall haue halfe a dozen men servants w'thin the said castle to doe the business of the said Lord Herbert, and three or foure maldes to attend his said daughter. And that if any thinge may be required for the further satisfaccion and contentment of the said Edward Lord Herbert, it shall bee lawfull hereafter to explaine and add the same.   JAMES TILL.

" *Witnesses :*

" Hugh Pryce.	Oliver Herbert.
Samuel More.	Rowland Evans.
Edward Price.	Daniel Edwards.

" Whereas there is a doubt that goods should be removed or carried away out of the Castle of Montgomery by Edward Lord Herbert. It is agreed that there shal bee left w'thin the said castle six beds for souldiers, one suite of hangings in the dyneing roome of the new castle, as also one suite of hangings and furniture for a chamber w'thin the said castle, wherein S'r Tho. Middleton shall please to lodge, and one bed with furniture for a captaine. And it is further agreed that there shall be noe person or persons enter into the library or study of the said Edward Lord Herbert, or the two next roomes or chambers adjoyning to the said study or library, during the time of the absence of the said Edward Lord Herbert, or at any time other time. It is further agreed that the said Edward Lord Herbert shall remove and carry all his goods out of the said castle, except the beds and furniture before mentioned, when the said Edward Lord Herbert shall thinke fitt.

" I am content to stand to all the above specified agreements in every point.   EDWARD HERBERT."

the leave of the House, to his castle of Montgomery for his health's sake, and there remained, rejecting all offers from Prince Rupert and others to join them in the execution of the array; and he has since preserved the peace in those parts, and assisted the well-affected from time to time; but was prevented by sickness from coming to London or disposing of his castle, which is of very great consequence and the key of Wales, and is now delivered up to the Parliament, as the accompanying papers will show."[1] Heath therefore prayed that the sale of his Lordship's goods in his town-house, and of a number of books which were in the petitioner's custody, might be stayed by order of the House. This request was not granted immediately, and some persons claimed leave to seize the goods. Lord Herbert therefore sent other representatives to protest that though his name might be "faulty" (so many of his relatives held high rank among the Royalists), his person was not, and he requested that an inventory should be taken of his London property, which should be left in his house, upon security to be forthcoming if required. On 23rd September the threatened sequestration was "dis-

---

[1] This and the other documents referred to are printed in the "Archæologia Cambrensis" (4th series), xii. 324 *et seq.* They are there abstracted from the Historical MSS. Report, vi. 27. The dates seem somewhat erratic, and it is clear that they are often made later than other facts warrant.

charged and taken off"[1] after Brereton's account
of Herbert's conduct had been read to both Houses.
Upon such terms Lord Herbert vainly imagined perfect peace was possible.

Having thus arrived at a settlement with those
who had deemed themselves his enemies, he had
now to reckon with those who had deemed themselves his friends. Lord Herbert had not only
broken ties of long standing: he had dealt his
Royalist neighbours a well-nigh deadly blow. He
had put into Middleton's hands a fortress that was,
as he himself rightly termed it, the key to North
Wales. Sir Michael Ernely, the Royalist commander at Shrewsbury, perceived that no time must
be lost if the position bartered away by "the
treacherous Lord Herbert" was to be retrieved. He
at once collected a considerable force of horse and
foot, and marched upon Montgomery. Middleton
anticipated some such manœuvre, and hastened to
the neighbouring towns and villages for provisions to
enable his men in the castle and town to stand, if
need were, a long siege. But Sir Michael's movements were too rapid for the Parliamentary general.
The Royalists fell upon his force while near the town
and utterly routed it. Middleton retired with his
horse to Oswestry, and made his way to Cheshire
and Lancashire to procure relief. His foot-soldiers

---

[1] Lords' Journal, vi. 712a ; Commons' Journal, iii. 636.

under Colonel Mitton managed to re-enter Montgomery Castle. Ernely straightway laid siege to
the town and castle; earthworks were hastily
thrown up and trenches dug all round them. For
ten days Lord Herbert and his neighbours suffered
terrible distress, and their peril grew with every
hour. Happily Middleton foresaw their critical
situation and wasted no time. He urged Sir
William Brereton in Cheshire and Sir John Mel-
drum in Lancashire to hurry with him to their
rescue. Sir William Fairfax, coming from Yorkshire, was also ready to offer some assistance, and
thus four detachments of troops, numbering about
three thousand men in all, arrived before Montgomery on the 17th September. Meanwhile Sir
Michael Ernely's force had been supplemented by
one small army from Chester under Lord Byron, and
another from Ludlow under Colonel Wodehouse,
and the Royalists had acquired a large numerical
superiority over their opponents. Both sides acknowledged the high importance of the issue of the
impending conflict and carefully laid their plans
for an engagement. At a council of the Parliamentary leaders held on the night of the 17th
September, it was resolved to revictual the town
and castle before taking the offensive. Next morning, therefore, a third part of the Parliamentary
forces was told off to bring in provisions and forage.
Lord Byron had, however, taken up a strong position

T

on the mountain overlooking the castle ; he perceived
the foraging party leave the enemy's camp, and, with
his customary precipitancy, resolved to open attack
on the stationary force.   His sudden onslaught met
at first with complete success, but this success was
not sustained.   After a desperate hand-to-hand conflict, the Parliamentary generals gained a signal
victory before nightfall.   Lord Byron fled to Chester and Ernely to Shrewsbury.   The victors' loss
included Sir William Fairfax, who was fatally
wounded, but it was slight compared with that of
the enemy, and the prisoners taken by the Parliamentary forces were very numerous.[1]

Lord Herbert and his companions, who had
anxiously watched the conflict from the castle,
were thus relieved.   The next step that it was to
his worldly advantage to take was obvious.   He
had to make an unmistakable profession of allegi-
ance to the Parliament.   Now that his own safety
was assured, he willingly left his castle at the
mercy of Middleton, and accompanied Sir William
Brereton to Oswestry.   The occupation of his castle
and its neighbourhood by a military force had, in

---

[1] For a full account of the battle see " Phillipp's Civil War in
Wales," i. 248–249, and ii. 201–209.   A very valuable collection of
despatches by the commanders on both sides is given under the latter
entry.   The result was watched in London with intense interest ;
and, according to the *London Post* for 1st October 1644, public
thanksgiving for the victory was held on the part of the Parliament
in the City churches.

spite of the terms he had previously made with
Middleton, deprived him of his means of livelihood,
and it was a thankless business to play proprietor
any longer. On 27th September 1644 *The Court
Mercurie,* a Parliamentary newspaper, announced :
" The lord of Cherbury, late Governour of Montgomery Castle, with Sir John Price, who came in to
Sir Thomas Middleton, are come as farr as Coventry,
and intend for London and to offer their persons to
the Parliament."   Well-nigh destitute, he made his
way to London, and addressed (2d November 1644)
to the Parliament a petition for relief which closely
resembles his former appeals to Charles I.[1] He
asserted that he had sustained his losses in the
service of the Parliament ; and he received a more
consoling reply than that with which his sovereign
had been wont to favour him.   On 19th December
the House of Commons instructed a committee to
consider " some way for his present maintenance
and subsistence." [2] Twenty pounds a week was
assigned him on February 25, 1644–45, and no
restrictions were set upon his liberty.[3]

From this time he made his London house, which
was situated in Queen Street, near St. Giles', his only
home.[4] Parted from almost all his old friends, he

---

[1] See Hist. MSS. Com. Report, vi. 34 and 48, and Lords' Journal,
vii. 241.
[2] Commons' Journal, iii. 727   [3] Commons' Journal, iv. 62.
[4] Lord Herbert frequently moved his London house. In his
autobiography he speaks of living near the Old Exchange at one

concentrated himself upon literary work. He had
not apparently the heart to take up again his autobiography at the point at which the clash of arms
had interrupted it: it was left unfinished in 1644.
But in 1645 he issued the elaborate appendix on
fallacies to his treatise "De Veritate," and published his work "De Religione Gentilium." He
gave the finishing touches to his History, and wrote
a bombastic dedication addressed to the King whom
he had deserted; but though he made all preparations for its publication, he was fortunate enough
to die before giving to the world this final testimony
to his insincerity. At the same time he corre-
sponded with foreign scholars, among whom he still
could claim the unblemished reputation of a philosopher, and in September 1647 went for a few weeks
to Paris on a visit to Gassendi, the famous French
philosopher, who had always appreciated his writings.[1]

---

time, and at another in Blackfriars. On 11th November 1633 he
dates a petition from his house in St. Bartholomew's. On 16th
January 1637-38 he was living at Islington (see Cal. State Papers
under date). He dated his last petition to Charles I. in 1639 from
"my house at Hackney" (see Cal. State Papers, 9th February
1638-39). In the references to his London house in the Parliamentary journals during the Civil War the building is entitled
Camden House.

[1] In 1635 Herbert had sent a copy of his "De Veritate" to
Gassendi through Diodati. In Gassendi's correspondence (Opera
Omnia, iii. 411) occurs the passage that establishes the fact of Lord
Herbert's visit to Paris: "Cum me invisisset illustrissimus Baro
postridie kalendas Septemb. 1647, et redditas sibi non_fuisse meas
litteras contestaretur."

But those final years of his life must have proved
dark and dreary even to one of his sanguine temperament. However he may have accounted to
himself for his recent actions, he must have learnt
that he was commonly called by both friend and
foe "the black Lord Herbert;" nor could he have
wholly freed himself of an inward suspicion that
he had renounced from sordid motives the chivalrous
ideals of his youth. His sons, grandson, and brother
had all suffered deeply in their sovereign's cause:
they had refused to qualify themselves for a Parliamentary pension; heavy fines and sequestrations of
property were their only rewards of loyalty; the terrible contrast between his condition and theirs must
at times have disturbed even his portentous self-
composure.

But to the end Herbert gave no outward sign of
remorse. He had become a Parliament man in all
outward show, and was contemplating taking office
under the kingdom's new rulers. On 26th October
1646 an ordinance was issued appointing him steward
of the duchy of Cornwall and warden of the Stan-
naries.[1] But Herbert does not appear to have taken
advantage of the appointment. On 25th March
1647 he pointed out to the House of Commons
that he was excluded from Montgomery Castle,
and petitioned for permission to appoint a governor

---

[1] Commons' Journal, iv. 704.

of his own choosing. He promised to be responsible
for the maintenance of the fortress in the Parliamentary cause, and his request was granted, although
he does not appear to have put in a personal
appearance at Montgomery.[1] A few weeks later
(12th May) Herbert was called upon by the House
of Lords to account for an assault made on the
castle by a Royalist band of soldiers from Poole,
to which his governor offered no resistance.[2] After
his return from France in October, he was fined
(9th November 1647) for absenting himself from
the House of Lords, but the fine was remitted the
next day on the ground of ill-health.[3] His last appearance in the historical arena was in his accustomed
character of petitioner for money. On 4th May
1648 he reminded his patrons "that much of this
money (*i.e.*, his pension) is now in arrear." If it
was not to be continued throughout his lifetime,
its payment ought, he urged, to be prolonged
"until he be satisfied for the losses he sustained
for two years and three months, during which
time he kept his castle until he submitted it unto
the Parliament, which losses appear by good certi-
ficate to amount to divers thousand pounds."[4]

---

[1] Commons' Journal, v. 125, 171, 564.
[2] Lords' Journal, ix. 186.
[3] Ibid. ix. 515, 516.
[4] Lords' Journal, x. 243; Archæologia Cambrensis (4th ser.),
xiii. 265.

His death was now close at hand. On 1st August 1648 he deemed it prudent to make his will,[1] and he there shows himself to unexpected advantage. He bore his two sons no ill-will for adhering to the faith which it did not become him to leave, and made generous provision for both of them ; but he specially favoured his grandson Edward, the son of Richard, the heir to all the entailed estates in Wales. To young Edward he left all the household stuff, books, arms, and ammunition in Montgomery Castle, "charging him upon my blessing neither to sell nor give away, nor so much as lend any of my said books and furniture," and only to allow his father the use of them, "he putting in good surety to my executors for the using of them, with good husbandry and without spoil, and for returning of them . . . with safety and without diminution." Bags of money kept by Lord Herbert in a trunk in his chamber, together with the plate of his London house, were appointed for Edward's "education in some one of the universities, or in travel beyond the seas." To his daughter Beatrice he left the plate remaining in Montgomery, and his clothes and furniture in Queen Street were to be sold for her benefit : to his granddaughters, Frances and Florence, young Edward's sisters, he bequeathed

---

[1] This interesting document is very long. It opens with a statement of his religious belief. I have made a transcript of it from the copy in Somerset House, where it is numbered "Essex 138."

a diamond hatband to be converted into "wearing jewels," and two bags of old gold. To his younger son, Captain Edward, the manor of Llyssin was left for life, with remainder to Edward the younger, besides sums of ready money in the hands of foreign merchants; but a quaint condition was annexed to this bequest. The legatee was to pay to "two maimed soldiers that have done something that is famous in the service of the kingdom or of any confederate thereof in the wars, the sum of ten pounds a year yearly," and these men were to "attend and wait with halberts in their right hands at the gate of my castle of Montgomery." His Latin and Greek books which were with him in Queen Street were to pass to Jesus College, Oxford, "for the inception of a library there." [1] Directions were given to his grandson to carry all his manuscripts and English books from London to Montgomery Castle. His autobiography was

---

[1] The original catalogue of this collection, consisting of twenty closely written folios, is still in the possession of the college, and it was my intention to have printed it here, but the necessary arrangements could not be completed in time. The books seem to have been in the keeping of Sir Henry Herbert at the date of his brother's death, and Selden, one of the executors of the will, had some difficulty in procuring their transference to the college. The following letter was sent by Selden to Sir Henry on the subject :—

"NOBLE SIR,—This gentleman, Mr. Williams, comes from Dr. Maunsell, head of Jesus College, in Oxford, about the legacy of

to be completed and published by "a person whom
I shall by word entreat." Richard, the elder son,
received his father's horses, with a special injunction
"to make much of the white horse," and the viols
and lutes went to Richard's wife, Mary, daughter
of John, Earl of Bridgwater. The final article in
the document breathes a very quixotic generosity.
"Near the sum," says Herbert, " of £2000 is due
to me from the Houses of Parliament as an arrears
of £20 settled to be paid unto me weekly. And
whereas by my capitulation with Sir Thomas
Middleton, my losses and other damages,—£12,000
and more,—were all to be made good unto me, I
do hereby totally remit the same, desiring the said
honourable Houses that, in lieu thereof, and for my
sake, that they will please to remit unto my said son,
Colonel Richard Herbert, the sum of £2500 imposed
upon him as a fine for his delinquency by the committee sitting at Goldsmith's Hall." Herbert concludes by entreating his three executors—his grandson
Edward, and his friends John Selden and Evan

---

books made to them by my Lord Herbert of Chirbury. I presume
he will take just care of the safe delivery of them, if he shall receive
them from your hand, which I desire he may, together with the
catalogue, to take a copy of it, and return it again. Sir, I
ever am,
      "Your most affectionate and humble servant,
                       "J. SELDEN.
"*November* 1, 1648, *White Friars.*
"The Hon. Sir HENRY HERBERT, Knight."

Thomas of Bishop's Castle, Shropshire—to present
a petition on this subject to Parliament in behalf
of his son, " whose great debts and numerous issue
are a burthen greater than my weak state can well
bear." [1]

On 20th August 1648 Lord Herbert died at his
house in Queen Street, nineteen days after his will
was drafted.   On his death-bed he sent for Usher,
the Primate of Ireland, with whom he had previously
lived on terms of intimacy.   He asked to receive the
sacrament at Usher's hand.   It might do him some
good, he added, and would do him no harm.   But
on such an understanding the Archbishop declined to
comply with the dying man's request.   Turning on
his side, Lord Herbert solemnly announced that in
an hour from that moment he should quit this
world ; and these, his last words, proved true.[2]   By
his will he directed that " his earthly parts " should be
committed to the earth at " twelve of the clock at
night in the parish church where I shall die, without
pomp or other ceremony than is usual."   He forbade

---

[1] The second Lord Herbert had four sons—Edward, John (died
young), Henry, Thomas ; and four daughters—Frances, Florence,
Arabella, and Alicia.

[2] Aubrey's *Lives*, ii. 387.   Aubrey also writes that Lord Herbert
" had constantly prayers twice a day in his house, and on Sundays
would have his chaplain read one of Snayth's sermons. . . . I have
seen him several times with Sir John Danvers : he was a black
man."

" all mourning or shew of mourning, . . . desiring
my friends nevertheless to love my memory." These
orders were faithfully fulfilled, and Lord Herbert's
body was buried in the Church of St. Giles-in-
the-Fields, beneath a stone bearing the inscription,
believed to be from the pen of his friend Lord
Stanhope:—" *Hic inhumatur corpus Edvardi Herbert equitis Balnei, baronis de Cherbury et Castle-
Island, auctoris libri, cui titulus est ' De Veritate.'
Reddor ut herbæ;* [1] *vicesimo die Augusti anno
Domini* 1648."

But this was not the only memorial which Lord
Herbert desired. He had Hamlet's horror of a bad
epitaph, and made every kind of provision to secure
at any rate a neutral one. One Mr. Stone of Long
Acre had received instructions from him in his lifetime to set up a monument either in Montgomery or
Cherbury church, " with a strong grate of iron . . .
eight feet high, before it every way " and " on the
pedestal of the pillar which is to stand in the middle
of the said monument" the following words were
to be placed : " *Quid aspectas, lector ? non iacet ullibi
Edwardus Baro Herbert de Cherbury et Castri*

---

[1] *Reddor ut herbæ* was Herbert's own anagram on his surname
and Christian name. Among his poems is the following *Epitaphium
in anagramma nominis sui :—*

"Quas turgens flos mane decet, quas aruit omnes
Una dies, quas morte cita, nova vita sequetur,
Non unquam moritura tamen, sic *Reddor ut Herba.*"

*Insulæ de Kerry sed meliori sui parte in beatorum
sedes abijt seram posteritatem testatus nihil ita relictum
nisi quod secum abducere noluit! Vale, lector, et
stude eternitati."*[1] If leave were obtained, Herbert
did not object (he said in his will) to the erection
to his memory of a little chapel at Montgomery
"adjacent to that . . . where my ancestors lie
buried." Among Herbert's poems appears one
other epitaph for himself, and this one is written
in his own language. It runs :—

> " READER,
> " The Monument which thou beholdest here,
>   Presents Edward, Lord Herbert, to thy sight ;
> A man, who was so free from either hope or fear,
>   To have or lose this ordinary light,
> That when to elements his body turned were,
>   He knew that as those elements would fight,
> So his immortal Soul should find above
>   With his Creator, Peace, Joy, Faith, and Love ! "[2]

---

[1] Lloyd in his Memoirs (ii. 340) gives the following account of this
monument :—" He had designed a fair monument of his own invention, to be set up for him in the church of Montgomery, according to the model following : Upon the ground a hath-piece of 14
foot square, on the middest of which is placed a Doric column, with
its right of pedestal basis, and capitols of 15 foot in height; on the
capitol of the column is mounted an urn with a heart flamboul, supported by two angels. The foot of this column is attended with
four angels, placed on pedestals at each corner of the said hath-
pace ; two having torches reverst, extinguishing the motto of
mortality ; the other two holding up palms, the emblems of victory."
The details which I quote are from Lord Herbert's will.

[2] Poems, ed. J. Churton Collins, p. 81.

But if Lord Herbert had little political influence
in his own times, his name had less in the years
that immediately followed his death. And the
march of events deprived his sons and executors
of all opportunity of carrying out his will; no
monument was set up in Montgomery Church, as
he had directed, nor was his landed property there
distributed as he desired. Montgomery Castle had
not passed through the late civil conflict without blemish ; like all fortresses in private hands, it
had been an object of suspicion to the new rulers
of the country, and when it passed into the possession of an avowed Royalist like Lord Herbert's
heir, it was doomed to immediate destruction. Its
end came peacefully. Richard Herbert, who succeeded his father in his titles, was allowed to com-
pound for his estates, but under a Parliamentary
order dated 16th June 1649 was forced to consent
to the demolition of Montgomery Castle.[1] In the
following months the ancient structure was levelled
to the ground, and the owner was granted the barren
privilege of employing his own wreckers, and of
selling the scattered stones for his own profit. He
gained, it is said, not a penny by the tantalising trans-
action. He apparently retired to London, and there
he died on 13th May 1655, while his enemies were
still in power. But his friends were able to secure

---

[1] Commons' Journal, vi. 228.

burial for him with his ancestors in Montgomery church. The old Lord Herbert's favourite grand-child, Edward, became the third Lord Herbert of Cherbury, and he lived to witness the restoration of the monarchy, in behalf of which he had loyally fought with his father throughout the civil war. He appears to have reciprocated his grandfather's affection. To him his grand-uncle, Sir Henry, dedicated the first Lord Herbert's poems when he printed them for the first time in 1665. Though twice married—first to a daughter of the very Sir Thomas Middleton who had caused his grandfather so much distress of mind and estate, and secondly to a granddaughter of his grandfather's early friend, Lord Chandos—he had no children, and on his death on 9th December 1678 the title passed to his brother Henry. With the death (without issue) of Henry, the fourth Lord, on 21st April 1691, the united baronies of Herbert of Cherbury and of Castle-Island of Kerry became extinct.[1]

---

[1] Burke's "Extinct Peerages," *s. v.* "Herbert of Cherbury." Three years later (28th April 1694) the single barony of Herbert of Cherbury was revived in favour of another Henry Herbert, the only son of Sir Henry Herbert, who survived his eldest brother five and twenty years. But this was a transient revival. The first Lord Herbert of Cherbury of this new creation died in 1709, and his only son, the second lord, left no issue on his death in 1738 to inherit the barony. When the earldom of Powis was created in 1748, and restored in 1804, the barony of Herbert of Cherbury gave its name to one of the minor titles.

APPENDIX.

APPENDIX.

I.

The early History of the Herbert Family.

The Herbert family has a well-ascertained genealogy, but Lord Herbert has not exhausted the subject, nor is his account at all points to be relied on.[1]

Dugdale, as I have noted above,[2] received assistance in his treatment of the history of the Herberts in his "Baronage" from Lord Herbert himself, and, like Lord Herbert, makes no real endeavour to trace the pedigree beyond the William Herbert who was created Earl of Pembroke in 1468. In his corrections of the "Baronage" (printed in *Collectanea Topographica et Genealogica,* i. 219 *et seq.*), Dugdale threw out the conjecture that "the common ancestor" of the family was chamberlain to King Stephen. But reference to the Domesday Survey (p. 48b.) really gives far more precise information. There we find that *Herbertus Camerarius*—one of the Conqueror's companions—held from the King two Hampshire manors, and that the Camerarius

---

[1] The subject has long formed an attractive field of labour for Welsh antiquaries, and they have derived no little satisfaction from the fact that they have been able to supplement and correct the usually accurate results of Dugdale.

[2] See p. 3.

had a son, Henry *Thesaurarius*—who held the office of roya treasurer, not only under William I., but under his two successors, and was, like his father, a Hampshire tenant *in capite* (Domesday 49b). It has been frequently stated that Henry the Treasurer was a natural son of Henry I.,[1] but his appearance in Domesday proves the absurdity of the statement. He was as old, if not older than Henry I. His father was alive as late as 1101,[2] and he himself died at a great age in Stephen's reign. Herbert Fitz-Herbert, his son, and therefore a grandson of William I.'s companion, held the office of chamberlain through Stephen's and Henry I.'s reign, and he, or his immediate successors, added estates in Yorkshire and Gloucestershire to the ancestral property in Hampshire. Herbert Fitz-Herbert's grandson, Peter, appears to have been the first of the family to secure land in Wales. When William de Braose was attainted in 1210, John granted to him the lordships of Blaenllyfni and Talgarth, together with the honour and castle of Dinas, Brecknockshire, and his successors were summoned to Parliament as lords of Blaenllyfni. Peter-Fitz-Reginald, the younger of two grandsons of Peter the first Welsh settler, identified himself with Wales. He died in 1323, having married Alice, heiress of the lord of Llanowell, Monmouthshire. Their son Herbert succeeded to this lordship, and married Margaret, heiress of the lordship of Llandwenin and Llandough ; and Adam, this Herbert's son, married Christina, the heiress of a third great landowner of Monmouthshire (Gwillim Ddû of Wernddû). In the next three

---

[1] In 1462, when the first Earl of Pembroke was created a Knight of the Garter, the oldest heralds and bards of South Wales were directed to "certify the lineage and stock of the said Earl," and in their anxiety to connect the family with the " Royal blood of the Crown of England," they made the founder of the family "son natural of King Henry the First." See Dugdale, ii. 256.

[2] Eyton's Shropshire, i. 244.

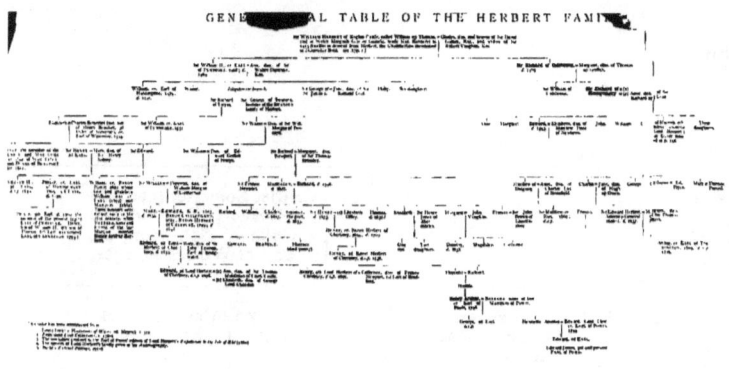

GENEALOGICAL TABLE OF THE HERBERT FAMILY

of Mach
bᵗless ᵃ
Lord H
:in Oliv(
ed in p.

Elizabeth＝Charles Somerset (nat. son
of Henry Beaufort, 3d
Duke of Somerset), *cr.*
Earl of Worcester, 1514.

HENRY, the ancestor of the
EARLS and MARQUISES
(*cr.* 1642) of WORCESTER,
and DUKES of BEAUFORT
(*cr.* 1682).

Sir HENRY,＝Mary, dau. of
2d EARL. Sir Henry
Sidney.

ᵃ

WILLIAM H.,
3d EARL,
d.s.p. 1630.

PHILIP, *cr.* EARL
of MONTGOMERY
1605, 4th EARL,
d. 1650.

William, *cr.* BARON
POWIS, 1629, whose
heir and grandson
William was *cr.*
EARL (1674) and
MARQUIS (1682).
These honours were
extinct early in the
18th century, when
BARBARA, niece and
heiress of the last
Marquis married
**Henry Arthur Her-
bert.**

PHILIP, 5th Earl, *d.* 1669, the
ancestor of the present (13th)
EARL of PEMBROKE. (Henry,
son of William H., 5th son of
Thomas, 8th Earl, was created
EARL of CARNARVON, 1793.)

Henry ?
nes of
er-
rles.

ᵗo
iters.

This table has been constructed from—

1. Lewis Dwnn's *Visitations of Wales,* ed. Meyric
2. *Powysland Club Collections,* v. 158–9.
3. The ten tables prefixed to the Earl of Powis' ed!
4. The notices of Lord Herbert's family given in h;
5. Burke's *Extinct Peerage,* 271–6.

generations the chief representatives of the family pursued their ancestors' domestic policy, and by persistently marrying neighbouring heiresses, consolidated their territorial supremacy in south-east Wales. Beneath the Welsh nomenclature, which they gradually assumed, they concealed their English origin. Maud, the daughter and heiress of Sir John Morley, married Thomas ap Gwillim ap Jenkin (who died in 1438), a great grandson of Adam Fitz-Herbert. She brought Raglan into the hands of the family, and was the grandmother of the two Herberts (the Earl of Pembroke and his brother Richard) whom Lord Herbert of Cherbury regarded as the founders of his family.[1] These men—of the thirteenth generation in descent from Henry, the Conqueror's treasurer—appear to have been the first of the family to acquire reputation for anything beyond great wealth and territorial influence.

I have given sufficient information in my notes as to the genealogy of the succeeding generations of the younger branch of the family to which Lord Herbert belonged; the accompanying table will help the reader to realise the relations of the elder to the younger branch. It is well to bear in mind that of the two Herberts who fell at Hedgecote Field in 1469, the elder, William Earl of Pembroke, is the common ancestor (1) (by the marriage of his grand-daughter Elizabeth) of the Earls and Marquises of Worcester of the seventeenth and eighteenth centuries, whose heirs bore the

---

[1] It is seldom that a family pedigree is so clearly traceable as in the present instance. The subject has been treated in a very scholarly fashion by Mr. Joseph Morris in the *Archæologia Cambrensis*, 3rd series, vol. iv. pp. 16–30. A very deliberate attempt has been made to connect the founder of the family in England—the companion of William I.—with Charlemagne, but the links await verification. The first of the Ten Tables prefixed by Lord Powis to his edition of Lord Herbert's Expedition to the Isle of Rhé professes to supply this pedigree.

courtesy title of Lord Herbert ;[1] (2) (through an illegitimate son) of the Earls of Pembroke (by a second creation)
of the sixteenth and succeeding centuries ;[2] and (3) of the
extinct Herbert family of St. Julian's, into which Lord
Herbert of Cherbury married. (The modern earldom of
Carnarvon was conferred on a son of the fifth son of the
eighth Earl of Pembroke in 1793.) Richard Herbert, the
younger brother of the fifteenth-century Earl of Pembroke,
is the common ancestor of Edward Lord Herbert of Cherbury and his successors, and of the Earls of Powis of the
latest creation (now represented by the third Earl). Thus
three English earldoms (Pembroke, Carnarvon, and Powis)
still remain in the family.

II.

Wales in the Sixteenth Century.

Throughout the fifteenth and sixteenth centuries England
was occupied in denationalising Wales. Owen Glendower
(Glyndwr) had made a desperate struggle to recover his
country's independence in the early years of Henry IV.'s
reign. His failure had been followed by a series of penal
enactments which deprived Welshmen of all political or
civic rights. Welsh customs were suppressed by law, and
intermarriage of the Welsh and English was made a capital
offence. But though the government of the country was
nominally divided between the stewards of the royal demesnes under the Prince of Wales and the feudal landowners

---

[1] Henry, third Marquis of Worcester, was created in 1682 Duke
of Beaufort, and he is the ancestor of the eighth and present Duke.

[2] The present Earl of Pembroke is the thirteenth in succession
from the first Earl of the second creation (1551.)

known as the Lord Marchers, it was practically in the latter's hands. The absence of a strong executive government combined with the new vexatious legislation to excite the people against their rulers more effectually than before ; and the rudimentary condition of Welsh society at the time intensified the evils of divided authority in the executive government. The patriarchal theories of life still regulated social institutions, and the right of a man to rob his neighbour of his property, were he strong enough to do so, was generally recognised. Every family was thus united through all its branches into a band of brigands, who marched at frequent intervals from their mountain homes to make raids upon the border-chieftains. Occasionally they made war upon each other, but their native turbulence of spirit was for many years kept in check at home by the strong bond of hatred of their common oppressors. In 1478 an attempt was made to meet the difficulties of the situation by organising a Council of Lords Marchers—a Welsh Star Chamber—with summary jurisdiction over the disturbers of the public peace. Its headquarters were fixed at Ludlow Castle, but the arrangement did not answer the expectations formed of it. The accession, with the assistance of many Welsh followers, of Henry VII., the grandson of a Welsh squire, to the English throne in 1485, led to the first improvement in the sentimental relations between the two peoples. But neither the political nor the social condition of Wales was thereby materially improved. As Lord Herbert points out in his " History of Henry VIII.," during the first years of the reign, "in about some 141 lordships marchers . . . many strange and discrepant customs " were still practised ; and although he insists that his great-grandfather, Sir Richard Herbert,[1] was a forcible administrator in a part of the Principality, he admits that "the lords marchers (who

---

[1] See p. 10 and note, *supra.*

conquered at their own cost) ruled yet by their own laws and customs, and substituted officers at their pleasure, who again committed such rapines as nothing about was safe or quiet." And the national antipathy had not yet exhausted itself. The Minister Cromwell believed that "in the trouble caused by the divorce" the Welsh were an element of weakness to England, and to illustrate England's power, he put to death Sir Rice ap Griffith in 1531, on the specious ground that he had countenanced a scheme for an invasion from Scotland in behalf of, Queen Catherine, in which the Welsh were to support the invaders.[1] In 1536 Parliament took the matter in hand. It was pointed out that "manifold robberies, murders, and other malefacts" were daily practised throughout Wales and the Welsh marches, and that justice was not administered there as in other parts of the realm. It was therefore enacted, (1) that Wales should be incorporated with England by act of union; (2) that all Welshmen should enjoy the privileges of Englishmen; (3) that all English laws were to be observed in Wales; (4) that the English language was to be alone recognised as the official language of the people; (5) that the Welsh national customs still adhered to outside North Wales were to be examined into by a special commission with a view to their extirpation. Thus the independent jurisdiction of the lords marchers was annulled: the Council was not abolished, but its functions were more distinctly defined, and it was given the new title of the Court of the Council of Wales (1543).[2] Steps were taken to form the territories of the marchers into counties. Monmouth became a new English shire, while Radnor, Brecknock, Montgomery, and Denbigh were formed into new Welsh shires. Justices of

---

[1] Letters and Papers of Henry VIII., v. 289.

[2] This court was suspended by the Long Parliament in 1641, re-established at the Restoration, and finally abolished in 1689.

assize and sheriffs were nominated for the whole Principality, and it was expected that Welsh turbulence would
straightway subside. But there were two serious defects
in this legislation. The statute affecting the Welsh language
excluded Welsh-speaking persons from political office, and
the Court of Wales adopted arbitrary modes of judicial
procedure which did little to conciliate a people which set
a high value on individual liberty. Roland Lee, afterwards Bishop of Lichfield and Coventry, entered on a
vigorous administration of the office of President at this
moment, and he resolved on forcible suppression of all lawless
outrage. "All the thieves in Wales," he wrote to Cromwell, "quake for fear," and "although," he said in another
letter, "the thieves hanged are by imagination, yet I trust
to be even with them shortly in very deed."[1] Lee forbade
the use of long strings of patronymics connected by the
syllable *ap* in personal nomenclature, and bade Welshmen
take a single surname. But the temper of the people was
not, and could not be, hastily changed. The brigands were
now outlawed, and ran risk of severe punishment. The
national feeling tolerated them, domestic ties protected
them, and the geographical features of the country made
their capture difficult. Lord Herbert's grandfather and
his father both suffered, as he tells us, from bands of
robbers, but their theories of government were little in
advance of those of their neighbours. To protect themselves, they did not appeal to the judges or to Ludlow
Castle ; they were content to summon their relatives and
retainers, to take the law into their own hands, and to
avenge themselves upon the families of those who had
offended them.[2] In 1557 Sir George Herbert of Swansea
marched upon the castle of Oxwich in the absence of its

---

[1] Ellis's Letters, 3rd ser., ii. 364, 370.
[2] See pp. 4 and 6, *supra*.

owner, Sir Rice Mansel, and in the fight an aged relation of the owner was killed. In the streets of Cowbridge, Glamorganshire, a veritable battle took place in 1576 between the supporters of the Bassetts of Beaupré and those of the Turbervilles of Penlline. In both cases the combatants were led by members of the lords marchers' families, who were infected by their neighbours' turbulent spirit. In 1580, Sir Henry Sidney, the President of the Council, intervened in a serious contention " betwixt the surnamed Thomases and Joneses," which threatened to involve all Wales.[1]

As late as 1607, a President of the Council of the Marches writes of such methods of procedure, that any man who is believed to have done his neighbour a wrong "shall hardly escape a cruel revenge, even unto death," and that the governors are powerless, because where private feuds were concerned, all men of influence combined to suppress evidence.[2] Lord Herbert himself never extricated his mind from a patriarchal belief in the right of every injured man to take personal vengeance with the aid of his family on his enemies and their families. The traditional wrongs which his relatives had suffered at the hands of the Vaughans he never forgot, and a Montague never regarded a Capulet with greater detestation than Herbert regarded any person bearing the hated name of Vaughan. The intermarriage of his sister with a Vaughan was vainly imagined by the more peaceful members of either family to be an effective treaty of peace ;[3] but readers of the autobiography will remark that the old spirit manifested itself in full intensity when Herbert met a few years later Sir Robert Vaughan.[4] Valiant as the Welshmen were admitted on all hands to be, their choleric

---

[1] Cf. the Stradling Correspondence, ed. Traherne, pp. 15–17.
[2] History of Ludlow, pp. 356–369.   [3] See p. 28, *supra.*
[4] See p. 186 *et seq. supra.*

temperament, the result of baffled national hopes, made them objects of ridicule among Englishmen till the close of the seventeenth century. Intercourse between the two peoples had by that time familiarised the one with some real knowledge of the good as well as of the bad qualities of the other. But Shakespeare's Fluellen (a satirical phonetic spelling of the Welsh Llewelyn) indicates the highest esteem in which an Englishman held his Welsh fellow-subjects. Less thoughtful writers concentrated their attention on "the rebellious attempts, the proud stomachs, the presumptuous stir, trouble, and rebellion of the fierce, unquiet, fickle, and necessitous Welshmen." [1]

The social condition of Wales owed its lasting reform to strong administrators of the stamp of Roland Lee, and to the growth of such civilising influences as commerce and education. Sir Henry Sidney, the father of Sir Philip Sidney, who was President of Wales from 1559 to 1586, did all that in him lay to suppress "brawls and contentions," both by persuasion and coercion, and affairs so improved under his regime that he could assert, with some obvious touches of exaggeration, in a letter to Sir Francis Walsingham in 1583, that "his great and high office in Wales" was "a happy place of government, for a better people to govern or better subjects Europe holdeth not." But successful as Sidney's rule undoubtedly was, it is to the translation of the Bible unto Welsh in 1567, to the establishment of free grammar schools like those of Carmarthan (1576), of Ruthin (1595), of Beaumaris (1603), of Hawarden (1609), and to the opening up of the metal and coal-mines that the country chiefly owed its future peace and prosperity. [2]

---

[1] Dedication of Powel's "Historie of Cambria" (1584) to Sir Philip Sidney.

[2] The general authorities for this chapter are Miss Jane Williams' "History of Wales;" "Documents Connected with the History of

III.

Walton's and Donne's accounts of Lord Herbert's Mother.

The following extract from Walton's "Life of George Herbert," the poet (Lord Herbert's brother), throws additional light on Lord Herbert's relations with his mother while a student at the university : he does her fuller justice than Lord Herbert does her himself (see p. 18 *et seq. supra*). Walton's description of Lady Herbert's relations with Donne is one of the most beautiful passages in seventeenth century prose literature.

"In the time of her widowhood, she being desirous to give Edward, her eldest son, such advantages of learning and other education as might suit his birth and fortune, and thereby make him more fit for the service of his country, did, at his being of a fit age, remove from Montgomery Castle with him and some of her younger sons to Oxford ; and having entered Edward into Queen's College [1] and provided him a fit tutor, she commended him to his care ; yet she continued there with him, and still kept him in a moderate awe of herself, and so much under her own eye as to see and converse with him daily ; but she managed this power over him without any such rigid sourness as might make her company a torment to her child, but

---

Ludlow," 1841 ; the first chapter of Mr. J. R. Phillip's " Civil War in Wales," and Lord Herbert's " History of Henry VIII," sub anno 1636. Churchyard, in his " Worthies of Wales," 1589, patriotically insisted on the love of peace inherent among the Welsh, but his poetical picture is clearly overdrawn in order to refute the contrary opinion current among Englishmen.

[1] This is an error. See p. 39, *supra*. Herbert was entered at University College.

with such a sweetness and compliance with the recreations
and pleasures of youth, as did incline him willingly to
spend much of his time in the company of his dear and
careful mother; which was to her great content; for she
would often say, 'That as our bodies take a nourishment
suitable to the meat on which we feed, so our souls do as
insensibly take in vice by the example or conversation with
wicked company;' and would therefore often say, 'That
ignorance of vice was the best preservation of virtue; and
that the very knowledge of wickedness was as tinder to
inflame and kindle sin, and keep it burning.' For these
reasons she endeared him to her own company, and
continued with him in Oxford for four years; in which
time her great and harmless wit, her cheerful gravity, and
her obliging behaviour gained her an acquaintance and
friendship with most of any eminent worth or learning
that were at that time in or near that University; and
particularly with Mr. John Donne, who then came accidentally to that place, in this time of her being there. It
was that John Donne who was after Dr. Donne and Dean
of St. Paul's, London; and he, at his leaving Oxford, writ
and left there, in verse, a character of the beauties of her
body and mind. Of the first he says,

> 'No Spring nor Summer beauty has such grace,
> As I have seen in an Autumnal face.'

Of the latter he says,

> 'In all her words, to every hearer fit,
> You may at revels or at council sit.'

The rest of her character may be read in his printed poems,
in that elegy which bears the name of 'The Autumnal
Beauty;' for both he and she were then past the meridian
of man's life.

"This amity, begun at this time and place, was not an

amity that polluted their souls, but an amity made up of
a chain of suitable inclinations and virtues ; an amity like
that of St. Chrysostom's to his dear and virtuous Olympias,
whom in his letters he calls his Saint ; or an amity, indeed,
more like that of St. Hierome to his Paula, whose affection to her was such, that he turned poet in his old age,
and then made her epitaph, wishing all his body were
turned into tongues, that he might declare her just praises
to posterity.   And this amity betwixt her and Mr. Donne
was begun in a happy time for him, he being then near to
the fortieth year of his age,—which was some years before
he entered into Sacred Orders :—a time when his necessities
needed a daily supply for the support of his wife, seven
children, and a family.   And in this time she proved one
of his most bountiful benefactors, and he as grateful an
acknowledger of it.   You may take one testimony for
what I have said of these two worthy persons from this
following letter and sonnet :—

"'MADAM,—Your favours to me are everywhere: I
use them and have them.   I enjoy them at London, and
leave them there ; and yet find them at Mitcham.   Such
riddles as these become things inexpressible; and such is
your goodness.   I was almost sorry to find your servant
here this day, because I was loath to have any witness of
my not coming home last night, and indeed of my coming
this morning.   But my not coming was excusable, because
earnest business detained me ; and my coming this day is
by the example of your St. Mary Magdalen, who rose
early upon 'Sunday to seek that which she loved most ;
so did I.   And from her and myself I return such thanks
as are due to one to whom we owe all the good opinion
that they whom we need most have of us.   By this
messenger and on this good day I commit the enclosed
Holy Hymns and Sonnets—which for the matter, not the
workmanship, have yet escaped the fire—to your judgment, and to your protection too, if you think them worthy

of it ; and I have appointed this enclosed Sonnet to usher them to your happy hand.—Your unworthiest servant, unless your accepting him to be so have mended him,

Jo. DONNE.

' MITCHAM, *July* 11, 1607.

' *To the Lady Magdalen Herbert, of St. Mary Magdalen.*

' Her of your name, whose fair inheritance
    Bethina was, and jointure Magdalo,
An active faith so highly did advance,
    That she once knew more than the Church did know,
The Resurrection ! so much good there is
    Delivered of her, that some Fathers be
Loth to believe one woman could do this,
    But think these Magdalens were two or three.
Increase their number, Lady, and their fame :
    To their devotion add your innocence :
Take so much of th' example, as of the name ;
    The latter half ; and in some recompense
That they did harbour Christ himself, a guest,
Harbour these Hymns, to his dear name addrest.—J. D.'

These Hymns are now lost to us ; but doubtless they were such as they two now sing in heaven.

"There might be more demonstrations of the friendship and the many sacred endearments betwixt these two excellent persons,—for I have many of their letters in my hand,—and much more might be said of her great prudence and piety ; but my design was not to write hers, but the life of her son ; and therefore I shall only tell my reader that about that very day twenty years that this letter was dated and sent her, I saw and heard this Mr. John Donne —who was then Dean of St. Paul's—weep, and preach her funeral sermon in the parish church of Chelsea, near London,[1] where she now rests in her quiet grave ; and

---

[1] On 1st July 1627. See p. 20, *supra.*

where we must now leave her, and return to her son George, whom we left in his study at Cambridge."

Dr. Donne's sermon gives similar testimony to Lady Herbert's sweetness of temper, and does not, with both Herbert and Walton, overlook the fact of her second marriage to Sir John Danvers. The following passages towards the close of the sermon are of special interest :—

"From that worthy family from which she had her original extraction and birth,[1] she sucked that love of hospitality (hospitality which hath celebrated that family for many generations successively) which dwelt in her to her end. But in that ground, her father's family, she grew not many years. Transplanted young from thence by marriage into another family of honour, as a flower that doubles and multiplies by transplantation, she multiplied into ten children,—Job's number and Job's distribution (as she would often remember), seven sons and three daughters. And in this ground she grew not many more years than were necessary for the providing of so many plants. And being then left to choose her own ground in her widowhood, having at home established and increased the estate with a fair and noble addition, proposing to herself, as her principal care, the education of her children ; to advance that she came with them and dwelt with them in the university, and recompensed them the loss of a father in giving them two mothers—her own personal care and the advantage of that place, where she contracted a friendship with divers reverend persons of eminency and estimation there, which continued to their ends. And as this was her greatest business, so she made this state a large period, for in this state of widowhood she continued twelve years. And then returning to a second marriage, that second marriage turns us to the consideration of another personal circumstance,

---

[1] The Newports.

that is, the natural endowments of her person, which were such as that her personal and natural endowments had their part in drawing and fixing the affections of such a person,[1] as by his birth and youth, and interest in great favours at court, and legal proximity to great possessions in the world, might justly have promised him acceptance in what family soever or upon what person soever he had directed and placed his affections. He placed them here, neither diverted thence nor repented since. For as the well tuning of an instrument makes higher and lower strings of one sound, so the inequality of their years was thus reduced to an evenness that she had a cheerfulness agreeable to his youth, and he had a sober staidness conformable to her more advanced years. So that I would not consider her at so much more than forty, nor him at so much less than thirty, at that time ; but as their persons were made one, and their fortunes made one by marriage, so I would put their years into one number, and finding a sixty between them, think them thirty apiece ; for as twins of one hour they lived. . . . God gave her such a comeliness as, though she were not proud of it, yet she was so content with it as not to go about to mend it by any art. And for her attire (which is another personal circumstance), it was never sumptuous, never sordid, but always agreeable to her quality and agreeable to her company ; such as she might, and such as others such as she was did wear," . . . Respecting her charitableness Donne says :—" She gave not at some great days or at some solemn goings abroad, but as God's true almoners, the sun and moon, that pass on in a continual doing of good, as she received her daily bread from God, so daily she distributed and imparted it to others. In which office though she never turned her face from those who, in a strict inquisition, might be called idle and vagrant

---

[1] Sir John Danvers.

beggars, yet she ever looked first upon them who laboured, whose labours could not overcome the difficulties nor bring in the necessities of this life, and to the sweat of their brows she contributed even her wine and her oil, and anything that was, and anything that might be, if it were not prepared for her own table. And as her house was a court, with conversation of the best, and an almshouse in feeding the poor, so was it also an hospital in ministering relief to the sick. And truly, the love of doing good in this kind, of ministering to the sick, was the honey that spread over all her bread; the air the perfume that breathed over all her house. . . . As the rule of all her civil actions was religion, so the rule of her religion was the Scripture; and her rule for her particular understanding of the Scripture was the Church. . . . In the doctrine and discipline of that Church in which God sealed her to himself in baptism she brought up her children, she assisted her family, she dedicated her soul to God in her life, and surrendered it to him in her death; and in that form of common prayer which is ordained by that Church and to which she had accustomed herself with her family twice every day, she joined that company which was about her death-bed in answering to every part thereof which the congregation is directed to answer to, with a clear understanding, with a constant memory, with a distinct voice, not two hours before she died. According to this promise, that is, the will of God manifested in the Scriptures, she expected this that she hath received, God's physic and God's music—a christianly death." [1]

---

[1] See Alford's edition of Donne's Works, vi. 271 *et seq.*, or the original duodecimo edition of the sermon (1627), pp. 137 *et seq.*

IV.

Duelling in France and England in the early years of the Seventeenth Century.

Duelling holds no more prominent place in Lord Herbert's autobiography than it deserves to hold in any full social history of James I.'s reign. The practice, although long discredited by men of sense, sprang into new life in England in the early years of the seventeenth century. The cause of the revival is probably to be found in the intimate relations existing between men of fashion in England and France. To impetuous Frenchmen like Balagny[1] the duello was indispensable, and when English men imitated French social customs, they adopted unconsciously the most characteristic feature of French social life—that sensitive regard for what Frenchmen called their honour. Henri IV. perceived the disadvantage of the practice of duelling, and in stern edicts denounced it as a capital offence. But the edicts were systematically disobeyed, and the King had not resolution enough to refuse a pardon to those who infringed them. He entreated his generals to discountenance the practice, but was himself unwilling to employ coercion in the matter. Between 1589 and 1607, it has been estimated that 4000 Frenchmen met their death in duels. Montaigne, illustrating the bellicose spirit of his fellow-countrymen, humorously states that if three Frenchmen met together in the Libyan desert, they would demand satisfaction of each other at the sword's point. It was left to Richelieu to inaugurate a determined policy of repression.[2]

---

[1] See p. 106, *supra.*
[2] Brantôme's Memoirs give the best account of duelling in France under Henry IV.

X

In England matters were little better. Every family of distinction lost some promising cadet in the early years of the century by duelling, and the foreign wars in which Englishmen were in the habit of engaging as free and independent volunteers encouraged in them a spirit of aggression without accustoming them to strict military discipline. The war in Cleves and Juliers was fertile in duels among Englishmen, in spite of the precautions taken both by Sir Edward Cecil and Count Maurice, and the quarrels, although invariably based on very flimsy pretexts, resulted in very many fatalities. In 1609 Sir Hatton Cheek killed Sir Thomas Dalton in a duel fought on the Calais sands, in which both combatants were armed, according to the French rules, with rapier as well as dagger.[1] Herbert's disputes with Lord Howard of Walden and Sir Thomas Somerset came happily to a spiritless and bloodless conclusion ; but a similar encounter between Edward, Lord Bruce of Kinloss, and Sir Edward Sackville was pursued in deadly earnest. The quarrel arose out of a love-suit, and after several abortive meetings in Holland and England, the two men fought on September 1613 under the walls of Antwerp, where Bruce was killed and Sackville severely wounded.[2] Steele has given a faithful account of this long and sanguinary conflict in Nos. 129 and 133 of the *Guardian*, from Sackville's manuscript narrative. Nicholas Charles, Lancaster Herald, writing to Sir Robert Cotton of the termination of this meeting, declares (10th September 1613) the world of London to be full of rumours of duels to be fought abroad. "A gentleman of [Lord Harington]," he says, "[was] very treacherously killed by the means of Sir Andrew Keith

---

[1] These weapons were to be used in Herbert's duel with Lord Howard. It was usual in France for the seconds to fight as well as the principals.

[2] Clarendon's " History," i. 60 ; Winwood's " Memorials," iii. 422, 454, 476.

master of the horse to the Lady Elizabeth.[1] But Keith is
in hold to be sent over into England. There is also a
quarrel between my Lord of Essex and Mr. Harry Howard,
and one of them is gotten over, but there were letters
sent to the Archduke and the French King to prevent their
desperate proceedings. There is also talk of a quarrel between my Lord of Rutland and my Lord Danvers, as also of
other noble and gentle men of good quality."[3] Chamberlain,
the well-known gossip, gave even more alarming proofs of
the prevalence of duels at this moment. "Though there yet
be," he writes (9th September 1613), " in shew a settled peace
in these parts of the world, yet the many private quarrels are
very great, and prognosticate troubled humours, which may
breed dangerous diseases, if they be not purged and prevented.
I doubt not but you have heard the success of the combat
between Edward Sackville and Lord Bruce of Kinlos. . . .
Here is speech likewise that the Lord Norris and Sir
Peregrine Willoughby are gone forth for the same purpose,
and that the Lord Chandos and Lord Hay are upon the
same terms : there was a quarrel kindling betwixt the Earls
of Rutland and Montgomery, but it was quickly quenched
by the King, being begun and ended in his presence. But
there is more danger betwixt the Earl of Rutland and the
Lord Danvers, though I heard yesterday it was already or
upon the point of compounding. But that which most now
listen after is what will fall out betwixt the Earl of Essex
and Mr. Henry Howard, who is challenged and called to

---

[1] The Electress-Palatine. Further particulars of this quarrel are
given in a letter printed in "Court and Times of James I.," i. 265.
Sir Andrew Keith was guilty of a murderous assault on a gentleman named Bashall, which closely resembles Ayres' attack on
Herbert at Whitehall.

[2] Brother of Lord Howard of Walden.

[3] Ellis's " Original Letters," 2d ser., iii. 234.

account by the Earl for certain disgraceful speeches of him. They are both gotten over, the Earl from Milford Haven, the other from Harwich, with each of them two seconds. The Earl has his base brother and one Captain Ouseley, or rather, as most affirm, Sir Thomas Beaumont, as one interested in the quarrel." In a later letter Chamberlain describes the action of the Council taken in this business.[1]

These practices ill assorted with James I.'s pacific temperament, and he took vigorous steps to suppress them. He directed his Ministers to collect information as to the mode of dealing with such breaches of the peace on the Continent, and then issued a proclamation, penned with his own hand, calling on his peaceable subjects to support his repressive policy.[2] The Star Chamber was directed to take the ·matter in hand, and, to make a preliminary example, two "base mechanical persons," named Priest and Wright, were charged by the Crown, the one with sending a challenge, and the other with accepting it. Sir Francis Bacon, the new Attorney-General, conducted the prosecution, and in a speech full of common sense and high principle illustrated the evils of the practice. "It is a miserable effect," he said in one of the finest passages, "when young men full of towardness and hope, such as the poets call *auroræ filii*, sons of the morning, in whom the expectation and comfort of their friends consisteth, shall be cast away

---

[1] Court and Times of James I., i. 272, 276.

[2] In a MS. volume in the Cottonian Library in the British Museum are many documents relating to the history of duelling in England at the time. In Ellis's Letters, 1st ser., iii. 107–110, is printed from the volume Sir Francis Cottington's account of the treatment of duellists in Spain. Sir John Finet, writing from Paris, 19th February 1609–10, is the author of another account there, treating of the duels in France.

and destroyed in such a vain manner ; but much more it is
to be deplored when so much noble and gentle blood shall
be spilt upon such follies, as if it were adventured in the
field in the service of the king and the realm, were able to
make the fortune of a day and to change the future of a
kingdom." Coke delivered judgment against the prisoners.
Priest was ordered to pay £500, and Wright 500 marks, and
both had to do penance at the next Surrey assizes, and to
remain in Fleet prison for some months. The Star Chamber
decree and Coke's judgment were printed and widely cir-
culated.[1] But the reader will remember that these proceedings had little effect on Herbert, who, until he was well past
middle life, was always anxious to find opportunity for a duel.
Massinger and Chapman, with other Jacobean dramatists,
continued to make duelling an important feature in their
portraits of contemporary society. That the practice died
hard in England, and temporarily revived whenever the
morality of the upper classes suffered serious deterioration,
students of the reign of Charles II. and of the Regency well
know. But when the thinness of the arguments in its favour
was once thoroughly exposed by Bacon and Coke, and re-
exposed by vigorous writers like Jeremy Collier and Steele,
it was virtually abandoned to the thoughtless and the idle.[2]

---

[1] Spedding's Life and Letters of Bacon, iv. 395–416.

[2] In Hearne's *Curious Discourses* (1771), ii. 225 *et seq.*, is a
singular paper signed "Edward Cook," entitled "Duello Foiled."
It purports to be a paper prepared before 1604 for a meeting of
the ancient Society of Antiquaries, originally formed by Archbishop
Parker in 1572, and recounts the device successfully adopted by
the friends of two would-be duellists to prevent a meeting. The
correspondence that passed between the disputants is given at length.
Jeremy Collier's "Dialogue of Duelling" in his "Essays upon
Several Moral Subjects" (1698), i. 113 *et seq.*, is an amusing and
vigorous piece of reasoning.

V.

Lord Herbert's quarrel with Lord Howard of Walden.

In the MS. Lansdowne in the British Museum (xcix. art. 99) is a copy of some of the correspondence that passed between Sir Edward Herbert and Lord Howard of Walden relative to their quarrel, together with an account of the curious incident by Peyton, Lord Howard's second. The document runs thus :[1]—

" Sr E[dward] H[erbert], his first letter.

"MY LORD,—Though for the matter in question between us I do not hold myself bound to seek you, yet, since I have withdrawn myself, I have thought fit to acquaint yourself that I will wait your leisure any time before your going into England, to give that honest account that I promised and shall ever maintain.

"E[DWARD] H[ERBERT].

" The answer.

"Sᴿ Eᴅ. HERBERT,—I have not withdrawn myself from the place you left me in : if you have anything to say to me, you may easily find me before my going into England.

"T[HEOPHILUS] H[OWARD].

" The second letter.

"MY LORD,—Since I perceive your Lordship satisfied so far that you have not any meaning to call me in question, which by your Lordship's offer to draw your sword I might have conjectured, and that neither by it nor any way else I find not myself to have

---

[1] I have modernised the spelling.

received the least hurt from you, I shall no longer trouble myself to satisfy your Lordship, unless you deny this in any particular.

"E[DWARD] H[ERBERT].

"Answer.

"S^R ED. HERBERT, — I am so well satisfied with my own actions that I will trouble myself no further.

"T[HEOPHILUS] H[OWARD].

" Upon this passed by me[1] from Sir Ed. Herbert to my Lord a courteous message, and afterwards a reconcilement between them made by my Lord General.[2] Some four or five days after Sir Ed. Herbert wrote a challenge in these words : [3]—

"MY LORD,—Having lately understood that a report of your Lordship's striking me is gone so far as to M. Betune and M. de Chatillon,[4] and that, for anything I know,. it may be so related in England, and that the authors of this report may be lackeys or people unworthy my revenge, to the end I may put my honour out of dispute, I have thought fit to require your Lordship so to clear this that I may be declared as free from any touch from your Lordship as I know myself to be, or that you would think of some time and place in your return to do me reason, protesting that upon whether of these your Lordship shall resolve, that neither malice nor desire to win upon your Lordship's honour causeth this, but only a necessity so to right myself, so that I may be held worthy

---

[1] The writer is Peyton, Lord Howard's second.
[2] Sir Edward Cecil.
[3] Herbert, on pp. 117-118 *supra* overlooks this correspondence, and admits no preliminary settlement of the dispute.
[4] Two French generals, see page 116, note.

in honest reputation. So attending your Lordship's answer at Dusseldorf, which, in regard of our reconcilement, I must make any way questionable, I rest your Lordship's humble servant,

"E[DWARD] H[ERBERT].

" *This 11th of September* 1610.

" This was sent by one Mr. Turner of my Lord Governor's company after Sir Edward Herbert had taken his leave of my Lord General and his Excellency [1] and withdrawn himself into the woods. My Lord would take no hold of the former reconciliation, as he might well have done, to refuse him, but, as soon as I could be called to him from his Excellency his quarter, returned this answer :—

" *The answer.*

"S[R] ED. HERBERT,—I thought you had been satisfied of the things passed betwixt us ; but since I find by your letter that it is not so, I will answer you at the time and place so appointed, as this bearer shall acquaint you with.

T[HEOPHILUS] H[OWARD].

" I found him by the woodside near his Excellency his quarter ; he withdrew himself with me from the company he had, being Captain Herbert [2] and a servant or too, and received the answer with much contentment at my Lord's honourable proceeding. Demanding of me the circumstances left to my relation, I first required to know his second, since my Lord had chosen me. He would fain have had none, but since my Lord's pleasure was such, he chose his own brother, which I accepted of, and told him my Lord would meet him the next morning on horseback with a single rapier. I had not the length of it with me, but

---

[1] Count Maurice.
[2] Either William or Thomas Herbert. See pp. 21, 23, *supra.*

desired that he would send his second to my quarter about dinner-time and he should see it : all which he accepted of, and desired me to tell my Lord that he would come up to him bravely without malice, to fight for his own honour and the honour of his nation, and desired me to be secret. I answered he needed not to doubt my secrecy, nor to be met with like resolution as he spake of. About dinner-time himself instead of his second came near our quarter, and sent in a gentleman, his servant, named Omerfielde (?), who told me his master desired to speak with me. I went to him ; he asked me the length of my Lord's sword. I told him I did expect his brother to fetch it, because he had so appointed. Nevertheless, if he would stay there, he should have it : he desired that that servant of his might bring it him. I said it had been more proper for his brother, yet I would not be therein curious : so we both together measured the sword, and I gave him the length of it. I told him the place should be on the farther side of that wood where I found him in the morning. He uttered some discontentment at his want of horses, yet said he would come on any he could get, how unfit soever, or on foot, and let my Lord use the advantage. I answered my Lord sought no advantage, but he knew how my Lord would come provided : that if he had challenged at the first, he might have had more time, but now my Lord being upon the point of departure, he had no reason to delay his own affairs for his satisfaction. He said he was sorry that his inquiry for horses might give suspicion of what was intended. About four of the clock in the afternoon the same Omerfielde came to me with a sword that was a thought longer than my Lord's, protesting that he could find no cutler in all the army, it being Sunday, but that he would use all diligence to make it even. I told him I did expect no less, and desired that Mr. Herbert might come to me : he said he should, and so afterwards he did, and we had a slight view of one another's weapons.

" Sir Edward Herbert guessed rightly that his inquiry for horses would spread the business. For he sought in likely places to be well furnished, [but would not have been discovered] if he had not been refused first of Sir Charles Morgan, to whom he was free of the end, and desired him to be his second, but was refused of both,[1] then to Count Henry,[2] and then M. de Chatillon and divers others to borrow horses. M. Chatillon sent for Sir Charles Morgan, and told him that he saw Mr. Herbert take leave of his Excellency, and now that he came to borrow great horses ; laying these things together, he could guess it was to fight with my Lord of Walden . . . [?], and that he being an officer in chief of the army, held himself bound to impart his suspicion to his Excellency. In the evening these bruits and others spread, I know not how, even unto the particularities of weapon (so that nothing but the time and place were secret), moved my Lord to leave the General's quarter and me to meet his Lordship, but I should have been stopped in our own quarter. We spent the most part of the night in Sir John Ratclife's quarter, holding as good watches as we could to prevent a surprise of any guard that his Excellency might have sent, and about three or four of the clock we went to the woodside appointed, where they were to fight by seven. We walked twice the whole length of the woodside and saw nobody, then withdrew ourselves into covert of the wood, lest some horsemen might discover and take us. When it grew lightsome, my lackey told us he saw two men walking by the woodside on whitish horses : my Lord, after a small pause, bade me look out to see if it were Sir Edward Herbert, and, if it were, to let him know he may hear from him. I walked out so far as I might discern the whole side of the wood, but [saw] no two horsemen ; yet thinking they might be covered for the

---

[1] *i.e.*, both request for horses and second.
[2] Brother of Count Maurice.

same purpose that we were, I walked there a pretty while that they might discern me. But seeing nobody show out of the wood, and considering it was yet before the hour, I returned to my Lord. About a quarter of an hour after, his Lordship bade me look out again, and then I was quickly driven back by the sight of a horseman, who passing by and keeping his course, I went out and saw another galloping towards, which I hoped to have been Mr. Herbert, but when he came near enough for me to discern my error, I returned to our covert.

" Then I sent out my lackey to discover the worst, who told me very soon that all the woodside was laid with horsemen ; and we might see them scour up and down, but kept ourselves as close as we could. About half an hour after this, being near the hour appointed, Mr. Selinger came directly to us, and told my Lord that he attended to no purpose, for my Lord General had taken Sir Edward Herbert long since in the middle of the wood, not far from the place where he seemed to have lodged that night ; that he was mounted upon a great horse of Sir James Erskin's, who being at Aix, his lieutenant had furnished Sir Edward Herbert [with horses] either voluntarily or receiving a letter from his Captain : further, that he had with him a Scotsman, and not his brother (who was intercepted in Reymester), that this Scotsman had a case of pistols, all which seemed very strange to us, that expected him with a second armed as I was, with rapier and dagger, and two lackeys without weapons. The colour of this Scotsman's horse being bay, it seemed to us that the two horsemen which my servant had seen were not these, and consequently that Sir Edward Herbert had not been on the very place appointed at all : but in truth, the wood was so laid before the time assigned, that it had been to no purpose, since they could not ˸fight in the woods, and any ground chosen without must have offered them to the full power of all the horse-men. Thus prevented by the care of his Excellency and

my Lord General, and being entreated by a messenger
from him to go home, we left the wood and came to our
quarters. J. PEYTON."[1]

VI.

The following were the instructions given to Herbert by
James the First on his first mission to France. The original
is preserved at Powis Castle.[2]

"JAMES R.

" *Instrucͨcons for our trustie and well beloved servant Sir Edwar
Herbert, Knight, our Ambassador with the French King.*

"Having occasion at this present to employ some person of
specialle quality, judgement, discretion and trust to reside as our
ambassador with our good brother the French king, we have out
of our princely favour been pleased to make choice of you as of one
whom we hold in all respects sufficient and capable of such an
employment, and of whose fidelity and zealous affection to our
service we have ever entertayned a gratious opinion.

"There be not many particulars that we have to give you in
charge by way of instrucc'n, nor shall it be greatly needfull if you
observe but this one generall end, and thereunto apply you endevors,
which is, to give that king the best assurance you may from time to
time of our brotherly friendship and affecc'on towards him, letting
him know that to this purpose principally we have sent you as our

---

[1] The indistinct signature may be T. Peyton, but another copy
of Peyton's account, described by Mr. J. C. Jeaffreson in the Hist.
MSS. Com. Fifth Rep., has the signature J. See p. 48, *supra.* The
paper is labelled, "Challenge betwixt my Lord Walden and Sir
Edward Herbert. September 1610."

[2] Powysland Collections, vi. 417. See p. 190, *supra.*

ambassador to reside near his person ; and you may tell him further
that howsoever by the meanes of all instruments and minist'rs there
hath been of late some misunderstanding between us, yet nevertheless there should never enter into our heart the least sparke of ill
affecc'on towards him, as on the other side this last honour and
courtisy that he hath done us by sending hither a gentleman so
qualified and every way accomplished as is the Marquis of Tresnel,
and so timely to declare his condolence with us for the death of
our late dearest wife the queen, hath imprinted in us that certaine
perswasion and assurance of his reciprocall friendship towards us ;
we thereupon being very unwilling to be prevented in courtisy or in
doing that honour which we desired, have made all the hast that
possibly we might to dispatch you away unto him before any
ordinary embassador should come from thence unto us.

"And because the meaning is not to be wanting in any good
office which may testify the reality of our professions unto him, you
shall let him know that we, understanding of the troubles in
governing his kingdom is at this present embroyled, have given the
order, as well out of our singular love unto him, as also in regard
of the promise wee made to the king his father of happy memory,
to offer him in our name the best assistance that we can afford him,
either by our faithful advice or otherwise, whensoever he shall have
at any time occation or use of our help, and shall think fit to
signify so much unto us.

"Next you shall take notice of the great obligation we have unto
him, and gave him thanks accordingly for the true sense he hath of
our present griefe and affliction by reason of the queen's death, our
dearest wife, as his ambassador (the Marquis of Tresnel) hath
expressed the same unto us, assuring him that, for our part, we
cannot be less sensible of anything that may befall him, but must
be equally affected, either with joy or sorrow, as the subject shall
give cause ; neither may you omitt to perform the like ceremony
unto the queen.

"And hereupon you may take a fitt occasion to congratulate him
in our name for the marriage of his sister, Madame Chrestienne,
with the Prince of Piemont, to which alliance we wish all honour
and happiness, as well for the interest which the king hath therein
of himself, as also in respect of the singular affecc'on we bear unto

the House of Savoy, and the strict amity which is betwixt us and that duke at this present.

"Lastly, whereas it was agreed and concluded by a treaty dated the 19th of August in the year 1610, betwixt certain commissioners appointed on our part, and Le Sieur de la Boderie, then ambassador from the French king, residing here with us, on behalf of the king his master, that forasmuch as the sayed king was at that time in his minority, he should therefore afterwards, when he came to be major, take a solemn oath for the observation of all things conteyned in the said treaty, being thereunto duly required by a ambassador sufficiently authorised for such a purpose. We have to that end enabled you, by a commission under our greate seale of England in his name, to require and to take the sayd oath, hereby willing and commanding you to see the same effected according to your commission in such due manner and form as is usual in like cases.

"GEO. CALVERT.

"*7th May* 1619."

VII.

Lord Herbert's Correspondence.

The earliest extant letters with which I have met are four addressed by Herbert to his guardian Sir George More of Loseley in 1602–1603. They have been already printed in Kempe's *Loseley MSS.*, pp. 143–146. In August 1602 Herbert was in his twentieth year.[1]

Lord Herbert to his Father-in-wardship, Sir George More.

Worthy Father, if I were persuaded that you did *amare ex judicio*, and not *judicare ex amore*, your good opinion of me would

---

[1] I have not printed the letters at full length, but given only the most important passages.

make me show more to deserve the continuance of it, than the greatest discouragement of my little abilities could prevail to the breaking of my weak beginnings.

Lest you should think this country ruder than it is, I have sent you some of our bread, which I am sure will be dainty, howsoever it be not pleasing; it is a kind of cake which our country people use, and made in no place in England, but in Shrewsbury—if you vouchsafe the taste of them, you enworthy the country and sender. Measure not my love by substance of it, which is brittle; but by the form of it, which is circular, and *circulus* you know is *capacissima figura*, to which that mind ought to be like, that can most worthily love you. Yet I would not have you to understand form so as though it were hereby *formal;* but, as *forma dat esse*, so my love and observance to be *essential;* and so wishing it worthy your acceptance, I rest—Your son that knoweth your worth,

HERBERT.

Scribbled *raptim* as you see, and hope will pardon.

EYTON, *this 17th of August 1602.*

To the right worthy and his honourable
friend Sir George More, Knight, his
beloved father, &c.

———

Noble Knight, I perceive your love placed in this our family to be as faithful in continuance, as it hath been excessive in greatness, when you will send to find us out in a corner among the *toto divisos orbe Britannos;* such a love in these days wants an example, and is not like to be paterned; only to us it is a comfort, that desire at least to be thankful, that seeing it was begun without our desert, we need not stand doubtful of ourselves, as knowing that his worthy disposition that began it of himself, will continue it as undeservedly as he did unmatchably enter into it. This small testimony doth your many kindnesses challenge at my hands, who doth more honour your virtues than the pied outside of an hereditary nobility.

I hear of your indeed royal entertainment of the King; a happiness able to make you forget yourself, much more your remote friends, were it not you.

I am very sorry to hear of the increase of the plague, which besides many inconveniences, will hinder our meeting this many a day, I fear. I pray God to stay His heavy hand, in whom I wish both our preservations, as—The son that lives more than half in his loving father,

HERBERT.

MONTGOMERY CASTLE, *this 28th of August* 1603.

I pray you present my due salutations to your lady, and Sir Robert Moore and his lady, not forgetting good Mr. Pulsted.

To that worthy knight, Sir George More,
at his house, Loseley, in Surrey, &c.

If absence (noble knight) could afford friends a better testimony of love than remembrance, or remembrance express itself in a better fashion than in letters, to you especially, to your nought-needing self (if either invention or example would have yielded me a newer means), my engaged love would not have omitted the execution of it to your worthy self, unto whom the greatest service I can profess is too little to be performed ; but where means scant the manifestation of more, let your acceptance make that good, which my ability could make no better. I pray you think not that, because my letter contains not any essential business, that therefore it is merely formal, but rather that my thankfulness would disclose itself in any shape sooner than forego the least occasion to show how many ways he is—Yours, HERBERT.

MONTGOMERY CASTLE, *this 12th of October* 1603.

To my much honoured father, Sir George
More, Loseley, in Surrey.

Your continual remembrance of us (noble knight), though it cannot add to the opinion of your worthy love (only in respect of yourself worthy) ; yet it may confirm it, if there can be a confirmation of that which is held most assured.

The barrenness of this country, as in all other things, is dilated into the scarcity of any occurrence fit your entertaining, much unlike your part, where all good varieties warring among themselves distract the mind in their choice, of some of which as you have made me partaker, so the most acceptable beyond comparison was to hear of your health.

If there be a Parliament shortly, if I can, I will be one of the number, a burgesse or something, rather than get out, for I think I shall give away my interest in this shire to another ; not making doubt to meet you there, though once in my hearing you seemed to be weary of your being of the House.

So with the protestation of an unfeigned affection to do you any acceptable service, I rest—Your adopted son in name, but natural all other ways, HERBERT.

MONTGOMERY CASTLE, this 4th of December, 1603.

I must give my lady great thanks (for in my letter I have testified of you) for my little brother.

Mr. Henry Morrice remembers his love to you, with many thanks for your kind entertainment of him when he was with you.

To his most honoured father, Sir George
More, Knight, at Loseley, give these.

In the British Museum is a valuable volume in manuscript containing Herbert's correspondence during his embassy in France for the years 1619 and 1620. It is among the Additional MSS., and is numbered 7082. I have had the whole of it copied, and give below some extracts likely to prove of interest to the reader of Herbert's life. The volume opens with a series of letters addressed by Herbert to the Prince of Orange and other English and foreign friends, announcing the writer's appointment to the French embassy. In the first letter addressed to the King (fol. 8) Herbert writes (under date 29th May 1619, *stilo Anglico*) that the distracting quarrel between Louis XIII. and his mother Marie de Medicis had been compounded, and the former

Y

released from her imprisonment at Blois.[1] Herbert concludes thus :—

I cannot omit to tell your Majesty of a circumstance which had almost broken this peace about the time that it was most treated of by the Commissioners. . . . For whilst these did negotiate there was discovered a design to give fire to the powder in the castle, the ruins whereof were likely to fall upon the Queen's lodgings, that were not far off. They lay the fault upon the Comte de Schomberg, but he excuseth himself. In the meantime the Queen made a long complaint thereof unto the King. It is much desired by the Prince of Piedmont, son of the Duke of Savoy, that the King and Queen-mother should meet : but some dislike it, as fearing natural affection should bring them too near : others dislike it, lest repetition of unkindness should put them further assunder : they therefore who labour this prescribe the words and behaviour on both sides. This is the substance of all I can learn as yet worthy your Majesty's knowledge.

Another letter (fol. 13) of the same date to the King begins with a characteristic apology for the writer's style :—

I must humbly desire in all my letters to be thus understood, that if the second do not contradict the first, your Majesty would be pleased to take it as a confirmation. For my last I find nothing in it to reform, if your Majesty be pleased to pardon the rudeness and ignorance of my style, which I therefore humbly submit unto your Majesty's good acceptation.

The settlement between the Queen-mother and the French King was menaced by the rude behaviour of the Queen's messenger to Luynes, the King's favourite, who had really instigated Louis XIII. to attack his mother, and whose true character Herbert soon came to know and detest. But at first he had only good words for Luynes.

The Comte de Bresne . . . being sent unto the French King on a message from her, did not only omit to salute Mons. de Luynes, having first saluted all the rest, but braved him in such a fashion that

---

[1] See p. 194, *supra.*

it was interpreted by some as a slighting of the favour the French King hath showed him, which I hear the King took very ill, and therefore dismissed him without answer. This hath made P. Benille travail again, and the labour is now to bring the Queen and Mons. de Luynes to accord. . . . I find Mons. de Luynes much envied, but cannot learn wherein his greatest enemies can justly tax[1] him ; for they avow his intentions are good : that so at most they can find no fault with him but that he cannot help, wherein they conclude him better than themselves.

. . . For myself, I am invited by the French King to come to him : for which purpose Mons. de Puisieux (secretaire des commandements du Roy) writ me a letter as in his Majesty's name. This makes me prepare to find him at Tours, though I have somewhat deferred it, in hope of your Majesty's further commandments. But on Monday, God willing, shall go, if I hear nothing to the contrary ; for so was your Majesty's pleasure at my departure. . . .

Herbert finally reports a rumour that the Prince of Piedmont is a candidate for the throne of the Empire which has just become vacant, and expresses a hope that the rumour is true.

"But," he adds, "we must not prevent[2] your Majesty's judgment and wisdom with our inconsiderations."

With this letter Herbert sends another note (fol. 15), stating that a man named James Haig had discovered to him a Jesuit plot against James's life.

Writing to the Secretary Naunton (fol. 26) on $\frac{10}{20}$ July 1619, Herbert refers to Count Henry of Nassau's visit to France,[3] and to the French jealousy of the Dutch. He points out in vigorous terms the advantage of a permanent alliance between Holland and England, and first notifies the approach of the plague to Paris :—

The estate of these parts is still alike full of change and uncer-

---

[1] *i.e.* censure.   [2] *i.e.* anticipate.   [3] See p. 200, *supra.*

tainty, and for those that look on of entertainment. . . . Comte Henry[1] going to see the King at Tours on his way to Orange, was invited nowhere but to the council table ; where after a chair presented him to sit down, he was expostulated about the death of Barnaveldt, and told in these express words the act was unjust and barbarous withal. I hear since (by the Holland Ambassador) there is a command given to seize on all the Dutch ships in French ports, and that the French take it very ill our new league with the Hollander, wherein they understand we have excluded the French from the East-Indies, which has made them to vaunt as to talk of sending out a fleet to right themselves. All I will infer out of this, is to beseech your Honour (as a true and noble English heart) to take this occasion to dispose the King and state to enter into a straight league with the Hollander, who alone on earth can either hurt or do us good.

I have not written at all unto his Majesty at this time, because I know not what news you may have of the plague here : there are but some twenty-four or twenty-five houses infected in all the town ; besides it is not very infectious nor mortal, for the one half escape, and I see no body dislodge ; yet the Parliament speaks of retiring, which if it much increase I will follow.

On 14th July 1619 Herbert informs (fol. 28) Sir Robert Naunton that he has

sent to Mons. de Luynes, to let him know his Majesty doth understand, and will accept of his services. All this I have chosen to do by letter, that I might not put his Majesty to unnecessary charges : yet if your honour think fit I should go, I doubt not to overtake any inconvenience the business may suffer by my absence.

On 23rd July Herbert sent a French letter to Luynes, expressing James I.'s high esteem of his proffer of friendship to England (fol. 30). Luynes replied on 27th July (fol. 32) and paid Herbert many high-flown compliments.

---

[1] See p. 200.

Herbert, on 29th July, found it necessary (fol. 34) to urge Naunton to hand over to the French government a French malefactor who had fled to England and been taken into Buckingham's favour. He argues that it is a mere act of international courtesy :—

I come to the latter part of your letter, which is concerning Gautier, who for having killed a brave French gentleman and of a noble house in a most base fashion fled to England, where for his excelling on the lute he was received into the favour of my Lord the Marquis of Buckingham. I therefore thought fit first to acquaint his Lordship (who I assure myself never understood his fault) what this King demands concerning him : but having received no answer as yet, I humbly beseech your Honour to represent unto his Lordship, that whereas the English could not lately walk the street without affront and injuries [in Paris], they are now restored to all the favours and good opinion they can desire : besides, since they have accorded all my requests both for our state and particular persons, that his Lordship would be pleased to think at least of some indifferent way for their satisfaction in this. In the mean I do not so much as incline your Honour any way, having no other design but, together with my due respects to my Lord the Marquis Buckingham, to acquit myself of my obligation to this place. But your Honour shall understand more at large of all these particulars by the Comte de Tillieres,[1] who set forth on Monday the 2d of August (*Anglico stilo*), and intends to be at Calais on the 6th following, and so to pass with the first commodity. I humbly beseech your Honour to give order for his good reception, and that all those courtesies I have received here may be returned on him, which will assuredly entertain all good correspondence. Your Honour will find him a discreet gentleman if I be not deceived, having no other acquaintance but a visit he gave me this day.

Herbert sends a postscript about the plague :—

The plague doth increase, but not much of 67,000 tecta or covered

---

[1] The French ambassador in London.

houses esteemed to be in this town, they account 300 only to be infected, which is but little in proportion ; yet because I have a great family, and that if (which God forbid) the plague should seize on any of them it would be too late to dislodge, I think fit to take the commodity of a fair house offered me in the country not far off.

In sending ($^{24th\ July}_{2d\ August}$) to Naunton a report of the likelihood of further warfare between the supporters of the Queen-mother and Louis XIII. (fol. 33), Herbert returns to the plague, which clearly caused him some anxiety :—

The plague does increase here, but not much : yet the academies are dislodged, whose example I think to follow, unless it decreaseth or be *in statu.*

Herbert withdrew immediately to Montmorency's palace at Merlou, and thence he reports to Naunton (fol. 35) the settlement of the civil disturbances in France (23d August).

There follow several letters of no great importance touching a misunderstanding which arose between Herbert and Sir Theodore de Mayerne, the well-known physician, (fol. 36–40). Mayerne had been engaged in some secret diplomacy in France in 1618, and had managed to offend the French King. He therefore asked Herbert to adjust their differences. But Herbert, taking the matter seriously, set inquiries on foot in both France and England as to what the nature of his offence had been; and Mayerne complained to James I. that Herbert had insulted him by taking for granted that he was in the wrong. Herbert declared (Sept.) to Naunton (fol. 41), that Mayerne had misunderstood him, and that he had secured full satisfaction for him at the French court. Mayerne was attending at the time Herbert's sister, probably Lady Jane of Abemarles, and Herbert wished "to comfort him to look to my sick sister, who hath long been his patient," and "to oblige him the more to procure her health." At the same time Herbert was much harassed by the French demand for the extradition of Gautier and was anxious to learn "whether his Majesty, on the examples of Tyrone and Bothwell (whom France had refused to surrender) was being inclined to keep him in England still." He asked for the removal of all ambiguity on this point (fol. 41). On 4th October 1619 he wrote a French note to M. de Puisieux, pointing out that James had never insisted on the extradition of Tyrone or Bothwell ; and that he wished to know whether a reciprocal agreement were possible by which malefactors of the one country, who had taken refuge in the other, should be handed over to their own government (fol. 51). Finally, on 25th October (fol. 64), Herbert informed Naunton that the suit was relinquished by the French ministers.

Another matter treated at length in Herbért's correspondence at this time (fol. 46–51), concerns one Pierre Hugon, who was believed to have stolen two coffers of jewels, belonging to the late Queen Anne, and to have entrusted them to the keeping of some French nobles. Hugon was in prison in England. At length Herbert obtained permission to break open the two trunks of Pierre Hugon "remaining in the Hotel des Orisons at Paris, in the custody of Paris, servant to the Marquis de Trenelle." He forwarded the inventory of their contents to Naunton (fol. 52–55) through his brother Henry, in October, and among the items were some of the missing jewels (fol. 64).

Herbert was an enthusiastic supporter of his friend the Elector Palatine, and was very anxious that he should accept the perilous offer of the throne of Bohemia. On 9th September 1619 he wrote (fol. 47) that " whether the Palatine will accept the offer," was the chief subject of discussion at the French court :—

But God forbid he should refuse it, being the apparent way His Providence hath opened to the ruin of the Papacy. I hope therefore his Majesty will assist in this great work, having by the means of winter approaching time enough to resolve, and prepare by treaties and other ways against the next summer. For my part, most faithfully and willingly I offer both life and fortunes to serve his Majesty this or any way I may be of use.

On 29th September Herbert recurs to the subject (fol. 55) :—

For the business of Bohemia I understand this King hath written to the King my Master and to the Palatine to dissuade the acceptance of that crown, at which some of this court take occasion to laugh. In the meanwhile his Majesty and the Palatine's Highness may be assured they have here a great party, and which if this King be indifferent will be certainly much the stronger side. . . . I cannot believe a state so unsettled and tottering [as this] is ready yet to declare itself on either side : besides, it is extreme needy at this present, the King having stayed his journey to Chartres from Ambois a great while for want of money.

The Elector desired to maintain his friendship with Lord Herbert, and on 21st October (fol. ·64), the latter writes to Naunton :—

I must acquaint your Honour that during my stay at Compiegne,[1] I received a letter from the Palatine's Highness, wherein his Highness was pleased to advertise me that the Elector of Treves (or Trier) would shortly come in person to this King : that his business was to accuse the Palatine's Highness for taking arms and disturbing the public peace ; to which his Highness desires me to answer : That (when there was on other consideration) he and the princes of the union were obliged to it for the defence of their countries, being so near unto Bohemia : that the ecclesiastics could not allege any such reason ; that, therefore, in them it was unjust to take arms, but in himself and the rest necessary : so that in general his Highness wishes me to do him all good offices in this court, and particularly to present the many helps and courtesies this King's father received from his Highness's predecessors upon all occasions, assuring me in conclusion that his Majesty would approve well any

---

[1] He had visited the court there.

service I could do his Highness in this kind. That which first occurred upon reading this letter, that I wanted instructions from his Majesty to treat in this business, yet when I considered, what and for whom I should speak, I recollected myself, and went immediately unto the King's principal ministers, the Chancellor, Monsieur le Guardesteau, and President Jannin, where, after I had protested that what I had to say was only in the name of the Palgrave's Highness, without that I had any such command from the King my master, I repeated his Highness's letter in substance, as I related that now : but found them wholly inclined to believe that his Highness had some further intention, and that the raising of those forces was to make himself King of Bohemia, insomuch that admitting the kingdom to be elective, which indeed they granted, they would needs argue by what right the Bohemians could depose Ferdinand. To which I answered that I had no commission to treat so far, yet that I had seen diverse copies of their motives : that, among many others, Ferdinand had treated with the King of Spain to make that kingdom hereditary to the House of Austria ; that, besides, he was never lawfully elected. In conclusion, after a long debate, I brought them to this, that they promised to advise with the King my master before they resolved on anything in the business, which was all I could expect to have obtained by the conference. Howsoever, at worst I hope his Majesty will find this state so unaffected and neutral, that if not their resolution, yet at least their irresolution will keep them indifferent : and that is enough, since whensoever his Majesty shall resolve to comfort the Palatine's Highness to the acceptation of this offered crown, his Majesty may be assured of many servants and honourers in this country that will voluntarily offer their lives in the quarrel.

On 31st October 1619, Herbert sends in a bill " for secret services," including " intelligences, and conveyance of letters," to the amount of £340 (fol. 66); and on 5th November a bill for his " late travelling between Merlou, Compiegne, and Champagne " amounting to £400 (fol. 69). On 4th November he implores James I. to send instructions concerning his behaviour towards the embassy coming to

Paris from Treves and from the Emperor to complain of the Elector Palatine. He declares that " his heart is as much affected to the advancement of his Highness's cause as any whosoever " (fol. 68). On 24th November he writes that the Protestants are growing rebellious in Bearn, and that France is not likely to interfere in German affairs. But he adds, " the French do all their business in compliment, the outward sense and meaning being only the cipher and dead letter of their intentions."

For my part, I have many reasons to induce me to believe they will be neutral : wherein I may come from words to more evident testimonies. I find this state first too poor, and then too unsettled to stir. Their poverty appears in that they have taken up three-fourths of a year's rent beforehand ; that they lay new impositions upon the people, that faint under the old ; that they expect from the Parisians a great sum of money (they say 300,000 crowns) as the price of the court's removing to this place (*i.e.* Paris), though the contagion (God be thanked for it) seems to be in a manner extinguished. And for their unsettledness, it is such as, when the King would send an army, I think they know not whom to trust.

On 23d November (fol. 73) Herbert sent an enthusiastic letter in French to the new King of Bohemia (fol. 73), expressing his own sympathy with him, and his belief that France would not join the Emperor against him. On 3rd December he told Naunton (fol. 74) that he was forming a strong party in the Elector's behalf among the French nobility, and that if the French King remained neutral, the German Protestants might count on many ardent volunteers from France. But complaints were being made that the Roman Catholics " were worse used than ever " in both England and Germany. On the $\frac{14}{24}$ December (fol. 77) Herbert states that "this King hath at last appointed the $\frac{20}{10}$ of January for the solemnity of the oath of alliance betwixt the two crowns"—a ceremony which had been repeatedly post- poned, but to take part in which Herbert had originally been sent from England. Monsieur Puisieux said that "it was expected I should put myself into an extraordinary equipage for the great solemnity." The French still hesitated with regard to Bohemia, and Herbert asked for fuller instructions. On 30th December Herbert described (fol. 83) some hot disputes current at the French court and the rising discontent of the French Protestants ; but the approaching ceremony chiefly occupied his mind, and he was anxious to be treated with extraordinary honour.

The oath of alliance is to be solemised the 20th of this month (new style), for which day, unless your Honour allow me the title of an Extraordinary Ambassador, they will diminish the outward ceremony of respect they gave in their last. I have therefore, by that extraordinary commission I had for that purpose, suffered them for that only day to receive me in the quality of an Extraordinary Ambassador, and in truth have already put myself into an equipage altogether extraordinary. I send your Honour the oath ; if your Honour dislike anything, I beseech your Honour to advertise me. I will hope to prolong the solemnity to three or four days further, which will be a sufficient time, if your Honour please to send me word, which I beseech your Honour not to fail ; for I am unwilling to proceed in anything for which I have not good warrant. But I think there will be no difficulty to suffer them to give me the respect of an Extraordinary Ambassador for one day. If I hear not from your Honour in a reasonable time I will proceed, for now they call on me. So hoping your Honour will not omit to let me hear from your Honour in this business with all possible speed.

On 31st December Herbert reviewed the attitude of France as to foreign affairs in a long and able letter to James I. (fol. 85–8). He urged Naunton at the same time (fol. 89) to lead the King to announce his own policy as one interested in the cause of the newly elected King of Bohemia. The French ministers refused to tell him the result of their negotiations with Furstemberg, the special ambassador from the Emperor, on the ground that the King

of England made no communication of his intentions to
their master. Herbert, however, saw that Louis was inclining
to the side of the Catholics, and that the German dispute was
coming to be regarded as a great religious quarrel (fol. 89).
The arrangements for the solemn signature of the treaty of
alliance were proceeding apace, and he was sparing no
expense to array himself to best advantage (fol. 91). He
writes to Naunton, 8th January 1619–20 :—

> Our ceremony goes on, and it is now too late at this present to
> recall my disbursements, having already. (indiscreetly enough) put
> myself so far into the equipage of an Ambassador Extraordinary that
> your Honour I think will hear no man was ever beyond me. But
> I confess I found it necessary at this time to oblige the people even
> by extraordinary shows to the solemnity, and due respect of this
> great alliance betwixt the two crowns, besides that I was in plain
> terms told that unless the same pomp were observed on our side
> we must not expect it on theirs. Wherein they did insinuate that it
> was a favour, that from an ambassador ordinary they did accept me
> in the quality of an extraordinary (even for one day) though at last
> they concluded my commssion apart did oblige them to it. These
> considerations made me enter into great expense ; and howsoever
> I shall never repent to have become my place in the best fashion I
> could. For the rest, I believe that if his Majesty be pleased to con-
> sider what an Ambassador Extraordinary would have cost .by
> itself, my'reckoning will be thought very easy.

On $\frac{13}{23}$ January 1619–20 Herbert reported that military
preparations were being made, whether or no to assist the
Emperor he did not know, but the Duc de Guise had said
to him that if the King of Bohemia's cause was a good one,
James I. would have publicly declared for it. The formal
ceremony was deferred till 2nd February (new style) " for
(it was stated) the more solemnity " (fol. 93) ; but public
policy in France was clearly very vacillating (fol. 95.) On
27th January Herbert describes the performance of a

preliminary part of the solemnity with much self-satisfaction (fol. 97).

The oath of alliance betwixt the two crowns was performed on Sunday last, in the Church of the Feuillans, with all solemnity. They would have much diminished the ceremony, as doubting whether I was honoured with such an extraordinary commission as was capable of it. But upon better perusal of my commission they thought good to make it public in the church, as when my Lord Wotton was here, and this being the reallest I thought I need not insist upon some less essential forms. In the fashion I appeared in, the opinion is, no man exceeded me of the most extraordinary that have been here; which I did the rather to meet with their objections. I shall take the boldness to write to his Majesty concerning the same business whereof my last advertised his Majesty, but have not herein desired his gracious pleasure, so that I will beseech your Honour to obtain it, which I do I protest for no other end but that the honour may remain to my posterity of serving his Majesty though but for one day, in the quality of an Ambassador Extraordinary. If your honour be pleased to use my most noble Lord the Marquis of Buckingham herein, I am sure his Lordship will be pleased to remember the honour his Majesty did me on this occasion.

On $\frac{20}{30}$ January 1619–20 Herbert sends to the King a copy of a letter from Louis to the Emperor, to which he had secretly obtained access. He points out that the French King is not sending succours to the German Catholics, but merely desires " to weigh the Emperor's propositions." [1]

On 3rd February 1619–20 Herbert returns to the question of his status (fol. 100).

And now for my quality during the ceremony, I hope your Honour knows how far I was from persuming, though it were the subject for which I was once designed extraordinary, and which (since they had no other allegation why they should diminish that ceremony)

---

[1] A copy of this letter is also in MS. Harl. 1581, f. 13.

I hoped I might most humbly desire his Majesty to confirm as a favour heretofore conferred upon me, in which since I beseech your Honour most particularly that his Majesty may understand me.

On 18th February 1619–20, Herbert renews his desire for precise instructions with regard to Bohemian affairs, complains that James I. had, without considering his dignity, been answering the current charges brought against him by continental politicians of having instigated his son-in-law to act on the offensive, and that popular feeling in France was inclining against the Elector Palatine; although Herbert's own affection for him was unchanged (fol. 100). On 21st February 1619–20, he writes that the relations between Louis XIII. and his Protestant subjects were very critical, and that Gondomar had arrived in Paris in the hope of preserving peace in Europe (fol. 100). On 25th February he perceives that the Bohemian cause is in jeopardy. "All I have to comfort me, next God's providences," Herbert writes, "is his Majesty's wisdom, which I assure myself will temper all for the best."

With these words the letter-book comes to an end. The only other letter of this period with which I have met is one in MS., Harl. 1581, fol. 11, addressed by Herbert to Buckingham from Merlou, 1st October 1619, in which he first broaches a marriage between Henrietta Maria and Prince Charles.

Since my writing this other, I understood the King passed near this place, on his way to Compiegne in Picardy. They made me repair to court, where I visited only M. de Luynes, who, among other speeches, told me they had given instructions to their ambassador in England, that if there were any overture made of a match for our Prince with Madame Henriette the king's sister, that it should be received with all honour and affection; and (if I be not mistaken in the meaning of his words) said, so much was already insinuated by their said ambassador.

I answered them as civilly as I could, having no instructions to speak of any such thing, and came to the business of Bohemia, wherein I desired to know how his master stood affected. He told me that he had not yet leisure to consider the consequences, and that he first desired to hear how the King my master did declare himself. I told him his Majesty did advise what was to be done, that in the meanwhile he did protest that when he sent his ambassador to compose the differences of the empire, that he knew nothing of the Palatine's election to the kingdom of Bohemia, or that there was any such design. That besides his Majesty's protestation, which was an argument above all that could be made to the contrary, there were many reasons to persuade that even the Palatine's Highness himself knew nothing of any such intention ; as, first, the unanimity of consent in the Bohemians, which argues there was no faction or labouring of voices ; secondly, the necessity, since they could not tell where else to put themselves under protection ; thirdly, that if it had been the Palatine's Highness's desire, that certainly he would have used both that and other means to prevent the election of King Ferdinand to the Empire. This was the effect of the reasons I gave, to which I added that, howsoever the King my master did resolve, I hoped at least his master would be indifferent—that they had no greatness to fear but that of the House of Austria ; that they might take the time to recover the countries detained from them ; that lastly, there was no other way, as matters now stand, to establish the peace of Christendom, since he might be sure the untamed Germans would never submit themselves to others. He, which seemed to hearken more to my reasons than to answer them, told me all these matters should be referred to the King's being at Compiegne, whither he desired me to come, which I promised ; as having the business of the King's renewing his oath, to require. I have written these particularities to Mr. Secretary Naunton, and attend your Lordship's further commandments.

The postscript runs :—

M. de Luynes doth much desire to hold correspondence with your Lordship, and desired me to tell your Lordship so much. I should be glad to have leave to use a little compliment to him on your Lordship's part.

On $\frac{14}{24}$ August 1620, Herbert returns to the theme in a letter to the King (MSS. Harl., f. 15) :—

Le Buisson is returned, and, as Monsieur Le Prince did tell me, hath made a proposition to your sacred Majesty concerning a marriage betwixt his Highness and Madame Henriette, to which, he said, your sacred Majesty did answer, that your sacred Majesty did desire it too, but that your sacred Majesty was so far engaged with Spain that your sacred Majesty could not treat thereof. This Monsieur Le Prince told me, and I thought it my duty to let your sacred Majesty know the report ; on which occasion, I cannot omit to tell your sacred Majesty that the match is generally desired by this nation, and particularly by Madame herself, who hath not only cast out many words to this purpose, but, when there hath been question of diversity of religions, hath said, that a wife ought to have no will but that of her husband's ; which words I confess have incited me to do her this good office. In the rest, being so far from having a voice that I will not so much as have a thought which is not warranted by your sacred Majesty's authority, which I hold in that infinite reverence that I am sorry I can say no more than that I will live and die your sacred Majesty's most obedient, most loyal, and most affectionate subject and servant,

HERBERT.

On 15th February 1620–1 Herbert described in a letter to the King the coming war with the French Protestants, and the plan of attack adopted by the King in council. Luynes, he stated, was in favour of peace, and his "averseness from entering into any war at home," would probably delay its outbreak. Herbert suggested that Luynes foresaw "that his enemies who dare not show themselves in time of peace will not fear to declare themselves in time of war."

Among the Egerton MSS. No. 2598, are a few letters addressed by Herbert to Lord Doncaster, Earl of Carlisle. In the first (fol. 173), dated 24th July 1620, Herbert describes the French people thus :—

This is a nation tied by no rules, and therefore there is nothing else can be affirmed of them; yet, in this irregularity, they will want neither example or excuse. If we compare them to those things which corrupt, wanting motion ; in the perpetual inconstancy and unquietness whereof they have left it more doubtful whether they will make either war or peace, at this present.

On $\frac{17}{27}$ October 1620 Herbert describes to Doncaster (fol. 254) the visit of Louis XIII. to Bearn, and his cold reception there by the disaffected Protestants.

During his temporary withdrawal in 1621 Doncaster took Herbert's place at Paris. When Herbert was returning in 1622 to the French court, he writes to Doncaster to thank him for having smoothed the way for him :—

It is not a work of Fortune that I am put into your Lordship's hands. For, to have put me into your Lordship's hands, were to have put me out of her own. It is therefore a higher Providence, which, foreseeing the disposition I have ever had to honour and serve your Lordship, would as well give me all just occasion for it ; On these terms I can nothing doubt of the success of mine or any affair, while, for being undertaken by these hands, I can do no less, than most humbly desire, as soon as possibly, to kiss them.[1]

After Herbert's return to Paris in December 1621, little of his correspondence is extant. On hearing that Doncaster was coming to Paris to excuse Prince Charles's and Buckingham's hasty passage through France on their way to Spain, Herbert wrote (Egerton MS. 2574, fol. 165) :—

Meeting so fit an opportunity, I would not fail to put your Lordship in mind with how much and true devotion I accompany your Lordship's journey, and withal give your Lordship notice that the Marquis Spinola is departed from Bruxelles, his cannon marching towards the Palatinat ; whither it is certainly believed he will lead his forces.

The letter is dated from Paris, 20th August 1622.

---

[1] From London, and not Paris, this $\frac{13}{28}$ April 1622.

z

When Doncaster had left Paris to follow the Prince into Spain, Herbert writes (Egerton MS. 2595, fol. 181) (23rd March 1622–3) :—

Your Lordship's letters of exchange I delivered Mr. Langherac, who hath sent them after your Lordship, to Bordeaux ; your Lordship's present hath been delivered to the King, who seemed much to esteem it. Your Lordship must have heard before now of the death of the good President Jannin.

The postscript runs :—

I desire infinitely to hear the success of his Highness' journey, whom God bless, but know not how far I may presume of your Lordship's leisure.

The last extant letter written during his embassy was addressed by Herbert to the King, and discussed the opinions held in France of the Spanish marriage treaty after the failure of the negotiations :—

MY MOST GRACIOUS SOVEREIGN,—Now that I thank God for it, his Highness, according to my continual prayers, hath made a safe and happy return unto your sacred Majesty's presence, I think myself bound, by way of complete obedience to those command-ments I received from your sacred Majesty, both by Mr. Secretary Calvert and my brother Henry, to give your sacred Majesty an account of that sense which the general sort of people doth enter-tain here, concerning the whole frame and context of his Highness' voyage. It is agreed on all parts that his Highness must have received much contentment in seeing two great kingdoms, and consequently in enjoying that satisfaction which princes but rarely, and not without great peril obtain. His Highness' discretion, diligence, and princely behaviour every where, likewise is much praised. Lastly, since his Highness' journey hath fallen out so well, that his Highness is come back without any prejudice to his person or dignity : they say the success hath sufficiently commended the council. This is the most common censure (even of the bigot party, as I am informed) which I approve in all but in the last point, in the delivery whereof I find something to dislike, and therefore tell them, that things are not to be judged alone by the success, and that when they would not look so high as God's providence, without which no place is secure, they might find even in reason of state so much as might sufficiently warrant his Highness' person, and liberty to return.

I will come from the ordinary voice, to the selecter judgment of the ministers of state, and more intelligent people in this kingdom, who, though they nothing vary from the above-recited opinion, yet as more profoundly looking into the state of this long-treated-of alliance betwixt your sacred Majesty and Spain in the persons of his Highness and the Infanta, they comprehend their sentence thereof (as I am informed) in three propositions :

First, That the protestation, which the King of Spain made to his Highness upon his departure, whereby he promised to chase away, and disfavour all those who should oppose this marriage, doth extend no further, than to the said king's servants, or at furthest, not beyond the temporal princes his neighbours, so that the Pope, being not included herein, it is thought his consent must be yet obtained, and consequently that the business is in little more forwardness than when it first began.

Secondly, That the Pope will never yield his consent, unless your sacred Majesty grant some notable privileges and advantage to the Roman Catholic religion in your sacred Majesty's kingdoms.

Thirdly, That the said King of Spain would never insist upon obtaining those privileges, but that he more desires to form a party in your sacred Majesty's kingdoms, which he may keep always obsequious to his will, than to maintain a friendly correspondence betwixt your sacred Majesty and himself. I must not, in the last place, omit to acquaint your sacred Majesty very particularly with the sense which was expressed by the *bons François*, and body of those of the Religion, who heartily wish that the same greatness which the King of Spain doth so affect over all the world, and still main tains even in this country, which is to be protector of the Jesuited and bigot party, your sacred Majesty would embrace in being Defender of our Faith. The direct answer to which though I evade, and therefore reply little more than that this council was much fitter when the Union in Germany did subsist than at this time ; yet do I think myself obliged to represent the affection they bear unto your sacred Majesty.   This is as much as is come to my notice, concerning that point your sacred Majesty gave me in charge, which therefore I have plainly laid open before your sacred Majesty's eyes, as understanding well, that princes never receive greater wrong than when the ministers they put in trust do palliate and disguise those things which it concerns them to know.   For the avoiding whereof, let me take the boldness to assure your sacred Majesty that those of this King's Council here will use all means they can, both to the King of Spain, and to the Pope (in whom they pretend to have very particular interest) not only to interrupt but if it be possible to break off your sacred Majesy's alliance with Spain.   For which purpose the Count de Tillieres hath strict command to give either all punctual advice, that accord- ingly they may proceed.   It rests that I most humbly beseech your Sacred Majesty to take my free relation of these particulars in good part, since I am of no faction, nor have any passion or interest, but faithfully to perform that service and duty which I owe to your sacred Majesty, for whose perfect health and happiness I pray, with the devotion of your sacred majesty's Most obedient, most loyal, and most affectionate subject and servant,

HERBERT.[1]

From MERLOU CASTLE, *the* 31*st of October* 1623.   *Stil. No.*

The Princess Elizabeth's gratitude to Herbert for his devotion to her cause is shown in the following undated letter which she addressed to him from the Hague :—"I pray be assured that my being in childbed hath hindered me all this while from thanking you for your letter, and no forgetfulness of mine to you to whom I have ever had obligations from your love, which I will ever acknowledge and seek to requite in what I can." — Warner's *Epistolary Curiosities.*

---

[1] Printed in "The Cabala," p. 231, and Ellis's Original Letters, 1st ser. iii. 1636.

INDEX.

———o———

PRINTED BY BALLANTYNE, HANSON AND CO.
EDINBURGH AND LONDON.

2 A

14 KING WILLIAM STREET, STRAND, W.C.,
LONDON, MARCH ·1886.

JOHN C. NIMMO'S

T OF NEW BOOKS

FOR

THE SPRING OF 1886.

A New Edition, in Three Volumes, medium 8vo, cloth,
fine paper, price 31s. 6d. net.

BURTON'S
ANATOMY OF MELANCHOLY.

THE ANATOMY OF MELANCHOLY:

WHAT IT IS,

WITH ALL THE KINDS, CAUSES, SYMPTOMS, PROGNOSTICS,
AND SEVERAL CURES OF IT.

In Three Partitions.

WITH THEIR SEVERAL SECTIONS, MEMBERS, AND SUBSECTIONS,
PHILOSOPHICALLY, MEDICINALLY, HISTORICALLY
OPENED AND CUT UP.

By DEMOCRITUS JUNIOR
[ROBERT BURTON].

Burton's Anatomy at the time of its original publication obtained a great
celebrity, which continued more than half a century. During that period few
books were more read or more deservedly applauded. It was the delight of
the learned, the solace of the indolent, and the refuge of the uninformed. It
passed through at least eight editions, by which the bookseller, as Wood
records, got an estate; and, notwithstanding the objection sometimes opposed
against it, of a quaint style and too great an accumulation of authorities, the
fascination of its wit, fancy, and sterling sense have borne down all censures,
and extorted praise from the first writers in the English language. The grave
Johnson has praised it in the warmest terms, and the ludicrous Sterne has
interwoven many parts of it into his own popular performance. Milton did
not disdain to build two of his finest poems on it; and a host of inferior
writers have embellished their works with beauties not their own, culled from
a performance which they had not the justice even to mention. Change of
times and the frivolity of fashion suspended, in some degree, that fame
which had lasted nearly a century; and the succeeding generation affected
indifference towards an author who at length was only looked into by the
plunderers of literature, the poachers in obscure volumes. The plagiarisms
of "Tristram Shandy," so successfully brought to light by Dr. Ferriar, at
length drew the attention of the public towards a writer who, though then
little known, might, without impeachment of modesty, lay claim to every
mark of respect; and inquiry proved, beyond a doubt, that the calls of justice
had been little attended to by others as well as the facetious Yorick. Wood
observed, more than a century ago, that several authors had unmercifully
stolen matter from Burton without any acknowledgment.

THE SONG OF SONGS.

SUPER ROYAL QUARTO.

Illustrated with Twenty=six Full=page Original Etchings from Designs

By BIDA.

ETCHED BY EDMOND HÉDOUIN AND ÉMILE BOILVIN.

Also Twelve Culs=de=Lampes from Designs

By GUSTAVE GREUX.

Bound in a new and original rich plush padded binding, price Three Guineas *net.*

NOTE.—"The Song of Songs" is printed trom the REVISED VERSION, the copyright of which belongs to the authorities of the Oxford and Cambridge University Presses, who have courteously granted the publisher permission to use it for this purpose.

The twenty-six full-page etchings are beautifully printed on fine Japanese paper, and carefully mounted on white vellum paper, same as the text is printed on.

No finer specimens than these of BIDA'S wonderful designs have hitherto appeared.

OCTAVE UZANNE'S NEW WORK.

The Frenchwoman of the Century.

FASHIONS—MANNERS—USAGES.

By OCTAVE UZANNE,

Author of "The Fan," "The Sunshade, Muff, and Glove."

Illustrations in Water Colours by ALBERT LYNCH.

Engraved in Colours by EUGÈNE GAUJEAN.

Super royal 8vo, elegantly bound in padded Japanese leather,
price Two Guineas *net*.

Only 500 copies are printed, 300 for England and 200 for America.
Type distributed.

NOTE.—"The Frenchwoman of the Century," written by Octave Uzanne,
gives a description of the principal fashions in France, its customs, manners,
and usages from the earliest years of the Revolution to the present time.
With the history of the dress is pleasantly intermingled a history of the most
notable people of this eventful period. The book sparkles with vivid allusions
to the principal men and women of the epoch. Napoleon is photographed in
his habit as he lived, and the inner life of the Empress Josephine appears as
in a delicate miniature. The work, comprehensive in extent, is at the same
time minute in detail. The fashions of the Directory and the First Empire
are, as it were, underlined. To the assistance of the letterpress has been
called, not without sufficient reason in description of the intricate complexity
of Parisian fashions, the able pencil of M. Albert Lynch, who has been careful
to supply his water colour illustrations exactly in those places where they
were most wanted. These pictures have been subsequently engraved in
colours by the skilful hand of Eugène Gaujean.

The work, careless and superficial it may seem, is in reality a marvel of
profound research and exact investigations. Though copious it is not pro-
digal, though anecdotal it is seldom trifling, though learned it is never dull.
Its expression is polished and lively, its plan precise and duly defined. The
best writers of the time for the subject in hand, such as George Duval,
Madame d'Abranté, Emile de Girardin, and others of equal reputation have
been diligently consulted. The volume is a suitable, almost indeed a necessary, appendage to the other works of Uzanne, viz., "The Fan" and "The
Sunshade, Muff, and Glove," recently published.

An elegant and choicely Illustrated Edition of

The Vicar of Wakefield.

By OLIVER GOLDSMITH.

With Prefatory Memoir by GEORGE SAINTSBURY, and One Hundred and Fourteen Coloured Illustrations by V. A. POIRSON (Illustrator of "Gulliver's Travels").

Royal 8vo, cloth extra, printed in colours and gilt top, price 12s. 6d.

NOTE.—This edition of Oliver Goldsmith's famous English classic is illustrated and produced in so sumptuous a form and at so moderate a price, the publisher feels confident the entire edition will be speedily disposed of. It is uniform in size and style of illustration to "Gulliver's Travels" recently published, and of which three thousand copies were sold in two months.

Edinburgh and its Neighbourhood

IN THE DAYS OF OUR GRANDFATHERS.

A series of Illustrations of the more remarkable Old and New Buildings and Picturesque Scenery of Edinburgh, as they appeared about 1830. With Historical Introduction and Descriptive Sketches by JAMES GOWANS.

Royal 8vo, Eighty Illustrations, fine paper, cloth elegant, price 12s. 6d.

NOTE.—The leading feature of this book will be a series of views of Edinburgh and its neighbourhood from the original steel plates after drawings by Mr. Thomas H. Shepherd, and published in 1833. Some of these views are of special interest, as they give vivid representations of historical and other edifices now swept away in the course of improvements which have so much altered the features of "the grey metropolis of the north." A few of the original descriptions of the views will be preserved, but most of the others will be superseded by fresh sketches, whilst the original introduction will be recast, and in great part rewritten. Numerous incidents will be supplied illustrative of the social life of the period, when Scott was still the typical representative of the literary life of Scotland, and Christopher North and his associates were exercising a mighty influence in the domain of literature and politics by their diatribes and searching yet sympathetic criticisms in the brilliant pages of *Maga*.

A new and beautiful edition of the "IMITATION OF CHRIST," in demy 8vo, with the text and quaint borders printed in brown ink, and illustrated with Fifteen Etchings, ten by J. P. LAURENS and five by CH. WALTNER, price 21s. *net*, bound in full parchment, gilt top.

THE IMITATION OF CHRIST.

FOUR BOOKS.

Translated from the Latin by Rev. W. BENHAM, B.D.,

Rector of St Edmund, King and Martyr, Lombard Street, London.

NOTE.—The etchings to this new edition of the "IMITATION," fifteen in number, and printed on fine Japanese paper, make it one of the most beautiful at present to be had.

𝔑ew 𝔖eries of 𝔥istorical 𝔐emoirs.

The Autobiography of Edward,
LORD HERBERT OF CHERBURY.

With Introduction, Notes, Appendices, and a Continuation of the Life.   By
SYDNEY L. LEE, B.A., Balliol College, Oxford.   With Four Etched
Portraits, fine paper, medium 8vo, cloth, 21s. *net*.

NOTE.—"Lord Herbert of Cherbury's Autobiography" is one of the most
fascinating and entertaining books of its class.   The author is devoid of self-
consciousness, and keeps no secrets from his readers.   He dwells as com-
placently on his failings as on his virtues; his childlike vanity keeps his
self-esteem intact in the least promising circumstances.   But the book does
more than throw a steady light on an attractive personality, it illustrates the
habits and customs of English and French society at the beginning of the
seventeenth century.   No other work so fully describes the contemporary
practice of duelling.   Abundant reference is made to politics, and it thus
forms an important commentary on the history of James the First's reign.
Incidentally Lord Herbert enunciates his religious, educational, and metaphysical theories, and substantiates his claim to be regarded as the father of
English deism.   The autobiography only carries the writer's life as far as the
year 1624, and Lord Herbert died in 1648.   The book has been reprinted
two or three times since its first publication by Horace Walpole in 1764, but
it has never been fully edited.   In the present edition the editor endeavours
to explain the allusions to the historical events, and gives brief accounts of the
numerous terms and books mentioned in the text, and interprets the obscure
words and phrases.   He will also continue Lord Herbert's life until the date
of his death, print some of his correspondence, and will attempt to define his
place in English literature, philosophy, history, and religion.

MEMOIRS OF
The Life of William Cavendish,
DUKE OF NEWCASTLE,

To which is added the True Relation of My Birth, Breeding, and Life.   By
MARGARET, DUCHESS OF NEWCASTLE.   Edited by C. H. FIRTH, M.A.
(Editor of "Memoirs of the Life of Colonel Hutchinson.")   With Four
Etched Portraits, fine paper, medium 8vo, cloth, price 21s. *net*.

NOTE.—The Memoirs of the Duke of Newcastle by the Duchess has
been judged by Charles Lamb a book "both good and rare," "a jewel which
no casket is rich enough to honour or keep safe."   The first edition of these
Memoirs is, however, difficult to obtain, and the later reprint in form hardly
worthy of the original.   The aim of the present edition is to supply a book
which shall be in type, print, and paper attractive.   At the same time,
preface, notes, letters, and an index are added to increase its use to the
student of seventeenth century history, and to all who are interested in the
records of our great civil war.   As in the corresponding edition of Mrs.
Hutchinson's Memoirs, the spelling is modernised and explanations of
obsolete words given.

The True History of the Life and Work of William Shakespeare,

PLAYER, POET, AND PLAYMAKER.

By F. G. FLEAY, M.A. With Three Etchings of interest. Fine paper, medium 8vo, half parchment, gilt top, price 15s. *net.*

NOTE.—The theatrical side of the career of Shakespeare has never yet received any adequate consideration, his connection with the theatres and acting companies in his earlier years not having been traced or even investigated. His relations with other dramatists, especially with Jonson, have also been grossly misrepresented. While every idle story of mythical gossip has been carefully collected, and the pettiest details of his commercial dealings have been garnered, little attention has hitherto been given to his dealings with the plays by other men with whom he was fellow-worker, and a large group of evidences bearing on the chronology of his work, derived from the early production of English plays in Germany, has been cast aside as valueless. In this work an attempt is made to collect this neglected material, to throw new light on the Sonnets, and to determine the dates of the production of all his works. A complete list of all plays published with due authority anterior of 1640 by any dramatic writer is given (from the Stationers' Registers. Many unfounded hypotheses of Collier, Halliwell, and others are for the first time exploded, and the work of ten years investigation is condensed in a single volume. In many instances one paragraph represents months of labour, and it is hoped that a permanent addition of value is thus made to Shakespearian literature. The arrangement of the book is made so as to appeal not merely to the specialist, but to every one who feels an interest in the greatest writer of any literature, and the crowning glory of our own.

VOLUMES RECENTLY ISSUED.

MEMOIRS OF THE LIFE OF COLONEL HUTCHINSON. By his Widow, LUCY. Revised and Edited by CHARLES H. FIRTH, M.A. With Ten Etched Portraits. Two Volumes, fine paper, medium 8vo, and handsome binding, 42s. *net.*
NOTE.—Only 500 copies are printed, 300 for England and 200 for America. Type distributed.

OLD TIMES: A Picture of Social Life at the End of the Eighteenth Century. Collected and Illustrated from the Satirical and other Sketches of the Day. By JOHN ASHTON, Author of "Social Life in the Reign of Queen Anne." One Volume, fine paper, medium 8vo, handsome binding, Eighty-eight Illustrations, 21s. *net.*

THE LIFE OF GEORGE BRUMMELL, Esq., commonly called BEAU BRUMMELL. By Captain JESSE, unattached. Revised and Annotated Edition from the Author's own Interleaved Copy. With Forty Portraits in Colour of Brummell and his Contemporaries. Two Volumes, fine paper, medium 8vo, and handsome cloth binding, 42s. *net.*
NOTE.—Only 500 copies are printed, 300 for England and 200 for America. Type distributed.

MEMOIRS OF COUNT GRAMMONT. By ANTHONY HAMILTON. A New Edition, Edited, with Notes, by Sir WALTER SCOTT. With Sixty-Four Portraits engraved by EDWARD SCRIVEN. Two Volumes, 8vo, Roxburghe binding, gilt top, 30s. *net.*

14 King William Street, Strand, London, W.C.

NEW SERIES OF HISTORICAL MEMOIRS—continued.

SOME NOTICES OF THE PRESS.

HUTCHINSON.
Athenæum.

" Is an excellent edition of a famous book. Mr. Firth presents the ' Memoirs ' with a modernised orthography and a revised scheme of punctuation. He retains the notes of Julius Hutchinson, and supplements them by annotations—corrective and explanatory—of his own. Since their publication in 1805, the ' Memoirs ' have been a kind of classic. To say that this is the best and fullest edition of them in existence is to say everything."

Times.

" Beautifully printed upon fine paper, with rough edges, and with margins which will delight the heart of the book-lover, we announce with pleasure a new edition of Colonel Hutchinson's ' Memoirs,' revised, with additional notes, by Mr. C. H. Firth. This edition, which is in two handsome volumes, contains ten etched portraits of eminent personages. As the editor remarks in his introduction, none of the ' Memoirs' which relate to the troubled history of the English Civil Wars have obtained a greater popularity than those of Colonel Hutchinson compiled by his wife."

OLD TIMES.
Daily Telegraph.

" That is the best and truest history of the past which comes nearest to the life of the bulk of the people. It is in this spirit that Mr. John Ashton has composed ' Old Times,' intended to be a picture of social life at the end of the eighteenth century. The illustrations form a very valuable, and at the same time quaint and amusing, feature of the volume."

Saturday Review.

" ' Old Times,' however, is not only valuable as a book to be taken up for a few minutes at a time ; a rather careful reading will repay those who wish to brush up their recollections of the period. To some extent it may serve as a book of reference, and even historians may find in it some useful matter concerning the times of which it treats. The book is in every respect suited for a hall or library table in a country house."

BEAU BRUMMELL.
Morning Post.

" The editor of the present edition has been enabled to add much new matter which had been excluded from the original by reason of many of the persons therein referred to being alive at the time. . . . And readers who plod through these two handsome volumes will be rewarded with an admirable picture of English and French society in the days of the Regency."

Notes and Queries.

" The book, which is on beautiful paper, is worthy of a place in most collections, and the privilege of possessing it in a form so artistic and handsome is a subject for gratitude."

GRAMMONT.
Hallam.

" The ' Memoirs of Grammont,' by Anthony Hamilton, scarcely challenge a place as historical ; but we are now looking more at the style than the intrinsic importance of books. Every one is aware of the peculiar felicity and fascinating gaiety which they display."

T. B. Macaulay.

" The artist to whom we owe the most highly finished and vividly coloured picture of the English Court in the days when the English Court was gayest."

An Elegant and Choicely Illustrated Edition of

Travels

INTO SEVERAL REMOTE NATIONS OF THE WORLD BY LEMUEL GULLIVER, First a Surgeon and then a Captain of Several Ships. By JONATHAN SWIFT, Dean of St. Patrick. With Prefatory Memoir by GEORGE SAINTSBURY, and One Hundred and Eighty Coloured and Sixty Plain Illustrations. Royal 8vo, cloth extra, price 12s. 6d., 450 pages.

SOME NOTICES OF THE PRESS.

The Saturday Review.

"Mr. Saintsbury, in editing the fascinating volume before us, wisely refrains from hinting at any matter that may become matter of controversy. The remarks with which he introduces this beautiful edition of one of the masterpieces of the world's literature breathe the very spirit of true criticism. . . . But we have barely alluded to the distinctive features of this edition which make it a book to be coveted and purchased by all true bibliophiles. M. Poiron's pictures, in their delicacy and subtle humour, are in every way worthy of the story. Those which illustrate the Voyage to Lilliput are perhaps the most dainty and delightful in their quaint poetical design and colouring. But there are some uncoloured head and tailpieces which, to all true lovers of art, will appear simply delicious."

Daily News.

"No handsomer edition of Swift's renowned work than that which Mr. Nimmo has just published of 'The Travels into Several Remote Nations of the World, by Lemuel Gulliver,' is recorded in the annals of bibliography. Mr. George Saintsbury furnishes a brief biographical and critical introduction."

Scotsman.

"The charm of the book, besides the excellence of the printing and generally attractive appearance, lies in the illustrations. They are charmingly drawn bits, some interwoven, so to speak, into the page, others of them occupying the whole page, and all of them marked by a delicacy and refinement which are delightful. Take the edition altogether and it is one of the most remarkable books of its kind that has been published."

Times.

"For this handsome edition of 'Gulliver's Travels' we have nothing but praise. Paper and type are unexceptionable, while there is a profusion of quaintly grotesque illustrations."

The Guardian.

"This is in every respect one of those sumptuous volumes which are now being devoted to our standard authors. Every luxury of paper and type have been freely spent upon it, and the numerous illustrations, both plain and coloured, especially perhaps the latter, display a spirit and humour and wealth of delicate and graceful fancy which it would be difficult to surpass. Possibly some of our readers may have a very vague remembrance of what Swift really allowed himself to write. If so, they will be tolerably certain to be attracted by the grace and beauty of this edition of his most popular work."

Spectator.

"Of all Swift's works, 'Gulliver's Travels' is the most satisfactory and complete, as it is the most famous ; and it follows, therefore, that all lovers of English literature will be pleased at the production of so handsome a reprint as that published by Mr. J. C. Nimmo. A special feature of this edition is the pictures. There is no doubt that the process by which they are produced is extremely delicate and beautiful, the colours being as transparent as water colours, and laid with perfect clearness of outline and precision of detail. And we reinvite those who have not read 'Gulliver's Travels' since childhood to study once more one of the profoundest and most brilliant satires, one of the greatest of imaginative creations, and one of the noblest models of style in the English language."

𝔗𝔥𝔢 𝔈𝔩𝔦𝔷𝔞𝔟𝔢𝔱𝔥𝔞𝔫 𝔇𝔯𝔞𝔪𝔞𝔱𝔦𝔰𝔱𝔰.

NOTE.—This is the first instalment towards a collective edition of the Dramatists who lived about the time of Shakespeare. The type will be distributed after each work is printed, the impression of which will be four hundred copies, post 8vo, and one hundred and twenty large fine-paper copies, medium 8vo, which will be numbered.

One of the chief features of this New Edition of the Elizabethan Dramatists, besides the handsome and handy size of the volumes, will be the fact that *each Work will be carefully edited and new notes given throughout.*

ALGERNON CHARLES SWINBURNE

(IN THE *NINETEENTH CENTURY*, JANUARY 1866)

ON THE

𝔈𝔩𝔦𝔷𝔞𝔟𝔢𝔱𝔥𝔞𝔫 𝔇𝔯𝔞𝔪𝔞𝔱𝔦𝔰𝔱𝔰.

"If it be true, as we are told on high authority, that the greatest glory of England is her literature, and the greatest glory of English literature is its poetry, it is not less true that the greatest glory of English poetry lies rather in its dramatic than its epic or its lyric triumphs. The name of Shakespeare is above the names even of Milton and Coleridge and Shelley; and the names of his comrades in art and their immediate successors are above all but the highest names in any other province of our song. There is such an overflowing life, such a superb exuberance of abounding and exulting strength, in the dramatic poetry of the half century extending from 1590 to 1640, that all other epochs of English literature seem as it were but half awake and half alive by comparison with this generation of giants and of gods. There is more sap in this than in any other branch of the national bay-tree; it has an energy in fertility which reminds us rather of the forest than the garden or the park. It is true that the weeds and briars of the underwood are but too likely to embarrass and offend the feet of the rangers and the gardeners who trim the level flower-pots or preserve the domestic game of enclosed and ordered lowlands in the tamer demesnes of literature. The sun is strong and the wind sharp in the climate which reared the fellows and the followers of Shakespeare. The extreme inequality and roughness of the ground must also be taken into account when we are disposed, as I for one have often been disposed, to wonder beyond measure at the apathetic ignorance of average students in regard of the abundant treasure to be gathered from this widest and most fruitful province in the poetic empire of England. And yet, since Charles Lamb threw open its gates to all comers in the ninth year of the present century, it cannot but seem strange that comparatively so few should have availed themselves of the entry to so rich and royal an estate. Mr. Bullen has taken up a task than which none more arduous and important, none worthier of thanks and praise, can be undertaken by any English scholar."

The Elizabethan Dramatists.

The Works of Christopher Marlowe.

Edited by A. H. BULLEN, B.A.

IN THREE VOLUMES.

Post 8vo, cloth. Published price, 7s. 6d. per volume *net ;* also large fine-paper edition, medium 8vo, cloth.

The Works of Thomas Middleton.

Edited by A. H. BULLEN, B.A.

In Eight Volumes, post 8vo, 7s. 6d. per volume *net ;* also large fine-paper edition, medium 8vo, cloth.

NOTE.—The next issue of this series will be *The Works of John Marston*, in Three Volumes, and *The Works of Thomas Dekker*, in Four Volumes. The remaining dramatists of this *Period* will follow in due order.

Some Press Notices of the Elizabethan Dramatists.

Saturday Review.

"Mr. Bullen has discharged his task as editor in all important points satisfactorily. Marlowe needs no irrelevant partisanship, no 'zeal of the devil's house,' to support his greatness. . . . Mr. Bullen's introduction is well informed and well written, and his notes are well chosen and sufficient. . . . We hope it may be his good forture to give and ours to receive every dramatist, from Peele to Shirley, in this handsome, convenient, and well-edited form."

Scotsman.

"Never in the history of the world has a period been marked by so much of literary power and excellence as the Elizabethan period ; and never have the difficulties in the way of literature seemed to be greater. The three volumes which Mr. Nimmo has issued now may be regarded as earnests of more to come, and as proofs of the excellence which will mark this edition of the Elizabethan Dramatists as essentially the best that has been published. Mr. Bullen is a competent editor in every respect."

The Academy.

"Mr. Bullen is known to all those interested in such things as an authority on most matters connected with old plays. We are not surprised, therefore, to find these volumes well edited throughout. They are not overburdened with notes."

The Spectator.

"That Marlowe should take precedence in Mr. Bullen's arduous undertaking is matter of course. He is the father of the English drama, and the first poet who showed the capabilities of the language when employed in blank verse. His line is not only mighty ; it is sometimes most musical, giving us a foretaste of what English verse was to become in the masterful hands of Shakespeare. We cannot part with Mr. Bullen without congratulating him on his success."

Contemporary Review.

"Mr. Bullen relates the little that is known of Marlowe's life with much care, leaving all that he tells us of him beyond the region of doubt ; for with great pains he has succeeded in verifying his statements."

---

14 King William Street, Strand, London, W.C.

The Elizabethan Dramatists.

SOME PRESS NOTICES—continued.

Athenæum.

"Mr. Bullen's edition deserves warm recognition. It is intelligent, scholarly, adequate. His preface is judicious. The elegant edition of the dramatists of which these volumes are the first is likely to stand high in public estimation. . . . The completion of the series will be a boon to bibliographers and scholars alike."

Pall Mall Gazette.

". . . Marlowe has indeed passed the age of simple eulogy, and has reached that of comment. The task set before him by Mr. Bullen is that of supplying a text which shall be as clear and intelligible as the conditions under which plays were printed in the sixteenth and early seventeenth centuries render possible. In this he has been successful. . . . If the series is continued as it is begun, by one of the most careful editors, this set of the English Dramatists will be a coveted literary possession."

Notes and Queries.

"Passages of Marlowe are as nervous, as pliant, as perfect as anything in Shakespeare or any succeeding writer. The same may be said of Marlowe's dramatic inspiration. Much mirth has been made over the grandiloquence of his early plays. None the less Marlowe is, in a sense, the most representative dramatist of his epoch. . . . Appropriately, then, the series Mr. Bullen edits and Mr. Nimmo issues in most attractive guise is headed by Marlowe, the leader, and in some respects all but the mightiest spirit, of the great army of English Dramatists."

Illustrated London News.

"It is perhaps, a bold venture on the part of the publisher, or would be if he had chosen an editor less competent than Mr. A. H. Bullen. Marlowe's power was felt by Shakespeare, and felt also by Goethe; and Mr. Bullen is not, perhaps, a rash prophet in saying that, 'so long as high tragedy continues to have interest for men, Time shall lay no hands on the works of Christopher Marlowe!'"

The Standard.

"Throughout Mr. Bullen has done his difficult work remarkably well, and the publisher has produced it in a form which will make the edition of early dramatists of which it is a part an almost indispensable addition to a well-stocked library."

The Quarterly Review.—*October* 1885.

"We gladly take this opportunity of directing attention to an edition of Marlowe's complete works recently edited by Mr. A. H. Bullen. If the volumes which follow are as carefully edited as this the first instalment of the series is, Mr. Bullen will be conferring a great boon on all who are interested in the Early English Drama."

The Spectator.—*October* 17, 1885.

"Probably one of the boldest literary undertakings of our time, on the part of publisher as well as editor, is the fine edition of the Dramatists which has been placed in Mr. Bullen's careful hands; considering the comprehensiveness of the subject, and the variety of knowledge it demands, the courage of the editor is remarkable."

The Antiquary.

"Mr. Swinburne calls Marlowe 'the greatest discoverer, the most daring and inspired pioneer, in all our poetic literature.'"

Manchester Examiner.

"Not Shakespeare, not Milton, not Landor, not our own Tennyson, has written lines more splendid in movement or more wealthy in sonorous music than these, from 'The Tragical History of Dr. Faustus'—

> 'Have I not made blind Homer sing to me
> Of Alexander's love and Ænon's death?
> And hath not he who built the walls of Thebes,
> With ravishing sound of his melodious harp,
> Made music with my Mephistophilis?'"

Uniform with " Characters of La Bruyère" and a "Handbook of Gastronomy."

Robin Hood:

A COLLECTION OF ALL THE ANCIENT POEMS, SONGS, AND BALLADS now extant relative to that celebrated English Outlaw ;

To which are prefixed Historical Anecdotes of his Life.

By JOSEPH RITSON.

Illustrated with Eighty Wood Engravings by BEWICK, *printed on China Paper.*

Also Ten Etchings from Original Paintings by A. H. TOURRIER and E. BUCKMAN.

8vo, half parchment, gilt top, 42s. *net.*

NOTE.—300 copies printed, and each numbered. Also 100 copies on fine imperial paper, with etchings in two states, and richly bound in Lincoln Green Satin. Each copy numbered. Type distributed.

This edition of "ROBIN HOOD" is printed from that published in 1832, which was carefully edited and printed from Mr. RITSON'S own annotated edition of 1795.

The Guardian.

"This reprint of the Robin Hood ballads will be welcome to many who have loved from childhood the rude romance of the famous outlaw ; it will not be the less welcome to them by reason of its excellent paper and print and the reproduction in China paper of Bewick's original woodcuts. A novel and interesting feature of the book is the old musical settings which are appended to some of the songs."

Pall Mall Gazette.

"Robin Hood has lived in the old ballads of England for many centuries ; his own exploits and those of his merry men have been sung in every town ; the Elizabethan dramatists made him the hero of many of their plays. Southey proposed to write an epic poem on him, Walter Scott delighted in him, Shakespeare brought a faint echo of his life into 'As You Like It,' his bower is still carried through the streets on the first of May, while Maid Marian dances on the pavement for pennies, and still in the pleasant summer afternoons worthy tradesmen flock to the Crystal Palace in doublets of Lincoln green, and with horns that won't blow and bows that won't bend wander through the refreshment-room and the Pompeian Court of that amazing structure in a laudable attempt to combine respectability and picturesqueness."

Notes and Queries.

"The shape in which this work is presented is uniform with La Bruyère and Brillat-Savarin, the appearance of which has already been noticed. Pickering's edition of 1832, which contains the additions of Ritson and of his editor and nephew, including the tale of Robin Hood and the Monk, the existence of which was ignored by Ritson, has been followed, and the woodcuts of Bewick have been retained. These are now printed upon India paper, with a view of communicating greater softness. To these indispensable illustrations have been added nine etchings which now first see the light, from original paintings by A. H. Tourrier and E. Buckman. Some of these, which are also on India paper, are very spirited in design and rich in execution. A handsomer edition of Ritson's Robin Hood, or a more coveted possession to the bibliophile, is not to be expected."

The Literary World.

"Any who cherish a love for mediæval lore will find much to delight them in Ritson's Robin Hood, and an edition more desirable than the one Mr. Nimmo has given us could hardly be demanded by the most fastidious of book collectors. The print and paper superb, and the illustrations have all the freshness of originals."

A. B. FROST'S NEW ILLUSTRATED WORK.

100 *Illustrations.*   *Crown 8vo, cloth, gilt top,* 5s.

Rudder Grange.

By FRANK R. STOCKTON.

The new "Rudder Grange" has not been illustrated in a conventional way. Mr. Frost has given us a series of interpretations of Mr. Stockton's fancies which will delight every appreciative reader,—sketches scattered through the text; larger pictures of the many great and memorable events, and everywhere quaint ornaments and headpieces. It is, on the whole, one of the best existing specimens of the complete supplementing of one another by author and artist.

SOME PRESS NOTICES.

The Times.—"Many of the smaller drawings are wonderfully spirited; there are sketchy suggestions of scenery, which recall the pregnant touches of Bewick; and the figures of animals and of human types are capital, from the row of roosting fowls at the beginning of the chapter to the dilapidated tramp standing hat in hand."

Scotsman.—"Externally it is an uncommonly pretty volume, and the pencil of Mr. A. B. Frost has been employed to brighten its pages with a hundred capital illustrations."

Daily Telegraph.—"Allured by the graphic illustrations, no fewer than a hundred, which the pencil of Mr. A. B. Frost has furnished, the reader who takes in hand Mr. Frank R. Stockton's 'Rudder Grange' will have no reason to regret the fascination, or to wish he had resisted it; altogether the book is full of quiet and humorous amusement."

Morning Post.—"It will be welcomed in its new dress by many who have already made the acquaintance of Euphemia and Pomona, as well as by many who will now meet those excellent types of feminine character for the first time."

Saturday Review.—"The new edition of 'Rudder Grange' has a hundred illustrations by Mr. A. B. Frost; they are extremely good, and worthy of Mr. Stockton's amusing book."

Court and Society Review.—"After looking at the pictures we found ourselves reading the book again, and enjoying Pomona and her reading, and her adventure with the lightning rodder, and her dog-fight as much as ever. And to read it twice over is the greatest compliment you can pay to a book of American humour."

Figaro.—"The volume contains no less than a hundred illustrations large and small, all charming, and what is even better, all appropriate. There is no doubt that it will be very popular."

Society.—"Mr. Stockton's story is quaintly conceived and thoroughly American in style, the characters being most amusing types, and Mr. Frost has provided a host of quaintly grotesque illustrations, large and small, adding much to the intrinsic merit of the work."

Guardian.—"The illustrations by Mr. A. B. Frost to the new edition are extremely humorous and the edition itself is handsome both in type and paper. No one who cares to know what American humour is at its best should be without a copy of 'Rudder Grange.'"

14 King William Street, Strand, London, W.C.

A VERY FUNNY ILLUSTRATED HUMOROUS BOOK.

Stuff and Nonsense.

By A. B. FROST,

The Illustrator of Stockton's "Rudder Grange."

Small 4to, illustrated boards, price 6s.

Mr. Frost has made a wonderfully amusing and clever book. There are in all more than one hundred pictures, many with droll verses and ludicrous jingles. Others are unaccompanied by any text, for no one knows better than Mr. Frost how to tell a funny story, in the funniest way, with his artist's pencil.

Standard.—"'This is a book which will please equally people of all ages. The illustrations are not only extremely funny, but they are drawn with wonderful artistic ability, and are full of life and action.

"It is far and away the best book of 'Stuff and Nonsense' which has appeared for a long time."

Times.—"It is a most grotesque medley of mad ideas, carried out nevertheless with a certain regard to consistency, if not to probability.''

Figaro.—"The verses and jingles which accompany some of the illustrations are excellent fooling, but Mr. Frost is also able to tell a ludicrous story with his pencil only."

Press.—"The most facetious bit of wit that has been penned for many a day, both in design and text, is Mr. A. B. Frost's 'Stuff and Nonsense.' 'A Tale of a Cat' is funny, 'The Balloonists' is perhaps rather extravagant, but nothing can outdo the wit of 'The Powers of the Human Eye,' whilst 'Ye Æsthete, ye Boy, and ye Bullfrog' may be described as a 'roarer.' Mr. Frost's pen and pencil know how to chronicle fun, and their outcomes should not be overlooked."

Graphic.—"Grotesque in the extreme. His jokes will rouse many a laugh."

Daily News.—"There is really a marvellous abundance of fun in this volume of a harmless kind."

Athenæum.—"Clever sketches of grotesque incidents."

Literary World.—"A hundred and twenty excruciatingly funny sketches."

CONTENTS.

The Fatal Mistake—A Tale of a Cat.

Ye Æsthete, ye Boy, and ye Bullfrog.

The Balloonists.

The Powers of the Human Eye.

The Crab-Boy and His Elephant.

The Old Man of Moriches.

The Bald-headed Man.

The Mule and the Crackers.

The Influence of Kindness.

Bobby and the Little Green Apples.

The Awful Comet.

The Tug of War.

The Ironical Flamingo.

&c. &c. &c.

14 King William Street, Strand, London, W.C.

LIMITED EDITIONS

OF

The Two Guinea Half-Bound Parchment Series of Choice Works.

A Handbook of Gastronomy.

(BRILLAT-SAVARIN's "Physiologie du Goût.") New and Complete Translation, with 52 original Etchings by A. LALAUZE. Printed on China Paper. 8vo, half parchment, gilt top, 42s. *net*.
NOTE.—300 *copies printed, and each numbered. Type distributed.*
[*Out of print.*

The Characters of Jean de La Bruyère.

NEWLY RENDERED INTO ENGLISH. With an Introduction, Biographical Memoir, and Copious Notes, by HENRI VAN LAUN. With Seven Etched Portraits by B. DAMMAN, and Seventeen Vignettes etched by V. FOULQUIER, and printed on China paper. 8vo, half parchment, gilt top, 42s. *net*.
NOTE.—300 *copies printed, and each numbered. Type distributed.*
[*Out of print.*

The Complete Angler;

OR, THE CONTEMPLATIVE MAN'S RECREATION, of IZAAK WALTON and CHARLES COTTON. Edited by JOHN MAJOR. A New Edition, with 8 original Etchings (2 Portraits and 6 Vignettes), two impressions of each, one on Japanese and one on Whatman paper; also, 74 Engravings on Wood, printed on China Paper throughout the text. 8vo, cloth or half parchment elegant, gilt top, 31s. 6d. *net*.
NOTE.—500 *copies printed.*
[*Out of print.*

Robin Hood:

A COLLECTION OF ALL THE ANCIENT POEMS, SONGS, AND BALLADS now extant relative to that celebrated English Outlaw; to which are prefixed Historical Anecdotes of his Life. By JOSEPH RITSON. Illustrated with Eighty Wood Engravings by BEWICK, printed on China paper. Also Ten Etchings from Original Paintings by A. H. TOURRIER and E. BUCKMAN. 8vo, half parchment, gilt top, 42s. *net*.

NOTE.—300 copies printed, and each numbered. Also 100 copies on fine imperial paper, with etchings in two states, and richly bound in Lincoln Green Satin. Each copy numbered. Type distributed.
This edition of "ROBIN HOOD" is printed from that published in 1832, which was carefully edited and printed from Mr. RITSON's own annotated edition of 1795.

14 King William Street, Strand, London, W.C.

Carols and Poems

FROM THE FIFTEENTH CENTURY TO THE PRESENT TIME.

Edited by A. H. BULLEN, B.A.

Post 8vo, cloth, elegant gilt top, price 5s.

NOTE.—120 copies printed on fine medium 8vo paper, with Seven Illustrations on Japanese paper. Each copy numbered.

Saturday Review.

"Since the publication of Mr. Sandys' collection there have been many books issued on carols, but the most complete by far that we have met with is Mr. Bullen's new volume, 'Carols and Poems from the Fifteenth Century to the Present Time.' The preface contains an interesting account of Christmas festivities and the use of carols. Mr. Bullen has exercised great care in verifying and correcting the collections of his predecessors, and he has joined to them two modern poems by Hawker, two by Mr. William Morris, and others by Mr. Swinburne, Mr. Symonds, and Miss Rossetti. No one has been more successful than Mr. Morris in imitating the ancient carol :—

> 'Outlanders, whence come ye last?
> The snow in the street and the wind on the door.
> Through what green sea and great have ye past?
> Minstrels and maids stand forth on the floor.'

Altogether this is one of the most welcome books of the season."

Morning Post.

"Good Christian people all, and more especially those of artistic or poetic inclinations, will feel indebted to the editor and publisher of this fascinating volume, which, bound as it is in elegant cloth, ornamented with sprigs of holly, may fairly claim to be considered *par excellence* the gift-book of the season. 'Carols and Poems' are supplemented by voluminous and interesting notes by the editor, who also contributes some very graceful dedicatory verses."

Spectator.

"Mr. Bullen divides his 'Carols and Poems from the Fifteenth Century to the Present Time' into three parts—'Christmas Chants and Carols,' 'Carmina Sacra,' and 'Christmas Customs and Christmas Cheer.' These make up together between seventy and eighty poems of one kind and another. The selection has been carefully made from a wide range of authors. Indeed, it is curious to see the very mixed company which the subject of Christmas has brought together—as, indeed, it is quite right that it should. Altogether the result is a very interesting book."

Notes and Queries.

"Mr. Bullen does not indeed pretend to cater for those who regard carols from a purely antiquarian point of view. His book is intended to be popular rather than scholarly. Scholarly none the less it is, and representative also, including as it does every form of Christmas strain, from early mysteries down to poems so modern as not previously to have seen the light."

The Times.

"Is very exceptionally a Christmas book, and a book at which we may cut and come again through this sentimentally festive season. It forms a 'Christmas Garland' of the sweetest or the quaintest carols, ancient and modern."

Athenæum.

"Is an excellent collection of ancient and modern verse, mostly religious and sentimental, formed with much learning, research, and taste by Mr. A. H. Bullen."

Illustrated London News.

"The atmosphere of these plain-speaking songs is of the rarest purity. They come from the heart, and appeal to it, when the way is not choked up by the thorns and briers of conventional propriety. The reader accustomed to more artificial strains may not see the beauty of these songs at first, but it will grow upon him by degrees ; and possibly he will look with something like regret to the old-world days when verses so pure and quaint were household words in England."

Old Spanish Romances.

Old English Romances.

Romances of Fantasy and Humour.

Illustrated with Etchings, crown 8vo, parchment boards or cloth,
7s. 6d. per vol.

The Times.

" Among the numerous handsome reprints which the publishers of the day vie
with each other in producing, we have seen nothing of greater merit than this
series of volumes. Those who have read these masterpieces of the last century in
the homely garb of the old editions may be gratified with the opportunity of perusing
them with the advantages of large clear print and illustrations of a quality which is
rarely bestowed on such reissues. The series deserve every commendation."

THE HISTORY OF DON QUIXOTE DE LA MANCHA.
Translated from the Spanish of MIGUEL DE CERVANTES SAAVEDRA by
MOTTEUX. With copious Notes (including the Spanish Ballads), and
an Essay on the Life and Writings of CERVANTES by JOHN G. LOCK-
HART. Preceded by a Short Notice of the Life and Works of PETER
ANTHONY MOTTEUX by HENRI VAN LAUN. Illustrated with Sixteen
Original Etchings by R. DE LOS RIOS. Four Volumes.

LAZARILLO DE TORMES. By Don DIEGO MENDOZA. Trans-
lated by THOMAS ROSCOE. And **GUZMAN D'ALFARACHE.**
By MATEO ALEMAN. Translated by BRADY. Illustrated with Eight
Original Etchings by R. DE LOS RIOS. Two Volumes.

ASMODEUS. By LE SAGE. Translated from the French. Illustrated
with Four Original Etchings by R. DE LOS RIOS.

THE BACHELOR OF SALAMANCA. By LE SAGE. Translated
from the French by JAMES TOWNSEND. Illustrated with Four Original
Etchings by R. DE LOS RIOS.

VANILLO GONZALES; or, The Merry Bachelor. By LE SAGE.
Translated from the French. Illustrated with Four Original Etchings
by R. DE LOS RIOS.

THE ADVENTURES OF GIL BLAS OF SANTILLANE.
Translated from the French of LE SAGE by TOBIAS SMOLLETT. With
Biographical and Critical Notice of LE SAGE by GEORGE SAINTSBURY.
New Edition, carefully revised. Illustrated with Twelve Original Etch-
ings by R. DE LOS RIOS. Three Volumes.

THE LIFE AND OPINIONS OF TRISTRAM SHANDY,
GENTLEMAN. By LAURENCE STERNE. In Two Vols. With Eight
Etchings by DAMMAN from Original Drawings by HARRY FURNISS.

THE OLD ENGLISH BARON: A GOTHIC STORY. By CLARA
REEVE. **THE CASTLE OF OTRANTO:** A GOTHIC STORY.
By HORACE WALPOLE. In One Vol. With Two Portraits and Four
Original Drawings by A. H. TOURRIER, Etched by DAMMAN.

THE ARABIAN NIGHTS ENTERTAINMENTS. In Four
Vols. Carefully Revised and Corrected from the Arabic by JONATHAN
SCOTT, LL.D., Oxford. With Nineteen Original Etchings by AD.
LALAUZE.

ILLUSTRATED ROMANCE SERIES—continued.

THE HISTORY OF THE CALIPH VATHEK. By WM. BECKFORD. With Notes, Critical and Explanatory. **RASSELAS, PRINCE OF ABYSSINIA.** By SAMUEL JOHNSON. In One Vol. With Portrait of BECKFORD, and Four Original Etchings, designed by A. H. TOURRIER, and Etched by DAMMAN.

ROBINSON CRUSOE. By DANIEL DEFOE. In Two Vols. With Biographical Memoir, Illustrative Notes, and Eight Etchings by M. MOUILLERON, and Portrait by L. FLAMENG.

GULLIVER'S TRAVELS. By JONATHAN SWIFT. With Five Etchings and Portrait by AD. LALAUZE.

A SENTIMENTAL JOURNEY. By LAURENCE STERNE. **A TALE OF A TUB.** By JONATHAN SWIFT. In One Vol. With Five Etchings and Portrait by ED. HÉDOUIN.

THE TALES AND POEMS OF EDGAR ALLAN POE. With Biographical Essay by JOHN H. INGRAM, and Fourteen Original Etchings, Three Photogravures, and a Portrait newly etched from a life-like Daguerreotype of the Author. In Four Volumes.

WEIRD TALES. By E. T. W. HOFFMAN. A New Translation from the German. With Biographical Memoir by J. T. BEALBY, formerly Scholar of Corpus Christi College, Cambridge. With Portrait and Ten Original Etchings by AD. LALAUZE. In Two Volumes.

Imperial 8vo, Extra Illustrated Edition of

The Complete Angler;

OR, THE CONTEMPLATIVE MAN'S RECREATION OF IZAAK WALTON AND CHARLES COTTON.

Edited by JOHN MAJOR.

Full bound morocco elegant (Zaehnsdorf's binding), price Five Guineas *net.*

This Extra-illustrated Edition of THE COMPLETE ANGLER is specially designed for Collectors of this famous work; and in order to enable them either to take from or add to the Illustrations, it is also supplied unbound, folded and collated.

The Illustrations consist of **Fifty Steel Plates**, designed by T. STOTHARD, R.A., JAMES INSKIP, EDWARD HASSELL, DELAMOTTE, BINKENBOOM, W. HIXON, SIR FRANCIS SYKES, Bart., PINE, &c. &c., and engraved by well-known Engravers. Also **Six Original Etchings and Two Portraits,** as well as **Seventy-four Engravings on Wood** by various Eminent Artists.

To this is added a PRACTICAL TREATISE on FLIES and FLY HOOKS, by the late JOHN JACKSON, of Tanfield Mill, with **Ten Steel Plates**, coloured, representing 120 Flies, natural and artificial.

One Hundred and Twenty copies only are printed, each of which is numbered.

14 King William Street, Strand, London, W.C.

The Fan. By OCTAVE UZANNE.

ILLUSTRATED WITH DESIGNS BY PAUL AVRIL.

Royal 8vo, cloth, gilt top, 31s. 6d. *net.*

The Sunshade—The Glove—The Muff.

By OCTAVE UZANNE.

ILLUSTRATED WITH DESIGNS BY PAUL AVRIL.

Royal 8vo, cloth, gilt top, 31s. 6d. *net.*

NOTE.—*The above are English Editions of the unique and artistic works,* " *L'Eventail*" *and* " *L'Ombrelle*," *recently published in Paris, and now difficult to be procured, as no new Edition is to be produced. 500 copies only are printed.*

Saturday Review.

"An English counterpart of the well-known French books by Octave Uzanne, with Paul Avril's charming illustrations."

Standard.

"It gives a complete history of fans of all ages and places ; the illustrations are dainty in the extreme. Those who wish to make a pretty and appropriate present to a young lady cannot do better than purchase 'The Fan.'"

Athenæum.

"The letterpress comprises much amusing 'chit-chat,' and is more solid than it pretends to be. This *brochure* is worth reading ; nay, it is worth keeping."

Art Journal.

"At first sight it would seem that material could never be found to fill even a volume ; but the author, in dealing with his first subject alone, 'The Sunshade,' says he could easily have filled a dozen volumes of this emblem of sovereignty. The work is delightfully illustrated in a novel manner by Paul Avril, the pictures which meander about the work being printed in varied colours."

Daily News.

"The pretty adornments of the margin of these artistic volumes, the numerous ornamental designs, and the pleasant vein of the author's running commentary, render these the most attractive monographs ever published on a theme which interests so many enthusiastic collectors."

Glasgow Herald.

"'I have but collected a heap of foreign flowers, and brought of my own only the string which binds them together,' is the fitting quotation with which M. Uzanne closes the preface to his volume on woman's ornaments. The monograph on the sunshade, called by the author 'a little tumbled fantasy,' occupies fully one-half of the volume. It begins with a pleasant invented mythology of the parasol ; glances at the sunshade in all countries and times ; mentions many famous umbrellas : quotes a number of clever sayings. . . . To these remarks on the spirit of the book it is necessary to add that the body of it is a dainty marvel of paper, type, and binding, and that what meaning it has looks out on the reader through a hundred argus-eyes of many-tinted photogravures, exquisitely designed by M. Paul Avril."

Westminster Review.

"The most striking merit of the book is the entire appropriateness both of the letterpress and illustrations to the subject treated. M. Uzanne's style has all the airy grace and sparkling brilliancy of the *petit instrument* whose praise he celebrates, and M. Arvil's drawings seem to conduct us into an enchanted world where everything but fans are forgotten."

Copyright Edition, with Ten Etched Portraits. In Ten Vols., demy 8vo,
cloth, £5, 5s.

Lingard's History of England.

FROM THE FIRST INVASION BY THE ROMANS TO THE ACCESSION OF WILLIAM AND MARY IN 1688.

By JOHN LINGARD, D.D.

This New Copyright Library Edition of "Lingard's History of England," besides containing all the latest notes and emendations of the Author, with Memoir, is enriched with Ten Portraits, newly etched by Damman, of the following personages, viz. :—Dr. Lingard, Edward I., Edward III., Cardinal Wolsey, Cardinal Pole, Elizabeth, James I., Cromwell, Charles II., James II.

The Times.

"No greater service can be rendered to literature than the republication, in a handsome and attractive form, of works which time and the continued approbation of the world have made classical. . . . The accuracy of Lingard's statements on many points of controversy, as well as the genial sobriety of his view, is now recognised."

The Tablet.

"It is with the greatest satisfaction that we welcome this new edition of Dr. Lingard's 'History of England.' It has long been a desideratum. . . . No general history of England has appeared which can at all supply the place of Lingard, whose painstaking industry and careful research have dispelled many a popular delusion, whose candour always carries his reader with him, and whose clear and even style is never fatiguing."

The Spectator.

"We are glad to see that the demand for Dr. Lingard's *England* still continues. Few histories give the reader the same impression of exhaustive study. This new edition is excellently printed, and illustrated with ten portraits of the greatest personages in our history."

Dublin Review.

"It is pleasant to notice that the demand for Lingard continues to be such that publishers venture on a well-got-up library edition like the one before us. More than sixty years have gone since the first volume of the first edition was published ; many equally pretentious histories have appeared during that space, and have more or less disappeared since, yet Lingard lives—is still a recognised and respected authority."

The Scotsman.

"There is no need, at this time of day, to say anything in vindication of the importance, as a standard work, of Dr. Lingard's 'History of England.' . . . Its intrinsic merits are very great. The style is lucid, pointed, and puts no strain upon the reader ; and the printer and publisher have neglected nothing that could make this—what it is likely long to remain—the standard edition of a work of great historical and literary value."

Daily Telegraph.

"True learning, untiring research, a philosophic temper, and the possession of a graphic, pleasing style were the qualities which the author brought to his task, and they are displayed in every chapter of his history."

Weekly Register.

"In the full force of the word a scholarly book. Lingard's history is destined to bear a part of growing importance in English education."

Manchester Examiner.

"He stands alone in his own school ; he is the only representative of his own phase of thought. The critical reader will do well to compare him with those who went before and those who came after him."

Imaginary Conversations.

By WALTER SAVAGE LANDOR.

In Five Vols. crown 8vo, cloth, 30s.

FIRST SERIES—CLASSICAL DIALOGUES, GREEK AND ROMAN.
SECOND SERIES—DIALOGUES OF SOVEREIGNS AND STATESMEN.
THIRD SERIES—DIALOGUES OF LITERARY MEN.
FOURTH SERIES—DIALOGUES OF FAMOUS WOMEN.
FIFTH SERIES—MISCELLANEOUS DIALOGUES.

NOTE.—*This New Edition is printed from the last Edition of his Works, revised and edited by John Forster, and is published by arrangement with the Proprietors of the Copyright of Walter Savage Landor's Works.*

The Times.

"The abiding character of the interest excited by the writings of Walter Savage Landor, and the existence of a numerous band of votaries at the shrine of his refined genius, have been lately evidenced by the appearance of the most remarkable of Landor's productions, his 'Imaginary Conversations,' taken from the last edition of his works. To have them in a separate publication will be convenient to a great number of readers."

The Athenæum.

"The appearance of this tasteful reprint would seem to indicate that the present generation is at last waking up to the fact that it has neglected a great writer, and if so, it is well to begin with Landor's most adequate work. It is difficult to over-praise the 'Imaginary Conversations.' The eulogiums bestowed on the 'Conversations' by Emerson will, it is to be hoped, lead many to buy this book."

Scotsman.

"An excellent service has been done to the reading public by presenting to it, in five compact volumes, these 'Conversations.' Admirably printed on good paper, the volumes are handy in shape, and indeed the edition is all that could be desired. When this has been said, it will be understood what a boon has been conferred on the reading public; and it should enable many comparatively poor men to enrich their libraries with a work that will have an enduring interest."

Literary World.

"That the 'Imaginary Conversations' of Walter Savage Landor are not better known is no doubt largely due to their inaccessibility to most readers, by reason of their cost. This new issue, while handsome enough to find a place in the best of libraries, is not beyond the reach of the ordinary bookbuyer."

Edinburgh Review.

"How rich in scholarship! how correct, concise, and pure in style! how full of imagination, wit, and humour! how well informed, how bold in speculation, how various in interest, how universal in sympathy! In these dialogues—making allowance for every shortcoming or excess—the most familiar and the most august shapes of the past are reanimated with vigour, grace, and beauty. We are in the high and goodly company of wits and men of letters; of churchmen, lawyers, and statesmen; of party men, soldiers, and kings; of the most tender, delicate, and noble women; and of figures that seem this instant to have left for us the Agora or the Schools of Athens, the Forum or the Senate of Rome."

14 King William Street, Strand, London, W.C.

In One Volume, 8vo, cloth, price 7s. 6d.

The Teaching of the Twelve Apostles

(ΔΙΔΑΧΗ ΤΩΝ ΔΩΔΕΚΑ ΑΠΟΣΤΟΛΩΝ).

Recently Discovered and Published by PHILOTHEOS BRYENNIOS, *Metropolitan of Nicomedia.*

Edited, with a Translation, Introduction, and Notes, by ROSWELL D. HITCHCOCK and FRANCIS BROWN,

Professors in Union Theological Seminary, New York.

Revised and Enlarged.

Extract from the Preface.

" Among the special features of this edition may be noticed the discussions as to the integrity of the text ; as to the relations between the ' Teaching ' and other early Christian documents, with translations of these *in extenso,* so far as seemed desirable for purposes of comparison ; the presentation, entire, with annotations, of Kramutzcky's now famous reproduction of ' The Two Ways ;' the sections on the peculiarities of the Codex, the printed texts, and the recent literature ; and the care expended on the history of the characteristic Greek words ' of the Teaching.'

" The editors feel sure that continued study will only add to the interest felt by scholars in this unique product of early Christianity, and enhance their estimate of its importance. "

Westminster Review.

" This enlargement of the hastily prepared edition brought out last year by the same editors seems to us one of the most complete and valuable of the numerous commentaries on the ' Teaching.' The matter of the discourse need not again be dealt with ; it may suffice to say that these introductions and notes show thoroughly sound and scholarly work, and the reproduction of the conjectural restoration of ' The Two Ways ' by Kramutzcky, with which our editors incline to identify the document, may be read with interest, even by non-theologians, as a justification of ' reconstructive criticism.' The commentary, too, though mainly for experts, may be read with profit by any who are interested in scholarship. We cordially welcome this new evidence of the activity of America in theological learning."

Spectator.

" Of the several editions of the ' Teaching ' none is more worthy of the student's attention than this. A very full introduction gives an account of this very remarkable work of Christian antiquity (certainly the first in intrinsic value of the sub-Apostolic writings), of the circumstances of its discovery, &c. Then follows, first, the text, with a translation on the opposite pages, then notes, and then an appendix."

The Scotsman.

" There are few literary discoveries of recent years which have been so interesting to ecclesiastical scholars, or which have aroused more discussion, than that by Bryennios, Metropolitan of Nicomedia, of a manuscript in the library of the Monastery of the Holy Sepulchre in Constantinople. Found in 1873, it was published in 1883, and for the first time scholars became acquainted with a work which they had seen tantalisingly referred to, quoted, and used by early Christian writers."

The Bookseller.

" If genuine, and apparently there is no reason to doubt its being so, this is one of the most important documents connected with historical theology that has been discovered for many years. It professes to be a summary of the Christian religion as taught by the Apostles themselves. . . . If the editors be correct in their conjectures, the ' Teaching ' must have been written about the end of the first century or very early in the second."

www.ingramcontent.com/pod-product-compliance
Lightning Source LLC
Chambersburg PA
CBHW022016110726
47901CB00006B/1551